An Original Dutch Master

A Story as Told by Baz

Mick Barrett

Grosvenor House
Publishing Limited

This book is published by
Grosvenor House Publishing Ltd
Link House
140 The Broadway, Tolworth, Surrey, KT6 7HT.
www.grosvenorhousepublishing.co.uk

This book is a work of fiction. Any resemblance to
people or events, past or present, is purely coincidental.

A CIP record for this book
is available from the British Library

ISBN 978-1-83975-960-4

IN FOND MEMORY OF
KEITH AND PAULINE

IN FOND MEMORY OF
PATRICK AND MARGARET REGAN
FOUNDER MEMBERS OF THE FRIDAY NIGHTERS

MANY THANKS TO THE
FRIDAY NIGHTERS
THEY KNOW WHO THEY ARE

THANK YOU TO MY DAUGHTER MARGARET
FOR ALL THE TECHNICAL HELP WITH THE COMPUTER

THANK YOU TO MY WIFE FOR ALL THE
UNDERSTANDING

ALL THAT GLITTERS IS NOT GOLD
OFTEN HAVE YOU HEARD THIS TOLD
MANY A MAN HIS LIFE HAS SOLD
GILDED TOMBS DO WORMS ENFOLD
HAD YOU BEEN AS WISE AS BOLD
FARE YOU WELL, YOUR DEATH IS COLD

CHAPTER ONE

'Same line and another three feet,' called PK to Don.

I was playing bowls, crown green bowls that is; not that sissy stuff, flat green bowls, as played by southern softies, but crown green, as played by real men. (And, er, some women.)

First match of the season. With the thrill of a new season in a new league (we were promoted last season from 4th to 3rd Div.), all the battles, all the tension, matches to be won or sometimes lost, I should have felt great but I didn't. I felt fucking miserable. This was supposed to be a summer game but it was bleeding cold and wet, with dark clouds hanging very low. Rain had been pissing down all day. It had now slowed to a steady drizzle; it wasn't raining enough to call the game off but enough to make anyone playing quite wet.

I'd just come off having lost my game 19/21. I was 19/15 up, cruising to a win with a wood no more than a couple of inches from the jack, my second wood less than a foot away, game shot. The bastard fired with his second wood and somehow removed both my woods from the head. This left him with his first wood on. He then went very long; I could not get the length right and he went on to win.

We shook hands as is customary and he offered to buy me a pint, which is also customary. As a consolation for the loser, the winner buys the drinks. The etiquette is to buy them one back after the match in the clubhouse where we have sandwiches, nibbles and a chat about the match along with other subjects that blokes talk about when out together drinking. The way I felt at that moment was *Fuck the etiquette*, (I'm a bad loser me). *You never know though, we could win the match, so by the time we get back to the clubhouse, I'll be in a better frame of mind.*

As usual, there was great difficulty getting a team together for the first match. The bowls section secretary put a sheet up on the

1

club noticeboard requesting interested parties to sign up for the forthcoming season. Always a waste of time, it only ever gets three or four names, occasionally it might get five or six. This season it got eight but several of them were fictitious, such as Joe Bollocks, Isaac Hunt, etc. The club's full of smart twats.

My name was on the list, along with that of Ron Mitchell, put there by Vic Davies. We are three mates of more years than I care to remember. We'd played football together as youths and have remained friends ever since, over 30 years to be honest. Along with our wives, who get on well with each other, we socialise several times most weeks. Our kids, who are grown up now, know each other and get on quite well. Over the years we have had holidays together and the three families can be regarded as being quite close.

The AGM of the bowls section took place a week last Tuesday. The meeting was called to order by the chairman of the bowls section, Pete Kenyon, who along with vice-chairman Bill Anderson and bowls secretary Joan Hutton organise the bowls section. I was there with Ron. Also there were Brian, Mark, Don, Harry and Fred. A grand total of 10, which is about average for the AGM; that's a bit of a surprise considering everyone who attends gets a free pint. You'd think the room would be packed to the rafters knowing what our bowlers are for drinking.

After going through the regular rigmarole of a meeting, minutes, balance sheets and such, as it's all done very professionally, we came to the next item on the agenda: election of team captains. I say captains (plural) as the club has teams in four different leagues. Monday evening, Thursday evening, Saturday afternoon and Sunday morning.

Saturday, Sunday and Monday team captain selection was a formality with the last season's captains remaining in post.

Before the election of a Thursday captain, Joan read out a letter she had received from Haakon, last season's Thursday captain. The letter stated that although he intended to bowl on Thursdays, he had a few problems at home and wished to be relieved of the captaincy for at least a month.

This was very much a surprise to me because I work with Haakon or Dutch as he is universally known. Me and Dutch are the plant maintenance men of the local Public Transport Department. We are responsible for repair and maintenance of all company buildings, garage machines and equipment. He is a carpenter by trade and is responsible mainly for the buildings such as the roof, drains and doors, while I am an electrician and look after the services, electric, gas and water. We work very much as a team, assisting each other on most projects.

Dutch is so-called because his real name is Haakon Van De Enks. He's not really Dutch being born and bred just south of Birmingham. His parents were Dutch they had come to England in the late thirties looking for work. The main reason was to get away from the trouble brewing in Europe at that time. I believe his dad got work at a large power station.

He had not said anything to me about not being at the meeting or of any problems at home. On reflection, I had not seen much of him that day. It was the Tuesday following Easter. We had both worked on Good Friday. Dutch had let it be known he wouldn't be available for the rest of the weekend; he intended to visit his mother who lived in Banbury and was celebrating a birthday.

He apparently arrived quite early that morning, had all his equipment loaded on a flat truck ready for tiling in the paint shop toilets by the time I got to work. I had said, 'Morning, had a good weekend?'

'Not really,' he had replied, and went off to get on with his work. I spent the day in the traffic office rearranging the lighting. During lunchtime he went into town on some sort of business. The result of this was very little contact between us, bit unusual, but not unknown.

For the very tenuous reason that I work with Dutch, Brian proposed that I should be stand-in captain. This immediately received a second. When I raised the issue of my not wanting to be captain, it was argued by Brian that it was only for a few weeks, and I worked with Dutch, saw him daily, could keep him informed of all situations till he was ready to resume as captain. My response was 'Bollocks' (very articulate, me). I knew once landed with the role, I would be stuck with it. After some good-humoured

3

debate, I accepted the nomination on the understanding I would get help from Ron, with no arguing from the rest of the team regarding my team selections.

So here I am, as I said, wet, cold and miserable, captain of my first match having lost my game. Am I the lucky one? Mind, it now looked like we could win. Apart from me losing, Kevin lost quite heavily at 8/21. The other two of the first four, Don and Joan, both won well 21/13 and 21/14. The second four were on, all doing well, Ron was going along nicely, leading 19/4. The other three were holding good leads. Maybe a result after all.

With the business of the AGM complete, we adjourned to the club's lounge. The main topic of conversation was Dutch and his problem. The consensus of opinion was Karen (his wife) had caught him with his trousers down and was giving him hell. I personally did not consider this to be the case; if it had been through hanky-panky, he would have just come out and told me. We'd have had a good laugh, as we had with past misdemeanours and got on with it.

The guys at the club knew Karen and how sensual she was. Karen was a tallish fit, well turned out woman of 42 but could pass for 10 years younger. She was about 5`8" with a square-shouldered upright stance, a shapely body with big tits, nice arse and long slender legs, which she liked to show. She also had a lot of long reddish-brown wavy hair. To go with all this, she possessed a pleasant, outgoing way about her.

She had chatted and flirted with the guys at last year's club sports presentation dinner, much to the delight of them all. Dutch had looked on with much amusement of his own.

Dutch himself was a big powerful bloke standing six foot four and weighing around 16 or 17 stone with not much fat, as befits a man who's been in the building trade all his working life.

He was powerful and strong, both physically and mentally, he had an assertive manner if required, but for all that he was a pleasant easy going nice to know type of guy. That's why he was team captain. He was also a charmer and did very well with the ladies.

Karen was his second wife. His first marriage had been when he was quite young, probably too young. Four kids, all in quick succession, as is often the case when people marry too young (can't leave it alone, see). He had worked hard and supported the family for 15 years or so but his wandering eye and love of the ladies became too much, and the marriage broke up.

The last games are almost complete. All the second four won, the last two, Mark and Vic, were going to win well. The match was won.

Ron, who was keeping track of the score, said we were likely to win by 40 or so. The rain had stopped but it had gone a lot colder. The night had drawn in so much we were struggling to finish the match as we had no floodlights around our green.

I feel a lot better now. My first win as captain, I think I will buy my opponent a drink after all.

Dutch had not put in a show at our first game. I had not expected him to as I had heard about his so-called few problems at home.

The morning after the AGM, I got to work at about my usual time, put the kettle on and made tea. Normally, Dutch would have arrived somewhat before me and have it ready by the time I turned up, but not this morning. It was just about 8 o'clock, our normal start time, when Dutch came in. I was going through the report sheets for the day and called out, 'There's tea in the pot.'

I then said, that note at the A.G.M. was a bit of a shock.

At this, I looked up; 'Fuck me, Dutch. What's going on?' He looked very out of sorts, miserable and I suppose a bit shabby. 'Haven't you been to bed? You look shagged out. Sit down. I'll get the tea.'

He hung his coat in his locker and sat at the small table we use for lunch breaks. I passed him the tea and sat down. 'Thanks,' he said, 'I need this.'

'I was surprised by your note last night. You didn't say anything yesterday.'

He sat there looking down at the floor. 'No,' was all he said.

After a moment I asked, 'Do you want to talk about it?'

'Not really,' he replied.

'It sometimes helps. Has she kicked you out? I assume it's about Karen.'

There was a long pause. 'Yeah,' he said, 'it's something like that.' Another pause. 'I've got rid of her.'

'What! You've thrown Karen out? I don't believe you'd do that.'

He just sat there for a while, then he seemed to just blurt out, 'She's fucked off with some cunt of a bloke.' Then after a few seconds, '*Why?* Why would she do this to me, the fucking bitch.'

I didn't think it would help the situation to point out the times he had played away. 'I really did love her, you know,' he said.

'Yes, I realise that. I'm very sorry, mate. I don't know what to say,' I replied.

We sat there for a number minutes in silence, he then pulled from his back pocket a piece of paper. He asked, 'Could you do me a favour? She left this note. Could you get a couple of copies for me from the office photocopy machine? I can't face going in there.' He added, 'Her family are going to need to know what has happened.'

'Sure,' I said. 'Is it OK for me to read it?'

'I suppose in the circumstance, you should,' he replied. 'But don't show it or let on to anybody else.'

'You can count on me, mate. It's your business,' I said.

On my way over to the office, I read the note. It was a single, handwritten sheet, which simply stated:

Dutch,

Sorry about this. We had some good times but it's time to move on. Don't try to find me as I'm with someone else. You don't know him. I couldn't help it, it just happened. Look after yourself.

Goodbye.

Karen.

When I returned with the copies, Dutch had his coat on. I told him, 'I've done four. Will that be OK? I've put them in this envelope for you.'

6

'Thanks, that's fine,' he said, and put it in the inside pocket of his coat. He noticed me looking at his coat and said, 'I can't deal with this, I'm going home.'

'Wouldn't you be better with people around you to take your mind off your problems?' I suggested.

'No,' he said. 'I need to be on my own for a while. Could you explain to the manager without going into too much detail, this is going to take some time.'

'Yeah, OK. I'll tell him you have some domestic problems to deal with.'

'Good. That'll be fine,' said Dutch. 'I might book some holiday or go on the box. I'll be in touch and let you know.'

As he was leaving, I said, 'I'll give you a ring in a couple of days and we'll go for a drink.'

'No! Wait till I contact you. *Please.*' Then he was gone.

CHAPTER TWO

Easter had been early this year, Good Friday falling on April 2nd. Since then, quite a lot seems to have happened. The AGM on Tuesday 6th, Dutch and his situation on Wednesday. Coping the rest of the week at work on my own. So, by Friday evening, I was looking forward to a quiet drink at the club.

Along with my wife, we were meeting up with Ron and Vic and their other halves in the lounge at the club. A regular arrangement for a Friday night. They were already there when we arrived. Vic said, 'My round; what you having?'

'The usual for me. What's yours, Doreen?' I asked.

'Could I have a white wine, please?'

Vic went to the bar. Ron put in with, 'Evening, Captain.'

'Don't you start,' I said light-heartedly.

'Oh, you've been voted in as captain, haven't you?' said Ron's wife, Eileen.

'Press-ganged rather than voted,' was my reply.

We settled down in our usual seating formation, the ladies along one side of the small seating bay, with us blokes on the other with a table between. This allowed for separate conversations. No way were we going to be sucked into their conversations about kids, grandkids and shopping.

Ron asked about Dutch and his so-called problems. I said, 'He's gone off work, on the sick, I think.'

'Any idea what's going on?' asked Vic.

'I think it's about Karen, but more than that I don't know,' was all I said.

'Yes, she's caught him out,' said Vic. 'It was only a matter time.'

Ron's said, 'If she was living with me, I don't think I would be out of bed much, let alone chasing around after anything else.'

'Yes, but you are a dirty old man,' came the reply. We all had a good laugh. I thought of Dutch and what he was really going through, but said nothing.

Ron pointed out, 'Our first game is next Thursday. Have you got a team sorted yet?'

'Good point,' I said. 'Get the round in while I go in the bar room and get the list of guys who are interested in playing Thursdays.'

We all settled down again with drinks replenished. Looking at the list, I said, 'Bugger me, this is disappointing. Only five genuine names. The three of us plus Joan Hutton and Pete Kenyon.'

Ron asked Eileen if she had a pen and paper in her handbag. 'She's always carrying stuff like that around,' he stated.

Eileen, reliable as ever, produced said pen and paper. 'Right, let's have a few names from last season's team, see if we can sort something out.' Ron had taken control.

Great, I thought, *if he keeps this up, being captain will be a doddle.*

The names put forward started with Brian Holmes, Don Steel, Sam Marshall, Will Earl, Markey Mason. I said, 'Well, that's 10. We are going to need another three or four at least. That's assuming these five are going to play this season. If we can put forward a few more, I'll get around them during the next day or two and confirm their availability. Kevin Sargent,' I suggested, 'he was a regular last year.'

Vic pointed out that Dutch would be back soon. I thought, *Yes, maybe.*

Vic then came up with Harry and Fred. Ron said, 'Worth a try, but they are both working shifts now and will only be available at weekends.'

Ron went on, 'What about that Dave who came out of nowhere last season, he played quite well.'

'Dave Boucher,' I put in, and asked if he had been seen lately.

Vic said, 'Haven't you heard? It was in Tuesday's *Star*, he was some sort of manager at the Midland Bank in Aldridge and had took off with a shedload of money. The story has been on the Midland News a couple of times.'

'I've seen that story. Was that him?' said Ron. 'He's probably in police custody by now. He always was a flash git anyway. A real obnoxious piece of shit, that bloke.

'Don't hold back, Ron; say what you think,' I said. We all had a good laugh at that. No need to add him to the list then.

Vic then came up with Paul Lee and his son Liam. Ron added these to the list. I said, 'That will do for now. I'll get the drinks in.' Before I left the club, I spoke with Pete and Will to confirm their availability.

Joan, who is captain of the Monday Night team, also accepted the offer. She countered by asking if I could play for her on Monday in the League Cup.

I said, 'This Monday the 12th?'

'Yes, it's five home and five away, and I need a couple more players at Chase Town. I thought you and Vic could cover it.'

I said I wasn't sure I was going to be playing regular Mondays, but I could cover this Monday and thought Vic would also be OK.

On the way home, I asked Doreen, 'Anything interesting come up tonight?'

'No, not really, it was mostly about Dutch. Chris (Vic's wife) had said she was hoping Karen had thrown him out; he was always chatting up women even if Karen was there. She had gone on to say, "I know he's a pleasant, friendly chap but he always looks smug and so pleased with himself. He's had it coming for a long while."'

'He obviously didn't make a play for her then,' I said. 'What was your response?' I asked.

'I just said I'm not sure it's like that, it could be quite a different problem. Eileen had enquired if you had said anything. I told them you didn't know any more than was already known.'

* * *

Saturday morning, I was at work till about 1.30pm. After work I went to the club. I had a drink and had a chat with Fred and Harry (they always seem to be together). Both were expecting to play weekends but wouldn't be able to play on week-nights. I next spoke with Markey, who said he would be playing.

On Sunday, I didn't work. Doreen and I went to visit our son, daughter-in-law and our six-year-old grandson, Daniel, the light of our lives. They live in Oxfordshire. We took our grandson to the local park and had an extremely pleasant day.

Back at work on Monday. No one had heard from Dutch. It had been less than a week so I wasn't really expecting any contact yet. Early that afternoon I was called to the office and informed a box note had been received from Dutch stating he was suffering with nervous exhaustion. I thought, *That's one way of putting it.*

That evening, I played for Joan's team. I won what was a very close game. After the match, Vic chose not to return to our club. I and the other three players did return. Joan was delighted, the away five had won by 12 shots and the home five had all won. We were through to the next round. I spoke with a few more of the guys, and put a team sheet on the club noticeboard ready for Thursday's match.

Which brings you all bang up to date to where I started.

CHAPTER THREE

After our first Thursday match, I did buy my opponent a drink and stood talking with him. He was going on about his win, saying when he fired, he was actually going for the jack, trying to push it through to his first wood. He said he thought he had failed. I thought, *You're boring the bollocks off me, mate.* I actually said, 'Yes, well played. It was a very enjoyable game.' And thought, *Now fuck off.* (Still a bad loser, me.)

When the visiting team had departed, our team carried on drinking and generally taking the piss out of each other. Mainly me, for losing as captain. 'Hurry back, Dutch,' was the regular line. Kevin as worst loser also took some stick. It was all good-humoured fun, we had won our first match. Nobody was going to get upset. At the end of the evening, I confirmed with Ron and Vic I'd see them tomorrow, called out to all the team, 'Well done, everybody. Keep this going and we could get another promotion. Goodnight.'

I was late finishing work on Friday, having had a fair number of problems to deal with at work on my own. When I arrived home, I only had a light meal, I then had a shower and lay on the bed to relax.

I must have dozed off. Next thing I know, Doreen is saying, 'What time are we going out?'

I asked, 'What time is it now?'

She said, 'Eight o'clock.'

I was feeling a bit groggy having been disturbed from my nap, so I said, 'Do you really want to go out tonight? I could do with a night in.'

Doreen, with a raised voice, started to give me earache about me not being too tired on Monday to play bowls, or Thursday, only tonight when it's her night out. Blah, blah, blah.

I thought, *Fuck me, what's a bloke got to do to get some peace?* Anyway, by then I was fully awake. I said, 'OK, OK, just give me 10 minutes.'

We arrived at the club not many minutes later than normal. Comments were still made. Like, 'Thought you weren't coming after losing last night.'

Doreen jumps in with, 'Oh, did he lose last night? He didn't say. Is that the real reason you wanted to stop in then?' They all had a good laugh.

'Yes,' I said, 'very droll, get the drinks in.'

Ron fetched the drinks, Chris asked if I'd heard anything about Dutch. 'Yes, he's gone on the box with nervous exhaustion,' I replied.

'Ah, him with nervous exhaustion? I don't believe that,' was her comment.

'That's what it said on the note.'

Vic suggested a game of snooker, and Ron and myself were up for that. Just at that moment, Dennis and his wife, June, came in. Dennis was a friend of many, many years, a regular member of the Friday night group. Although not every week, and he is not a member of the bowls team; at only nine months older than me, he claims to be too young for bowls. (Cheeky sod.)

June settled down with the other girls, and we four blokes went to the snooker room. We tossed for partners, Dennis with me to play Vic and Ron.

After about 10 minutes or so, Pete came into the room. 'Hi,' he said, 'just the mob I've been looking for.'

'PK. How's it hanging?' answered Vic.

He's known as PK all over the club. He likes it. I think it makes him feel important to be known by his initials. He was voted in as club chairman 18 months ago. I personally think when they nicknamed him PK, they forgot the middle RIC. However, he does put in a lot of time for the club and all the activities in and around the place.

I was in the middle of my best break ever. The most I'd potted in sequence before was three balls. This time I had potted red, brown, red, blue, red and blue again with another red. 'Hang on a bit,' I said, 'I'm in the middle of a superb break here and playing like Ronnie O'Sullivan.' I took my shot at the pink and missed. 'Fuck it. Thanks, PK, you've played a blinder as

13

usual, you prat. What can we do for you, now you've stopped play?'

'Bollocks.' he said, 'you've never been any good.' There was plenty of laughter along with banter.

He said, 'I'm thinking of getting up a trip to Blackpool for the Waterloo in September. Can I count you in?'

Vic said, 'Hold it right there while I get the drinks in.'

While Vic was out, Ron asked, 'Is it just for blokes?'

'Yes,' said PK.' We always took a coachload years ago, but haven't done for the last few years, so I thought it's time we did.'

'Count me in,' I said, 'but it looks like Ron's got to ask Eileen's permission.'

'No, I haven't. I was just thinking if it's loaded with women, how many blokes do you need?'

'Yes, we believe you, Ron, if that's what you say,' put in Dennis.

'Bollocks,' was Ron's reply.

Vic returned with the drinks. 'We're all game for a wild weekend. You in, Vic?'

'Absolutely. I haven't been to Blackpool in years.'

Ron added, 'No women.'

'What? All weekend? I think I'll change my mind,' said Vic and we all had a good laugh.

'No, with us on the trip,' explained Ron.

'I shouldn't think so, talk about coals to Newcastle,' said Vic.

PK said, 'I need round about 30 or so to make it financially viable. Anybody else that you know who might want to go? What about Dutch?'

'Yeah, put him down for a seat. He's got a few problems just now but should be OK long before September.'

As he was about to leave, PK informed us that if he got a sufficient number, he would ask Barry the Bus (club member and coach owner) if he would allow us to hire his coach and drive for us. Book the required rooms at Tolley Towers (the regular boarding house). Sort out a cost and let everybody know. He also said he could collect money each week.

'Yeah, great. I think you should get a deposit off everyone who signs up,' said Dennis, 'Otherwise, you'll find a number will drop out.'

'That's right,' said PK, 'leave it with me. I've got to go now. I'm calling the bingo in the big room.' At that, he left.

'Well, that's something to look forward to throughout the season,' I said.

'The girls won't be happy if they miss out,' said Ron.

'I knew you needed to ask Eileen.'

'No, it's not that, you know they'll all start going on when they hear. So are you going in to tell them?' he added.

'Like fuck,' I said.' I'll let my misses know later on in the year. I'll tell her it's blokes only, and I'm just making the numbers up, and may I suggest we all do the same.'

'Ha.' put in Ron, 'you're more worried than me.'

'He's got more reason to be worried; he's married to Doreen,' said Vic.

'Bollocks,' was my reply, 'but you are right.' We all had a good laugh.

Dennis said, 'Are we still playing snooker or what?' We got on with the game still taking the piss out of each other as to who was most henpecked and generally having a good evening.

After finishing the game, and before leaving the snooker room, I said, 'No need to say anything about Blackpool, we might not be going yet.'

Ron asked about the team sheet for next week as we went back into the lounge. I said I'd put it up over the weekend.

CHAPTER FOUR

That weekend, I worked Saturday morning. I spent the afternoon mowing the back lawn and doing various other jobs around the garden. In the evening we went out with Ron and Eileen to a skittles night organised by someone Ron worked with, turned out to be a very good evening.

Sunday morning, I arrived at work at my usual time. I was immediately aware that someone had been messing about in our workshop. Things had been moved about. The overalls belonging to Dutch were on the workbench.

After checking, I didn't find anything amiss, so I came to the conclusion that Dutch had been in. Perhaps he needed something from his locker or some tools. I knew he had bought a new shed, maybe he was working on that. Having come up with that theory, I gave it no more thought.

When I'd finished work that morning, I went to the club to put the Thursday team on the noticeboard. I had put the eight winners from last week plus four to be selected on the night. Among the four was my name. I would be playing, but putting it this way made it look, er, well fairish.

Also, on the board, Joan had posted the Monday team; I had been selected to play. The match was at home so no problem there.

I didn't stay long at the club after the match on Monday. I'd bought my opponent a drink (once again I'm a winner). He offered to get me a drink. I said no thanks and gave the excuse I was driving. He said, 'OK, thanks for a very good game and well played.'

When I returned home, Doreen greeted me with, 'There's been a phone call for you.'

'Oh yes, who from?' I asked.

'Have a guess.' she said.

'I don't want to fucking guess. Who was it?'

'Oh, you're in a bad mood. Did you lose again?'

'No, I didn't lose and I ain't in a bad mood, just tell me who called.'

'Well, don't use that sort of language here. You are not with your bowling mates now.'

'Yeah, OK, I'm sorry, now who called?'

'That's a bit more civil. I don't know why you do it, I can't imagine what your mother would think if she could hear it.'

I'm losing the will to fucking live, I thought. 'Yes, yes, yes, I know. I've said sorry, now please tell me who called?'

'Dutch,' she simply stated and stood there with a look that seemed to say, *and fuck you.*

'Oh yeah, what did he have to say?'

'He wanted to talk to you. I told him you were playing bowls. He said he would ring you tomorrow.'

'Is he any better?' I asked.

'He didn't say. I asked if he was OK and that you had said he was off work on the box. He just said he was OK and he would speak to you tomorrow.'

On Tuesday at work, I didn't hear anything from Dutch.

During the morning, I decided to clean and tidy the shop. I went to put the pair of overalls belonging to Dutch into his locker, only to find he had put on a new padlock, and a pretty formidable lock at that.

So, I was correct with my theory, he had been in the workshop. No problem with that, but why when I wasn't there?

In the evening I had been toiling in the garden, anything to keep out of the way of the she monster that dwelt within.

I finished in the garden, had a shower and was settling down in front of the telly; it was somewhat after 9 o'clock when he rang.

'Hello, it's me,' he said.

'I know it's you,' I replied. 'Are you OK?'

'Yeah, listen. I was in the shop Saturday afternoon.' he said.

'I know you were in the shop. Any problems?' I asked.

'No, I put some personal things in my locker.'

'Yeah, I noticed the new lock.'

'Oh,' he said, he then added, 'Could you make sure no one messes with it? It's all very personal.'

'No problem, mate. Nobody goes in there anyway. Forget all that, how are you? That's the main thing.'

'Getting there,' he said. 'I might be back at work sometime next week.'

'Great,' I said. 'Have you heard from Karen?'

'I'll talk about all that when I'm back at work.'

'Yeah, OK. You need to get out for a pint at all?' I asked.

'No, I don't think I want to face up to people yet.'

'That's OK. Give me a call if you need help with anything.'

'Yes, I will thanks.' At that, he hung up.

'Hmm. Something very strange going on, that phone call was just to say keep out of his locker.'

Doreen said, 'What do you mean?'

I said, 'Well, the phone call wasn't about anything other than to say keep out of his locker. It must be really important for him to be so secretive.'

'Perhaps it's stuff which belongs to Karen,' she said.

'Yeah, like her sexy underwear or something, do you think?'

'There's something wrong with your head,' said Doreen.

'Well, what do you think it is?' I replied.

'I don't know, something quite innocent. You've just got a dirty mind.'

'Yes, I know.'

It's probably only porn books. Well, no, not really. If it was porn, he wouldn't bother to hide it, unless it's kiddie porn. No, not Dutch, I argued with myself. *Don't know, anyway very strange.*

* * *

We played our second bowls match on Thursday against the same team as last week, as that is how it works. Home one week then away the next. Then it's reversed with the next team, away then home. I happened to draw the same bloke as last week. Gave him a right thrashing, winning 21/9 on his home turf. (Great. Yes!)

The team also won. A good result, winning away from home, promotion form this.

The team selection had not been a problem. I left Kevin out, which he accepted, having been the biggest loser last week. I gave Paul Lee a game in his place, who had won. (What a captain.)

We met up on Friday as usual. Sat in our regular formation. Ron having lost last night took a bit of stick, not much because losing away is the norm. It was mainly congratulations regarding the team win. In the midst of all this, Doreen calls across. 'Has he told you Dutch rang Tuesday evening?'

'He didn't, did he?' called Chris in an all too excitable way. 'Is he alright?'

'Yes, he did call, and yes, he is alright, he's hoping to be back at work next week.'

'Has he sorted everything out with Karen?' was her next enquiry;

Hello, I thought, *too much interest here*. I just said, 'I don't know, he didn't say anything apart from saying he was expecting to be at work next week.'

'Will he be captain next week?' asked Vic. 'If he is, I'll buy him a drink as soon as I see him, make sure I'm picked for the team. Ha, ha.'

This prompted Chris to scold Vic with, 'You should show a bit more compassion for people who have problems.'

Ron said, 'He's never had compassion for anything in his life.'

All this was said with good humour as is all our conversations on nights out (apart from what Chris had said). Well, that's what I thought.

I went on to say, 'I intended to carry on with things as they are. Until I know or hear different. When Dutch returns to work, be it next week or sometime later, I'll let him know what the situation is and work out what will happen after that.'

I went to the bar to get the round in. While I was standing there, PK came in. As he approached, I offered to buy him a drink. 'Yeah, great, I'll have a pint please. I'm calling the bingo again tonight, so I haven't much time.'

19

I handed the drinks all round and said to PK, 'Come and sit with us.'

He said, 'OK, but I haven't got long.'

I asked how the trip was coming along.

Ron's eyes almost popped out of his head. Vic, with a big smirk on his face, looked at me and said, 'Oooh!'

PK, not noticing any of this, said, 'Yes, it's all go, we've signed up well over 30. I've still got to speak with Barry the Bus and contact Walter at Tolley Towers.'

'Walter,' I said, 'at Tolley Towers. What the hell's that?'

PK said, 'It's Walter Tolley. He's the owner. He's very good, the food's terrific and he always does us proud. I've got to go now. I'm on the bingo.'

When he left, it was very quiet for a few seconds. Ron looking at me, Vic looking at Ron, and me looking towards the wives.

The three of them sat there looking at me with puzzled faces. I was wondering who would speak first. Surprise, surprise, it was Ron. He called out, 'Shall we play snooker?' I immediately said yes and we three blokes stood up.

It was Eileen who opened up with, 'What trip?'

I replied, 'Ah, it's a run up to Blackpool PK's organising for the Champion of Champions. He does it every year.'

'Are you going?' she asked.

'Er, I haven't given it a thought, he's only just started to sort it out.'

'Well, why do you all look so guilty then?'

'Why am I being interrogated by your missus, Ron?'

'Well, she's always like that,' he said. We then took off speedily to the snooker room.

Once inside, Vic said, 'Why did you invite PK to sit with us then ask him about the trip?'

'Don't worry,' I said. 'They are in there now going over all possibilities and permutations of what might or might not be the situation. Give it 10 minutes or so and I'll go in to get the drinks.'

Vic said, 'It's my round next.'

I said, 'Well, you go in and—'

'Fuck off,' interrupted Vic, 'this is your mess. You sort it.'

'Yes, OK, give me the money and I'll go and get the round if you are that worried.

'This I've got to see,' said Ron. 'When you go, I'll be right by the door.'

We set up for a game, it was agreed Ron would play Vic, and then I should play the winner. I said, 'Before you start, let me have the money, and I can go and get the round while you are playing.'

Twenty minutes later, I said, 'Ready for the next drink?' and went into the lounge. Ron and Vic rushed to the door to watch.

I asked the girls what they would like. It was Chris who opened with, 'Wait a minute. Tell us about this trip to Blackpool.'

'What's to tell? it's just a trip to the Waterloo at Blackpool to see a bowls match.'

'When?' Eileen asked.

'A Saturday in September, that's as much as I know,' I said.

'Are you going?' Eileen again.

'I'd like to. PK is attempting to sort it all and to arrive at an approximate cost.'

'What about Vic and Ron?' again Eileen.

'Yeah, they've both said they would be interested, but it all depends on cost. OK, what drinks do you want?' I went to the bar, got the drinks, and returned to the girls.

Chris said, 'We could all do with a day at Blackpool.'

Oh fuck, I thought. 'Erm, I ain't sure who it's open to. I've been led to believe it was for the bowls teams because of limited places.'

'I might have known,' she replied.

I said, 'I'd better get back with these drinks,' and quickly departed.

Back in the snooker room, they were very anxious to know the outcome of the encounter as they could not quite hear the conversation. 'What did they say?' Ron asked.

'Not much,' I replied, 'just: What is the trip? Where is it going? Are we three going? How much is it? Can they go?'

'Can they fucking go!! Oh shit, I knew this would happen,' said Vic.

'What did you say?' asked Ron.

21

'Hold on, don't panic. I've told them it's a trip to the Waterloo to see a bowls match in September, and only open to club bowlers owing to the number of seats. I've also said that we three had expressed an interest, but only if the price is right.'

I went on to say, 'Now they're sitting there working out what questions to ask of us when we're on our own. So, remember, yes, we would like to go; no, we don't know how much; and, yes, it is for blokes only. Also try to suggest it's only for the day without actually saying it's only for a day. Certainly, no mention of a weekend. OK, all agreed?'

Ron said, 'I thought we all had agreed not to say anything for a couple of months and then say we were making the numbers up.'

'That's right, it's still the case, only now they've been primed and have time to get used to the idea. Shall we play snooker?'

'Hold it, what about this Tolley business?' Ron asked anxiously.

'I think it's the place we're having lunch,' I said.

'Yeah, OK, let's play,' agreed Ron. 'If push comes to shove, I can always get a divorce.'

On the way home, Doreen said, 'Right, tell me all about this trip. I want the truth this time.'

'What are you on about? You heard all there is to know. There's nothing more to tell.'

Doreen, not accepting this, said, 'I know you, you're not telling the truth or at least not all of the truth.'

'OK,' I said, 'there isn't much to say yet. When there is more information, I'll talk it all through with you, but don't go gossiping about it with the others.'

'I never do,' she said.

I thought, *like fuck you don't*, but said, 'It might cause a few problems this one so don't get involved, OK?'

'Why? What are you all going to be doing?' she asked.

'Nothing,' I said. 'It's just Vic and Ron seemed a bit worried, that's all, so leave it at that, OK.'

CHAPTER FIVE

On Saturday morning, our daughter came around with the intention of going to Oxfordshire with Doreen and me. As we were about to leave, I received a phone call to say I was required at work. (Problem with the bus wash machine.) They went without me. I went to work, which was OK by me.

Just before 12 o'clock when all problems were solved and everything hunky–dory, I was ready to leave work. I decided to call Dutch.

'Hello, mate. How are you?' I said when he picked up his end.

'Oh, hi,' he replied, 'I'm not too bad, I'm OK. What's everybody saying?' was his next response.

'Not much; they've been told you're off with stress, although most do not believe you'd have any stress about anything.' I then asked, 'Fancy a pint?'

'Oh, I don't know,' he said, 'I don't think I want to go to the club, not with that lot going on at me.'

'OK,' I said, 'how about the Boat? We could use the lounge; it's quiet in there at this time of day.'

'Hmm, yes, er, OK. I'll see you there in half an hour or so if you like.'

'Great,' I said, 'I'll see you there, OK.'

When I arrived at the Boat, I went into the lounge, paid for a pint and sat at a table by the window. Apart from me, the lounge was empty. I sat there for almost an hour. I was thinking, *He is not going to turn up.* I was debating with myself as to whether to have another pint or just go when the door opened and Dutch walked in. 'I was just about to give up on you. What's your pleasure?'

'I'll have a pint of bitter.'

I ordered two and we sat down.

'So, how's everything?' I asked.

'Not so bad, I suppose,' he said. 'What's everybody think about it all? I bet there is a huge amount of tittle-tattle going on.'

'Not really,' I said, 'they all think it's about Karen and a bit of falling out.'

'It's a bit more than that,' he said.

'Have you heard from her?'

'I won't be hearing from her again,' he said.

'Think it will be a final split then.'

'Yeah, very final,' he said.

'Even to a divorce?' I asked.

'We were never officially married; I just gave her a ring to wear and everybody seemed to accept that we were married,' he said. 'Doesn't anybody know she's gone?'

'Nobody at all,' I replied.

'Ah shit,' he said, 'I don't suppose you could let it be known that she's gone. I don't want to explain the situation to everybody when I get back.'

'Yes, OK, I'll do that. I'll tell Doreen, by Monday, the world will know.' He laughed at that. I thought, *That's better*. He then got up to get the drinks in. As he went to rise, he winced. 'What's that, a bit of old age creeping in?'

'No, I've strained a muscle in my shoulder, I think.'

When he came back, he asked how Doreen was. I told him she had gone with our daughter to see our grandson; I had been called to work and as a consequence I was here.

'Everything OK at work?' he asked.

'Yes, all under control. The manager wants a meeting sometime next week to discuss work plans for the summer. When are you going to return?' I asked.

'My box note is till Wednesday. I should be back then,' he said.

'Great, I'll arrange the meeting for Thursday, so have a think about what is required this summer. I'll make a few notes and between us we can have a good input to the meeting. That will settle you in nicely.'

'That's if I don't get bogged down explaining my problems with everybody.'

'OK,' I said, 'I'll let the girl in the garage office know about Karen, she's quite a good gossip, and in no time, everybody will know.'

'I'm not sure about her,' Dutch said. 'She's always flirting and giving me the come on. God knows what she is going to be like when she knows I'm on my own.'

'Since when have you been bothered about females flirting?'

'I don't know, I think all this lot has left me a bit sensitive,' he said.

'Bollocks,' I replied, 'you haven't changed at all. You can't wait to get back at it, can you?'

'Well, no, I haven't had any for a few weeks and I'm getting desperate.' We had a good laugh about this and I knew things were getting back to normal.

I next spoke about me being temporary captain of the Thursday bowls team and asked what his thoughts and plans were. 'Oh shit,' he said, 'I haven't given any thought to that at all. To be absolutely honest, there's more to this situation of mine than you know.'

I looked at him and could see he was still troubled, maybe all was not back to normal. He said he would appreciate it if I could carry on with things for a few weeks, just till things settled down.

'Yeah, OK,' I said,' no problem. Is there anything you want to talk about?'

'No,' was all he said.

'Right, that's OK,' I said, 'I'm thinking of going up the green later. You fancy coming?'

'Not just yet, I'll wait till everybody is aware of the situation with Karen,' he replied. 'I'll leave it at that and see you at work next week.'

I said, 'OK, see you next week.'

He then left.

Ron and Vic both bowl on Saturday. As I arrived at the green, the match had just started. Ron was on the green as one of the first four. Vic was marking his card. I acknowledged Vic with a raised hand. He called over, 'What's all this? You after a game?'

I didn't respond to his remark and went over to the pavilion where a number of our bowlers were. 'Afternoon all,' I called. They all responded in good humour, with remarks such as 'come to see a good team bowl?' and similar witticisms.

I sat and watched Ron's game. He hates it when Vic is marking his card, as Vic is prone to be distracted by anything and everything else that goes on around the green. It's quite amusing to see the frustration build in Ron as he signals to Vic and often doesn't get a response. Ron won his game quite comfortably 21/14.

Vic handed in the card to Markey and came over. 'No Oxford?' he inquired.

'No, I had an emergency call from work. Doreen and our Elizabeth have gone.'

We were then joined by Ron. 'Hello. what's all this then on a Saturday?'

'We're all entitled to a bit of relaxation.' I replied.

'With your job and lifestyle, you don't need any relaxation, whereas I have to put up with him marking my card.'

Vic had a laugh at this, then said, 'Anyway, what you doing here?'

I went through what had happened this morning. 'With nothing to do after work, I then arranged to meet up with Dutch in the Boat.'

'Oh, how is he? Has everything been sorted with Karen?' The questions came thick and fast.

'Slow down a bit,' I said. 'Yes, he is OK, and no, things with Karen are not sorted. Apparently, she's fucked off for good and he doesn't expect her back.'

'What, you mean we won't see her here again?' exclaimed Ron. 'Bloody hell, she's the main reason I bowl at this club.' He went on to ask, 'Where has she gone to, do you know?'

By now a number of the team were gathered around listening to Ron and laughing at his response to the news.

'Slow down, Ron,' I said. 'If your missus hears about your reaction you'll be in deep shit.'

'I'd swop her for Karen anytime,' he said. This statement was greeted with cries of 'and me' all round the pavilion, followed by raucous laughter and comments as they all ran images and scenarios through their minds.

'Well, she's gone and most likely won't be back,' I informed them all. I went on to say, 'Dutch expects to be back at work sometime next week, and hopefully back playing bowls shortly after.'

Markey called out, 'Come on, you lot, let's get around the green and support the team.' They drifted away, still making ribald comments as to what they might do with Karen if such a situation should ever arise. What a pathetic bunch of deluded dreamers they all were.

I stood the far side of the green with Vic; he wasn't marking a card as he was due on next. In a quieter and more relaxed conversation, I told Vic I thought Karen had most likely gone off with someone.

His reaction was, 'Bloody hell, no wonder Dutch is so fucked up about it all. Does he know where she's gone?'

'No, I don't think so,' I replied.

'Perhaps it's as well,' said Vic. 'If he did know, I think he would go round and do some damage to him or her or probably both.'

I said, 'Yes, I think you're right.'

When Vic was called on to play, I strolled around to Ron and said, 'I'm not hanging about much longer. You and Eileen out tonight?'

'Yes, I should think so,' he replied.

'OK, we'll see you in the Boat if Doreen's back in time.'

At that, I went into the club and put the team sheet up for next Thursday. I then went home for some food as I suddenly realised I was bloody starving. Driving home, I was thinking, *If Dutch thinks the situation with Karen being out in the open is going to give him an easy ride, he's in for a bit of a shock.*

27

CHAPTER SIX

Monday morning, I arrived at work as normal and began to complete my worksheets for the previous week, which I then took along with my timecard to the garage office. As I completed this task and was about to leave, Samantha, the girl from the garage office, arrived. 'Ah,' I said, 'I was just on my way over to your office with the sheets and cards.'

'Yes,' she said, 'but I am a bit in front of myself this morning, so I thought I would come and collect them.'

'Great, thank you very much,' I answered. 'Have you got the report sheets with you?'

'Oh, no, I haven't,' she said, 'I never gave them a thought, shall I go and get them?'

'No, don't worry, I'll pick them up when I do my inspection walk-around later.'

Sammie was a very clean, crisp, neat sort of woman aged about 32 to 34, had been married for about 10 years, I had been led to believe. She was always well dressed but never used makeup, well not at work anyway. She seemed a very virtuous person, bit reserved like a Sunday school teacher or a librarian, or what the popular image of them seems to be. She would always speak and be polite with people but never rude or crude and certainly no swearing or any bad language. She gave the impression of being a very nice person.

She then seemed to suddenly blurt out, 'Have you heard from Dutch?' in an embarrassed sort of way.

I told her I had spoken with him over the weekend. 'Oh yes, and how is he?' she asked in an all too nonchalant way.

I thought, *Fuck me, Dutch is right, she is keen.* I informed her that his wife had left him, and he felt it was a final split and that she would not be returning.

'Oh dear, no wonder he is so upset, poor love,' was her response.

I went on to say, 'He expects to be back on Thursday, as he feels he's over the worst of it.'

'Yes,' she said. 'he's due a sick note that day, I wondered if he would bring it in himself, or not.' At that, she said, 'You sure I can't get the report sheets for you?'

'No, it's OK, I'll collect them.'

She then left with a brisk, 'Bye.'

The rest of the day went by without any major problem occurring. In the evening I played bowls and lost (got no more to say about that) apart from it was away from home.

On Thursday morning when I got to work, a cup of tea was waiting for me. Dutch had returned. He greeted me with, 'Morning. Your tea's ready.'

'Great,' I said, 'good to have you back.' While I hung my coat up, I said, 'How are you?'

'I'm OK. I'm good, ready for work and I'm pleased to be back.'

'Do you want to go to the garage office for the report sheets?' I asked.

'Already done,' he replied.

'Bloody hell, you're off to a flier.'

'Yeah, I thought I'd get there before all the day staff was in; anyway, I did need to hand in my return-to-work note, so all done.'

'Good. When we've finished our tea, we'll do the inspection; do you want the workshops or the sheds?'

'I'll do the workshops,' he said, 'may as well go around and say hello to everybody.'

After I had completed my inspection, which had taken about an hour owing to the fact I had cleared a couple of drains that were blocked, I returned to the shop and found Dutch manoeuvring an extra personal locker into the workshop. 'Hello! What's all this then?' I inquired.

'I need to keep all that separate and secure for a while.' he said, referring to his original locker.

'Where is it from?' I asked.

'The drivers' rest room back of the traffic block. There's half a dozen spare in there.'

'Yeah, I know them.' I thought, *I won't ask about his original locker, he'll tell me when he is ready.* 'You should have called me, I'd have given you a hand.'

'That's OK; it's done now.'

We cleared all the jobs on the report sheets, had our mid-morning break. After which we reported to the manager's office for our arranged meeting. The meeting was quite fruitful in so much as we arrived at a full programme of work for the summer months.

Later that day, I mentioned to Dutch about the bowls match that evening and suggested he might attend. He declined the offer, saying he would leave it for now, maybe sometime next week.

I played and lost.

The team won. Vic and Ron both won. As a result, it was merriment all round, with a load of piss-taking of me that I bore with good humour (the bastards).

On Friday evening the abuse continued to a slightly lesser degree, the fact the team had won tempered their comments.

Dennis and June were with us, it was Dennis who suggested we play snooker. In the snooker room, PK was playing Bagatelle. As we set up to play, he came over. 'Evening, guys. I was hoping to see to see you lot. I've got all the details for the run to Blackpool.'

'Great,' said Dennis. 'How much?'

Ron looked round as if he expected Eileen to be standing behind him. His gesture raised a little snigger from me and Vic, to which Ron responded with, 'Bollocks, you pair.' This comment caused a roar of laughter all round. Even from Ron.

PK went on to say he had 34 applicants, the coach was booked and he had made bookings with Tolley Towers, so it was all go.

Dennis said, 'Yes, but you still haven't said how much.'

'Well, all in, around £70 should cover it.'

'Seventy quid!' Vic exclaimed.

'What, do you think that's too much?' said PK.

'No, I was expecting it to be somewhat more.'

'What are we to get for this £70?' I enquired.

'It's £22.50 for bed and breakfast per night.'

'Wow, sounds like a real class place,' said Vic sarcastically. 'How's he doing it for that?'

'He's got two, three and four-bedded rooms,' said PK. 'This means he gets £45, £67.50 or £90 each room each night.'

'You mean we don't get a room each, I'm expected to sleep with this lot? Well, fuck me,' I said.

'You want to be careful that don't happen,' chuckled Vic. This started laughter and crude remarks all round.

'Never mind all that,' I said, 'what other goodies are we to look forward to?'

'On Saturday evening, we have dinner at a cost of £7.50.'

No comment from anyone.

'Barry the Bus said for £100 plus his board and evening meal, he is willing to do the whole trip. That makes his charge about £150. Divided by 30 is £5.00 each.'

No comment from anyone again.

PK went on to say, 'I thought another £12.50 for drinks on the coach was about right, bringing the total cost to a nice round figure of £70.00.'

'Yes, that sounds just about right, very good, I can accept all that. I'm in,' I said. This sentiment was echoed by the rest of the group.

'How do you intend collecting the money?' Dennis asked.

'I'll get a payment book, a page for each person. Pay whatever you want whenever you want. When anyone pays money to me, I shall enter it in the book and have it signed by everyone. If it ain't in the book and signed, it ain't been paid, OK? So don't just pass me money when we are around the green. It's up to each individual to make sure it's in the book and signed.'

'Great,' said Vic. 'Shall we play snooker?'

We settled into the game, the atmosphere was very relaxed and all going swimmingly when Ron suddenly said, 'I'm going to have to tell Eileen about this trip.'

'Why?' asked Vic.

'Well, I'm no good at keeping secrets. Something is bound to slip out, and if she hears it like that, she'll assume there is something to hide. I've got to tell her.'

31

We all stood looking at Ron in silence. 'Sorry,' he said.

I said, 'OK, let's talk this through. I'm not all that bothered about it all coming out. The situation is, it's all booked up and it's only 70 quid. The story is we get there late Friday night, have a couple of drinks, have a bite to eat, off to bed. Next morning, breakfast, Waterloo Bowls all day. Evening meal, a few more drinks and bed. Come home Sunday. Where is the problem? Tell her you can't back out now, do you want everyone to think you always tell me what I can or cannot do.'

'Do we tell them now, tonight?' asked Ron.

'No! Not when they are together. As a group, they are sure to find some sort of argument against it. Tell them at home or even tomorrow. We all OK with that?' I asked.

Both Vic and Dennis agreed with this strategy, Ron accepted with less enthusiasm.

I then put forward the suggestion, 'Tomorrow night, owing to the fact it's a holiday weekend, there's a show and dance in the big room. We could meet in there and discuss the whys and wherefores of it all, if that's OK.'

Vic said he couldn't make it owing to other commitments, Dennis and Ron thought it a good idea. On with the game.

CHAPTER SEVEN

All went well Saturday evening, lots of questions asked, lots of careful answers given. No problems.

Monday was May Day bank holiday. Me and Dutch were at work to give the spray booth a complete overhaul and service. It was very hard and dirty work, and by the end of the day I was well knackered, and I think Dutch felt the same way.

On Tuesday morning I was working on some lighting in the bus parking sheds. I was up quite high on the lighting tower. I was at the far end by the entrance doors, and I suddenly noticed someone at the other end of the shed by the exit doors into the wash bay. I had to lower the tower slightly then I could see it was Dutch talking with Samantha. Nothing in that apart from them being there for a good 10 minutes, now that will require some answers.

At our mid-morning break, I said, 'I saw you talking with Sammie early this morning. Is she OK?'

'Yeah, she's OK.'

'What has she got to say for herself then?' I asked.

'Oh, er, nothing much, just enquiring if I was settled in and if I was glad to be back and that sort of thing.'

Looking at him, I could see a semblance of a smile. 'Come on, out with it,' I said. 'I can see there's more to it than just good morning, how are you.'

He then came out with, 'I told you she always came on to me. Well, I said was having some difficulty meeting with people and having to explain my situation so I don't go out much. She replied with "You should go out somewhere quiet with someone." Then she said, "I'm at a loose end tomorrow evening."' He said, 'I just stood there not knowing whether to believe what I had heard. She went on, "You could ask me to go out for a meal with you."

'I didn't know what to say. If I turned her down, it would be very embarrassing. My problem is it's too close to home. If it goes arse up, I've got now where to run.' He then said, 'Don't breathe a word of this to anyone or I'll be well fucked.'

I said, 'You know me better than that.'

'Yeah, OK.' He then went on, 'I said to her what about your husband? She said, "We're only going for a meal; why should that concern him or anyone for that matter." I asked where she would like to go. She said, "Could we go somewhere a bit out of the way." The end result is I'm taking her for a meal tomorrow night.'

I said, 'I'll give you this, Dutch; you fall off your bike you're straight back on it. I don't know how you do it but I take my hat off to you.' I went on to say, 'But seriously, be careful. As you say, it's close to home, wrong move, major problems.'

I changed the subject to bowls and in particular the Blackpool trip. I explained the situation and the cost; I also told him I'd provisionally booked him a place. 'So how do you fancy a wild weekend in Blackpool?'

'When is this outing supposed to happen?' he asked.

'Not till September, so plenty of time to prepare.'

'Yeah, I think I'll have some of that,' he said.

'Great. I'll confirm it with PK. He's running the show; he's collecting the money throughout the season. You can pay what you like when you like, but make sure you sign every time you give him some money.'

'I should think so,' he said. 'He is trustworthy, though, isn't he?'

'Oh yeah,' I said. 'Pete's a bit OTT about most things but he's sound alright. It's just that whenever anyone collects money, there is always an argument about who's paid what, so it's for PK's protection as well as ours.' I went on to say I intended to pay £20 on Friday as a show of commitment and the rest sometime in August. Dutch said he would do likewise.

This prompted me to ask, 'Are you coming down the club then?'

He said if things go OK tomorrow, he might look in on Thursday.

'Oh good, we are at home,' I said.

'I don't want to be involved with the game but I'll probably be there.'

On Wednesday, everything went along as normal. A few problems, nothing major. At our lunch break, I said, 'Everything alright for tonight?'

'Yes, I think so,' he answered.

'A bit nervous?' I asked.

'No, not really. It's not like I haven't done something similar before, I'm a big lad now, I can handle this sort of thing.'

'Yeah, you can say that again. Where are you taking her?'

'I'm meeting her on the car park of the Four Crosses on the A5. I'm thinking of going to that place in Acton Trussell; that's far enough out of the way for anyone.'

'Yeah, it's nice there. Good luck with it all,' I said.

That evening at home, I said to Doreen, 'If I say something to you, will you keep it to yourself?'

'Yes, I always do.'

'No, I mean really keep it to yourself.'

'Why? What's going on?'

I said, 'Dutch is taking the girl from the garage office out tonight.'

'I thought she was married,' she said.

'She is, but she as good as asked him out.'

'I thought you said she was a very nice, quiet, shy sort of a girl.'

'Well, she is,' I said. 'They are only going out for a meal. She said she wanted to help him through his problems.'

'Ha!' was Doreen's reply. 'Any married person who meets up with a member of the opposite sex for an evening out is up to no good. As for him, nothing has changed, has it? He's soon back at it. I thought these last few weeks might have had some effect on him, but it doesn't look like anything has changed, does it?'

All this was said with an amount of anger and a hint of disgust. 'Whoa,' I said, 'what's your problem with this? It isn't anything to do with us, just leave it there, and don't say anything to anyone about it, OK? Do you understand the sort of problems it could raise?'

'Well, he can't keep away from women and any trouble he gets, he deserves; not only that, he gets you involved as well.'

Bloody hell, I thought *I didn't expect a response like that. I wish I hadn't said anything at all now.* I changed the subject and said, 'He's coming to the bowls match tomorrow.'

To this, she responded with, 'I suppose you'll all have a good laugh at that poor girl's expense, with him going through all the gory details just to entertain you lot.'

Fuck me, give it a rest, I thought.

'No, it's not like that, nor is Dutch like that, so let's leave it. Remember, not a word to anybody, OK?'

'Yes, alright. I understand the situation, but he does ask for everything he gets.'

Jesus! Just leave it.

The next morning when I arrived at work, Dutch was there as usual. Tea made. 'Morning,' I said, 'everything OK?'

'Yeah, all in order,' he said.

I didn't want to dive right in asking about his night out, but it came out anyway. 'How's it go then? Last night?' I bumbled out.

'Oh, a disaster,' he said. 'Don't ask, it's too much, I don't want to talk about it. Let me wallow in my own misery.'

'As bad as that?'

'Worse than you can imagine.' He had a little resigned laugh to himself.

I thought, *I'll leave it there. He'll tell me when he's ready.*

CHAPTER EIGHT

I was late finishing work that evening. I didn't go home; I went straight to the bowling green. I wrote out the score cards and put them in my chosen order of play; Ron hung the scoreboard outside the pavilion. The opposing captain came into the room and we exchanged pleasantries and selected the order of play.

The game was on. I as usual started in the first four. About halfway through the game, the noise level around the green suddenly increased, and a spontaneous round of applause broke out. Dutch was back.

We stopped our game for a short while because of the disruption. My opponent asked what was happening. I informed him our original captain had been unwell for a few weeks and this was his first appearance at the green this season.

Looking at Dutch, he seemed somewhat embarrassed by the attention he received. On with the game.

I won my game 21/17. The team won quite comfortably; the world was good.

In the club house after the match, all the usual pleasantries were observed, the opposition finally took their leave. Everyone seemed to turn to Dutch with questions about his life, and then someone mentioned Karen.

Dutch looked at all of them with a stern face and said, 'That's my business and fuck all to do with any of you lot, OK.'

It was Brian who had mentioned Karen. He immediately apologised to Dutch and almost grovelled for forgiveness. No more questions about Karen then. From then on it was a normal after win bowls night. Vic had lost, very unusual for him to lose, especially at home. Brian had also lost. Not a good night for him all round.

Vic wasn't very happy with the ribbing he received and left quite early.

Because I hadn't been home after work, I left shortly after. When I arrived home, the first thing Doreen said was, 'How was his date last night? Did it go well?'

'Hello and good evening to you as well,' I replied.

'You in a bad mood, have you lost again?'

I thought, *It's my own fault I should have stayed at the club till she had gone to bed.* 'No, I'm not in a bad mood. No, I did not lose, and no, his night out did not go well. It was a total disaster.'

'*Good,*' was her only reply.

Friday was just a steady normal day. During the morning I said to Dutch, 'You OK with last night?'

'Yeah, it was good to be back. I was a bit surprised by the reception, I was touched by that.'

I said, 'Yeah, you looked a bit embarrassed by it all.'

'Yes, I was,' he replied, 'but nevertheless it was a pleasing show of support and much appreciated, it settled me in nicely.'

I then said, 'I thought you were a bit hard on poor old Brian; he just happened to say what everyone else was longing to ask.'

He said, 'Yeah, you're quite right, I was. I had it in my mind to jump on the first one to mention it and be sure everyone was aware of what my reaction would be to any reference to her, hoping it will stop continual questions about the situation.'

'Yes, I understand your motive and I'm sure it will work, but I still feel a bit sorry for Brian.'

'Yes, OK, you're right,' he said. 'What I'll do is buy him a drink and apologise for my behaviour towards him.' He went on, 'As long as everyone understands it don't mean it's open season on my business.'

'I'm sure they all got the message,' I said.

I then changed the subject. 'Have you spoken with Sammie at all since Wednesday?'

He took a deep breath and blew out with a sort of a sigh, 'Yes, but only for her to say she had not got time at the moment but she needed to talk with me. You know when I said I'd have nowhere to run; I think this is exactly that.'

'When are you having this talk?'

'At lunchtime,' he said.

'Any idea where?' I asked, saying, 'You will not want an audience, and you don't want to be too isolated.'

'No, you're right. I was thinking of the canteen but that gets a bit crowded, especially on a Friday.'

I said, 'I'll tell you what, I'll go to the canteen for my lunch, you contact her and ask her to talk with you here.'

'You'll do that?' he said.

'Only if you pay for my lunch,' I replied.

'You tight bastard,' he said, and we both had a laugh and agreed that's what we would do.

I added, 'I'll hear all the details this afternoon.'

'Like fuck you will,' was his reply.

In the afternoon we were very busy and very much occupied, so we never got around to discussing the events of lunchtime.

Friday evening as usual we gathered together, seated in regular formation at the club. Conversation, sport in general, bowls in particular.

PK appeared and sat with us. I paid him £20, which he with great aplomb recorded in his book and requested me to sign. This was all done to the sound of derisory scorn and comments such as 'you'll never see that again'. The commotion went up another notch when I produced a small card of my own and wrote paid £20 on it and asked PK to sign it. To his credit he signed the card and agreed it was a very good idea. He went on to say he would get some cards himself to hand to everyone who paid.

It was PK who was first to mention Dutch and his arrival last night. All agreed it was good to see him back and how much he seemed himself. It was Ron who said he thought he was a bit strong in his reaction to Brian. I said, 'Yes, I spoke with him today about it. He agreed it was a bit much and said he will apologise, as long as you all don't think it gives you the green light to bombard him with questions on what he regards as his business.'

It was at this point that Doreen opens up with, 'He's soon back chasing after women.'

To which Chris put in with, 'He ain't, is he?'

I thought, *Oh fuck! What do I say now?*

Chris went on to ask, 'Who is it? When was it?'

I said, 'Whoa, I never said he was chasing anybody, all I said was I saw him talking to one of the female cleaners at work. For goodness' sake, cut the bloke some slack.' I said all this while trying not to look threatening at Doreen.

At this, PK said, 'Well, I've got a lot to do, so if you'll excuse me, I'll carry on,' and moved away. Vic turned the subject back to last night's bowls and started to give an explanation as to why he lost. The evening carried on in the normal, easy going, jocular way.

On the way home, Doreen was unusually quiet, just sort of sat there as if waiting for the eruption. Eventually, I just said, 'Why?'

'Just shut up, will you,' was her reply.

I left it at that.

It's always a more relaxed atmosphere at work on weekends, far fewer people about, main workshops not in operation, paint shop and spray both closed. Only a few running repairs done in the shed pit area.

Dutch and I usually have a programme of maintenance work to carry out each weekend. It's all sorted and agreed with the manager during any given week.

While having our early morning cup of tea, I asked how his tete-a-tete went yesterday. 'Well, it was a bit embarrassing actually. She said it was all a very bad mistake, it should never have happened and certainly never happen again and would be grateful if it was never mentioned again.' She was aware the situation was of her own making and was very sorry if it caused him any problems. She hoped he could forgive her and would like them to remain friends and let things go on as before.

I said, 'Why? What the fuck happened?'

He said, 'It's a long story, let's burst the back of the work for today, then have a break, and I'll tell all.' He said, 'I've got to tell someone, it's all too much for me to keep in any longer.'

We worked very hard for three and a half hours and achieved a lot of our targets. Back in our workshop, we settled down with tea and sandwiches, and Dutch began his story.

They met up on the car park at the Four Crosses as arranged, travelled to Acton Trussell. On the journey, they conversed in a happy, relaxed mode, no sign of any nervousness. At the table when asked, she said she didn't drink much and would only have an orange juice. They sat there talking about everything and nothing for a while. Dutch then requested a menu and said, 'What do you fancy?' To which she replied, 'I'm not really hungry.'

After another 10 minutes or so, she suddenly said, 'Do you think we could find somewhere a bit more private and secluded.'

He said, 'I looked around, there were only three other couples in the place, so I said, 'Like where?'

She said there were a lot of quiet parking spots along the lanes. I said, 'Right, OK, drink up and we'll go.'

'Normally on first dates, I set the pace. I like to think I'm a good judge and take it along according to the character and demeanour of the person I'm with. Here I was just swept along by this woman who I'd thought of as gentle, quiet, reserved and a little bit shy. What the fuck's happening to me and my judgement?'

'Anyway, I headed towards the Chase (Cannock Chase). As we travelled along, she said, "It's very nice along here, don't you think?" Just at that moment, we came to a small lay by. I thought *Bloody hell, she knows this spot.* She said, "This is very secluded, shall we stop?"

'I pulled in and parked. She said, "How far back do these seats recline?" As she was reclining the seat, I reached over and kissed her. Her reaction was unbelievable; she had all her clothes off in seconds. She was phenomenal; I would not believe it was possible to undress that quickly in such a small space. I was struggling to match her performance, my shirt was off, my trousers were trapped by my shoes, my pants stuck around my knees. She was all over me, preventing me from most movement. I thought *Fucking hell, slow down,* it was like she was possessed. I finally managed to kick my shoes off, free myself of my trousers followed by my pants.'

He went on to say, 'My seat was fully reclined with her on top of me. I was thinking *Wow, who would have thought this seeing her at work?*

'Then it all happened, because I suddenly had a picture of her (he means Karen, he never seems to say her name) in my head with another bloke. This knocked me for six; I thought *This isn't right; I need to get out of this.* As I was about to ask her to stop, a car pulled up right behind us and switched on their main beam. The whole area seemed as bright as day.

'Every movement in the car stopped. Sammie was rigid, staring at the back window. Nothing could be seen; the windows were all steamed up.

'She let out a loud cry, "Ahhhh, it's my husband, he's followed me, he'll kill me, don't let him see me." At this, she leapt off me, grabbed all her clothes off the back seat and seemed to disappear under her coat as quick if not quicker than she got out of them.

'I sat there thinking, *Oh, I hope this isn't anyone looking for trouble.* It couldn't be her husband; he would have intervened long ago. While these thoughts were going through my head, she is whimpering away under her coat, saying, "Don't let him see me, he's going to kill me. I know what's going to happen."

'Suddenly the blue lights start flashing. *Bollocks, it's the fuzz, what the fuck do they want?* A thought went through my head, I wondered if they had come to ask questions about her (Karen).

'A shadow appeared at the window, then a knock. I grabbed my trousers and lay them over my lap with the legs covering over my legs.

'I lowered the window about an inch and said, "Yes, how can I help you?" The cop replied, "This your car, sir?" "Yes," was my short reply. "Can I ask what you're doing here, sir?" If you must, I said, "We've come to look at the stars, mate." "I'm not your mate, and I don't advise smartarse replies. We can do this here or at the station." "Sorry, officer," I quickly put in.

'He then asked, "Are you a member of the dogging fraternity?" I said, "Am I a member of the what-in-what?" "Dogging, don't try telling me you've never heard of it, there's a lot of it going on around here," he said in a sneering sort of way. "I don't doubt it, but I haven't, nor have I any wish to have anything to do with it."

'He said, "Is the lady OK? I assume it is a female." To which I answered, "Bollocks." "Can you lower the window so I can check?" I let the window down another four inches. "Are you OK?" he called to Sammie. "I want to go home," she droned, still covered by her coat. I said, "She is very embarrassed by it all. She's a colleague of some years and this is our first date." "First date, you have done well or were doing well." He smirked to himself. *Yes, you dirty-minded bastard*, I thought but kept my mouth shut.

'He then said, "Have you been drinking?" I said, "No, not really, I had a pint about an hour ago, that's all," "Would you mind stepping out of the car, sir," was his next command. "Oh, fucking hell, mate, you can see the situation I'm in." "Understand this," he replied, "I'm not your mate, and moderate your language when addressing an officer. Remember, here or the station. Now out of the car please."

'"This is farcical, we're consenting adults, miles away from anyone else doing no harm, why am I being harassed like this?" I whined to no effect. I got out of the car and stood there holding my trousers in front of me with my two hands.

'"Driving licence," he barked out. "It's in my coat pocket on the back seat." "Just get it," he said. "I haven't got any hands left," I said. "Too late for modesty," was his best offer of help. "Well, tell your mate to turn down his lights or is he after a cheap thrill as well?" "Get your licence," was his reply, given with a very stern look.

'Fuck it all, I tucked my trousers under my arm and with just my socks on opened the back door, reaching inside my coat produced my driving licence and passed it to the copper. To this, he replied, "Thank you. I'll go and check it against the computer records," and returned to his car.

'I took this opportunity to get dressed, slipping into my trousers and shirt, leaving my underpants somewhere under the seat. I was able to rescue my shoes and slip them on. Looking across the car, I could see Sammie had used the break in the process to do likewise. She was sat there with her coat all buttoned up, sitting very upright, staring straight in front with her hands on her lap, as if waiting to go out on a Sunday afternoon drive.

'The police car door opened, but it was the other side from where the first copper had entered. I thought, *Hello, the other plod's coming to get his view on the situation, so back at the station he can join the fun of telling the story.*

43

'To my amazement it was a policewoman. Who looked as though she was having trouble keeping a grin off her face. "All your documents and everything else seems to be in order." She looked into the car and asked, "Are you alright, ma'am?" To which she got the reply, "No, I want to go home."'

He then said, 'The policewoman looked at me with raised eyebrows and drooping mouth and said quietly, "Silly girl." She then went on to say, "You're a big boy now. You should get a room, it's the least I would expect." She then handed me my licence. With my licence was a small piece of paper. I shoved it into my pocket without looking at it. Jumped into the car, watched the police car move away, and set off back to reality.'

Throughout all of his story, I had hardly spoken or even murmured, but as he looked at me, I roared with laughter and said, 'Fuck me, you don't half tell a story.'

'No,' he said, 'every word is absolutely true.' He then produced the note from the policewoman. It read WPC *Evans telephone number*, and the legend: *Like what I saw. Call me.*

'So off one bike and on to another,' I said.

'I don't think calling them bikes is a very gentlemanly thing to say of these ladies, or very flattering to me,' said Dutch in an amused sort of way.

'No, as I said before, you fall off one, straight back on. That's all I meant,' I said. 'You are taking up this offer from this policewoman, I assume?'

'Well, the problem is, as I said, my reaction to the image that came into my head at the very point of attainment is falling off a bike that I'm not sure I can get back on. I would not have been able to complete the task, and had it not been for the police car arriving at that precise moment, I'd have been in a very embarrassing situation. It would have been one I would not have known how to deal with. As it happens, I got away with it, but with my reputation and belief in myself, it won't take many failures before it's gone.'

I said, 'Bollocks. It was only a momentary lapse. Given a few seconds to gather your thoughts, you would have been OK, back to your old self and on with the job.'

'Not really, it shook me a lot,' he said. 'I can't get it out of my head; it keeps popping up for no reason at all.'

I said, 'Well, hopefully, time will help with that one.' In an attempt to take his mind away from Karen, I asked what else Samantha had said during their 'clear the air' talk yesterday.

'Oh,' he said and started to laugh. He went on to say, 'She got in her car and just headed off home. As she started to calm down, she realised how uncomfortable she was. Under her coat, she had got dressed in complete darkness by touch and feel and now realised it was probably not quite right. Her topcoat was OK and all buttoned up, and outwardly she looked neat enough. When she arrived home, her husband was apparently in the back working on something for his Scout group. She ran to the bathroom and discovered her blouse had buttons in the wrong buttonholes, her bra was unfastened and her knickers were on sideways, whatever that means.'

'Sounds like she's alright with it though, no real damage done. She's got away with it, hasn't she,' I said.

'I don't think we'll be repeating the exercise. She's got all the lust out of her system now.'

'So onwards and upwards, we're back to the policewoman,' I said.

'Ooh, no, not yet,' he said. 'You see, it was a bit more than just that image in my head. I also thought about Sammie's husband and the effect it would have on him; I've never had a thought like that before.'

'Kin hell, you've developed a conscience, now that's a turn up for the book.'

As we were laughing about this, he said, 'I've always had a conscience; it's just never bothered me before.' We laughed some more then decided to get on with our work.

CHAPTER NINE

During the afternoon, we were working on a modification of the water recycling system of the bus washing machine when suddenly Dutch let out a gasp and very nearly dropped a motor and pump unit he was lifting. He managed to hold on and placed it on the floor without any damage.

'What's the problem?' I enquired.

'It's this shoulder; I told you a couple of weeks ago I'd strained a muscle.'

'Yeah, I remember, but I would have thought it would have healed by now.'

'I would have thought so as well, but I aggravated it wrestling in the car the other night.'

'Oh, so it's a combat wound now, is it,' I said.

'Bollocks to you,' he replied.

'If you'd let me know you were struggling and still had a problem, I'd have done the heavier lifting work.'

'Well, that's it, it doesn't always play up. It only happens when my arm is in a particular position and trying to move in an awkward direction.'

'Right, OK, for the next week or so, you favour your shoulder and don't do any heavy lifting, and we'll see if we can alleviate the problem.'

The following week, workwise, all went well. Socially, not quite so good. Played bowls on Monday, lost again. Shit. Only saving grace was that several others also lost. The team lost by 27; back to the drawing board.

On Thursday, late in the afternoon, I was writing out the team for the evening match when Dutch came into the workshop. 'Ah, just the bloke I was thinking about. Will you be available this evening?'

'For what?' he asked.

'Bowls,' I replied.

'No, I won't be able to play for some time yet. Two reasons, one my shoulder and secondly, I have not had my bowls out of the bag yet this season.'

'Yeah, you're right, we'll have to get down the green a couple of times for some practice when you've rested your shoulder.'

'Will you be at the green?' I asked.

'I haven't given it much thought,' he said.

'The reason I ask is early next month I'm off on two weeks holiday and need someone to take over the captain's role. How do you fancy being non-playing captain? In your letter to the AGM, you said you needed a few weeks.'

'That's right; I think I will get involved again. Tell you what; I'll come along tonight and for the next couple of weeks and assist you in the role as non-playing vice-captain, it will allow me to get a feel of things. I will then be in a position to take control when you go on holiday.'

'Great,' I said. I thought to myself, *Once he's in the job, he'll remain in the job.*

I said, 'Have your bowls with you this evening and we'll have a roll before the match starts.'

'Yeah, I'll give it a go,' he said.

That evening we were the first at the green. As the rest arrived one by one, various comments were made by each and every one on seeing Dutch on the green. Mostly suggesting he should immediately take over as captain. Also intimating, I will now have to play for my place in the team. Mainly from members I had left out at one time or another over the last few weeks.

After half a dozen ends or so, I came off the green. In the pavilion, I prepared the score cards, welcomed the visiting captain and sorted the order of play. During this time, Ron came and got the scoreboard to hang outside the pavilion. I let him know Dutch was taking over as vice-captain for a few weeks with a view of becoming captain again soon.

His response was, 'Fucking marvellous. Cast aside like an old broken toy as soon as someone else comes along.'

I said, 'Don't you start, that is unless you want to take over as captain. Ah! Is that what you're angling for?' I asked.

'Like fuck,' was his reply as he went out to fit the board.

I went through the order of play with Dutch and left him with it. I as usual went on with the first four. Dutch took over, calling players to the mark, issuing score cards to team members, encouraging them to get around the green. In general, ran the match with the same aplomb as always.

Back in the club house after the match, I said, 'What did you think of that?'

'Great. I'm really pleased to be here and involved again.'

I asked, 'Fancy taking over as of now?'

'We can talk about it at work next week but I think I just might do that.'

'Will you want Ron as vice-captain?' I asked.

'Yes, if he's happy to do it but as I'm non-playing captain, he isn't that vital,' he said.

'Yeah, but in a couple of weeks, you'll probably want to play yourself.'

'Yeah, like I said, we'll talk it over next week.'

So, Dutch is in charge. Mission accomplished.

During lunch time on Friday, I said to Dutch, 'I'm off to Oxford this weekend as you know.'

'Yeah, I know, so what?' he said.

'Well, a team for next week needs to be selected and a team sheet put on the board at the club. You fancy taking charge and doing this?'

'Yeah, I don't mind, but I'll need all the records of who's played and how they got on as a guide.'

'Great, no problem. I've got them all here.' I handed them over to him. I said, 'Oh and just one thing more, I'm only away for the weekend and will be available for selection on Thursday.'

'Well, I'll have to see what the record shows before I can make any decision on that,' he said with a hint of a smile that seemed to say *I'm in charge now*.

I replied, 'Oh, in that case, I'm in.' We had a laugh along with our little exchange of dialogue.

* * *

On Friday evening, a darts competition had been organised. Dennis and Vic had entered as a team, and Ron and I had also entered. The draw had been made; Dennis and Vic were playing Paul and his son Liam in the first round.

While waiting for our game to be called, Ron and I sat in the vicinity of the dartboard and conversed about sport in general and last night's bowls in particular. The subject inevitably turned to Dutch and his role as vice-captain. Ron said he had taken to it as though he had not been away, which is what you would expect from him, he added.

I said, 'Yes. exactly as you'd expect.' and went on to say, 'he's taking over as non-playing captain as of today as well. He's got all the information and will be selecting next week's team. He wants you to be his vice-captain.'

'Me!' said Ron. 'Why has he said that?'

'Well, he thought you put a lot of effort in last night in helping to organise the game and said you were a natural organiser.'

'Yes, I think he's right,' said Ron in a jokingly proud posture. He then said, 'Wait a minute, if he's non-playing captain, he does not have much need of a vice-captain.'

'Yes, but in a week or so when he's had a few practice games, he's going to want to play,' I said.

'Maybe,' he replied.

I said, 'Think of the kudos you'll gain as the right-hand man of Dutch.'

He said, 'Kudos is no good to me; my missus won't let me use it anywhere.'

This raised a laugh from me. I said, 'So you're OK with that then, I'll let him know.'

He suddenly asked, 'Why not you?'

'Why not me what?' I replied.

'You for vice-captain.'

'Well, I'm off on holiday soon, that's why he's taking over.'

'Oh!' he said. Then after a short while said, 'Yes, that's right, where are you going? I've forgotten where you said you were going.'

'We are staying in a small villa between Benalmadena and Mijas. We've got our own swimming pool and a car, so a good time should be had by all.'

'It's way down south of Spain, isn't it?' Ron asked.

'Yes, not far from Gibraltar, actually it's quite near Marbella.' I went on to say, 'We're off to Oxfordshire this weekend, so I'm taking it easy with the beer tonight.'

Just then we were called to the oche. Dennis and Vic had lost, so commiserations from us as we approached the darts area, given with a hint of sarcasm and a little snigger. We were up against Bill Anderson and Don Steel. Ron was a noted darts player, so we fancied our chances. Sure enough, we won and were through to the semi-final.

In our semi-final, we came up against the favourites, Barry the Bus and an exceptional darts player, John Roberts. In a very tight game that I had the chance to check out with one dart at double 16, we lost.

After the final, which Barry and John won, we returned to the lounge. There Ron filled everybody in with the news of his elevation to vice-captain to Dutch. Eileen put in with, 'I thought you were already vice-captain?'

To which he answered, 'Er, yes,' accompanied with a look of total defeat.

After a while, I said, 'OK, Doreen, get your coat, time for us to leave these to it.'

This was greeted with, 'Wahey, you on a promise or what?' from Vic.

I responded with, 'Can't think what you mean, and if I did, I could not possibly say.'

At this Doreen interrupted with, 'No, we're going away to Oxford for the weekend, we need to sort out all the luggage and stuff we're taking.'

'Yes, we've heard all the excuses for leaving early before,' said Dennis.

'I never need an excuse for that,' I said. 'Anyway, we're playing away in Stafford on Monday, see you there, tatty bye,' and we left.

The weekend was very much a success. We had visited Blenheim Palace on Saturday, had a picnic in the grounds, played cricket with our grandson and generally had a very good time. On Sunday, we had gone to Bicester in the morning. In the afternoon, we went into Oxford and had a punt on the river, all in all a very satisfactory break.

On Monday back at work, Dutch gave me a résumé of the weekend's work, all planned projects completed, no real problems. (Didn't miss me.)

Later while chatting to Dutch, I said, 'We're playing in Stafford tonight. Fancy a run up there?'

'No, I'm thinking of going to our green and getting in some practice.'

'Oh great, you'll be after a place in the team soon then.'

'No, I haven't put me down to play, not this week,' he said.

I arrived at the green in Stafford with minutes to spare. I had travelled to the green directly from work, having been a bit late finishing. I was still early enough to play in my customary first four. I also won, although it was a close game. Unfortunately, the team lost, also to a very close score.

I hadn't intended to hang around after the match, but suddenly realised I was very hungry, so I went into their club house. I had furnished my opponent with a drink while the match had been in progress. In the clubhouse, he returned the compliment and got me a drink. I acquired a plate of sandwiches, pork pie and a sausage roll. I went and sat with a group of our guys. The talk was of how we could have, should have, won the match! It was there for the taking. I received a number of congratulatory remarks, which was nice. Just then, I think it was Bill Anderson, said, 'Did you see on the Midland News this morning, that bloke who played on Thursdays last season. You know the one who nicked the money from the bank.'

Joan said, 'No. What about him?'

Bill said, 'They found his car at Birmingham Airport; it's been there for weeks apparently.'

'Bloody hell, haven't they caught him yet?' said Markey.

'No, he's away and gone,' said Vic,' after this amount of time, the trail's gone cold, they won't get him now.'

Bill went on to say, 'The police are quite certain he hasn't departed from Birmingham and his car being there was just a decoy to confuse the issue.'

'That's typical of him; he always thought of himself as James fucking Bond,' said Don.

At this, the group started to prepare for the off. 'Are you going back to the club?' Vic asked,

'No, I came straight here from work, so I'll head home.'

'OK, I'll see you Thursday if not before,' he said.

It was Wednesday at lunchtime when Dutch said, 'You'll never believe what happened to me last night.'

I said, 'Whatever it was, if it happened to you, Dutch, I'll believe it.'

'A phone call; WPC Evans, no less.'

'Yeah, what was she after?'

'Well, exactly that actually.'

'What do you mean?'

'Her being after something: me. She opened with, "This is WPC Evans here." I said, "Oh yes, how can I help you?" She said, "That sounds a bit formal. What's the matter with, 'Oh hello, how are you?'" I said, "I rarely open up with that sort of statement when speaking to the police." She said, "This is not an official call, just a social call." I said, "In that case, hello, how are you?" "Very well," she replied.

'She then said, "I've been waiting for a phone call from you." "Have you, why's that?" "You got my little note, didn't you?" "Yes, but I didn't quite know how serious it was." "It was a genuine invitation," she said. "I don't go passing notes like that out to just anyone." "No, I don't suppose you do. I'm sorry if I gave that impression." "OK, I'll believe you, so when are we going to meet?" she came out with it just like that.'

'So, when are you going to meet her?' I asked.

'No, what I said to her was, "Well, you see, it's a bit difficult at the moment, I've got a lot of commitments right now." She said, "You're not still seeing that whinging skinny little slapper, are you?" Meow. "I don't think a remark like that is called for or even worthy of you," I said as a retort. She just said, "I didn't think she was your type at all."

"No, my commitments are not to any person, I have other things in my life." She said, "Yes, but don't neglect your social life. You will see I look a lot different out of my uniform." I said, "I bet you do." She said, "Cheeky, I meant in my civilian clothes." I said, "Too late, the image is already in my head." To which she came back with, "Good; what are you going to do about it?"

'I responded with, "Well, I've had, still have, a number of problems I need to deal with. Why don't you leave it with me and I'll call you when things are a bit more settled."

'"You didn't seem to have many problems the other night, I get the feeling you are giving me the brush off. I feel cheap now." I thought *Well yes, perhaps you ought*; I actually said, "No, I'm not against the idea; I'm just postponing the event for a short while."

'"Yes, that's what I'm saying; you're giving me the kiss-off. I don't think I will hear from you at all." "You've got me all wrong," I said, "I'll call you next week, regardless of whether I'm ready to take you up on your proposition. I should be in a better frame of mind to organise my social life then." "Alright, I'm going to trust you. I'll wait on your call, don't let me down."'

I said to him, 'What problems have you got that stop you taking her out?'

'Oh, I don't know. I just worry about what she's after.'

'What she's after? A man of your experience knows exactly what she's after.'

'No, I mean, is she trying to find information about her.'

'Her being Karen, I presume?' I said.

'Well, yes, of course, who else?'

'Why would she be interested in Karen?'

'Oh, I don't know, I don't know. I just know she's the police and that one has gone missing.'

'The police aren't bothered that she left you, and even if they were, they wouldn't send WPC wet knickers to interrogate you, would they?'

'Her name is Barbara.'

53

'Who!'

'WPC wet knickers.'

'Oh, OK then, what you need to do is get this silly idea out of your head and give the girl what she obviously wants.'

'Yeah, I'll give her a ring next week and sort something out. I hope I can cope and it doesn't happen again.'

'Hope what don't happen again?'

'What happened last time with Samantha.'

'For the world-class stud that you are deemed to be by all who know you, you're certainly lacking some belief in yourself.'

He said, 'Bollocks, you know my situation.'

I said, 'Yeah, and as I've said before, off one bike and on to the next, it's the only way.'

'I know; you're right; the worst that can happen is one disappointed wet-knickered policewoman and my reputation in ruins.'

'Now you know that won't happen. Your reputation won't suffer because if – and I do emphasise if – you did disappoint, you wouldn't tell anybody, would you?'

'Too fucking true,' he said.

CHAPTER TEN

Thursday evening, we played away at Rugeley. Dutch had selected the team, posted his selection on the noticeboard and took total charge of proceedings. It was always going to be a tough match and chances of a result quite slim. I won a very close game 21/20. Ron lost an equally close game 20/21. The clincher was a very good and somewhat unexpected win by Vic, as he was playing one of their better bowlers. Plus, a very good win for Markey. The result was a win for our team by two, would you believe. The lads were ecstatic, generally crediting Dutch and his ability to lead for our win.

I took these beliefs as detrimental to my term as captain but kept that thought to myself and joined in the merriment that goes with a win of this magnitude.

Friday, we gathered as usual, the main topic of conversation, the win last night. Chris led the praise for Dutch and his input to our win. I thought, *What the fuck does she know about it?* and then thought, *Yes, always in praise of Dutch is Chrissy, hmm.* I in turn gave due recognition to Vic and his game as the main factor for our win. Vic with false modesty said he agreed with me. The happy banter carried on with Vic stating my win along with Ron's score were also contributory factors in our win. All in all, we were very pleased with ourselves and the result.

Sometime later, Doreen mentioned our forthcoming holiday. This prompted Dennis to ask, 'Is it next weekend you go?'

'No, another four weeks before we're off, I haven't even started to think about it,' I said.

'Where are you actually going?' asked Dennis.

'The Costa del Sol, we've rented a villa outside Fuengirola, in the hills going towards Mijas.'

Dennis said, 'You know who you'll bump into down there, don't you?'

'Lots of people I expect,' I answered.

'No, the Banker, him that skedaddled with all the money. That's where he will have taken himself off to. All the criminals head for that area.'

'Well, if I see him, I'll get him to buy me a drink. Then report him when I get back.'

This raised a laugh all round with Ron putting in with, 'Yes, get all you can out of the bastard then grass him up to the Old Bill.'

'I take it you don't like him then,' said Vic.

'No, I don't. I was dropped a couple of times last season just so he could have a game.'

Over the weekend, during conversations with Dutch, I confirmed the lift everyone had seemed to have had from our win on Thursday and how it was put down to his influence on the team. To his credit, Dutch didn't believe he had much to do with the result. He had only put out the same team as last week and played them in the same order.

He thought several of our players had been quite extraordinary. Where he hoped to be of some influence was next week when we played the same team at home because he felt they would come seeking revenge. I very much agreed with his reasoning. We discussed the merits of altering the order of play and tried to think of anything that might give us a slight advantage. The discussion ended with me saying, 'Well, that's all the advice I've got, over to you, Captain.'

To which he said, 'Yes, and thank you very much.'

Later that weekend, a conversation turned to Barbara (WPC wet knickers) Evans. I don't know why but that name seems to be stuck in my mind. I asked Dutch if he'd had any thoughts about her or that particular situation. What he said surprised me somewhat. He said, 'I don't think I want a casual relationship. Not anymore, I think I've grown out of that part of my life. I'm getting too long in the tooth to be running around chasing females, dodging husbands or boyfriends. I just need a quiet life.'

I said, 'Fuck me, Dutch. What are we going to talk about if you're living the quiet life? Your life is the only excitement in my life.'

This made him smile. He said, 'To be honest, I would love to have your life. You've got a lovely attractive wife, a very pleasant home, surrounded by a wonderful family, and a great social life with really good friends. What more could you ever want?'

'You make me feel guilty for being jealous of your riotous lifestyle, and I thank you for your thoughts on how you perceive my life and existence. I suppose it's always greener the other side of the fence.'

'Well, I would be quite happy to live your sort of life,' he said.

I put forward a suggestion that maybe this policewoman was the answer. 'She's not married, is she?'

'I don't know,' was his reply.

'OK, here is a plan of action. You phone her, fix a date for Tuesday or Wednesday, treat her to a meal and only a meal. Check her marital status, if single, still just a meal. Then, leaving her with a promise of better things to come, offer to take her out again on Friday. Bring her to the club and spend an evening with us and our wives. Do you think she would be receptive to an idea such as that?'

'I haven't got a clue. I don't know her, do I?' he said.

'Is she alright, I mean is she a looker?' I asked.

'Well, once again, I'm not sure. I only saw her in her uniform. But you know me, if it's female and warm, that'll do.'

'You're a callous bastard as far as women are concerned, ain't ya,' I chuckled.

'Yes, I suppose I am, but that's what I'm on about. I've had enough and need to change, give more respect to these women.' He went on to say, 'I think it all started at that moment with Sammie, or possibly before then when that bitch did the dirty on me.'

My thoughts were: *As you sow, so shall you reap*. I said, 'Maybe a lesson learned, it could encourage a change for the good.' I followed up with, 'I still think you should make a date with your WPC, and consider my suggestion about Friday and remember it will be Spring bank holiday weekend.'

He said, 'Yeah, I'll give it some thought.'

Monday's match was away again. I lost; the team lost; Joan was not best pleased and hinted at some changes for the future.

It's bank holiday next week so there will not be a match. Maybe by the next match she will have calmed down a bit.

It was Wednesday at our lunch break when Dutch came out with, 'I made a phone call to WPC Evans last night.'

'Oh yes, and what's the outcome of that?'

'You might well ask because I'm not sure.'

'Oh, why's that?'

'Well, I started by apologising for seemingly messing her about, said it was not intentional and my problems were very real. She said, "You didn't seem to have much in the way of problems on that night." She went on, "You've made me feel very vulnerable and unwanted."'

I cut in at this point and said, 'Fuck me, she's a bit thin-skinned for a copper, ain't she? What did you say to that?'

He said, 'I just went into bullshit mode. I said, "I might have seemed trouble-free on that night, because up till the moment you and your colleague arrived on the scene, I did not realise I had a problem." She came back with, "Oh, so it was all my fault, was it?" "No, no, that's not what I'm saying."' He said, 'I then asked her to meet up with me and I would explain everything. She said, "Maybe, I'll think about it." She wants me to ring tonight at about six o'clock.'

To all this, I said, 'Seems like she's cooled down a bit. Are you going to follow it through?'

To which he replied, 'Oh yes, it's just a ploy on her part, she was doing all the chasing, now she wants to play a bit hard to get. Gains a bit of pride back this way, know what I mean. Read them like a book, I do.'

'You sure do,' was my reply.

The next morning, I could tell by the look on his face everything had gone well. 'So! How's it go then?' I asked.

'How did what go?' he replied with a smirk all over his face.

'Miss WPC wet knickers,' said I.

'It went surprisingly well. I made the phone call, she let it ring a regular four rings. I knew she was standing there waiting but didn't want to seem too keen.'

'In your dreams,' I put in.

He said, 'The upshot is, we went out for a meal.'

'Only a meal?' I asked.

'Woo, slow down a bit,' he said.

'Remember, I've already said your life is the only excitement in mine, so how can I slow down.'

As we laughed about this, he said, 'Well, it's not that exciting, actually. We went for a carvery along the A5. She is a bit of a looker, quite attractive, more so than I remember when seeing her in uniform. She's very pleasant and easy to talk with and listen to. I told her I'd had the dirty done on me by my last partner and that's why I was feeling a little out of sorts.'

He said, 'I didn't go into too much detail as its fuck all to do with her. For her part she said she had been married for eight years. Her husband had been killed four years ago in a road accident while at work. He had been a policeman and was in a car chase when it happened. This was the first time she had gone out on a date since then.'

'Kin hell. You're going to have to be very careful with this one, mate. I hope this doesn't end badly, she sounds OK. I'd advise you not to mess her about too much. I feel guilty now for giving her the nickname wet knickers.'

'I don't intend messing her about. The longer I was with her last night, the more I realised what a nice person she was. I went as far as taking up your suggestion of inviting her to the club on Friday evening.'

'Are you going to let them know at the match tonight?' I asked.

'No, I shouldn't think so. What the fuck's it got to do with any of them who I go out with,' was his reply.

The match turned out to be a disaster, only two winners at home. Ron was a winner as was Markey, the rest all lost. Me, I lost 21/13, the worst loser. Most of the other games were close but still games lost. The opposition were every bit as pleased with their win as we had been with our win last week.

I saw Dutch congratulate their captain and wish him well for the rest of the season, saying he thought they had a good chance of winning the league title. I thought *Smooth talking bastard, our*

Dutch, that's how he does so well with the ladies, apart from being tall, good-looking, and well turned out, he's full of charm and bullshit.

Anyway, it's only a game, so onwards and upwards, we'll be back next week for another match.

In discussions next day, Dutch came up with, 'The first four losing set the trend.'

'Oh, so it was all my fault, was it?' I said.

'No, they put their top four on the first ends and it paid off for them.'

I agreed they had come up with a good strategy, but I should have done a lot better. I went on to say, 'The problem with our green is that it's not a good home green. Anyone who can play a bit can soon get the feel of our green, it doesn't have any real tricks in it. The crown is small and quite even. Their players last night were all good bowlers, bowling at the top of their ability. Best put it down to experience and start to plan for our next match.'

'Yes, I'm afraid that is all we can do,' he replied.

Later that afternoon, I said to Dutch, 'Everything OK for tonight?'

'Yeah, though I'm a little uneasy about introducing her into a crowd of close friends as you all are.'

I said, 'I'll tell you what; most of the gang don't get to the club till around 8.30ish. I'll arrange to be there with Doreen at 8 o'clock. If you and Barbara arrive at about that time, you can make the introductions and settle in without too much pressure. As the other couples arrive, you can make them aware of the situation separately, thus avoiding any confusion, with little if any embarrassment. How's that grab yah?'

'Yeah, that sounds like a plan. I'll go with that, OK.'

When I arrived home, I said to Doreen, 'We're out early this evening. I've arranged to meet up with Dutch and his new friend Barbara in the club at 8 o'clock.'

'Yes, that's right, put yourself out for him. If it was me wanting to go out early, you would be accusing me of being an alcoholic.'

'Now don't start, all I'm asking is to help a mate to change his life around. You know he's had and still has a lot of problems to cope with.'

'Mostly of his own making,' she stated.

'I think that's a bit unfair. I know he's not always been the best role model, but I think he really is now trying to be a better person. Let's help a little bit if we can. Anyway, what's with all this hostility? He's never done you any harm. To be absolutely honest, he always seemed to hold you in the highest regard. He thinks you are a good-looking nice to know person.'

'I don't doubt he says these things, and he does always treat me very well, but he's the same with any woman he meets. I don't trust or believe anything he has to say or does. Well, I bet he thinks it's nice to know he has some friends who he can rely on when times are tough.'

'OK, just for tonight, try to be your usual pleasant self, and next week I'll tell him what you really think.'

'You keep your big mouth shut,' she stated, most eloquently.

When we arrived at the club, it was just after 8 o'clock. Dutch and Barbara were already there. Dutch made the introductions then went to get the drinks.

Barbara opened with, 'I've heard a lot about you over the last couple of days.'

I said, 'If it's from him, only about 10 per cent is true. If it's what you've read in the *Police Gazette,* none of it's true; it was just a misunderstanding, and the lady withdrew the allegation anyway.' This made her laugh, even Doreen had a smile. Result, a pleasant atmosphere gently settling on the event.

We sat and chatted about anything and everything, with Doreen slowly engaging Barbara in conversation regarding our kids and in particular our grandson. Barbara had contributed to the conversation with a brief history of her marriage and subsequent death of her husband. Dutch and I had our own chat, mostly about work. Yeah, you're right, we are two very boring old buggers.

First to arrive was Dennis and June, a bit unusual, normally they were last to arrive on a Friday evening. Nothing very dramatic

61

about that; they had been to visit an elderly relative in a home who was thought to be close to the final door. Introductions were made, and before we could settle, Ron and Eileen came in, closely followed by Vic and Chris.

Introductions were made all round, I called a round of drinks. While I got the drinks, Vic and Dennis acquired an extra table from the centre of the room to extend our drinking area, as it was a bit of a squeeze with 10 of us in there.

We blokes sat ourselves around the newly acquired table, with me on the outside looking in towards our seating bay where the ladies were sat.

Our conversation mainly revolved around last night's poor showing on the green and a wood-by-wood assessment of what had gone wrong. Ron for his part, would from time to time chime in with statements along the lines of 'I don't know what the problem was, us winners didn't seem to have any difficulty, did you notice that, Captain?' Which were greeted with remarks such as, 'Somebody has to draw the rabbit from Vic, and stop sucking up to the captain, we all know you had a bit of luck, if his dog hadn't run off with his white stick, it could have been a very different story.' The evening rolled along in that manner, all jocular banter.

From my position, I could see that Barbara seemed OK sat there chatting with the ladies who were all about 10 or 15 years older than she was. What I could also see was that Doreen was in her element acting as guardian and closest ally to Barbara, having been first to meet her.

I could not hear their conversation, nor did I wish to, but it seemed Doreen was encouraging her to relay the story of her husband and his shortcomings to the rest of the group.

We had been there about an hour when PK suddenly popped up. 'Anybody want to pay in any money?'

'Is that all you ever think about?' said Dennis.

'If I don't chase after you lot, I can't imagine you looking for me to pass over money.' He then suddenly realised Dutch was with the group. 'What are you doing with this lot on a Friday?'

'I'm sorry, I didn't realise I had to consult you as to where I went on a Friday, Mr Chairman,' replied Dutch.

62

'Bollocks,' was his short reply.

'Language,' put in Vic, 'not before the ladies.'

'Sorry,' said PK, 'I didn't know it was their turn.' This raised hoots and comments all round. 'Don't mess me about, I haven't much time, I'm calling the next session of bingo.' Ron and Dennis paid in money, all suitably recorded. We then settled down again and carried on with our usual banter.

I became aware that Chris was holding court at the far end of the seating bay. She was pontificating on the fact that we were all going off to Blackpool for a weekend. Not asking but telling them when it had all been sorted. She was being supported by June and Eileen on the injustice of the situation. In fairness to Doreen, she didn't seem to get too involved in slagging us off.

Then it happened, Barbara said, 'Instead of moaning about it, organise an outing of your own.'

Four miserable little faces lit up like beacons. *Kin hell*, I thought, *that's going to cost.*

Eileen asked, 'Like where?'

Barbara seemed to take charge now and said, 'Well, somewhere like Chester, Sheffield, Leeds, Bristol, or even London for a weekend's shopping.'

I'm watching this unfold before me, sat there with my mouth gaping open, not listening to what was being said around our table. Suddenly I'm aware of Dennis saying, 'What you nosing at?'

'Oh! er nothing, shall we retire to the games room?'

Dutch was a bit reluctant to leave his date after such a short acquaintance. Dennis said, 'I'll get a round in; you can tell them what we're doing.'

I said, 'Thanks, mate, why is it always me doing the dirty work?'

'Because you called for the move,' put in Ron.

Dennis checked what drinks were required and went to the bar. I tagged along to transfer the drinks to the table.

I put all the ladies' drinks on a tray and approached their table. It was at this point I heard the words 'health spa'. 'There you go, ladies,' I said, 'everyone all OK now? Right, we are just going to pop into the games room for a short while, is that OK?'

Chris stated, 'As long as you don't neglect our drinks, you can stop in there as long as you want.'

'Oh, thank you,' I replied, 'but Dutch is a bit reluctant to leave Barbara alone with you wild young things, as you might lead her astray.'

Barbara said, 'It's quite alright. I think I'll be safe with these pleasant young ladies for a while.'

I, looking up to the ceiling, said, 'Forgive her, Lord, for she knows not what she says.'

Doreen's comment to this was, 'Bugger off and give us some peace.'

'Language, dear,' was my parting shot.

In the games room, Vic was already trying to book a table. I said, 'Hold on, you know what's being planned in there?'

This was greeted by blank faces. I told them they were planning a weekend away as retribution for our Blackpool trip. Absolute silence and looks of disbelief.

'What are you on about?' asked Ron.

'Well, when PK came to collect money, Barbara enquired as to what it was for. That started them off on a tirade aimed at us and our dastardly deeds in going to Blackpool. Then Barbara put forward a suggestion, instead of moaning about it, organise an outing of their own.'

'Is that much of a problem?' asked Vic.

'Not if it was just an outing, but with talk of a weekend in London, or as the last suggestion was a few days at a health spa, it'll cost a fortune.'

On hearing this, Dutch was a bit embarrassed. 'Fucking hell, the first night I bring her to meet friends, she fucks it all up. Sorry, I should not have put you in this situation. I'll go and tell her we've got to go.'

'No, no, don't do that, it's not down to her, they were bound to reach the same conclusion sooner or later. It's really my fault, I panicked. Vic's quite correct it ain't much of a problem. It was just the mention of a weekend in London that spooked me. I had visions of sightseeing trips, top shows, top hotels, expensive shopping and a whole host of costly jaunts throughout a long weekend and I overreacted.'

I went on to say, 'I think we all need to remind our wives before they come to a final decision on where or what they might do for their little outing that our entire trip is only costing £70. I for my part will suggest a maximum of a similar cost.'

'You've got no chance of getting away with that,' said Dennis.

I replied, 'Maybe not, but I intend to try.' The atmosphere lightened somewhat as they all had thoughts and comments as to what Doreen would say to me about my restrictions on her. My reaction was to say, 'You would all do well to follow the same line of reasoning and hope they make a sensible decision.'

Dutch said he still felt Barbara was culpable and would be having strong words with her about putting forward ideas as to create such problems.

Ron said, 'Don't fall out with her over what's been said here, none of this is her doing.' This sentiment was echoed by Vic and Dennis.

Dutch said, 'You might think that but all the same, I'm not so sure, but we'll leave it and see how it all progresses.'

Vic said, 'The tables are all booked with a substantial list of guys waiting to play, we'd better go back into the lounge.'

Ron asked, 'How are we going to play it?'

'As if nothing has happened,' put in Dennis.

'Quite right,' was my comment.

Back in the lounge, it was Doreen who buoyed up by alcohol said, 'You're back early. Wouldn't they let you play?' in a Mumsie to little boy sort of way. To this, they all roared with laughter as if it was the funniest thing they had ever heard.

I nearly let a smile slip out but managed to control myself and replied with a hint of disdain, 'Yes, something like that.' This started another bout of laughing, which seemed to be more raucous than the situation warranted. I took this to be a symptom of how pleased they were with their perceived rebellious plan.

The rest of the evening went along in a pleasant, relaxed way as Friday evenings tend to go.

On the way home, I was informed by Doreen that the ladies were going to organise an outing of some sort for the weekend that we were in Blackpool. I said I thought it was a very good idea. 'Yes,' she said, 'it'll probably be to a health farm.' She went on to say, 'Barbara was getting a load of information for tomorrow night, and we are meeting up in the concert room to have a look at it.'

'Great, you've been to one before, haven't you? Ain't they're a bit pricey to just keep you amused while I'm away for a couple of days.' I then added, 'Just remember, we're going on holiday in a couple of weeks, and also my trip to Blackpool is only £70 all in.'

When I arrived at work the following morning, Dutch had the tea ready and had started to sort out the tools and equipment for the morning's work. I greeted him with, 'Morning. How's things with you then?'

'Oh, I don't know, alright, I suppose.'

'Hello,' I said, do I detect a note of despondency?'

'Last night was all wrong; we should not have gone.'

'Bad as that then. I thought it was OK.'

'No, it was a disaster. We had a right row after we left the club, I don't think I'll be seeing her again.'

'Well, that's a shame,' I said.

'Too fucking right,' he said. 'I never got around to giving her one.'

'You're a callous bastard where women are concerned,' I said with a slight laugh.

'They get from me exactly what they deserve. I always try to deliver that much.'

'Well, here's another problem for us to ponder on. My good lady is expecting you and your lady friend at the club again tonight with information regarding the last night's discussed outing.'

'Well, that's out the window, I'm afraid, because we won't be there, so all problems solved, right.'

'Not really because it's now in their minds. So, with or without Barbara, some sort of outing will be arranged. It was said last night it was not down to Barbara; the conclusion would have been reached regardless of who actually put the idea forward. Best thing you can do now is to give her a call and say you were wrong for creating an argument last night and you're sorry.'

'Like fuck I will,' was his reply. At that we got on with our work.

I finished work in mid-afternoon. When I arrived home, Doreen was cooking a meal. While eating, she asked, 'What time will we be going out tonight?'

I said, 'I've no idea, why?'

She said, 'We're all meeting up at the club in the big room.'

I think that's all cancelled. Dutch and Barbara had a falling out last night so they won't be there.'

'Ha! I knew he would try and put his oar in, I suppose he felt she got on too well with us. Is that what upset him?'

'No, he's not like that, as you well know.'

'I don't know at all,' she replied. 'I've always thought he could be awkward and vindictive.'

'Well, no, he isn't, is he? You've known him long enough to know that. You've never known him to behave in that way, have you?'

'No, I suppose not.'

After a short break in the conversation, she suddenly said, 'Barbara might just turn up on her own.'

'Yeah, and pigs might fly,' I replied.

The upshot of it all was that we arrived at the club at about 8 o'clock. All our usual gang were there. Apparently, a pop group and a comedian were about to entertain us for the evening. It was Chris who was first to inquire as to what time Dutch and Barbara were due to arrive.

Ron put in with the fact that Dutch had turned up at the bowls during the afternoon but had not said anything about the evening. I informed them of the situation as I knew it to be. Chris looked a bit surprised and said, 'Why? What happened?'

This sent all the ladies into a close huddle to exchange thoughts about what might or could have caused the breakdown of the relationship. We blokes just got on with our conversation regarding the afternoon's bowls match and the day's football results.

After we had been in the club for about an hour and a half, surprise, surprise, in walked Dutch and Barbara. She had a sort of guilty look about her. Ron, who had just got the last round in, asked what they were drinking and went to the bar. Barbara sat right opposite me across the table and said, 'I think I owe you an apology.'

I said, 'Stop right there; you do not owe me or anyone else anything, let alone an apology. It was all a misunderstanding on my part. If anyone should apologise, it should be me, so let me say I'm very sorry for my part in the misunderstanding. If you can accept that from me, please don't give it another thought.'

She went to say, 'But I feel I should.'

I put my finger to my lips and said, 'Shhh. It's all in the past, OK?'

She nodded, smiled and said, 'OK.'

I turned to Dutch, raised my eyebrows and said, 'So?'

He just said, 'I took your advice, thanks.'

'No problem,' said I.

On the way home and at home for that matter, Doreen blasted me with insignificant details of the night's conversations, to which I responded with lots of 'yeahs' and 'ohs', along with some 'did shes' and 'oh rights' without really taking in anything she was saying. She had drunk more than she should have, so I got away with it.

It had been agreed at work, Sunday should be a day of rest as it was a bank holiday weekend.

Both Dutch and I were at work on Monday, the three compressors in the main workshop were to be stripped and overhauled. When I first arrived, I could see he was in good spirits. 'Good weekend then?' I asked.

His face said it all. 'Yeah, OK.'

'OK, bollocks,' I said, 'you look like the cat that got the cream. So, I presume you got the cream, yeah.'

'Let's crack on with the work. If we can make good progress, I'll fill you in with some of the details when we have a break.'

The work was hard with a number of problems cropping up, and progress was much slower than I'd anticipated.

So consequently, it was nearly five hours before the compressors were ready for testing. I suggested to Dutch he went and made the tea, and I would monitor the machines charging up.

By the time I sat down for the break, I felt I was really ready for it. As we consumed our food and drinks, we discussed what was left to be accomplished. After due consideration, we agreed about another hour and a half should do it.

I started with, 'So OK, what happened?'

'After you left on Saturday, I was at a bit of a loose end. What you had said about it not being her fault had started me thinking maybe I'd got everything wrong. Anyway, I knew the Saturday bowls team were playing at Bloxwich, so I popped in to watch for a short while. I got talking to Ron, who was saying how good it had been on Friday evening and how much he and his wife had enjoyed meeting Barbara and what a nice person she was. This convinced me I had fucked up.

'It was very apparent you had been correct and what I should do his call her and apologise and admit I was at fault. When I called, there was no answer. I wasn't sure if no one was there or if she refused to pick up. So, I left a message on her answering machine saying I needed to speak to her and would ring back at 5.15 and hoped she would be available.'

He went on, 'I had not said what I wanted to speak about, whether it was to apologise or carry on with the disagreement of the night before. If she thought it was to ask for forgiveness, it would give her the upper hand right from the start.'

I interrupted at this point to say, 'You don't give much ground in these little battles, do you?'

'No, always keep in control, that's my way,' was his response.

'Anyway, I did phone at exactly 5.15. I thought the regular four rings to show she's not anxious, sure enough, four rings she picks up. "Hello." "Hello," I put in, "it's me." "Oh! is it?" she responded. "Look, about last night, I got it all wrong, I'm ringing to say I'm really sorry." "Yes, but why did you turn on me like that?" she asked with a very hurt sounding voice.

'"I don't know. I just panicked. I so much wanted everyone to like you." I took a pause. No response came from her. I thought

Wow, that must have been a good line, it's slowed her down a bit. After a moment of silence, I added, "When it was realised it was you that had put forward the suggestion of an outing, they were all a bit critical of the idea. At that, I became quite disappointed about the evening." I then added, "Since she let me down (he means Karen), I'm all confused, unsure of myself, feel vulnerable, even a bit frightened."'

'Wow! Hold on,' I interrupted. 'This, the type of bloke who is everything I hoped I'd turn into when I was a youth. A bloke shagging them as quick as they could throw them under him, running around without a care in the world, is now confused, unsure, vulnerable and!! And frightened, do me a favour.'

'No, you twat, this is what I'm saying to her. This gets me all the sympathy needed to make forgiveness acceptable.'

'Ha, you've certainly got a way with words, ain't yah?' I said.

'Oh, I don't know, I am what I am,' he replied.

He went on to say, 'With her on the back foot, I suggested I take her for a meal, where she could allow me to carry on begging forgiveness. She agreed, so that's what we did and it all went very well. Later, it was Barbara who put forward the idea of going on to the club, as she had promised to meet you all and didn't want you to think she'd let you down.'

'And!!' I prompted.

'Well, after the club, I took her home.'

'AND!!' I prompted again.

'Well, I stopped the night.'

'Now that sounds a bit more like the bloke I work with. So how did it go?'

'I'm saying nothing,' he answered.

'Is a repeat performance in the pipeline? If you'll pardon the pun,' I inquired.

'Already performed. I stayed all of yesterday.'

'So, all is good and everything is OK then,' I said.

'Yeah, it's all great,' he replied. Then, after a moment or so, he said, 'On Saturday night, as we were relaxing after the bout of physical stuff, I was suddenly aware she was weeping, all very gently and quietly with tears running down her cheeks. This startled me; I wasn't sure what was happening. I asked what the problem was. She said it was the first time she had made love with anyone since her husband had died, and she had just thought about him and hoped he understood.'

'Fuck me,' I put in, 'that's a bit delicate, what did you say?'

'Just that I thought he would understand, it was done for all the right reasons and that I was sure he would not have wanted her to not have any life after he had gone.'

'Was she OK with that?'

'Yeah, eventually.'

'I told you from the very start this would need to be carefully handled, but in fairness to you, I think you did it all absolutely right.'

He then added. As they were all quiet and cuddling, she had said she now understood the problems he was having about her (meaning Karen) when they were first trying to get together, and she was sorry for mistrusting him. He went on to say with some bitterness, 'She doesn't know the first thing of how I feel about that fucking bitch.'

I did not venture a comment on this, I just said, 'Time to get back to work or we'll never get home today.' Later, thinking about our conversation, I came to the conclusion his confused, unsure and vulnerable line was closer to the mark than his response to my comments would suggest.

It was several days later when I asked how things were with Barbara.

'She's on late evenings for the next week or so.'

'Oh, bad luck,' I said. 'When are you expecting to see her next?'

'I wanted to talk with you on that. She finishes this shift on the 10th of June, which is a Thursday, and we were thinking about having a few days away somewhere. Only a long weekend in North Wales probably.'

'Oh great, so it's all systems go with this bird, is it?' I said.

'*Bird!!*' he said, 'You're talking about the lady I'm presently in love with.'

I said, '*Presently*, you be careful with this, OK?'

'Yeah, I'm just being frivolous, it's all under control,' he replied.

'Yeah, a weekend away sounds good. I assume it's the 11th to the14th, right?'

'Yes, those are the dates. You OK with that?'

'Sure,' I replied. I said, 'You realise I'm off for a couple of weeks the following Friday, and we are programmed to complete all the roof gutter cleaning during June.'

'OK,' he said, 'the sides of the first and last bays are definitely two-handed, so we crack on with those when the two of us are here, and we can get on with the valleys when on our own.'

'Good, all settled. Go and see the manager, put in your holiday request, explain our ideas and let's get this show on the road.'

CHAPTER ELEVEN

On Friday at the club, all were keen to know if Dutch and Barbara would be putting in an appearance. We had played bowls Monday and Thursday, all three of us had won on both occasions, but no one had raised the issue of Barbara.

I informed them all Barbara was on evening shifts till the middle of next week, so no, they wouldn't be joining us. As it turned out, Chris had enlisted our daughter Elizabeth to help her organise their outing, it involved spending some time at Silverdale Hall, a health spa, apparently.

Dennis and June were not with us tonight. June had phoned Eileen to say they were babysitting the grandchildren.

In conversation with Ron, I asked if Dutch had mentioned next week's match. He said, 'Oh, yeah, he might not be available, he'll let me know on Monday.'

'So, there you go then, captain of the Thursday bowls.' We all had a laugh as Ron strutted his stuff with exaggerated pride. Vic put forward the suggestion it might be permanent now Dutch was walking out a new lady friend.

Chris enquired as to whether she should include Barbara in their jaunt to Silverdale. I said I didn't know but thought it likely she would wish to go as Dutch would be with us.

On the following Tuesday, Dutch and I were working on the gutter of number one bay. Dutch was at the top of a ladder with a bucket and a trowel, scraping and scooping up dirt and plant life that had started to grow. I was below preparing the coating which was to be applied when the gutter was clean.

I wasn't taking too much notice of him or what he was doing when suddenly he let out a loud cry. 'Arrrr! BELOW,' he called. I looked up just in time to see the bucket come flying down and managed to scramble out of the way.

Dutch, still at the top of the ladder, was just standing there with his head down on his chest. He remained like that for several seconds. I called out, 'You OK?'

Suddenly, he looked down. 'Sorry,' he called and started to descend the ladder.

'What happened? You OK?' I was quite concerned. I thought he was going to follow the bucket when I'd first looked up.

Quite calmly, he said, 'I'm OK, it was this shoulder again. As I was lifting the bucket, my shoulder locked out, and the pain shot right through my body, I lost all control and the bucket just went.'

'Good job you called out or it would have hit me.'

'I didn't realise I'd called out,' he said, looking a bit sheepish. 'I had a bit of a blackout, I think. I just hung on for a second or two, but I'm OK now.'

'Well, I ain't. Let's go for a cup of tea and a break. I'm all of a tremble,' I said.

Back in the workshop with a cuppa, I suggested he should have his shoulder looked at as it had been troubling him for a good number of weeks now.

'It'll be OK, it only happens occasionally. In fact, that's the first time for a long while.'

'Maybe, but it seemed to be more severe this time, you looked to be in real trouble up there.'

'No, it was just a couple of seconds, it's OK now.'

'I still think you should get it looked at. When we start again, I'll go up the ladder.'

'No need, really, I'm good to go,' was his statement as we returned to our work.

Over the next couple of days, despite a considerable number of interruptions with problems elsewhere that required immediate attention, the work on the end gutter of the first bay was completed.

On Thursday, Dutch left for his weekend break. He's too cool a guy to show much feeling but I thought he was quite excited about the prospect of spending a few days with Barbara. He went with a 'best of luck' endorsement ringing in his ear from me.

The bowls match that evening was away at Willenhall. I lost, as did Ron who was captain. Despite us two losing, the team won, a very good result. Back at the club, Ron blamed the pressure of being captain for his loss. This seemed to be acceptable to everybody as they congratulated him and were overjoyed with the win.

Unfortunately, this left me as the target for piss-taking as the only loser without an acceptable excuse. It was all in good spirits as the teams win overrode all other emotions.

At work on Friday, I got into conversation with the works manager. He was asking about progress with the summer programme. I explained our present position and our expectations and said I thought we were on target. I went on to say that after next Friday I was on holiday for two weeks. And added that Dutch and I had discussed this situation and had been quite confident we could still deliver.

'I'm quite sure you can,' he said. 'I've got every confidence in you two. I'm in no doubt you will achieve whatever you promise.'

I then said, 'Well, actually, there is a slight problem.' I explained the difficulty Dutch was having with his shoulder.

'Is he safe to be at work?' he asked.

Oh fuck, where am I going with this? I thought. 'Yes,' I answered, possibly too quickly, and followed up with, 'I would not have raised the issue but for the fact that we are doing roof work and Dutch will be up there on his own, working to keep up with the programme while I'm away.'

'I see, so there is a problem keeping up to schedule. What do you suggest we do?'

'I had thought it would be acceptable to acquire some assistance,' I said.

'And where do you think this assistance is to come from?' he asked, looking worried at the thought it was going to cost him money.

'I've given this some thought and would like to suggest we use an apprentice, namely Mickey Reynolds. He's the senior auto-electrical apprentice. He's just finished his exams for this year, it will give him some experience in other aspects of working environments, give good support to Dutch, and his electrical knowledge will also be very useful in my absence.'

'My goodness, you have given this some thought, haven't you? Leave it with me. I'll have a think about what you've said and come back to you.' With that, he departed.

It was quite late in the afternoon when Samantha came looking for me to say the manager wanted to see me.

He said he had thought through my idea, could not fault the logic. He had had a word with young Michael who had found the prospect of the new challenge exciting. The manager thought it would be an advantage for the lad to work with me on Monday as I was on my own that day. 'Yeah, OK, if you think that,' I said.

In the evening when at home, I'd phoned our daughter. I asked what progress had been made regarding the ladies outing.

She told me the cost of a weekend at Silverdale Hall had been several hundred pounds; talking with Chris it was thought to be more than they were willing to pay. She had got costs for a one-night stay and also costs for a Saturday visit with various treatments that seemed more in keeping with what they were prepared to pay.

She then added she had suggested a day at Silverdale followed by a meal at a good pub. Chris was going to put it to all the ladies tonight and see if a consensus of opinion could be reached. I had said, 'When you talk with your mother about this, try to make her see reason regarding the cost.'

She said, 'Don't be so miserable, you know my mom does not take advantage of you in any situation.'

I said, 'Oh! Yeah, OK.' I actually thought, *Shit, she's on her mother's side in this.* Well, I'd done my best to exert some control over the cost of this anarchy and show of female liberation.

At the club we had a full team. The main topic of conversation was last night's win. I put forward the theory that I had drawn the only good bowler they had and was unlucky to lose even then. This was greeted with howls of derision. To this I said, 'Please yourselves, but that's my opinion and I'm sticking to it.'

Eileen then informed the blokes that they, the ladies, were going into the big room to play bingo and would like a round of drinks to take with them. 'Some bloody equality we get here,' said Ron as he went to fetch the drinks. We all nodded in agreement, but the ladies still all looked pleased with themselves.

When on our own I explained the conversation I'd had with our Elizabeth. I'd said I thought a day out at Silverdale with some treatments and meal in the evening would cost between £125 and £150. 'Any comments?'

'That's twice what our costs are,' was the first remark from Ron.

'Yes, but the cost of Silverdale on its own is only in the region of £70,' I ventured to say, 'and if you take in what we will spend on extras like beer and such, it might be closer to their costs or with a bit of luck even more. So, I don't think we've got much of an argument.'

Dennis said, 'If that's what it is, so be it. We'll just have to go along with it.'

Vic added, 'You do realise this will be used as a precedent every time we go on an outing.'

'Too fucking true, it will,' was Ron's comment. We sat there all quiet and a bit defeated for a moment.

Then Vic said, 'Get the dominoes out and let's play,' all financial worries forgotten.

We were suddenly disrupted by the return of the ladies, all overexcited owing to the fact that June had won the big one, whatever that should be. They all laughed and giggled and went on about everyone else's disappointment with remarks like 'did you see the look on so and so's face' and other such remarks.

It was Dennis who said, 'Calm down, ladies, you're causing a disturbance.'

This was greeted with, 'Oh shut up, misery guts, go and get a round in on me,' by June.

Dennis said, 'I don't know about a round. You should save your money for your weekend outing.'

'Is that what you've been moaning about while we've been in there?' said Doreen, looking directly at me. They all roared with laughter at this, we just sat there looking a bit sheepish.

June once again insisted that Dennis should get a round out of her winnings.

Later on, in the evening I spoke with Ron about the team selection for next week. He said Dutch had not said anything about next week. 'He won't be back till Tuesday and a team sheet needs to go up sometime over the weekend.' I went on to say, 'Leave me out as I lost last night.'

He said, 'So did I. Do I leave myself out or what?'

'No, I will be going on holiday next Friday so it's no problem for me. The team will accept you keeping your place as you were captain and have took the decision to leave me out, OK.'

The weekend all went smooth enough. Sunday morning I was at work to clean the filters of the bus washing machine water reclamation scheme. Quite dirty and smelly but everything went to plan, no problems.

Early Monday morning, young Mickey reported to our workshop. While having a cup of tea, I put forward the plan of action for the day. First, he was to report to the garage office, get the report sheets, and not to hang around there all day chatting to the young girl. To which he replied, 'Who me?'

I thought, *Hello, we've got another character here along the lines of Dutch*, and answered, 'Yes, you.' As he laughed about the situation, I said, 'While you sort the sheets out, I'll do the walk-around inspection. We'll then clear the reports and any items I pick up on, that should take us up to break time.'

All went to plan, at break I informed him as to why he had been temporarily transferred, that we had some roof work to complete, and Dutch had a slight shoulder problem. Added to this, the manager was concerned about health and safety with one or the other being on holiday, leaving the other to work alone on a roof. I went on to say, 'His shoulder is not a major concern, but keep an eye on him, especially if he's in a vulnerable position.'

'Yes, I understand the situation, and sure I will cope.'

During the afternoon while working on the roof, I'd asked Mick to go and fetch the battery drill. When Mick came back, he said Samantha was after me, as someone had come to the office asking to see me. Not wanting to leave him up there on his own, we both went to the office. I knocked and entered; a young woman who had been sitting on a chair stood up. *Kin hell!!* I thought, *What the fuck could she ever want with me?*

She was gorgeous, but that's an understatement. She was quite tall, slim, leggy, expensively dressed with shiny dark hair. For all this, there was a ring of familiarity about her.

'Hello,' I said.

'Hello. I'm Mrs McDonald,' she said, holding out her hand.

I took her hand thinking, *Go steady or you'll be showing signs of sexual excitement,* but said quite calmly, 'And what can I do for you?'

'I need to speak with you about Dutch,' she said, without any hint as to why.

At that point I decided a bit of privacy was called for. I turned to Mick to ask him to return to the workshop and wait for my return and said, 'Close your mouth, Mick, you look like you're catching flies.' He half smiled and looked a little bit embarrassed, which is a bit unusual with today's 19-year-olds. As he returned to the workshop, I escorted Mrs McDonald to the canteen. She had coffee, I had tea, and we sat in a quiet area of the dining room.

'Right, what is your concern with Dutch?' I asked.

'I'm Karen's sister.'

Oh, that's what was familiar about her, I thought. She went on to say she had been trying to contact Dutch for some time now but did not seem to be able to locate him.

'For what reason do you wish to contact him?' I inquired.

'I have not heard from my sister for several months, which is very unusual. Actually, I haven't heard anything from the day she left him.'

'What do you think he might be able to do about that?' was my next question.

'I don't know,' she said. 'I was wondering if he'd had any contact with her or if he knows where she might be.'

I said, 'It's not my place to go telling you what Dutch knows or does not know. What I will say is that he was very hurt by the episode, he doesn't speak well of Karen if he even mentions her at all. I think he's made a great effort to put it all behind him and now appears to be getting on with his life. He has not left the planet; he's just taking a short break and is out of the area at the moment.'

'So, you don't think he'll be able to help me contact her?' she asked.

'No, I personally don't think he knows anything about her whereabouts or even wishes to know. I'm sorry I can't be any more helpful, what I will do is let him know you were making enquiries. I assume he'll know how to contact you if that's what he wishes.'

'Yes, that will be fine,' she replied.

'OK, Mrs McDonald, once again, sorry I could not be of much help.'

'My name is Ruth, please; Mrs McDonald sounds so formal.'

'OK, Ruth, very nice to have met you, and for what it's worth, I thought Karen was a very pleasant person to be around and nearly as attractive as her sister.'

She looked at me with a half-smile and a look that seemed to say, *Don't you dare try it on with me*, and said, 'Sorry to have troubled you at your place of employment but I did not know what else to do.'

'No problem,' I said and held out my hand as she said thank you.

I said, 'The pleasure was all mine, bye.'

When I returned to the workshop, Mick greeted me with, 'Who the fuck was that?'

'Never you mind, and get all those filthy thoughts out of your head.'

'No way, I think I'll be dreaming of her tonight,' was his reply.

Tuesday morning, Dutch was back, looking very happy and pleased with life. 'Good break?' I inquired.

'The best,' was his reply.

'I suppose you spent all the weekend in bed shagging, right?'

'Not at all, we were out and about every day, I actually climbed Snowdon.'

'Fuck off, you mean you went up Snowdon on a train.'

'No, not with this girl, she insisted on climbing. The start was from a place called Pen-y-Pass, up and along something called the

80

Pyg Track. This took us all the way to the top, it was brilliant,' me, I'm a Mountaineer said with a big grin. 'On the Sunday we did go on a train, the Ffestiniog Railway with a real old-fashioned steam train; it was absolutely great.' He seemed genuinely pleased with life.

'Sounds great, a good time had by all then. Afraid it's back to work time now,' I said.

'Oh, wonderful,' was his response. I brought him up to date with work and the situation regarding young Mickey and the manager's concerns with H&S. I didn't say it was at my suggestion because of my worry about his shoulder.

It was at this point I informed him of Ruth and her visit. 'What the fuck is she after now? This is harassment. Why don't she just fuck off and leave me alone.'

I was taken aback by his reaction and said, 'Whoa, she's concerned owing to the fact her sister has not contacted her since she left.'

'What the fuck's that got to do with me? I'm no longer her keeper. I hope you told her to fuck off. She's got no business coming here and imposing on my colleagues.'

'Calm down, she was told you did not know anything of her whereabouts and that I didn't think you were at all interested in anything to do with her, OK?'

'Yeah, you are right. I shouldn't have reacted like that, it ain't your problem, sorry.'

'I told her I would ask you to contact her if you had any information.'

'No fucking chance,' he said.

'She only wants to keep in touch with her sister,' I remarked.

'I'll tell you what, I'll give you her number and you call, tell her I don't know anything, don't want to know anything, so don't contact me again, OK?'

'Yeah ,OK, if that's the way you want to play it. Shall we get to work?'

Later that day, I was letting Dutch know what had happened at the bowls on Thursday and that Ron had put up a team sheet for this week's game. When told Ron had left me out of the team, he had laughed and said, 'With mates like that, you don't need enemies.'

He then said, 'Do you think Ron would like to take over the captaincy as a permanent position?'

I asked, Why? Have you a problem with doing it?'

'No, it's just that at the moment my life is a bit overcrowded, plus I don't think I will be playing at all this season. I mean it's halfway through and I ain't played yet. I haven't had any practice to speak of, so I think it would be better if a regular player was in charge, don't you?'

'Well, yeah, maybe,' I responded. 'What you need to do is talk it through with Ron and see what he's got to say.'

'Will you see him on Thursday because I won't be there,' he said.

'Oh, why's that?' I asked.

'Barbara has insisted I go and get this shoulder checked and made me an appointment for Thursday evening.'

'So, something good has come out of your break.'

'There was plenty of good that came out of it,' he said with a big smile.

'You dirty boy,' I said. 'Do I get any details?'

'No, you fucking don't.'

Then after a slight hesitation, he said, 'This is a bit different from those casual encounters I used to have when I'd tell you all the gory details; this is love not lust.'

'Kin hell,' I replied, 'my encounter with the wilder side of life is over.'

That same evening, I called Ron to let him know Dutch would be absent on Thursday due to his medical appointment, thus making him captain for the evening. 'Yeah, no problem, as long as it's OK with the rest of the team.'

'I'm sure it will be, if anyone questions the situation, just say Dutch had told you to do it.'

'Are you going to put in an appearance?' he enquired.

'I just might but I won't be staying long. I will have to get back home and sort out my packing.'

'Will you be out on Friday?' he asked.

'Probably not. We are flying out of Birmingham at 6.30 on Saturday morning, we need to be at the airport by four which means a very early start.'

After the phone call to Ron while still by the phone, I decided to call Ruth McDonald. I dialled the number given me by Dutch, and after a couple of rings it was answered by a male voice. 'Could I speak to Mrs McDonald?' I asked.

'May I ask who is calling?' he replied.

'I'm a colleague of her sister's ex-partner Dutch.'

'Oh, that cunt,' was his sharp reply.

'I wouldn't advise you to say that any time you're in his company,' I said.

'He doesn't bother me, and tell him if you see him to keep away from my missus.'

Kin hell, he's only been there as well, I thought. 'Look, mate, none of this has anything to do with me. I just wanted to pass on a bit of information regarding Karen to your wife if I may, please.'

'Yeah, just hang on. I'll get her,' he said in a very dour tone.

A few seconds later she was on the phone. 'Hello, any news?' sounding full of expectation.

'Afraid not,' I replied, 'I've spoken with Dutch regarding your concerns with not hearing from your sister. His comments were it's nothing to do with him anymore.'

'Oh dear,' she said,' is that all he's got to say?'

'Well, no, not really, I told you he was very bitter about the whole situation. He had said he didn't know nor wanted to know anything about her and seemed to resent the fact that you had had the audacity to try and contact him about her.'

She said she was sorry and had not realised he was so sad and hurt by it all, as he appeared to be a happy go lucky sort of guy whose feelings rarely get touched by the actions of others.

'Yes,' I said, 'his response has surprised a good many. I suppose we never know how an individual will react in any situation.' I went on to say, 'Like your husband's remarks to the very mention of Dutch'

'Ooh, take no notice of him; he thinks every man I speak with is going to whisk me off to some exotic faraway place.'

'And are they?' I enquired.

'Some chance,' she said in return.

I then added,' It's like the old saying, when you have a beautiful bird, clip her wings.

She said, 'Are you trying to flirt with me?' and added, 'You've been working with Dutch too long, you're beginning to sound like him.'

It was my turn to reply with 'some chance' with an added laugh, hoping this would cloud my embarrassment of being caught out in my feeble attempt at small talk.

'Anyway, I'm sorry there's no good news. I just thought you should hear what Dutch knows and feels regarding your sister's whereabouts.' I added, 'If I do hear or obtain any information on her, I will endeavour to pass it to you.'

'Thank you for your efforts and for letting me know, please keep me informed of any developments you hear of. Bye,' and she was gone.

On Tuesday, Wednesday and Thursday of that week we managed, despite some inclement weather for a considerable part of Wednesday, to complete the cleaning and re-coating of the gutter of the end bay.

On the Wednesday, I had spoken with Dutch of my two telephone chats the night before, and told him Ron was OK for the match on Thursday. I went on to say I had not said anything about him taking over the captain's role as a permanent position. He said Barbara had declared an interest in going to the club on Friday, so he would sort it then.

Of my call to Ruth, I said, 'Her husband ain't a fan, is he? In fact, he was quite hostile.'

'Ooh that little shit, he's a prick and five-eighths, he is. He accused me of dallying with his missus.'

'And had you?' I asked.

'You've seen her, what do you think?' he said with a laugh.

'You jammy bastard, I don't think you ever mentioned that one.'

'No, it was a good number of years ago. In fact it was her who introduced me to Karen.' *(Kin hell, he actually said her name, things are improving.)*

84

I told him Ruth had been made aware of his feelings on the situation and seemed to understand. 'I don't think she will bother you again on the subject.'

'Fucking good,' was his comment to end that discussion.

On Thursday evening I did put in an appearance at the bowls, the match was away at Cheslyn Hay. Ron had roped in Vic to assist and all was under control.

I chatted with both Vic and Ron said I was off shortly. I also informed them that Dutch and Barbara would be with them at the club on Friday.

With best wishes for a good holiday from them and most of the team for that matter, I left to go and start my packing.

On Friday the manager had decided young Mickey should spend the day with us in an attempt to familiarise himself with the layout of the complex, which was just as well, for I had demob fever, and in my mind already off on holiday. On the morning inspection, I had Mick tag along with me. I gave him a quick rundown of the electrical distribution, gas and water isolation valves, most of which probably went in one ear and out the other, but as Dutch knew where everything was, it wasn't all that important.

At our morning break, I asked Dutch how things had gone at the doctors. 'The bloke's a quack,' he said. 'He had no idea what the problem was, he poked and prodded, had me doing all sorts of arm and shoulder movements of which I had no problem, and he said he didn't think it was anything for me to worry about. I then informed him of the number of incidents that had occurred at work, and in other areas that had caused embarrassment and very nearly accidents. He had said I'd better have an ultrasound scan; he's going to arrange for me to see a specialist at the hospital.'

'Good,' I said, 'that's a step in the right direction, a scan should show if there is any real damage.'

For the rest of the day, I left Mick to work along with Dutch while I cleared away all the equipment and general rubbish that had accumulated around the workshop and gave it all a general tidy up. I answered phones, passed on messages, made tea and just helped things roll along. Eventually the long-drawn-out day ended. I said, 'See you all,' and left for my holidays.

Our son Thomas, daughter-in-law April and grandson Daniel were already at our house when I arrived home. Doreen had cooked a roast chicken dinner, and with much excitement we sat around the table to eat. Most of the chatter was about the holiday; no, all the chatter was about the holiday. Explaining things like how big the swimming pool was to an overexcited little boy. Confirming everything was sorted, money check, tickets check, bank cards check, sun cream.

'Whoa!' exclaimed Doreen. 'Stop all this worrying, everything has been thought about and packed,' but the excited chatter still prevailed. There seemed to be suitcases everywhere. Eventually, we all retired to bed, hoping to be up again by 2.00am.

Everything went to plan; we all travelled to Birmingham Airport in Tommy's people carrier, enough room for everyone plus luggage. We arrived at the airport with plenty of time in hand. The plane took off just three or four minutes late.

CHAPTER TWELVE

After a good flight we landed at Malaga Airport. Tommy and I went to pick up our hire vehicle. It turned out to be a small Fiat Uno. I said, 'What the hell is that?'

The Spanish lady from the hire company said, 'It's your hire car.'

I informed her we had booked a big car, something like a Mondeo. The Fiat would not be any good to us as there were five of us plus our luggage. She said it was all she had left. I said to Tommy in quite loud terms, 'The Fiat's no good; we'll cancel this agreement, get a taxi, then hire locally when we get to the villa.'

On hearing this, the lady said, 'If you have an upgrade, I could fix you up with something, I'm sure.'

I said, 'No thanks. I think we were paying as much as I am prepared to pay already.'

She said, 'Hold on. I'll go and talk to the boss, see if there's anything we can do.'

While she was out, I said to Tommy, 'I think they were just trying it on, she will come back with a far better deal.'

Sure enough, on her return, she said, 'The boss has agreed, owing to the fact that we haven't a car as you booked, you can have a Mercedes Diesel 5-door estate for the same cost as your original request.'

Accepting the situation, and with all relevant paperwork completed, we were on our way. We had detailed instructions on how to find the villa. Allowing for the fact we were in a strange car and on strange roads, we did OK and arrived at our destination in just over an hour.

You know when you have a picture in your mind of something and the reality generally doesn't quite live up to it. Well, our villa was the exact opposite of that, it looked fantastic. White walls, with a red-ridged tiled roof, all inside a large, walled area.

The entrance was through a double wrought iron gate, with a red gravel drive up to a car port. On the right-hand side was the swimming pool, although it wasn't an Olympic size pool it was plenty big enough for us at about 15m long and 8m wide. On the other side of the drive was a spacious lawn and garden area with a number of trees, bushes and shrubs along the back by the wall. Between the lawn and the house there was a barbecue area.

Inside the villa there were four good sized bedrooms, a large lounge and a very acceptable kitchen, two bathrooms and a separate toilet, all clean, well decorated and tastefully furnished. Bedrooms were allocated, and within minutes one little boy and one granddad were in the pool.

The first couple of days were spent seeking out local shops, restaurants, cafes and bars. The centre of Marbella was only some 15 to 20 minutes car ride away, affording us lots of scope for shopping and entertainment.

As the holiday progressed, we ventured further afield to such places as Gibraltar, and even a trip as far out as Granada during the second week.

It was on the Tuesday of the first week. We were in a bar along the front at the Marina in Marbella. I got into a conversation with a very nice couple Jack and Beryl, who were apparently in a similar villa to ours.

We chatted, and as you do on these occasions, spoke about where we lived. They were from Tamworth, which is not that far from where I live. (I thought, *be careful or they'll be inviting themselves round*). When I told them where I came from, they responded by saying, 'That's close to Brownhills, isn't it?'

I said, 'Yes, well, reasonably close.'

They then told us of a chap who hangs around the bars in the area who said he came from Brownhills or rather just outside Brownhills as he had put it, he'd been living in this area for a good number of months. They went on to say he seemed to be guarded and a bit cagey about his origins, but for all that, he was pleasant company and quite amusing with his repertoire of tales.

At this, I immediately thought of the Banker. Someone had said this was where he would be hanging out. Yes, it was Dennis,

I thought. *Wow, if it is him, that'll create some excitement when we meet.*

I said to them, 'I'm looking forward to meeting him already. If you see him again, let him know of us and tell him we are interested in meeting him.' I thought, *If he gets that message, it'll frighten the shit out of him.*

As it was, our holiday continued unabated. We tended to spend one day at the villa swimming, sunning, barbecuing and generally just relaxing. On alternate days we would run out in the car, visiting places along the coast or venture into the surrounding hills, finding and exploring little hidden villages. Then late in the day find a nice restaurant for our evening meal.

It was Saturday in one of these restaurants that we next came across Jack and Beryl. After the meal while having a drink, Tom and April were playing with Daniel on the various pinball type machines that were dotted about the place. Doreen and I engaged our two newfound friends in conversation.

The subject soon got around to the Brownhills man. They had come across him last night (Friday) at a bar in town.

He had told them he had come into a substantial inheritance and had decided to move to a warmer climate. They also said, when he was approaching them, he had a very attractive female with him. She had not stopped at the bar and had just carried on along the street. When asked about who she was, he had said, 'Oh, just a friend.'

I put in with the fact that I was still interested in meeting him. Doreen asked, 'Why do you want to meet him?'

I said, 'Well, he's a local from home and we might just know him. Anyway, if he's got all that much money, he could treat us.'

Jack said, 'No chance! He's very careful and doesn't splash his cash, not as I've noticed anyway.'

Beryl said, 'We told him about you being in the area and that you were from where he had lived in England.' She said, 'He asked what your names were, when told he said he didn't know anyone of that name.'

Jack said, 'Shortly after that, he finished his drink and left.' He then added, 'We haven't seen him at all today.'

89

Beryl said they were leaving for home the next day, so good luck and goodbyes all round at the end of the evening. Off we went back to the villa for coffee or even a glass of wine on the porch.

With Daniel in bed, the four of us settled on the porch with a glass of wine apiece. It was Doreen who said, 'You were more than just interested in meeting that bloke, why was that?'

I explained the role of the Banker, how he had played bowls for the team last season, what he was thought to have done in taking the money from the bank. What Dennis had said of his whereabouts, and said I just wondered.

'Do you really think it could be the same bloke?' asked Tom.

'I don't know, but it certainly sounds as if it could be.'

He said, 'Would you recognise him if you saw him?'

'I think so, though I haven't seen him for nigh on a year and didn't have much to do with him when he was playing for the team. But yeah, I think I would.'

The holiday progressed, and though we put ourselves about quite a bit and met with many people, who spoke of many things, including supposed criminals in the vicinity, who were deemed to be on the run. No one spoke of or claimed to know the man from Brownhills. Although I looked, I never saw him, or anyone who I even thought might be him. So finally, this wonderful, glorious, sunshine-filled holiday came to an end.

BACK TO REALITY.

I found it difficult to settle back at work the next week. At nights when in bed, I would drift back to the villa, my dreams were full of our holiday adventures. Every morning I'd wake up disappointed when realising we were back home. I know it's normal to have thoughts like this after a holiday, but this time it seemed a lot more severe and prolonged. I wondered if it was old age creeping up, or was I just unhappy with my job, my life perhaps?

At work everything had gone really well, I had not been missed. (Maybe that was the problem). The roof work was complete, Dutch and Mick had got along very well and had enjoyed working together. Mick had been expressing a wish to be transferred to the section to complete his apprenticeship with a view to eventually becoming a maintenance man.

But for now, it was back to just Dutch and me. At break times I gave an account of our holiday. Probably a bit boring, all this family life, to a bloke like Dutch with his wilder type of living, but he persevered with it and didn't show any lack of interest.

He, for his part, informed me of the progress made and problems that had cropped up at work over the last couple of weeks. Where we are in the summer programme and that our next target was the overhaul of the heating systems.

He also gave me a rundown of the bowls. Both Monday and Thursday teams had been quite excellent, winning all games while I was away. Not missed there neither, possibly not even wanted. Oh well, nothing for it but to just push on. (What a miserable old shit I'm becoming.)

On Monday evening, I had to practically force myself to go to the bowls. I knew I would not be playing, if you miss a game for whatever reason, you are expected to sit out at least one or even two games. You are expected to turn up, mark cards and await someone to be left out for losing a game or perhaps even going on holiday.

When I arrived, the match was just about to start. Joan greeted me with, 'Wow! Look who's here, all tanned up and looking fit.' Then without taking a breath, added, 'Mark a card.'

I responded with, 'And hello to you. Yes, I did have a good holiday, thank you.'

To which she replied, 'Oh yes, but I haven't got time for that now, the game is just starting.'

Taking the card, I said, 'It's OK, I do understand. Whose card have I got?' It was Ron's.

I called to Ron to let him know I had his card. 'Oh, you're back, good holiday?'

Before I could reply, he had turned to his opponent ready to start their game. *Not a lot of interest in my holiday there,* I thought. Unfortunately, though a tight game and both bowled really well, Ron lost.

He came over to me and asked, 'How many did I get?'

'Very close 21/19,' I replied.

'Bloody hell, you've only been back an hour and I've lost.'

'And is that my fault?' I asked.

'No, I don't suppose it is,' he declared.

The team won not as convincingly as had been hoped for but a win. I went into the club after the match as usual, all the talk revolved around the bowls as is the norm. I felt left out, not really part of it, rejected, I suppose. I did not stop long, I left about the same time as the away team did.

CHAPTER THIRTEEN

On Tuesday I suddenly remembered the appointment Dutch had with his shoulder and asked how it had gone.

'How's it gone?' he responded. 'I haven't even had an appointment yet. It's all OK now anyway so when I do get a call I probably won't go.'

That evening I went up the bowls green and had a roll, just to get a feel for the green, it also helped put me in a better frame of mind. I was only there for 45 or 50 minutes and I must admit I did feel better for it.

When I arrived home, Doreen informed me Ron had called wanting to speak with me. After having a drink and a bite to eat, I called Ron, and it was Eileen who answered. 'Hello, Eileen. Ron's been after me, I believe.'

'Oh yes, hang on, I'll get him, but first, how was your holiday?'

'Fantastic,' I replied, 'but the trouble with holidays, you have to come back. But we'll see you on Friday. Doreen's got loads of photos, plus any amount of tales to tell, so by the end of the evening you'll wish you had not asked.'

To that she answered, 'Yeah, you're probably right, hang on, I'll get Ron.'

'What oh, matey! Just a quick one, are you expecting a game on Thursday?' he said.

'No, not particularly, why, what's the problem?'

'Nothing really, it's just you seemed well pissed off on Monday with not playing. I wondered how desperate you were to have a game.'

'Ooh, take no notice of that, it was only post-holiday blues. Leave me out, it will only create an argument if you find a place for me; you know you will be accused of favouritism. That is unless you are struggling to get a team, in which case count me in.'

'No, I can get a team, so if you are OK with it, I'll leave you out.' He then quickly added, 'You will be turning up, won't you?'

'Yeah, I'm OK now. Like I said, it was only a hangover from the holiday. In fact, I've been up the green for a rollup, that's where I was when you phoned earlier. I think it's improved my outlook quite considerably.'

With that, he signed off with, 'OK then, I'll see you Thursday, bye.'

On Wednesday morning, Dutch suddenly said, 'Oh you know yesterday when you asked about my hospital appointment, well you must be psychic because when I got home last night, there it was, an appointment. It must have arrived at just the time you were asking about it.'

'Good, at least it's some progress,' I said.

'Not really, it's not till the 18th of August, that's six weeks away by then I'll have forgotten all about it.'

I thought, *Yes, maybe*, and said, 'You keep it in mind, and make sure you attend. It won't do any harm even if you do feel everything is all okay.'

* * *

I did attend the game on Thursday, we played away at Hammerwich. We lost, fortunately by less than we had won the week before when playing the same team at home. Even so, it was still suggested by Brian that I was an unlucky omen. To which I replied, 'Bollocks.' (Still as eloquent as ever.)

Brian then said, 'Well, we didn't lose while you were away.'

'Say whatever you want, it's still bollocks,' was my reply. *Yes, I'm truly back, nothing has changed. The holiday is beginning to feel a long way off.*

On Friday evening, Doreen, armed with several dozen photographs, accompanied me to the club. We arrived some 10 minutes later than usual so she could make an entrance, allowing her to show off her tan, which she did with aplomb, quite a show. The next hour or so was totally filled by the showing of photos and a little anecdote to explain the circumstance surrounding each one. To their credit, all our gang showed genuine interest throughout it all.

Showing a photo of Jack and Beryl, I was giving a spiel regarding the characters Jack had met and how any number of them were supposed to be slightly dodgy. Dennis immediately jumps in with, 'Did you come across the Banker?'

'Hang on a bit, I'm coming around to that. He was there.'

'I knew it, I told you that's where he'd be. Did you meet him, what did he say?' Dennis was just a little bit overexcited.

'Whoa! Hold your horses, it was not quite like that.'

I then related the story of the bloke Jack and Beryl had met, how they had described him and where he had said he originated from and how he seemed to have disappeared when told of our presence in the area. 'It sounds a lot like him, flash with his stories, his secrecy as to his history and he went missing when he heard about you. Yes, I think it probably was him.' said Vic.

It was at this point that Dutch and Barbara came in. A fresh round of drinks was called, it was Vic who did the honours. Barbara took up a seat with the ladies. We blokes pulled in a spare table as we did whenever there was this many of us.

As Vic got the drinks, Dennis said, 'We were just talking about the Banker, you know the one who got away with all that money.'

Dutch, to everybody's surprise, reacted quite aggressively. 'Oh that cunt. I don't want to know.' This was said quite loud. All the females in the group were too involved with the photos to hear what happened. That is except Barbara, who looked at Dutch with a look of astonishment and a hint of concern at his outburst. After the initial surprise, the blokes relaxed and didn't seem to be too bothered as the feeling expressed was mutual.

The following morning, I mentioned the incident of last night and asked what it was all about. 'I just don't wish to talk about it, OK,' was his response said in a rather more aggressive tone than the situation warranted.

'Oh, OK then,' I said, which seemed to end the conversation on the subject.

I could not recall any incident from last season that would provoke such sentiment. As captain, Dutch had selected this bloke often and as far as I could remember he had not been let down. But then what do I know, I know he is disliked by all, but the reaction from Dutch boarded on hate. Something must have happened to trigger such resentment.

Over the next couple of weeks, I settled back into the routine of life. Work went well, bowls not so well, home life was good, social life good. The weather had also been very good, all of which helped lift my mood of melancholy.

It was towards the end of July, Tuesday the 27th to be precise. Not that the date is significant, I just thought it would help with the chronology of this little piece of history. While on our mid-morning break, I said to Dutch, 'How's your romance going these days?'

'It's getting a bit tricky.'

'Oh, how's that? You're not looking for pastures new already.'

'No, it's not that, it's just the closer we get, the closer she wants to be. She now wants us to move in together.'

'So, where is the problem?'

'That's just it, she doesn't see a problem. She thinks her house is too small for the two of us. She's put forward a proposal that she sells her house and moves in with me. There is no way she is moving into my house.'

'Why is that?' I asked.

'Bad vibes, too many memories, wrong ambience, everything is wrong about it, she ain't moving in, full stop.'

'Only one other solution, sell both houses, buy another and start afresh,' was my final suggestion.

'Can't sell my house,' Dutch countered.

'You can't, why not?' I asked.

'Reasons, there are any number of reasons, I just can't sell.'

'So where do you think this will lead to?' I asked.

'I don't know. I suggested we put off any decision until I've got my shoulder fixed, that should buy me some time.'

He never did elucidate on the reasons he couldn't sell his house. I for my part didn't push for any explanation, believing he would inform me when good and ready.

Our Elizabeth had kept me updated on the proposed Silverdale escapade. As I have already said, she had been enlisted by Chris, originally to help with the organising of the day. Help which had subsequently turned into her becoming sole organiser.

For her part, she had included herself in the party. She was in regular contact with the proprietor of the establishment and had booked up for a party of six and the various treatments that each of them had specified. She was also acting as their accountant, collecting monies off each of them from time to time, when and wherever she could. With this task she had cajoled her mother into assisting her. So much so, that a fair amount of time on Friday evenings was spent by the ladies debating who had paid what and who was paying in what.

Us blokes tended to ignore the frequent excitable squabbles that arose. We got on with our discussions, bowls, football, sport in general, or retired to the games room.

My only concern was that when all this financial jiggery pokey was finalised, any discrepancy found, which there surely will be, who do you think is going to be held to account and who is going to be expected to foot the bill? Yes, you've got it! Mind you, knowing our Doreen and Elizabeth it might just show a profit. In which case, I won't hear anything about it.

As July turned to August, the end of the bowls season starts to rear up, with league position in everybody's mind. The Monday team, after a promising start, were now very much mid-table. No real chance of promotion or relegation for that matter.

My team or what as former captain I regarded as my team, the Thursday team, were well clear of any relegation problems, but in need of a minor miracle to get into the race for promotion. But not impossible, after the last two games which had been at home where we had been successful. We were in fifth place; the next game was away to the team we beat in our latest game at home quite convincingly. So, we had high expectations with that one. The final two games were against the team directly above us. If we could win the first one at their place, and either team above them dropped points, we would be in with a good chance to procure a promotion spot.

Throughout July on numerous occasions, Dutch and I had made a visit to the green directly from work to give him some much-needed practice. So much so that come the first of our last three must-win games, he felt ready to be considered for selection.

When speaking with Ron on the availability of Dutch for selection, Ron's only concern was as to whether he would want to be captain. I said I didn't think so, not at this stage of the season and Ron should expect to remain as captain for the rest of this campaign.

Ron did select Dutch, with real approval from the rest of the team. Even Sam, who was left out to accommodate him, did not voice any objection to the selection.

The match was won by a comfortable margin. Dutch played a blinder and in doing so won the pin money. (Money paid to the best winner; half the subs paid by each member who plays). It's not big money but carries a lot of prestige.

The next morning at work, I said, 'Good game last night, pleased that's out of the way.'

'Oh yes, I was dreading coming in this late in the season and letting the team down.'

'Yeah, I can appreciate the pressure, but not only a win, the pin money also,' I said.

With modesty, he replied, 'I was fortunate with the draw, I got probably their weakest bowler.'

'Yes, there is that,' I said with a laugh and added, 'you still have to get your shots in even if the opponent is weak, so well done.'

I then asked what Barbara had thought of his achievement. 'Yeah, she was pleased I'd re-joined the team.'

'And what about you winning the pin money?' I asked.

'I never gave her that information.'

'Why ever not?' I enquired.

'Well, you know me, didn't think it was that interesting or important.'

I thought, *Not important? That just about sums up the character of the bloke. His first competitive game, this late in the season, with a dodgy shoulder, not only wins but wins well. That shows a mental toughness not many possess.*

On that same Friday evening the usual gang gathered in the club. The early conversations were about last night's match and in particular Dutch. Chris led the euphoria surrounding the return of Dutch with statements such as 'If he'd been playing all season, you would have won the league.' I thought, *Yes, still carrying a torch.*

Eileen came in with, 'It was down to the captain who selected him; he should be getting some praise as well.'

In the midst of all this, PK appeared, the conversation turned to the more important topic of our league position and our chances of a promotion. Ron suggested our next fixture was perhaps the most critical match of the season because anything other than a win and all hope would be gone.

Ron was asked if he had any thoughts on what team he intended to put out next week. He said he was thinking of much the same team as last night, we had three who had lost, but we were away, so it hardly warrants any of them being dropped. 'Having said that, I think Sam perhaps should be given a place,' he said as if debating with himself.

The discussion continued for some time; the consensus of opinion was that whoever played it was going to be tough to get any kind of result. They weren't in that position in the league for no reason, for although their away form was very average, they had not lost any of their home games this season.

I became aware the females of the group were having their usual squabble regarding monies for their outing. It reminded me that I intended to pay my outstanding balance for our trip to Blackpool.

I side-lined PK and handed him the £50, which he duly recorded. I asked what the precise date of our eagerly awaited excursion was. 'We actually go on Friday 24th of September.'

'What's that, six, seven weeks from today?' I asked.

'Yeah, it's seven weeks exactly,' he replied.

'Everything in order, all under control, everything booked up?' I enquired.

'Yes, no problems at all, that is apart from Barry worrying about the price of diesel. He's saying he might have to raise his charges a bit.'

'That's not a problem, though, is it? I mean it can't be a lot surely.'

'No, it'll be OK but I ain't telling him that,' announced PK.

On Tuesday of the following week, it crossed my mind that Dutch had an appointment at the hospital for a scan sometime about now. At break time I mentioned it to him. His response was,' Oh, I'm OK now, I shall not be attending.'

He went on, 'I haven't had any trouble with it for weeks, I'd forgotten all about it.' He then added, 'Don't let on to Barbara. I don't need her going on at me.'

'Doesn't she already know of your appointment?'

'Yeah, she does, but if she isn't reminded, she'll probably forget.'

'No chance, mate, you'll be keeping that appointment, I'll guarantee.' I then asked, 'What date is your appointment?'

'A week tomorrow, 2.30 in the afternoon,' he said.

'I think you should go and get it done, it certainly won't do you any harm and it might do a lot of good.'

'Yeah, we'll see,' seemed to be his final comment on the matter.

The day of our crucial penultimate match of the season arrived. Ron had been in consultation with me regarding team selection. Between us it was decided to reinstate Sam and rest young Liam on the grounds that although he had not let the team down at any time, his lack of experience and youth could leave him vulnerable to the pressure and the atmosphere that would surely be generated during the match.

Before the match started, Ron, at my suggestion, gave a team talk. He reminded everyone of the importance of the match, how he wanted everyone to get around the green and encourage each other and be supportive at all times, he then wished us all best of luck and said, 'OK, let's go to it,' all this said with a fair amount of passion. I thought, *Kin hell, Ron, I didn't think you had it in you*. I felt quite uplifted myself.

As usual I was on with the first four, along with Don, Kevin and Sam. On reaching the starting footer (small mat used to denote starting spot), I called out, 'OK, let's show this lot how to play bowls.' This was greeted by rousing cheers from all our team. I thought that should intimidate the opposition a little bit.

My game went quite well, reasonably close but I won 21/18. After the first four we had a lead of two shots. Sam had won 21/16 Kevin lost 14/21 and Don had scraped a win 21/20.

The second four were now on: Ron, Dutch, Brian and PK. I didn't have a card to mark, so I had picked up the strings and made ready to measure any time a call went up.

All four of the games seemed to be going along fine, and each seemed to be closely contested. I was taking a particular interest in Dutch and his game. He had started well but his opponent was making a strong comeback. His opponent had won the last end, making it 11 across and put both his woods in close proximity to the jack.

Dutch called 'coming through', meaning he was about to fire at the head in an attempt to remove either the jack or his opponent's bowls. He pulled his arm right back and let fly; as he did, he gave out a loud cry and slumped to his knees. As luck would have it, his bowl remained true, striking the head and scattering woods and the jack all over the place. The only problem being the jack remained on the green, as did one of his opponent's woods.

I along with others immediately went over to Dutch, who was shouting, 'Leave me, I'll be alright in a moment,' but was still on his knees.

The opposing captain was calling non-players off the green. To which PK answered, 'Bollocks, can't you see we've got a man injured?'

I then became aware of their vice-captain, a short, stocky bloke saying to the bloke playing Dutch, 'You've won that end, quick send the jack, if he can't make it to the footer, you can claim the game by default.'

Brian, who was closest to them, said, 'Don't touch anything till it's been verified by our player or we will claim two shots.'

Their bloke said, 'If he can't make the footer, he will have to forfeit the game, so fuck off.'

Brian, who does not take shit from anyone, replied, 'I'll punch your fucking head off your shoulders, you obnoxious little shit.'

101

At this stage, all play had ceased. I said to Ron, 'Have you got a copy of the rules with you anywhere?'

'Yes, I think I have.'

'Good, go and get them as I think we're going to need them.'

I spoke to Dutch and asked, 'Are you OK? Can you continue?'

'Give me a minute, I'll be good to carry on; it just caught me unawares.'

I said, 'You can say that again, but are you sure you want to finish the game?'

'Yes, I'll be OK in a few seconds.'

Brian and his new archenemy were still caught up in their slanging match. Only with pressure of restraint on Brian from Don had stopped a more physical altercation taking place.

When I arrived in that area, Ron was calling along with their captain for everyone who wasn't playing to clear the green so play could resume. I asked the short, stocky bloke why he was there. He said, 'What's it got to do with you?'

I answered, 'I thought so, no reason at all, so if you don't mind, go away and let the captains clear this issue up.'

He just stood there looking at me for quite a number of seconds, then said, 'Twat,' and walked away.

I said to Ron, 'Dutch will be alright to carry on in a couple of minutes.'

He said, 'I've looked at the rules. Can you do a quick check? It's rule 8.12; make sure I'm right. I need to get on with my game.'

Rule 8.12 states: [any incident which necessitates a player having to stop play or leave the green and is <u>unable to resume before the finish of the match</u>]. In other words, Dutch had till the end of the match to recover and return to the footer.

I then engaged their captain; I explained that our captain needed to get on with his game and as former captain, I would deal with this incident. I asked if he was familiar with rule 8.12. He said not off hand, no. So, without showing the rule book, I quoted the said rule with an air of total authority and added the game will resume as soon as our player is ready. I could see he didn't feel he was in a position to offer any alternative proposals and just said OK.

We shook hands, and as he went to walk away, I said, 'Oh, by the way, I'm going to report that little fat bloke for ungentlemanly conduct.'

'What do you mean, it was your bloke who was at fault; he threatened Clive with physical violence.'

I replied, 'Only after receiving a torrent of abusive language from him,' and then added, 'just because he suggested the fat bloke should stop encouraging your player to cheat.'

'Cheat!!! Are you saying our player was cheating? You'd better be able to substantiate that or you could be in trouble.'

'Don't try to intimidate me, mate; go and ask the little fat cunt why he was trying to claim the game.'

With that, he walked away shaking his head. I turned my attention to the match.

Dutch though playing well had dropped a few shots behind but didn't seem to be having any difficulty with his shoulder.

Ron on the other hand was leading 20/11. The other two games were very close. After checking on all cards, I went back to Kevin, who was marking Ron's card. 'Ain't he off yet? What's happening?'

'Their bloke is fighting back, it's now 20/16.' Just at that point, Ron raised his hand to signal the point he required.

The score was plus seven in our favour, five games played, five to go. Dutch was next to finish, with a losing card 17/21. Our lead was down to three shots. Next off the green was Brian, who had also lost 18/21. Leaving the total score exactly even at 113/113. Then it was PK who came in with another very close but losing card 19/21.

Two shots behind, two games to play. As it turned out, Vic was drawn against the little stocky bloke and Markey against their captain.

Vic started very well and developed a substantial lead; he was 12/3 up. Markey on the other hand was struggling at 5/10 down. Still all to play for.

Round the green the tension was high with both sets of supporters calling and encouraging their guys to ever greater efforts.

Vic's game was first to finish, a win for Vic 21/16. Clive, the little stocky guy, had made a strong late charge and closed the score up considerably, but Vic had held out for a good win. We were now three shots to the good.

The last game was still very close at 17 across. Only two shots more needed for Markey and we would win.

It had gone quite dark with heavy clouds around, and suddenly the heavens opened. Both players sought shelter in the pavilion, Markey seemed relaxed with the situation. Their captain put on his waterproof clothing and said he was ready to restart, Markey said he was happy to wait a while for the rain to ease off. The ensuing discussion involved Ron and their captain. His argument was the green is playable so the game should restart. Ron, on shaky ground, put forward the claim that it was them who had requested to come off the green. 'Only to put on my waterproofs,' their captain countered.

'Yes, but that's what stopped the game,' put in Ron.

As this little debate ebbed and flowed, the rain eased considerably. Markey suddenly said, 'OK, I'm ready,' and went on to the green, closely followed by their man, and the game resumed.

Their man had the jack, but with the excessive water now on the green, he failed to set a mark. This gave Markey the upper hand, he had the jack. He sent it across the green and then put his first wood within inches of it. His opponent, having failed to set a mark with the jack, overcompensated and sent his wood off. Markey's second wood was well short. The other bloke put his second wood just a foot short of the jack. One shot to Markey, we can't lose.

Next end, Markey dropped both his woods quite short, two shots down. Their captain sent the jack quite long to a spot he obviously knew, took two more shots, game over. Match drawn.

The mood around the green changed from excitement and aggression to quiet sullen brooding. This result didn't please either team.

As their captain prepared the final results card, I said to Ron, 'Go and make some friendly gestures towards him when you sign off the results card. Let him know it was only good-natured banter and no real animosity was intended.'

Ron responded with, 'I can but try.' The look on his face said he was not hopeful of any success with that ploy.

I approached my opponent and offered to get him a drink as during the match everyone was too caught up in the tension surrounding the game to bother about the small matter of drinking. He was OK with the situation, had no hang-ups at all. He accepted a drink, we shook hands, I commiserated with him and said it had been a very enjoyable game. He said, 'Yes, it was well done, you bowled very well.'

Ron and their captain had shaken hands and were in what seemed to be polite conversation. I thought, *Good, it's all calmed down and relaxed, can't think what all the fuss was about.*

I went and sat with Dutch and Vic. Dutch appeared to want to take the blame for the result, saying it was his fault, his injury, and the shots dropped after that were the difference between a win and a draw. Vic made the point that the shots he gained after the injury were the difference between a draw and a loss.

I came in at this stage and said, 'It's always like that after a close game, everyone can see possibilities where they could have won or even lost the match. At one stage you, Vic, had a very big lead but their bloke managed to close it up. Markey had a chance to win us the game, and Ron had a very substantial margin over his opponent at one stage. We can all think, whether we won or lost, IF only I could have got just one more, or, IF only I had not let their bloke get that easy shot. It's the same old quandary and as they say, IF my aunty had had bollocks, she would have been my uncle. Nothing can be done now.'

Brian, I could see, was still busting a gut to have a go at the little stocky guy. I went over to him and said, 'Leave it, he ain't worth the worry.'

He replied, 'I'm still going to get the little shit one way or another.'

I said, 'The games over, it won't make any difference now, he'll be playing at our place next week, wind him up then before the game, that may have some effect on his game.'

'Yeah, maybe, but I do intend to have him.'

My opponent offered to buy me a drink, an offer I thanked him for but declined on the grounds that I was driving. He said, 'OK, I'll treat you next week.'

As I was leaving, I spoke with their captain and said, 'Sorry for all the aggro, it's just part of the game, especially important games like this one.'

His comment was, 'It's not the way we play, but knowing your lot, it was what we were expecting.'

I said, 'What do you mean by that?'

He answered by saying, 'From all accounts, it's what you lot always do, try to upset your opponents to gain an advantage.'

I said, 'Well, in that case, from us lot, you can go and fuck yourself,' with that I left.

The following morning (Friday), Dutch still seemed to carry the guilt for us not obtaining the required result in last night's match. This is very much out of character for Dutch, he never has any concerns when it comes to his responsibilities in any part of his life. He tends to just swing along expecting everyone else to accept him and whatever he has done as being for the best.

His reaction to the situation gave me cause for concern. I put it to him that his problem last night settled any argument regarding his hospital appointment. 'Yeah, I think I shall have to get it looked at; it does appear there's a problem. It can't be much though; it's only troubled me two or three times, but it doesn't seem to be going away.'

He then went on to say, 'Will you see Ron tonight?'

I said, 'Yeah, most likely.'

He said, 'Could you let him know I won't be available for selection next Thursday.'

'Oh, why's that?' I asked.

'Well, next Wednesday I've got my hospital appointment. I don't know what the outcome of that will be, but I also let the team down, and I don't want to do that again, do I?'

'For a start, you didn't let the team down, if anything your determination to carry on and the five extra points you gained were very much the reason we managed to scramble a draw. As for your appointment, you're only going for a scan, you won't have any treatment, so there will be no barrier to stop you playing on Thursday, will there?'

'Possibly not but I still ain't going to play.'

'Yeah, OK, it's up to you, but I still think you should play.'

In the evening we all gathered as per usual. The topic of conversation was as is often the case Dutch or, more accurately, his shoulder injury. I suddenly realised none of our gang nor any of the bowls team knew of his shoulder or at least the extent of his problem with it.

I was then obliged to give them all a full account of the history of said shoulder. Chris seemed to think I should have given her all this detail quite some time ago as if she had some vested interest in the situation. I politely told her and the rest of them it was not down to me to give an update on a regular basis of his health. He's not royalty, and as such, a regular bulletin will not be issued. This all said with an amount of humour, did little or even nothing to dispel the concern as to how serious his problem might be. There was an amount of speculation as to what it might be.

Vic thought it must be tendon related, owing to the fact that it had been going on so long. I said, 'Maybe, but when it has happened before he claimed that the problem is deep inside his shoulder and down towards his shoulder blade.' I went on to say, 'Whatever the problem, he now knows he needs to get it looked at and has an appointment for next Wednesday, so it's quite useless us worrying anymore.'

From that point on our talk, by our, I mean the blokes' talk, centred on last night's result and the fact that we would not now get a promotion. Ron said he had checked a couple of other teams' results and said we would not have had a promotion spot even if we had won. He went on, 'What we need to do now is make sure we win next week just to shut them up, not only that but if we do win, we will finish above them.'

I had already told of Dutch and his decision not to play next week. With this information, Ron had made his provisional selection. The last game was at home so we would normally expect a win. I said, 'After last night's problems, we must put in a top performance,' and asked, 'Are you going to speak with Brian regarding his spat with their vice-captain?'

Ron said, 'I actually considered leaving him out but thought that would give them too much satisfaction, but I will have to speak with him.' He then said, 'Brian was not the only concern I had.'

Vic said, 'Why, who else have we got to worry about?'

'Him,' said Ron looking at me.'

'ME!!' I exclaimed, 'What have I done?'

'I was called to task by their captain before I left last night. He said you had behaved in a disgraceful manner and had used threatening and abusive language at him.'

'Me? Abusive language? What a load of bollocks. I don't use that sort of language ever, the little twat. Wait till I see him, he'll find out what abusive and threatening language is.' This brought about a great swath of laughter from the rest of the gang.

I then went on to tell them exactly what had transpired between me and their captain. How I had gone over to him and offered an apology for any perceived aggression, and said it was only part of the game. He had answered by saying all our team were widely known for ill-mannered and aggressive behaviour, so it was no more than they had expected. It was only then that I told him, from all of us, what he could go and do with himself.

Vic said he thought my reaction to the bloke was quite mild against what his response to such a statement would've been. He also thought an official complaint from the club should be sent to the league committee.

Ron, as ever the diplomat, said at this stage of the season he didn't think it wise to start creating a fuss over what was really nothing more than just name-calling. He went on to say unless they make an official complaint to the league, we should just leave it at that. The best way to make them pay for their inappropriate behaviour was to beat them next week, not just beat them but give them a really good thrashing.

I thought, *Kin hell, Ron, you've got it spot on again.* I said, 'Give a team talk like that next week before the match and we're halfway there.'

So, the scene was set for a last match of the season showdown.

CHAPTER FOURTEEN

At work things had gone pretty much to plan. The summer work programme was as good as complete, just one hot air blower in the body-shop requiring a replacement motor, and a new valve to be fitted in the machine shop boiler house.

Owing to the fact that the summer programme was so advanced, Dutch had requested a two-week break which had been accepted. He and Barbara were going away to Turkey. She had suggested that after his hospital appointment they should take a holiday; some relation of hers had this apartment in a place called Akbuk, which was situated somewhere near Bodrum. They were to fly out on Tuesday the 24th and return on the 7th September. He said he would finish work on Friday, the extra days would be made up by the August bank holiday.

If he had any worries regarding his shoulder, it didn't show. Sometime late on Wednesday morning, I suddenly thought about his appointment and called to him, 'What time are you leaving for your scan?'

His response was, Oh, it's not till 2.30. I've told the manager I'll work straight through till 2 o'clock. It'll only take 15 minutes to get there and 5 or 10 minutes to find the treatment room, so plenty of time.'

Yeah, I thought, *I seem to be more concerned about his situation than he is.* The upshot was at around 2 o'clock, he departed for his appointment.

It was somewhat after 4 o'clock when he returned. I said, 'I wasn't expecting you back today.'

'No,' he said, 'I just wanted to finish the undercoat on all the woodwork around the cash counting office today so I can get all the gloss on before I go away.'

I said, 'If you had said, I could have sorted that out.'

'It's OK, I'll manage; I'll only be an hour or so late finishing, so no worry,' he said.

'How did it go at the hospital?' I asked.

'Not too bad I was only waiting about 20 minutes, so it felt like I was in and out in no time. It's the reason I decided to come and get this done.'

'Yes, maybe, but what did they say about your shoulder?'

'Er, nothing, just to see my doctor next week and he will have the results. I told them I was going on holiday, and they said that's OK; see him when you get back.'

'So, they did not appear very much concerned at all then?' I asked.

'No, why should they have been?'

'No, I don't suppose so. I'm near enough done for the day unless you want me to give you a hand with that painting,' I said.

'No, you go and get off home, I'll be OK,' he said. With that, I prepared for home.

* * *

Throughout the week I had several conversations with Ron and for that matter Vic regarding team selection for our last match. A consensus of opinion had been reached between us. We were ready.

Most of our team arrived at the green quite early. We were all having a practice roll which is allowed for the home team before the start of the match.

When the away team arrived, I purposely sought out their captain. I challenged him with, 'I hear you made a complaint about me to our captain after I'd left last week.' This was said in quite a brusque manner and seemed to unnerve him somewhat.

His response was, 'Yes, I'm very sorry, I was wrong. I should not have responded to your apology in the way that I did.' He went on to say it was all down to the tension that surrounded the game. 'Not that that is any reason for my behaviour or that of Clive, who incidentally has been left out of our team this week.'

All this totally threw me. I didn't know how to respond. I just said, 'Yeah, you're right, it was a lot of silliness. It is after all only a game,' and shook his hand.

I relayed the conversation to Ron, who then informed me he had spoken with him on the phone last night and tried to come to a better understanding of the situation. I said, 'Oh great, I wish you had said, I practically engaged him in a punch up. But anyway, well done, you've relaxed the atmosphere considerably.' I then said, 'I'll go and explain to Brian what's happened so he can calm himself down and see if we can get through this game without any more aggro.'

The game was a very relaxed affair, we won quite comfortably. Only two losers, of which I happened to be one. I lost to their captain, their captain!! Of all the people to lose to. (The bastard.) (Still a bad loser.)

On Friday, Dutch was saying I might have to come in tomorrow if I can't get a good run at the cash office today. The problem being the cash from last evening and the cash from the morning rush had to be counted before they would allow any access to any other person, be it maintenance, the manager or anyone else. The only exception was me, and only then if the cash counting machine had broken down.

I said, 'You don't want to do that, we'll clear this morning's reports, let them know we wish to get in there as soon as possible. They are normally finished by midday; if we both get stuck in, we should be able to finish it or be very close by knocking off time. What's left, I can clear up while you're away.'

'Yeah, but you know I don't like loose ends, so I'd rather it is complete before I go.'

'OK, let's give it a go and see what happens.'

Just after 2 o'clock, the phone in the cash counting office rang, it was Sammie to say the garage manager wanted to see me in his office. I said, 'What? Right now?'

She said, 'Yes, right now.'

I said, 'Kin hell, don't he know we've got work to do.'

Anyway, when I got there, he said he had arranged for young Mickey Reynolds to work with me while Dutch was on holiday.

I told him I didn't think it necessary; Mickey had covered for me when I was on holiday only because we were doing roof work. It had not been a requirement at any other time. He said he thought it a very useful exercise and would give him a bit more security and cover for the role in case of emergencies.

I suddenly changed tack and said, 'Yes, because you know the last weekend in September, both me and Dutch will be out of the area on a bowling weekend, and Mick will have to be your emergency cover.'

He looked over his glasses and said, 'No, I didn't realise you were both unavailable for a weekend; have I agreed to this situation?'

'Well, not in so much as agreed, I don't think it has been put to you in quite those terms till now.'

He said, 'Dear me, I sometimes think I must be running a charity show here. I suppose it's all booked and finalised this weekend?'

'Well yes, it's only a one-off once in goodness knows how many years, and I had spoken with the shift foreman who thought it would be alright.'

'Right, that settles it. Young Reynolds with you for the next couple of weeks and make sure he'll be fit for purpose come that weekend, that's all.'

It was well turned six when we finished. I said to Dutch, 'That'll do. Go and have a good relaxing holiday, plenty of sunshine, lots of good food, not too much alcohol and get nicely loved up. See you in a couple of weeks or so.'

He said, 'You'll see me long before that, Barbara has insisted we put in an appearance at the club tonight. She says she needs to check the details for the ladies outing, as when we get back it will be only two weeks left.'

'Great, I'll see you there, but everything I've just said still stands, OK.'

When I arrived home, Doreen was beginning to get agitated. 'Where have you been? I was just about to ring your works to find out where you were.'

'Whoa, calm down, we had a little bit of work to clear before we finished. I'm only a bit later than my usual time.'

'It's almost two hours later,' she said, 'you usually call and let me know if you're going to be late, especially on a Friday.' She went on, 'And no, we will not be stopping in, it's my night out. Anyway, Barbara has phoned and said she and Dutch will be out. She wants to pay the balance of her money for the trip to Silverdale Hall tonight, as next time she will be able to meet up it will be very close to the date of the outing. I've already phoned Eileen and Chris and also June, so we are expected to be there. So, you can't make any excuse for not going.' She said all this at full throttle, without taking a break or slowing down in any of it.

'Whoa.' I said again, 'slow down, you're using everybody else's oxygen talking that fast. First, I haven't said we aren't going out; secondly, I know Barbara and Dutch will be out; thirdly, if that's a word, I know she intends clearing her outstanding payments and finally, I'm going out to celebrate the end of the Thursday bowls season. So, get my dinner on the table while I go and shit, shave, shampoo and shower, right?'

'Well, why didn't you just say?' she replied and went to the kitchen.

We arrived at the club at about our usual time, certainly no more than a couple of minutes later than normal. They were all already there, a full Friday night team, extra table in position. Vic said it was his round and fetched the drinks. Doreen settled in and immediately started to drone on about me being late from work and how everything had been a rush.

I lost interest in her ramblings and turned my attention to what the guys were conversing about, which was last night's match. Vic who had returned with the drinks was saying how surprised he was with the lack of fight put up by the opposition as he had expected more from them.

I said, 'The bloke I played showed quite enough fight, thank you.'

'Yeah,' replied Vic, 'but he is one of the best players in this league.'

I thought, *Wow, that's better than the usual piss-taking I get after losing.*

Ron said from what he had managed to find out about other results from last night, it did look like we probably finished third.

He went on to say after he had done his final calculations, he thought Vic had finished top of the averages for the Thursday team. 'This hasn't been confirmed by any officials from club or league,' he said, 'but that's my assessment of the situation.'

Vic with face beaming said, 'That's good enough for me. I'll buy a celebratory round on the strength of your calculations, Ron.' He then added, 'I'll get a receipt, then if it turns out you're wrong, you can reimburse me.'

To which Ron replied, 'No chucking fance,' or words that were very similar.

Vic did get a round in to celebrate his achievement and with good heart, we retired to the games room.

After an hour and a half or so we returned to the ladies in the lounge. They had been kept supplied with drinks throughout the games room period. They had not played bingo but had entertained themselves calculating and collecting moneys to finalise their payments for their outing to Silverdale Hall. Also, Barbara had given them a very detailed description of the holiday apartment and its surrounding area and had hinted that it could possibly be available for friends in the future.

The evening concluded with a good, relaxed, happy gang wishing Barbara and Dutch a good holiday and a safe return and all other platitudes spouted out on these occasions.

On the way home, Doreen was rabbiting on about the possibility of having a late holiday at this apartment, and how wonderful it all sounded. I for my part was thinking how quiet Dutch had been all night. It was not the usual assertive, controlling, even domineering Dutch who normally accompanied us on nights out.

On Saturday morning, just after I had arrived at work, young Mick Reynolds appeared. 'Morning,' he says.

'Morning,' I replied and stood there looking at him. He just looked back with a half-smile on his face. 'Anything I can do for you?' I enquired.

'I'm working with you till Dutch returns from holiday.'

'Oh, are you?' I put in.

'Yes, old Billy called me to his office yesterday afternoon.'

'You mean Mr Williamson, the garage manager, do you not,' I said.

'Yeah, old Billy,' he replied.

'Fuck me, that's the trouble with the world today, no respect for anyone,' I said.

At this he laughed, and said, 'Respect? He was in a right mood. He spoke to me like I was a bit of shit that had fell off his shoe.'

I said, 'Don't take too much notice. I think someone pissed on his chips, I don't think he was upset with you.'

Mick said, 'He was quite adamant that I should make sure I was totally familiar with all aspects of the garage and how it works.'

At this I told him of our proposed trip to Blackpool, which would mean the whole garage and fleet being able to function that weekend would rest on him. 'Fuck me, I didn't realise I was going to be that essential to the whole operation.' He then went on, 'I think I'll have to tell him I can't do it.'

'Stop right there,' I said, 'it's up to me to make sure you can. 'First, you don't panic, not like that anyway. The manager's reaction to the news was panic, exactly like you. That's why he was in a bad mood, but the reality is much simpler. First, there are very few things that are really needed to get the fleet on the road. The main one is fuel; we have four fuel pumps, they can just about function with two, so not likely to be a problem there, right. Next priority is water; not likely to be a problem, is it? Same with air for tyres, lighting around the garage. Everything covered, OK?'

'Well, put like that, I think I should be alright,' he said.

'Good, so during the next week or so we'll make sure you are familiar with all the main problem areas, don't go telling the manager it's that easy or we'll all be out of a job.'

A much more relaxed young man roared with laughter.

Back at home later that day, Doreen said, 'Our Elizabeth has been round and I've paid her all the money I've collected; she wants to have a word with you about it. I think there is a small problem with the final amounts, and she would like you to go through it with her.'

'Why am I not surprised?' I said.

I phoned Elizabeth and said, 'What's the problem?'

She said, 'Can you get all the pieces of paper mother's got and go through them, see if you can put them in some semblance of order. I'll be round tomorrow to go through it all with you. I'm sure it's nothing more than an accounting error.'

Doreen was able to find eight papers with payments entered upon them, surprisingly all were dated.

On Sunday morning, I set young Mick the task of doing the garage inspection, explaining what to look at and what to do if any small nuisances found, and off he went.

I settled down with the eight payment sheets. I first put them in date order. Then on a separate A4 sheet I wrote the six names of the participants. Then starting with the earliest payment sheet, recorded each payment made against the name of the payee.

The first sheet had been done by Chris on 25th June, while we were in Spain. The second also by Chris on 2nd July was also while we were on holiday.

The one for the following week 9th July was missing. The next six were all completed by Doreen. I listed all payments against each recorded payee. Having done all that, there was nothing more to be done till the missing payment sheet turned up.

I finished work at 12.30 and went to the club. Vic and Ron were there and had played for the Sunday team. I only stayed for one drink then went home.

Elizabeth had come around for Sunday lunch, which is quite usual, and while Doreen was preparing it, we set about identifying the anomaly in the accounts of the proposed Silverdale outing.

Our daughter had the missing payment sheet dated 9th July. Chris had recorded each individual payment of that day and had then added total payments for each person over the last three weeks. Elizabeth said she had expected £125 off each of the five giving a total of £625, but she had only received a total of £560, and her mother had said she paid her all that she had collected and everyone seemed to think they had paid all that was required.

I spent the next 10 minutes or so going over the recorded payments. I then said, 'Yes, it looks like all four ladies that your mother has collected off have paid the correct amount.'

'Well, why am I £65 short?' she asked.

I said, 'Your mother was so concerned about recording and making sure she got everything correct, she forgot to pay any money herself, apart from her first payment of £60 to Chris on our return from holiday. Hence your mother owes you £65, now are you going to tell her or am I expected to do that?'

'Has she got that sort of money available?' asked Elizabeth.

'When do you need it by?'

'Not till the day we go.'

'That's OK then, another five weeks at £10 or £15 each payment and she's there, no problem. So, you can tell her,' was the suggestion I put forward. Knowing that if I gave her the news, she would immediately put forward the proposition that I should pay for her.

During the next couple of weeks, on a daily basis, I went over the most important aspect of keeping the garage running and the fleet on the road with young Mick. I was confident he could cope for a weekend, but convincing the manager was another thing.

What I proposed to do was to visit my son and his family in Oxfordshire at the weekend as it was August bank holiday. This would allow young Mickey to practice his newly acquired skills and knowledge unaided. I would only be a couple of hours away should anything untoward happen.

I put this plan forward to the manager. He seemed a bit reluctant at first but eventually agreed on the understanding that Mick and the shift foreman knew exactly how to contact me at all times.

While I was in conversation with him, I asked why he had been so hard on Mick last week when informing him he was to work with me. He replied, 'I wasn't aware that I was particularly hard on him.'

I said, 'Well, he was quite upset by your attitude and general tone toward him and wondered what he had done wrong.'

'Well, I sometimes wonder who's supposed to be running this garage, as you seem to go around telling everyone what to do, when to have their holidays, where they are to work, without any reference to me or anyone else.'

I replied by saying, 'Well, yes, I do take on a lot of decisions and put forward a number of proposals and try to organise my work, and all it affects the competent running of the garage. As a result of that, I'm here asking for your acceptance of my proposal.'

'Yes, OK, go ahead, put it all into action,' he said with a look of total capitulation.

I finished with, 'And by the way, in answer to your question who runs the garage, both you and I know that I do,' a pause, 'but only with your approval and guidance.' All this said with a hint of piss-taking.

'Fuck off,' was his only comment, said with a bit of a grin. I had never heard him use language like that before, not with anyone and especially not at anyone. I suspected there was a lot more meaning behind it than the grin tried to portray.

The first week went by without any major incidents. Come the weekend, Doreen and I went into Oxfordshire. I didn't receive a single call from young Mick, or anyone else for that matter. So, a very good time was had by all.

We returned home late Sunday evening refreshed and rejuvenated. We were particularly pleased with having spent time with our grandson, plus his loving response towards us throughout all our time with him.

Knowing I wasn't at work on Monday (it was bank holiday), Doreen had been in touch with our friends by phone and arranged to spend the day at a Town and Country Fair in the grounds of the local arboretum.

Not a problem, but for the fact I had intended to call in at work, although not officially on the payroll, to check that all was well, owing to the fact that I had set up the present scenario. Knowing the manager was not too pleased and that I had more or less forced him into agreeing to the situation, I felt I should take the responsibility and check that all was indeed OK and as it should be.

On hearing of my intentions, Doreen went ballistic. 'You can't do that; arrangements have been made. Vic and Chris are picking us up at 11 o'clock, Dennis and June are picking Ron and Eileen up and will also be here so we can all travel together.'

'I'll only be half an hour at most, I'll be back long before any of them get here.'

'Yes, I know,' she replied. 'I've been in this situation before; once you get there you lose all track of time, you're going to ruin everything. You always do this, work first, me second, it's always the same. This is the first weekend we've had to ourselves for a long time, and you've had to go and spoil it. What am I going to tell them when they get here? Answer me that.'

I said, 'For fuck's sake, I'm only going to be a few minutes.'

'That's right, start swearing. How many times have I told you about using language like that. It's got now so you don't know you're doing it.' At that I left and went to work.

When I arrived, surprise surprise, the manager was there. 'What are you doing here?' he enquired.

'Well, being a conscientious employee, and knowing you will hold me responsible for anything that might go wrong, I thought being as I'm available, I'll just look in and check everything is OK. Why are you here? Is there a problem?' I asked.

'No, like you, I'm here just checking. Now that you're here, are you staying for the day?' he asked with a look of expectation on his face.

'I intend to check with Mick. If he's OK and got no worries, I was prepared to leave him to it. Where is he anyway? He is here, isn't he?' I asked.

'Yes, I presume he's inspecting the garage,' he replied. He then said, 'OK, I'll leave you to oversee things, bye,' and he was gone.

I waited about 10 minutes for Mick to return to the workshop. When after that time he had not appeared, I decided to go and look for him. I found him in the female cleaner's cabin drinking tea.

'I might have known this is where you would be; this, the kid who wanted to tell the manager he didn't think he could carry the responsibility of the garage on his own. I now see you not only can do it but have time for drinking tea and entertaining all the young female cleaners as well.'

'No, I was just passing and they asked me if I wanted a cup of tea; they said you and Dutch always pop in for a drink at weekends. Anyway, what are you doing here? I thought you were going away for the holiday.'

'I was but I'm back. Me and the manager thought we should check on you to make sure all was well.'

'The manager? Is he here as well? What has he said?' Mick stammered out.

'Relax, he's gone now. When I first got here, I found him skulking around the place looking for you. He was not expecting me to be here. So being a good manager, with an amount of concern and some worry, he just popped in to check all was well. Once he became aware of my presence, he relaxed and fucked off, leaving me to cover his arse as usual. Enough about me and the manager, how's things with you, any major problems?'

'No, everything is going fine. I had a minor hitch with the bus wash on Saturday afternoon, the breaker for the brush motor tripped out. It all seemed OK upon being reset and hasn't shown any fault since. Yesterday a fuel hose split on number 3 pump so I fitted a new hose, other than that everything is good.'

'Great,' I said, 'if you're OK with everything, I'll leave you to it.'

He responded with, 'Has there been a complaint or is it that I'm not trusted?'

'What do you mean?' I asked.

'Well, you and the manager coming to check on me, I just wondered.'

'No, it's not that at all. I told you the manager wasn't happy with me setting up this arrangement; he wasn't sure you were experienced enough to carry all the responsibility. I had argued you were and the best way to prove my point was to let you have a go. He had eventually agreed but with reservations, I think he was more worried about the situation than I imagined. He does have to explain all his decisions and appease the directors. Consequently, he puts in an appearance to satisfy himself and to alleviate his concerns, OK?'

'Yeah, OK, but you know I won't let you down.'

'Yes, I know,' and with that I left.

I arrived back home still sometime before 10 o'clock. Doreen was upstairs beautifying and preparing herself ready for the day out. I called up to her. 'Honey. I'm home.' To which she replied with the single syllable, 'Huh.' I thought *and bollocks to you too.*

The day went well. By the time our friends arrived, Doreen was talking to me as if the early morning spat had not occurred.

The weather was warm and quite sunny and remained so until the middle of the afternoon when it suddenly clouded over and began to rain. At the outbreak of the rain, we left the show and retired to a pub, to wine and dine.

We remained at the pub till evening time then eventually moved on to the club. In the big room, a free and easy night had been organised, with a DJ and dancing, which rounded off a pleasant day.

The following day at work, I felt a bit jaded and far from refreshed after my weekend break from the regular slog of my work routine.

Young Michael was happy with the way things had gone and seemed quite proud of himself. The manager was less pleased with the situation, he more or less suggested I had misled him regarding my availability over the holiday period. After a short debate, he calmed down and accepted it was probably all for the best.

The week and the weekend that followed passed without any major incidents.

Dutch wasn't expected back till next Wednesday. Mick was continually expressing his disappointment at the prospect of having to return to his original role in the company and saying how much at home he now felt in our department. All the same his time with the section came to an end on Tuesday evening. I thanked him for his support and effort and said if the need arose again, I would definitely request his assistance.

Wednesday morning saw the return of Dutch. He seemed changed somehow, certainly tanned but something else, he seemed to have lost some weight. 'How's it go? Happy to be back?' I asked.

'Yeah, it was good, I really enjoyed it. Mind you, I'm well fucked and glad to be back for a rest.'

'Too much horizontal tango, I reckon,' was my comment.

'I don't know about too much; just about enough,' he suggested with a big smile across his face.

'Yeah, well, you look to have lost some weight from all this sexual activity.'

'It wasn't just all bedroom, you know, we did a lot of touring and sightseeing, that bloody woman just would not stop.'

I said, 'OK, I'll tell you what, let's crack on with the outstanding jobs then at break time you can give me a full run-down of this exploration of Turkey and all the gory details.'

'Yes, OK, but some of the gory details are governed by the official secrets act as laid down by the Ministry of Barbara.'

At break time Dutch gave me a pretty comprehensive run-down of his holiday. No bedroom secrets, though, not even a hint of them. It was an itinerary of Turkish ancient historical sights, such as Ephesus, Hierapolis, Pamukkale, Izmir and many more. He claimed this was what Barbara considered a holiday in that region of the world should be about. For his part, he said he would have been happy to just relax by the pool with the occasional visit to the bar. Precisely what had happened on numerous days.

Overall, he had enjoyed the experience even if it had been very tiring. He said on reflection he was pleased Barbara had pushed him into visiting all these interesting historical sites as now he could pass himself off as an experienced world traveller when in the company of pleasant young ladies. I said, 'You don't change, do you?'

'Not one bit,' was his reply. At which we had a good laugh before returning to work.

Later that day, he reminded me that tomorrow evening he would have to leave directly his shift ended to attend an appointment at his doctors for the results of his scan. 'Ah yes, I'd forgotten your shoulder,' I said, 'how is it, have you had any problems with it while away on holiday?'

'Not really, it played up a bit when swimming a couple of times so I think it'll need some attention.'

He then went on to eulogise on the swimming pool and its surrounding area. He sounded very enthusiastic and pleased with the apartment and the complex in general. He made it all sound very agreeable.

On Thursday Dutch was away very quickly at the end of the working day. He did seem to be a little bit concerned and more worried than he would normally let show. This was not like Dutch. It made me wonder what had happened to make him appear so troubled.

CHAPTER FIFTEEN

Friday morning was chaotic. I had received a phone call quite early at about 5 o'clock, saying there was a major incident at the depot. A garage mechanic had driven a bus into the parking bay doors, severely damaging them to the point that they could not be operated. This prevented a large percentage of the fleet from being operational.

When I arrived at the garage, everyone seemed to be just standing around looking at the scene. I said, 'What's going on? Why hasn't this vehicle been moved?' I was told the shift foreman had said it was to remain there till H&S had inspected everything. I said, 'Fuck the health and safety, the fleet must be allowed to go into service.'

I then asked if anyone had informed the manager of the situation. To which I was told the night foreman had said he was going off duty as he finished at six, and anyway the manager would go ballistic when he heard about this. I told the mechanic not to be such a prat and go and call the manager and let him know the situation and also let him know Dutch and I were on site.

At that stage, Dutch arrived, I quickly informed him of the situation and said, 'We need to get the vehicles out on the road as soon as possible.'

Dutch said to me, 'You get this lot sorted, and I'll go and try to get the back gates open.'

One of the shift cleaners said, 'You can't get them out that end, they are all parked sideways onto the door.'

To which Dutch said to him, 'What a load of bollocks. I'll open the doors, you go and get the motorised vehicle lift buggy and a couple of rolling jacks and we'll soon shift them. Once two or three are removed, you'll have room to manoeuvre the rest.'

Dutch and three of the male cleaners took off to the other end of the bay. I sent the mechanic, who had returned from phoning the manager, to fetch the breakdown tow wagon. While he was away, I assessed the damaged gates. These gated operate by running on rollers in a U-shaped channel at the top and bottom and are powered by electric motors. The rollers top and bottom had been knocked out of their tracks, the bottom track had also been damaged and raised out of the floor.

The mechanic, who for some reason was known as Wacker, returned with the tow truck. Between us we managed to get the truck in a position, which enabled us to attach chains to the rear of the bus and free it from the doors. It was then possible to tow it away from the area.

I then reset the breakers and tried to move the gates with the electric motors. It very nearly worked and came within a gnat's knacker of pushing the gates back, but the breakers tripped,

'Fuck,' was my reaction to that failure. I next disconnected the drive chain from the door opening mechanism, fastened the chains from the tow truck to the gates to force an opening to allow the trapped vehicles out.

At this point, the traffic superintendent arrived on the scene in a total panic, demanding that the vehicles be made available for service immediately or heads will roll.

One of the cleaners who had been assisting Dutch came to say they had managed to clear the back exit and were now freeing buses.

I said to the traffic superintendent, 'Hear that, and see this. It's a bit late to come here in that sort of mood, shouting, moaning and issuing threats. If you felt like that, why weren't you here a couple of hours ago?'

Dutch then appeared and said, 'How's it all going?'

I said, 'It was OK until he turned up issuing threats.'

Dutch said to him, 'Have you got anything useful to add to the situation?'

The traffic superintendent said in a quite pompous manner, 'Well, now that everything is under control, no.'

Dutch said, 'In that case, fuck off.'

The superintendent nearly bust a gut with indignation, then with veins showing in his neck and face bulging red, he departed.

We thanked the mechanic and the cleaners for their help and told them we would clear the overtime payments with the garage manager as they had been due to finish their shift at 6 o'clock.

The time now being somewhat after seven, Dutch and I went to the canteen for breakfast. I suggested we order the Full Monty, then claim it back as expenses, I thought the manager would accept that.

As we sat there consuming our food, I remembered his medical appointment and asked what the results were. 'Inconclusive,' was his response.

'What's that supposed to mean?' I asked.

'Not really sure, they suspect there is a problem but aren't sure what.'

'Well, we know there's a problem from the discomfort you've experienced, so full marks to them. What's next?'

'I'm being booked in for a biopsy.'

'Oh, what on? I mean like where, your shoulder, back or what?' I asked.

'They intimated they wanted a snippet from my lungs.'

'*Your lungs!*' I more or less shouted out, 'What's that going to tell them?'

'I don't know but I've also got to have another blood test.'

'When is this to take place?'

'I don't know, the hospital will send me an appointment, so till then I just carry on regardless.'

The garage manager entered the canteen, ordered himself a drink, then came and sat with us. 'Morning,' was said all round.

He then opened with, 'Had a little bit of excitement, haven't we?'

'Yeah, you could say that,' said Dutch. 'Could have done without that twat from traffic coming and issuing threats and ordering everyone around when the situation has already been dealt with.'

The manager said, 'Yes, he has already been onto me about you being abusive to him.'

I then said, 'He got no more than he deserved, in fact he didn't get as much as he deserved. I don't appreciate being called out in the middle of the night only to find people already here who are more than capable of dealing with the situation. But no, they would rather be raising issues of health and safety and generally being obstructive to the solution. Then to have traffic storming in like that did not lend anything to the task at hand.'

The manager asked, 'Who was quoting H&S and being obstructive?'

'Your shift foreman,' answered Dutch with an amount of disdain in his voice.

'What was his reason for this stance, had anyone been injured or anything like that?' asked the manager.

'You'll have to ask him to answer for himself, but ask him you must, all he seemed interested in was going home. Oh, and by the way, the mechanic Wacker and the three shift cleaners stayed over to give us a hand after their shift had ended. I said I'd ask you to sanction their overtime payment; they certainly deserve that, along with a formal thank you from yourself.'

'There you go again ordering everybody around, even issuing overtime now.' This was all said in jest (I think). He then added, 'Anyway, thanks, I think you pair saved the day.'

Friday evening, we all gathered as is usual, Barbara and Dutch also joined us, a full team. Most of the conversation revolved around their holiday. Lots of photos, lots of stories of adventures, tales of trips to exciting and mysterious sounding places again with photographs aplenty.

The blokes escaped to the games room as soon as it was deemed an acceptable time had been spent listening to holiday tales. We stayed in the games room later than we normally would, for no other reason than we just did. On our return to the ladies, who had been supplied with drinks throughout our absence, no comment was made.

On the way home, I casually asked Doreen, 'Anyone have anything exciting to say tonight, or was it all about the holiday in Turkey?'

'It was mostly about the holiday; it all sounds very nice. Barbara once again said she thought it could be made available for close friends.'

To which I replied, 'Yeah, maybe, it's something to think about.'

Doreen then said, 'Barbara is very worried about what is happening to Dutch, she had said his shoulder gave him so much trouble he could hardly swim. In the evenings he regularly wanted to leave the bar early as he was tired. When they went on trips to historic places, which were often quite long coach rides, he would invariably nod off. Plus, the uncertainty and confusion surrounding the scan, and now having to go for a biopsy on his lungs. What's it all mean?'

I said, 'I think she is overreacting to the situation. One, his shoulder is giving him a bit of gip, which curtailed his ability in the pool, that's common knowledge. Two, they were virtually on honeymoon, so early to bed. Three, we've been on those long coach trips in hot climates, they can be very boring. As for the hospital, let's wait and see.'

'Yeah, I suppose you're right, maybe she is reading too much into it,' was all she said.

CHAPTER SIXTEEN

It was the following Thursday, at our midday break that Dutch said, 'I went to see the manager this morning.'

'Oh yes, what was that about then?' I asked.

'I had the appointment for my biopsy come yesterday, it's for next Wednesday. I needed to book the day off as I've no idea how long it'll take.'

'That's great, quick progress, should make finding an early solution to your problem a formality.'

He next said, 'Old Billy wanted to sound me out about a situation that is going to present itself shortly. He said he is approaching retirement age, and in less than 18 months will be finishing. He wondered if either of us would be interested in being made assistant manager and being trained up to take over when he goes. He went on to say he could put in Mick Reynolds to replace whoever took the role on.'

My reaction was, 'Kin hell, that's a surprise, did you grab it, when do you start? Wow, that's great. Will I have to call you sir?'

'Whoa!!' said Dutch, 'I didn't volunteer for the post.'

'You didn't, why not?' I asked, 'You'd be an ideal manager.'

'I think he is looking for you to take the position.'

'Me? What makes you think that?' I asked.

'Well, like I said, he only wanted to sound me out as to what you might make of the idea.'

'That's bollocks, if he did not want you for the job, why did he put it to you? It seems quite obvious to me he was offering you the position.'

'I don't want the job. I have neither the aptitude nor interest, so it's over to you.' He went on to say, 'I told him I would put the situation to you and have a full discussion on the proposals. Which I now have done, that's me finished with the subject, OK.'

'That's your final word on the subject, is it?' I asked.

'Yes,' was his curt reply.

I said, 'Well, for my part, I don't think I want the job either. I don't mind suggesting what course of action should be taken at any particular time in any particular situation to any persons who happen to be involved. Like the manager is always accusing me of doing. But that's a lot different from taking responsibility for running the whole shebang. So are you going to tell him or what?' I asked.

'No, it's fuck all to do with me now. I told you, I was asked to discuss the situation with you, that's what I've done. As I said, that's me finished with the subject, over to you.'

'I can't go and tell him I don't want the job, it ain't been offered to me. If I go and turn down a post that's not been offered to me, I'm going to seem a right prick.'

'No comment,' said Dutch with a laugh.

To which I responded with, 'Bollocks.' I then said, 'We'll leave the next move to the manager.'

It was the middle of Friday morning when the message came via Samantha, the manager wanted to see me in his office ASAP.

I knocked on the door and entered without waiting for a reply to my knock. 'Morning, I've been informed you wish to see me.'

'Ah yes,' he said, putting aside whatever he was reading. 'Has Dutch told you I spoke with him yesterday regarding a situation that is about to present itself shortly.'

'Yes, we had a discussion about it,' I said and looked at him with a sort of blank face that was supposed to convey the message *I don't know what the fuck you want me to say.*

He looked at me with a similar expression. After a few seconds, he said, 'Well?'

I said, 'Well what?'

He came back with, 'Which one of you wants the job, or are you both going to apply for it?'

I said, 'It's probable that neither of us will want the post because we don't consider we have the relevant experience or knowledge to do the job.'

He explained that at his next monthly meeting with the directors, it was his intention to update them of his retirement plans and to put forward a proposal of continuity by suggesting a replacement who could be trained by him to continue the role he had pursued over the last few years.

He went on to say, 'I've always admired the dedication both you and Dutch have shown towards the job, how you are willing to turn out at any time to any type of emergency plus your willingness to propose actions to anybody and everybody to alleviate such emergencies. This is what made me think one of you would be ideally suited to a role as manager.'

'It's nice to know we're appreciated, but Dutch said he's not interested in the role. I think some of that feeling is down to his ongoing shoulder problem. As for me, I think I'm too long in the tooth to be changing professions, I'm less than 10 years younger than you. I think you should go for someone younger.'

I then added, 'If you do manage to convince Dutch to take on the role, I'm not sure Mickey Reynolds would be a suitable replacement, as I would require someone with building and construction experience.'

He came back with, 'Yes, but if I convince you to take the role, Dutch and young Reynolds will make a very desirable team.'

'Put that down as a non-starter. I've made up my mind. I don't want the job.'

'OK,' he said, 'that gives me plenty to think about. We'll leave it at that for now, thank you for being so open with me about the situation, it's much appreciated. I'll be in touch.'

That evening at the club, neither Dutch nor Barbara put in an appearance. The main topic of conversation was next week's jaunt to Blackpool.

I got into conversation with PK. 'Everything set for next week?' I asked.

'Yeah, I spoke with Walter yesterday actually; he's ready for us and said he was quite looking forward to our arrival.' PK then went on to say, 'He's given me a list of bedrooms that are available with numbers of beds in each. He asked if I could allocate persons to rooms before we arrive and make sure everyone knows which room they are to be in.'

'That shouldn't pose a problem, should it?' I said.

131

'No, there's plenty of scope with two, three and four-bedded rooms. I should be able to accommodate everybody to their satisfaction.'

I said, 'I wouldn't take a bet on that if I was you.'

'Yeah, you're probably right, please some of the people some of the time, but not all of the, well you know, any number of them will moan whatever I do. My main worry is who do I get to bunk up with Jumbo Jennings.'

Jumbo was in his early forties and was a big bloke, and I mean big. He stood about six-foot-six and weighed around 28 stone, quite possibly more. Not only that, he was also a grumpy, miserable moaning old sod, nothing was ever right for him.

'Well, just remember there's five of use, a two and a three, and we will be happy enough. And I don't give a fuck who you put with Jumbo as long as it's not me.'

'Yeah, see what I mean?' he said with a bit of a laugh. He then said, 'OK, I'll see what I can come up with over the next few days. I intend to let everyone know the arrangements when we're on the coach.'

It was at this point I informed him of the biopsy Dutch was to be subjected to next Wednesday. 'Fucking hell, what's that for?' was his reaction to the news.

'Oh, it's just that minor problem with his shoulder.'

'Will he be OK for Blackpool?'

'Yes, he's only attending the day clinic at the hospital, he shouldn't be there for more than a couple of hours. I don't think the recovery time is very long either.'

When I re-engaged with our mob, they were discussing the travel arrangements for the ladies. June had agreed to collect Eileen and then pick Chris and they would all travel together. Doreen had said our Elizabeth was to pick her up, and they were aiming to arrive at Silverdale Hall as early as possible, certainly no later than 9 o'clock. Between them it was agreed that Doreen would phone Barbara and check her travel plans.

I told them Elizabeth was to drop me at the club next Friday and intended to stay at our house over Friday night. This statement seemed like news to Doreen, who immediately put forward an idea of the girls having a night out

On Saturday morning, Dutch explained why they weren't out last night. He said Barbara was doing extra shifts to cover next week's days off. As apart from the health spa trip, she also needed time off to take him to the hospital.

'Wouldn't you be alright on your own?' I asked, feeling a bit surprised by this revelation.

'Apparently not. I've been advised not to drive for at least 24 hours after they have finished.'

'You are going to be OK for Blackpool, aren't you?'

'I should fucking hope so,' he said. 'If not, I'll cancel the appointment.'

'Listen, if you have any problems, any at all, you know I'm always here, make sure Barbara also knows. If you had said earlier, I could have had a word with the manager and we could have covered this.'

'I know that but it's all sorted now. Talking of the manager, how did your little tete-a-tete go?'

'Oh, not so bad, he asked if we had had a discussion regarding his proposal. I said we had, and the outcome was that I consider myself too old for the job, and you were too preoccupied with your shoulder to give it any serious thought.'

'I hope he understands I've given it all the serious fucking thought that I'm going to give it. Anyway, you're not too old for the job. You aren't all that much older than me.'

'That maybe so but there is a big difference between late forties and being in your fifties.'

'Yeah, but it's still less than five years, and I told you as far as I'm concerned, the discussion is closed.'

'Yes, I know, but he said he would replace whoever he moved with Mickey Reynolds. I told him if you went, I'd want someone with building and carpentry expertise, not Mick.'

'Fuck me, how many more times have I got to say it. I am not going anywhere.'

'Whoa,' I said, doubling up with laughter, 'I'm sure he'll get the message.'

On Monday evening, Doreen phoned Barbara. The conversation had gone along the lines of Barbara was willing to go on her own if necessary but would rather travel with someone else if possible. It was finally decided she would travel to our house and then travel to Silverdale with Doreen and Elizabeth.

On Tuesday, if Dutch was concerned about his forthcoming appointment, it didn't show. He carried on in much the same unassuming way as normal. When I asked him how much he knew of the procedure. He referred to it as a simple procedure known as a needle biopsy, only requiring a mild sedative; it should only take half an hour or so, with a couple of hours' recuperation.

Later that same day, the manager seemed to seek me out. He found me in the paint shop repairing a portable lighting stand. 'Ah, just the person I've been looking for,' was his opening statement. 'I'm putting young Reynolds with you from tomorrow. It is this weekend both you and Dutch will be absent from duty, isn't it?'

'Well, absent from duty is one way of putting it,' I said, 'yes, it is.'

'Right,' he continued, 'I'm still a bit unsure with this situation, so I've arranged for him to stay with you throughout the rest of the week. Please do your best to make sure he's up to date with all events happening over this weekend, I don't want any comebacks from this situation.'

'He won't let you down,' I said, which sounded more confident than I actually felt.

'Is Dutch going to be OK on your weekend excursion?' he suddenly asked, with a look of genuine concern.

'Oh yes, he's back at work on Thursday. It apparently is quite a small and very frequently used procedure. No one is expecting any complications or lasting effects.'

The manager changed the subject to the role of assistant manager and asked if any more thought had been given to the situation. 'No, not really,' I said. 'I'm quite sure I don't want to take on that amount of responsibility at this stage of my life. And Dutch is most adamant that it's not the role for him. But,' I ventured, 'if his shoulder continues to give him problems, if an answer cannot be found, if it turns out to be one of those things such as a cold shoulder or something of that sort, he may have to rethink his whole future work prospects. So, if I were you, I'd hold fire on seeking to get a conclusion till this little situation is played out.'

'Yes,' he said, 'but my thoughts are that where you deal with situations with tact and assertion, Dutch is inclined to use intimidation and aggression, and I'm not altogether sure he would be suitable for the position.'

I cut in at that point and said, 'I don't agree with your interpretation of Dutch. He can be aggressive, and he will intimidate because he can, but he is much more than that. If there is a problem, he is very analytical in looking at the situation. He is very logical in assessing the action required. He makes his point of view very clear, so there is no misunderstanding. People do accept this and will follow; he is a natural leader.

'If your understanding of how Dutch operates is based on his reaction to that bloke from Traffic the other morning, he was exactly right; the bloke got what he deserved. That's where his intimidation and aggression are used, only where it is needed. It is not the only tool in his box.'

'Yes,' he said, 'I hear what you say, but what you've said and the way you present your thoughts only convinces me more and more that you'd be a shoo-in for the role.'

Dutch left work on Tuesday, saying, 'OK then, I'll see you on Thursday. We can then start to plan for our Blackpool trip; I'm beginning to look forward to it. See yer.' And with that, he departed.

Mick turned up on Wednesday, all excited about the prospect of once again being a member of the maintenance section. I welcomed him with a statement intimating a difficult few days of concentration and application to the task ahead. I explained that the manager was still showing some concern regarding his ability to successfully see this weekend through.

'So, I intend for you to take charge of all decisions, I will only interfere if I think it will be disastrous, and by that, I mean really disastrous, OK.'

'Great, so I'm in charge, am I?'

'Yes, take it away.'

'Right, can you go and collect the report sheets?'

'Whoa, fuck off, I'm not here just to run around for you. You go and fetch the report sheets, then you decide in what order you are going to deal with them.'

'Oh, so I'm not really in charge after all.'

'In your fucking dreams,' I replied.

The day went well, Mick made a number of decisions, none of which were out of place with requirements. He handled himself and all inquiries with a maturity that belied his age. He was able to fob off people who requested unreasonable assistance, and be very accommodating to anyone with real needs. His ability to fob off the less needy was quite reminiscent of Dutch; I could see from where he had acquired this particular skill.

At our midday break I had given a recap on priorities and made sure he knew the importance of various aspects of the job. To boost his confidence, I said his decision-making had been quite excellent.

Thursday saw the return of Dutch, all bright-eyed and bushy-tailed, showing no effect of his hospital visit. 'How was it?' I inquired.

'Good, everything went as expected. Mind you, when they had finished and I sort of came around, I didn't know or realise I'd been out. It felt really weird. It took some time to get my bearings. People seemed to be talking to me and be halfway through a statement when I became aware of them. All a bit strange but no lasting effect.'

He then realised that Mick was in our workshop. 'What's he doing here? Weren't you expecting me back or what?'

'No, it's just the manager is still unsure about this weekend. He thought Mick would benefit from being with us for a few extra days.' I went on to say, 'I thought if he took charge for a couple of days, made all the decisions while we were here, it would be good training.'

Dutch said, 'As long as he doesn't try telling me what to fucking do, he'll be alright.'

Mick looked mortified. I said, 'No, he's not going to tell us what to do, he's going to be doing all the doing, we only keep a watching brief.'

'Oh, that's great. I can do that "watching".' said Dutch and started to laugh. Mick looked very relieved.

Dutch then said, 'OK, Michael, off you go, get the garage sorted out.' Mick took this as his cue to remove himself and collect the worksheets.

Dutch next spoke about a drain outside the battery house. He said he had noticed it some days ago, saying it had started to break up, and if it didn't get some attention, it was in danger of collapse. He suggested it was just the job to keep us ticking over till the end of the week. With Mick dealing with all other problems, we could relax and just concentrate on the drain.

Dutch suggested I should do the breaking out with the Kango hammer as he was a little bit unsure as to how his shoulder would hold up under that amount of stress. I said yes, no problem, and went to get the large electric hammer.

My thoughts gave me some concern, this was the first time Dutch had acknowledged his shoulder impeded his ability to carry out his job. Or was he just being ultra-careful after his hospital appointment? Only time will tell.

The work went well, me breaking out, Dutch reclaiming the bricks, he prepared the mix to re-do the benching, I then dressed the bricks ready for relaying. Nice steady progress.

Late that afternoon, Dutch asked,' What are you packing for this weekend away? Because I need to do mine this evening, as tomorrow we'll be in a bit of a rush after we leave work.'

'Yeah, you're right. I intend to travel in clothes I would normally be out on a Friday in. I shall have a couple of polo type shirts, a pair of jeans and trainers for fucking about in the day; I also have a lightweight fleece for just in case. Mind you the weather forecast is very favourable. Add to this a couple of good shirts (I've no idea what sort of state I might get in) and a spare pair of trousers. Toiletries plus shaving gear.'

'Shaving, fuck that, I'm on a lads-on-the-piss weekend, I shan't be too worried about having a shave.'

'Is your shoulder going to be OK, only you showed some concern earlier on?'

'Oh yes, it's all good. I'm really looking forward to a real wild weekend with a good gang of blokes like I haven't done for a long, long time.'

Friday, we completed the drain at a very leisurely pace. Wished Mick all the best and departed. Next stop, Blackpool.

A DUTCH MASTER PART 2

Friday Evening 24th Sept.

Elizabeth dropped me at the club just after 5.30. The place was buzzing; it seemed that everyone was already there. Most had had the day off from work, or at the very least the afternoon and were already quite boisterous.

Of our gang, Dennis and Dutch were sitting in our usual seating bay. Dennis immediately said, 'My round. You having the usual?' and went to the bar.

I sat down and said, 'Great, I'm ready, are you?'

Dutch nodded. 'Yeah, I'm ready.'

'Shoulder going to hold up?' I asked.

'Yes, and don't ask again, not at all throughout the weekend, OK?'

'Point made and taken, will not mention again.'

I'd only asked as during the afternoon at work, I asked why he had shied away from using the electric jackhammer yesterday. He had said, at the hospital, when he had first become aware of things around him and had requested a cup of tea, he had had a very strange occurrence; he said all the inside of his chest seemed to tremor. He had likened it to a crystal chandelier quivering in a small earthquake. It had only lasted for four or five seconds but the thought of using the jackhammer had worried him, thinking it might have started the tremor again, so better safe than sorry.

Dennis had returned with my drink. I'd only just taken the top off it when in walked Vic. Dutch said, 'Drink up, I'll get a round in.' I thought, *Kin hell, it's going to be like this all weekend.*

At about quarter to six, PK shouted up, 'OK, last drinks, we're starting to load up in five minutes, we must be away by six.'

Vic said, 'OK, last one before we go.'

I said, 'Where's Ron? He's cutting it a bit fine, ain't he?' at that very moment he entered the room. Vic got the round in.

I had not been in the room for more than 15 minutes and I was on my third pint. *At this rate, I don't think I'll last the weekend, never mind anyone else.*

Dennis asked Ron, 'Why you this late?'

To which Ron replied, 'I have to work for a living, I can't just stop and walk away when I feel like it.'

'Oooh,' came the response from all in hearing distance of this exchange. 'Who's pissed on your chips?' was the comment from Don, who was standing close by.

'Fuck off, all of you, and let me get my drink.' This raised great roars of laughter; the weekend was off to a flier.

PK called, 'OK, you've got seven minutes to get on the bus or we go without you.' This started a stampede, like a gang of school kids, a number of them all rushed out, aiming to be first so as to get the back seat. All to no avail, when after all the pushing, pulling and shoving they finally got on the bus, the sight that greeted them was that of Jumbo Jennings sitting right in the middle of the back seat.

The coach was a 43-seater, so plenty of room for 30 people, or you would think. We finished our drinks and were practically last out of the club. After stowing our luggage, took up seats in the middle of the coach, it seemed like no one else wanted to sit in that area. Dennis and Vic took up a seat on the offside of the vehicle, me and Ron sat immediately behind them. On a seat right opposite me was young Liam, spread out across the seat in an attempt to claim it all to himself. Dutch looked at him and said, 'Fuck off, Liam, that's my seat.'

Liam jumped up and went and sat by his dad. After a short while and a bit of seat swopping it, all settled down. Then a quick head count and PK announced to loud cheers, 'That's it, we're off.' It was just two minutes past six.

Beer was being passed around before the coach had got out of second gear. I thought, *You greedy bastards,* as I reached out for tins for me and Ron, owing to the fact that I was in the aisle seat.

Five minutes after the start, it suddenly went quiet for no apparent reason. PK took this opportunity to inform everyone there was a slight problem with the finance of the trip. Owing to the exceptionally large rise in fuel prices, he needed to raise some extra cash for Barry. This was greeted with shouts of derision. Not put off by this, he went on to say he intended to run a raffle. Thirty tickets at £2 each would raise £60. He would pay £20 to the winner and £40 for Barry.

All the time he was making this little speech, various witticisms were spouted. Then, I think it was Brian called out, 'The cunt couldn't organise a piss up in the old proverbial.'

Dutch stood up and said, 'Who called the organiser a cunt?' To which the whole of the coach answered, 'Who called the cunt an organiser?' Raucous laughter was abundant.

Throughout all of this abuse, PK remained aloof, did not rise to the baiting and carried on issuing tickets and collecting money as if nothing else was happening.

More drinks were passed around and the merriment flowed on. When the 30 raffle tickets had been sold, making sure it was only one ticket per person, PK settled to set up the draw. Bill Anderson started to distribute the food. It was all packed in boxes, the sort you buy small cakes in, one for each traveller. For all the derision aimed at the organisation, I personally thought it was all planned and executed very well. Each box contained a couple of sandwiches, a sausage roll, a chicken drumstick, a slice of quiche, a scotch egg and a small amount of salad in a plastic container. Plus, a plastic knife and fork, it was at this point I realised I was indeed hungry.

The atmosphere on the coach calmed and relaxed with the introduction of food. Then just as the noise level started to increase, PK said, 'Before we all kick off again, we'll get the raffle drawn.'

He asked young Liam, as the youngest and supposed most honest and innocent body on board, who was thought beyond corruption, to make the draw. I said to Ron, 'PK's covering all bases with this one.' Someone at the back coined a phrase 'L.I.AM' by calling, 'Am I feeling lucky? The L-I-AM.' The bus roared.

He made the draw, pulling out ticket 29. A drone-like sound spread along the coach as tickets were checked and blokes confirmed with neighbours that they didn't have the winning ticket. It slowly dawned on everyone that PK had started at the front with the first ticket number one and moved towards the back, selling as he went along.

As this was realised, all eyes turned to the back seat, 'Jumbo fucking Jennings' seemed to be murmured by everyone on the bus. 'Don't look at me,' he said in his most belligerent tone, 'I've only got 28.'

All eyes shot round on to PK. Don called, 'I hope you ain't pulled a fucking stunt on this one, PK.'

PK looked back and said, '*Me*, no chance I've got the last one, number 30.'

Then it struck, Barry the Bus had won the raffle held for his very own benevolence. This realisation was greeted with the usual cries of 'What a fiddle' and 'fix' along with such statements as 'them that have got will always get'. The reality was no one was that concerned, but these guys always feel they have to say something but can rarely think of an original line.

The coach rolled on at a fair rate of knots. The queue for the internal toilets was permanent, seemed never less than six. The drinks were still consumed at an ever-steady rate.

As we were approaching Preston, PK called for order. He asked that everyone should pay close attention to what he had to say. He was now about to inform everyone of their room numbers and who was in rooms with who. In fairness to all on board, total attention was given.

PK started by stating that 12 rooms had been allocated to us. There were six doubles and six three-bedded rooms, situated on three separate floors. He said, 'I'll start from the first floor. In room 1.1, a two-bedded room, Jumbo,'—you could almost hear the intake of breath and the gritting of teeth as everyone awaited the next name—'and myself.' PK had sacrificed himself for the cause, a piss-taking cheer went up along with a huge sigh of relief, followed by coarse remarks such as 'watch out, Jumbo, he's after your arse'. This turned out to be the format that accompanied each announcement, or at least something similar.

To his credit, PK took little or no notice of these remarks and carried on to announce the rest of the arrangements, namely: 1.2 Harry and Fred. 1.3 Bill, Brian and Don. 1.4 Markey, Kevin and Will. 2.1 Sam and Barry. 2.2 Ron and Dennis. 2.3 Dutch, Vic and me. 2.4 John, Jim and Roy. 3.1 Paul and Liam. 3.2 Keith and Tony. 3.3 Jerry, Duggie and Carl. 3.4 Cyril, Derek and last but not least, Nick.

Everyone seemed reasonably happy with what had been called out, and the noise once again rose to an excitable level. The clamour for drinks did not seem to abate even though we were close to the end of our journey. Blackpool Tower had been spotted, almost there.

It was Dennis who first said, 'Right, what are we doing tonight? It's just after half eight.'

Vic said, 'It will take a while to get to our rooms, sort out who's in what bed, make arrangements with clothing storage, cleaning and washing facilities. I suggest we meet up in the bar at no later than quarter past nine and take it from there.'

'Sounds like a plan,' said Ron. 'All agreed? OK, let's do that.'

Barry the Bus seemed to know Blackpool quite well and found his way to Tolley Towers by cutting through the back streets and missing most of the heavy evening traffic.

As we pulled up outside our destination, PK was first to alight our vehicle, he was immediately greeted by a bloke who I supposed was Mr Tolley. The welcome from where I was situated looked genuine, with a firm handshake and even a hug thrown in. I suddenly thought, *I wonder if PK is on commission?* Having had that thought (suspicious sod that I am) I thought *if not, perhaps he should be. He put in a lot of real graft on this project. I'll have a chat with him sometime over the weekend.*

We were all marshalled into the lounge bar. Mr Tolley called for order, then gave a little spiel. 'My name is Walter, Walter Tolley, the proprietor of this establishment. May I take this opportunity to welcome you to Blackpool; It is always a pleasure to receive members of your bowling club, I hope you all enjoy your stay. Please respect my property, and please try to keep noise levels down as a token of respect to my neighbours, particularly late at night.

If you experience any problems do not hesitate in informing me. Once again, I hope you all have a very enjoyable stay.'

He then finished with saying, 'I believe you all know your room numbers, you can collect your room keys from Molly over at the bar, thank you.'

Some drunken sot somewhere in the middle of the room called 'three cheers for Wally, hip-hip' and about six of the guys joined in with 'hooray'. The rest like me thought, *Here we go showing respect for the establishment and neighbourhood.*

Vic said, 'I'll get our keys,' and piled into the melee that seemed to be developing around the bar. It didn't take him many seconds to acquire the said booty, and with a call of, 'OK, follow me,' grabbed his bag and made his way to the stairs.

At this point, I said to Dennis, 'When we come back down, don't get a drink in, we'll go straight out and find some nightlife.' A number of the party were already downing quantities of various shades of the amber nectar. Ron was still in the middle of the scrum around the bar, attempting to collect keys for their room.

I picked up my bag and, closely followed by Dutch, ran up the stairs after Vic. At room 2.3, Vic unlocked the door and opened it, he then braced himself against the door frame preventing access to anyone else. He scanned the room, weighing up the possible sleeping arrangements. I then realised why he had been so willing to collect the keys.

Ever the schemer, he had probably been working this out since the allocation of rooms was announced. After a very few seconds, he made his choice, throwing his bag onto a bed closely followed by himself, thus making his claim on said bed.

I being next in line, adopted the same strategy. As I viewed the room from the doorway, I could see a double bed on my left-hand side, a single bed in the middle, which was the bed Vic had commandeered, and on the right-hand side was a two-tier bunk bed by the front window.

Understanding Vic had chosen the single bed to prevent having to share with anyone else, realising Dutch would rather sleep in the bunk bed than with me, I made claim to the double bed in much the same way Vic had claimed his bed.

Dutch, on entering the room, said, 'I suppose I'm expected to be in the bunk bed then, am I? Thanks a lot, guys.' He then settled on the lower bed and said, 'Yes, this will be OK. I can make myself comfy on this.'

We each lay there feeling relaxed just for a very short while. I then jumped up and said, 'I'm going to hang up my trousers and decent shirts before we go out.' As I was doing this, there was a knock on the door. Dutch called, 'Yes!! Come in.'

PK put his head round the door. 'Hi,' was his opening, with a slightly embarrassed look on his face.

'What the fuck do you want, PK?' asked Dutch in a tone that was there to intimidate him, as was the way with Dutch on most occasions when addressing the club president. It greatly amused the guys at the club to see PK's reaction when spoken to this way. It was why it was done, and only as a joke.

But PK was never quite sure how to take it. 'I need to move in here with you lot,' said PK.

'No fucking chance,' put in Dutch in much the same tone.

'Why, what's the matter with your room?' I asked.

'It's only a very small room, with just a three-quarter bed. When Jumbo's in there, it's full with no room for anyone else, let alone trying to get into bed with him.' Just the image of Jumbo in bed and PK trying to get in had the three of us rolling with laughter. I had tears running down my face. PK went on to say, 'Our bed ain't as big as that one,' pointing at my bed. With each utterance, our laughter went up a notch.

He then said, 'I put you blokes in here, the biggest room. I had thought about putting the five of you in here but then thought that was a bit unfair.'

Vic stopped laughing enough to say, 'I'm OK with that, how about you, Dutch?'

Dutch said, 'It's OK with me, but will he (meaning me) let him into his bed?' That started the pair of them rolling with laughter again.

I said, 'You've got less chance of getting into this bed than you had getting into Jumbo's. So, it's the top bunk, or you fuck off and try somewhere else.'

Dutch said, 'If you're getting up there, don't put your foot or any part of your body on my bed.' PK took this to mean acceptance and slung his bag up onto the top bunk.

At this point I checked my watch and said, 'Bloody hell, look at the time, come on, it's time to hit the high life.'

Vic chucked the keys to PK and said, 'Lock the door on your way out,' and at that, we three left.

When we entered the bar, Dennis and Ron were waiting. Dennis called, 'Come on, you're late.' It was exactly nine fifteen.

Dutch said, 'Yes, sorry about that, but we've had a squatter move in on us.'

Dennis said, 'That sounds like a tale worth hearing, but wait till we find a house of ill repute in which to while away our evening.'

Outside found us several hundred yards south of the Tower and two or three streets back from the seafront. Dennis, who seemed to be leading this foray into the wild side of Blackpool, said, 'That way towards the Tower, I think,' and set off to the left as we came out of the building.

We strolled along; Dennis, Dutch and Vic in front with Ron and I following just behind. As we walked, I related the tale of PK and his request to move into our room. The image of Jumbo in a small room was enough to start Ron off laughing. He then came back with, 'We're in the same situation, me and Dennis, our room is only small with a small double bed. If I had known you had a spare bed, I'd have been in with you.' The thought of Ron and Dennis in bed together gave me a fit of the giggles.

Ron's response to my laughing was, 'Bollocks to you.'

What I was really thinking was, *Bloody hell, this can't be right, the whole set-up is unacceptable. No wonder it's only costing £70. It's a good job we'll all be well pissed for most of the weekend.*

After covering about 150 yards, on a corner of a road junction there was a likely looking pub. The main door was open, it looked quite full, with music drifting out and a bouncer at the door. Vic said, 'This will do for a start, won't it?' This received nods of approval all round, and in we went.

It was a bit of a struggle to make our way round to the bar. I said, 'My call, what you having?'

'What they got?' was the reply. I noticed a pump pull along the bar with a badge saying "Black Sheep" I said, that will do and called five pints.

As we moved away from the bar, a group of blokes who were standing around a pillar with a drinks shelf around it decided to drink up and move on. Vic, sharp as ever on the uptake, put his glass on the shelf, claiming said area as ours.

At very much the same time, a young chap the other side of the pillar did likewise with his glass. Potential for conflict. Vic looked straight into the chap's face in what could only be described as a challenging manner.

The guy, a long, gangling, twenty-something, responded in a light singalong Welsh accent, 'Are we OK here?'

Dutch said, '*We?*'

The chap with a nod of his head indicated a young lady and said in the same light Welsh lilt, 'Me and my wife.'

Dutch, with his eyes nearly popping out of their sockets, said, 'Yes, sure, mate, it's OK.'

Ron, who by now is standing at the side of the young man, well actually between the chap and his wife, said, 'Are you Welsh?'

Vic said, 'Stands a good fucking chance with an accent like that.'

The young man answered without any sign of being upset or embarrassed and said, 'Yes, my name is David, that's David Llewellyn, and this is my wife, Myfanwy.'

Ron, with the beer getting the better of him, said, 'Your fanny,' and roared with laughter at what he obviously thought was a funny line.

'No, Myfanwy, it's a Welsh name meaning my little lovely.'

Dennis cut in with, 'Take no notice, mate, we've all had a drink or two.'

Young David's reply was, 'It's not a problem. I usually get referred to as a sheep shagger by people from your country.'

Dutch said, 'With a wife like that, I don't suppose you have that said when she's with you.'

Myfanwy then spoke and with the same soft Welsh lilt, said, 'Don't take too much notice of him, he's had more to drink than he should. It's his birthday, see; he's 25 today.'

Ron drinks up and asks David, 'What you drinking, Taffy? And you, Blodwyn? It's my round.' It was lager for Taffy as he was now and for evermore known and a Jack Daniels with Coke for Blodwyn, a name that also became a permanent fixture, and five pints for us.

Myfanwy was a tall slim girl as all young women seem to be these days. She was dressed if I could call it dressed in a black strapless bodice type of top, supporting what can only be described as an ample bosom, not huge and certainly not small but ample as I said, with a layered lace very, very short rah-rah sort of skirt also in black. Carrying all this around were the highest heeled, deep red shoes I'd ever seen anyone wearing.

I was suddenly aware of a lone piper in full Scottish regimental regalia standing in the middle of the dance area, making one hell of a noise on his bagpipes. He was playing 'A Scottish Soldier'. Going round the room were two menacing-looking individuals with plastic buckets collecting money. There was nothing to say what it was for, but they went on cajoling everyone to contribute.

They arrived in our vicinity and stood in front of Taffy, who was nearly out of it. He just looked at the bloke. The bloke said with an amount of menace, 'Come on, mate, cough up.'

Vic said, 'Leave him alone, he's had too much to drink.' The bloke stood there staring at Vic in a challenging sort of way. Vic just held his stare. After a few seconds, the bloke backed off, only to face Dutch, who just flicked his head as if to say, *on your way, mate*. The bloke moved away.

Dennis got the next round in and came back with a tray of our beers and Jack Daniel's chasers all round. This set the standard for the rest of the evening. The group on stage started to play a Buddy Holly song, I asked Blodwyn if she could rock and roll, she said not very well. I said, 'Well, that makes two of us. Come on, let's have a go,' to which she agreed.

As the evening had progressed, she had acquired a high stool to sit at our shelf. As she stepped down from her stool and made her way to the dance floor, Ron immediately stepped forward and inspected the seat. I said, 'What you doing, you dirty old man?'

He said, 'I don't think she's wearing anything under that frock and was wondering if she had left a snail trail.'

I said, 'Kin hell, where do you get your thoughts from?' Making my way to the dancing area, I could hardly walk straight for laughing at Ron's remark.

On catching up with Blodwyn, she turned around to face me and said, 'What you laughing at?'

'Oh, nothing. It's just that this room is full of some very amusing characters.'

As we started to dance, I was still laughing to myself. A lot of the folk around the dancing area seemed to be amused by the sight of a chunky greying middle-aged bloke dancing with a very elegant, attractive, leggy young lady. She was quite a good mover, and I, even if I say it myself, can put it about a bit. So, a performance to behold.

The five or six other couples who were on the dance floor slowed down and slowly but surely left the floor, leaving just Blodwyn and me. The crowd by now were all cheering and clapping along to the music.

As we swung around, I became aware the keyboard player was on his knees looking under his keyboard, I assume to confirm or dismiss the theory Ron had put forward regarding Blodwyn's underclothes.

On my next spin, I noticed the drummer and the guitarist were similarly positioned. The laughter and excitement in the room was mainly of their making, but centre stage was the leggy Welsh girl and me.

As the music came to an end, I spun round and dropped onto one knee, and Blodwyn, like a real professional, also did a spin and sat on my other knee with a hand raised to accept the adulation from the crowd, which was loud, enthusiastic, and seemed to me genuine.

We returned to our drinking station; I found another round had been purchased. I was falling behind the pace even though I'd only been on the dance floor for three or four minutes. I quickly downed my drink supplied by Dennis, closely followed by my Jack Daniels and took the top off my fresh pint, and said, 'I need a piss. where's the bog?'

In the toilet I quickly relieved myself, then splashed my face with cold water in an attempt to freshen me up. Feeling somewhat refreshed, I returned to the bar.

On my return, I realised the beer was taking its toll. Ron's speech was beginning to slur, Dennis was becoming a little bit unsteady on his feet, Vic was talking considerably louder than was required, and Taffy was asleep. Dutch, well Dutch was just standing there, relaxed, in control, looking much the same as he did before we started. How he manages this, I've no idea, but he always behaves the same when all about him are beginning to wilt.

Next minute the music strikes up with someone's achy-breaky heart not understanding. Blodwyn immediately suggests we all join the line dancers who are strung across the dance floor. Ron grabs her hand and heads for the floor, followed closely by Dennis and Vic. Dutch and I stand our ground and watch.

It's a magnificent performance. Blodwyn, step perfect. The three stooges hadn't got a clue. But in fairness they did entertain the audience, who cheered their every move, much to the annoyance of the accomplished line dancers. They seemed to look upon our three heroes as if what they were doing was sacrilege (but that's line dancers for you). Blodwyn did throw in a few variations in an attempt to keep the lads in the loop of what was supposed to be happening, without much success, but it all looked good fun.

While they were dancing, I thought I'd better get another round of drinks in as it was getting close to last orders. On returning to our drinking station, Ron, in a drink-fuelled all too excited state, insisted on getting his round in, saying, 'I've missed my round and I know you lot won't let up if that happens.'

Blodwyn said, 'Don't get me any more. I've got three drinks lined up already,' and despite protests from Vic and Dennis, Ron charged up to the bar.

The crowd had started to thin out slightly and we had acquired a table, which was very much needed now with the number of drinks that remained to be consumed. Blodwyn devoured two of her drinks and said, 'Excuse me,' as she shot off to the toilet.

Dennis and Ron sat on chairs at the recently acquired table, both seemingly to be feeling the effects of the consumed alcohol. Vic, Dutch and I preferring to stand, in a show of masculine pride, showing we could still stand. (Well, that's what I was attempting to do.)

As Blodwyn returned, the group announced the last dance. Vic stepped forward and asked Blodwyn if she would have the last dance with him. At much the same time, Ron, on staggering to his feet, said, 'I was going to ask you to dance with me.'

Vic gave a look of annoyance and said, 'Ron, you can hardly stand, let alone dance.'

Ron, buoyed up by drink, replied, 'Fuck off, you, course I can,' and promptly bumped into the column with the drinks shelf.

Blodwyn at this point turned to Dutch and said, 'You haven't had a dance yet. Why don't you have the last dance with me?'

Dutch said, 'Yeah, why not?' and they went to the dance floor.

Vic stood there with his mouth open, Ron sat down again. Dennis and I just laughed. Vic said, 'That's your fault,' to Ron. Ron answered, 'Bollocks,' and we just carried on laughing, which soon turned into all four of us laughing almost hysterically. I'm not sure we knew just what we were laughing at.

After the bar closed and the music had stopped, it took us at least 20 minutes to finish our drinks. Most of that time was spent trying to get Taffy to wake up and get on his feet. Blodwyn had suddenly realised she had to get him back to their hotel. She was not very steady on her own legs, particularly in those shoes. Dennis came up with the idea of getting a taxi as the best means of getting Taffy back.

When we finally did get out of the building, Dennis asked the doorman where a taxi could be found. The doorman pointed to a queue of 20 or 30 people. 'At the back of that,' was his only comment.

Blodwyn's response to the sight of the queue was, 'Bloody hell, he'll be asleep again if he has to stand still for more than a couple minutes.'

Vic asked, 'Whereabouts is your hotel?'

'Just past the North Pier. It's not that far but I don't think I'll be able to manage him even just that far.' Vic proposed that we give her a hand as it's only 10 minutes' walk. Dennis thought we should go to the front and walk along there as it might enable us to flag down a passing taxi. All agreed this was a good idea, so off we set.

It was hard work; Ron had linked arms with Taffy. I'm not sure who of the pair of them was most capable of walking unaided. On either side of this pair was Vic and Dennis, giving the group some stability, not a lot but some. As they rambled their way along the front, they were singing 'dear old palls, jolly old palls' to the amusement of many passers-by.

A few yards behind them walked Dutch and I with a tottering Blodwyn sandwiched between us. She was becoming very unsteady on her feet.

Not many yards past the North Pier, the quartet in front decided to take a break and seemed to just collapse onto a convenient bench. It was at this stage that Blodwyn suddenly decided she was feeling bilious and rushed over to the sea wall.

As she draped herself over the parapet of the sea wall and braced herself against it, feet set at least 18 inches apart, the sight set before us left nothing to the imagination. Ron's theory of the underwear was dispelled but only just. A black thong, hardly visible to the naked eye, was all that was there.

I was standing there with my mouth hanging open, thinking, *Kin hell, what a sight,* when a gang of blokes came strolling along. On seeing what I could see, their reaction was that of any bloke when faced with such a sight. They could hardly believe their luck. One of them stepped forward and lifted her skirt right up over her back. Dutch by this stage was almost upon them.

Encouraged by his mates, the bloke started to unzip himself. Dutch said, 'Hold it right there, mate. Go on, leave her alone, you've had your fun, now go away.'

The main man of this outfit said, 'Fuck off, mate, find your own, I was here first,' and all his mates roared their approval.

As he stepped forward, still fully intent of having his way with the draped young woman, Dutch hit him hard with a punch straight between his eyes. He dropped like the proverbial sack of potatoes.

His mates quickly squared up to Dutch, who just stood there in fighting pose. Dennis was now at his side, closely followed by Vic, and I was closing in fast. The gang of blokes were still threatening but were hesitant with the four of us standing ready to do battle.

Dennis was first to speak, 'You had better look after your mate, he looks like he needs some help.' This seemed to bring a little bit of sanity to the situation.

They started to relax, then turned to their fallen comrade and lifted him away from our area. Dutch had not moved from his original position. I then realised he had a problem. 'You OK?' I asked.

'No, it's my shoulder, make sure they (meaning the gang of blokes) don't know.'

'Fuck them, are you going to be alright?'

'Yes, just give me a moment.'

Ron, who had quickly sobered up owing to the little altercation, was attending Blodwyn. He had pulled her skirt down off her back and helped her into an upright position. Taffy had remained on the bench, oblivious to events going on around him.

Dutch regained his composure and said he was OK. He then said he wanted to get off the streets as he was concerned there might be repercussions following his twatting of that bloke. 'Repercussions?' I asked. 'Like what?'

'Well, the authorities, police or some other busybody asking questions as to who or what I am. I just want out of here.'

I suggested someone should go with him. 'Fuck off,' was his response, 'I ain't a kid, I'll be OK on my own.'

'What if they are waiting for you down the road?' I looked towards Dennis and with a flick of my head sort of suggesting he should go with Dutch.

Dennis, quick on the uptake, said, 'I've had enough of this lot. I'll come back as well,' the pair of them set off towards Tolly's place.

Blodwyn, still not fully aware of what had transpired all around her, linked arms with Ron and Vic; they just set off up the road without giving a thought for poor old Taffy and even less of a thought for me being left to cope with him on my own.

But cope I did. I suppose I was a little bit unkind in handling him the way I did. I quite aggressively shook him and pulled him onto his feet, he was several inches taller than me but considerably lighter. I raised his left arm and slipped underneath it. Then with his arm resting across my shoulders and my right arm around his back, I sort of frogmarched him along the road. Demanding and bullying him into walking as strong and quickly as possible considering his condition.

It only took a few minutes to reach their hotel. The forced march had revived Taffy to some extent; he became most adamant that we should join him and his wife in their bar, the fact that they were residents allowed him to drink till whatever time he wanted. Well, that's what I think he was trying to say, as he had major problems saying residents and any number of other words come to that.

Suddenly Blodwyn realised people were missing. 'Where's Dutch and er, er the other one er, Dennis?'

'They are where I intend to be very shortly, at our hotel.' With that, I started to walk back the way we had just come. Looking over my shoulder, I witnessed Ron getting a farewell snog with Blodwyn. *You randy bastard* was my immediate thought. I didn't look to find out if Vic did likewise but assume he wouldn't miss an opportunity to grapple at close quarters with Blodwyn.

Strolling back south towards our digs, I realised I had no idea what street Tolly Towers was in and neither did Vic or Ron. Ron was also asking, 'What's Tolly Towers?' I don't think he even knew he was in Blackpool.

Knowing it was a few streets back from the front and some way south of the Tower, we turned off the front into the streets that are behind the Tower, hoping to see something we could recognise.

A definite aroma of fish and chips filled our nostrils, all three of us seemed to say at the same time. 'I'm fucking starving.' There in bright neon was a sign bearing the legend 'Licensed Fish Bar'. Stumbling in, we were greeted by shouts of, 'Bloody hell, here's

154

trouble.' Half our coach appeared to be there. Or at least Don, Brian, Bill, Kevin, Markey and the reason it looked like half the coachload, Jumbo.

Don called, 'You had better be quick, Jumbo has nearly finished his first plateful and will be back for seconds.' This brought forth great wails of laughter as if it was the funniest line ever spouted. (Pissed as we were, the lot of them.)

'What you having?' asked Ron.

'Just get your own, whatever you want,' answered Vic. I being first in the queue, ordered steak and kidney pie plus chips and mushy peas with a can of Tetley's Bitter. I sat at a vacant table facing the counter. Vic followed and sat opposite with his back to the counter. Before I really got started on my food, I said, 'I need a piss,' and went to the toilet.

When I returned to the room, four of the blokes who had been with the bloke who got thumped by Dutch were gathered around Ron, who was still by the counter. 'Oi!! Leave him alone, you lot,' I called very loud and aggressively. This alerted everyone in the place. Don, Brian and Kevin were up and right behind me in seconds. Vic, on turning around, quickly followed.

The four blokes looked startled by this onslaught of guys. Their shock quickly turned to total fear as Jumbo Jennings loomed down on them.

Ron, who seemed as startled as the four blokes, shouted, 'Whoa, what's happening? These chaps are only talking to me.'

'You OK?' I asked.

Ron answered, 'Yes.'

One of the blokes said, 'We ain't looking for trouble, mate, we only wanted to know if the girl was going to report our mate, as he didn't mean any harm. He was well pissed, and your mate was absolutely right in giving him a smack like that.'

Our lads who were already in the place when we walked in, looked on in total bewilderment as they had no idea what the guy was on about. Vic, on the other hand, knew exactly what the situation was and decided to wind things up a notch. He said, 'Our mate, as you call him, was that girl's father. He and his daughter are going to the police in the morning to report the incident. They want him caught and put on the sex offender's register.' He went on to say some of his mates may find themselves also in trouble for egging him on. The four of them went white.

One of them said, 'But it was only a joke, just a laugh, he wasn't going to do anything really.'

'That's easy for you to say, but it ain't what it looked like from where I was standing,' replied Vic.

At this point, I interrupted their dialogue and suggested it would be sensible for them to leave town as soon as possible. They seemed to stand there shuffling their feet and taking sideways glances at each other. Looking very guilty, they slowly edged towards the exit. It was all very quiet in the Fish Bar with everyone just staring at the four blokes, making them even more uncomfortable.

As they got to the door, they quickened their pace and disappeared into the night, never to be seen again. A huge roar emanated from the building, which slowly turned to laughter, so much so that I couldn't speak when asked by the others who were from our team but not aware of the night's events, what it had all been about.

In our inebriated state, everything seemed so much more hilarious than it actually warranted. (But ain't that the reason we drink.) Anyhow, we relaxed enough to finish our meals and explain, well after a fashion, explain the night's little escapade.

In this happy state we eventually found our way back to Tolly Towers.

On approaching the entrance, I suddenly recalled Wally's request that we all respect his neighbours and keep the noise down. When I mentioned this, the amount of shushing that went on seemed far louder than the bawdy boisterousness that preceded it, that started me laughing again. In this state we entered the bar of Tolly Towers.

There to greet us was Dutch and Dennis, once again a request was made to keep the noise level down as it was now 2.30am, an amount of shushing started up again, but it was less than the first time and didn't last many seconds.

Dennis looked at me and asked, 'Everything alright?'

I replied, 'Yes, all sound, no problems at all.'

At this Dennis said, 'OK, that's it for me, I'm off to bed.' Everybody seemed to follow suit, suddenly there was only me and Dutch standing there, leaning on the bar.

I opened with, 'You OK, how's the shoulder?'

'It's not too bad, still a bit sore. It usually goes away after a few minutes but seems to be a little reluctant to ease this time.' He then asked, 'Is anyone looking for me out there?'

'*No!*' I replied, 'Who would be looking for you?'

'Well, the police for a start, I hit that bloke quite hard. Do you think he's OK? He looked like he might need some medical attention; if he has to go to hospital, the police will be informed, then I'll be right in the shit.'

I then related the events of the night after he had left and how the whole gang were now in fear of being branded sexual predators and being put on the sexual offenders register and last seen rushing away in a bid to leave town before the authorities could catch up with them.

With that information, he relaxed and said, 'I do hope it turns out that way.'

I said, 'Of course it will. Let's call it a day and get some rest; big day tomorrow.'

In our bedroom, PK was snoring his head off. Vic said, 'If he doesn't stop that, I'll hold a pillow over his head till he stops, or till he stops breathing.' I was laughing as my head hit the pillow.

Next thing, it's morning.

Saturday 25th Sept.

'Aw, what the fuck's happening?' were the words that awakened me. It was PK struggling to remove a pillow that was strapped over his face with a leather belt around his head. It was long ways on, stretching from about six inches above his head down to his chest. I was guffawing like a drain, I was laughing so much I couldn't breathe. I thought *if he doesn't stop, I'll pass out.* Vic and Dutch were also awake by now.

157

PK didn't seem to be able to grasp or comprehend why the pillow would not come away from his face. As he struggled and twisted, seemingly forgetting he was on the top bunk, he suddenly fell with a loud yelp of fear as to what was happening. Fortunately for him, Vic was able to grab hold of him, breaking his fall and saving him from serious damage. Vic then took hold of the bottom end of the pillow and lifted it up and over PK's head, allowing the belt to slip off.

PK was not a happy bunny. He was enraged and kept on saying that was fucking stupid, that was fucking dangerous, I could have suffocated, it was fucking stupid. As he ranted on, he was getting dressed. The three of us were all rolled up in laughter and as such didn't reply to any of his utterances. He then stormed out of the room, slamming the door behind him, only to reappear a few seconds later, holding on to his trousers; he had forgotten his belt. This only added to the hilarity of the moment.

We must have laughed for fully five minutes after PK had left the room, every time I started to relax and get some control, the vision of PK sitting up with that pillow stuck to him entered my head and started me off again.

Eventually, washed, brushed and reasonably presentable, we entered the breakfast room. On seeing PK, I almost started laughing again but was able to control myself. It was at that point I realised I was still pissed from last night.

Jumbo, Don and Brian were propping up the bar with a pint each (I thought *you dirty disgusting bastards*) but said, 'How the fuck do you do that?' I had a cup of tea, a bit of a ritual with me first thing in the morning. After that, I decided I needed to dump a load. (Too much information, I suppose.) I was now ready for my breakfast.

Wally duly arrived with a full English. As he placed it in front of me, I was pretty sure he then sucked his thumb. I looked around, no one else appeared to have seen anything, they all carried on scoffing away as though it was a race to see who could eat their meal the quickest. I thought I must be still pissed, I'm seeing things now.

The conversations were now in full flow, with tales of stupidity that could rival anything that had happened to us last night.

158

Markey then asked what was all that about in the Fish Bar last night. Ron was trying to explain what had gone on, but it didn't make much sense to me, probably because of the amount I'd had to drink. It was something to do with Dutch and a bloke having his lights punched out.

Dutch jumped in at this point and said, 'It was nothing, and certainly nothing to do with you, so don't refer to it again, OK?'

'I was only asking,' replied Markey, 'I'm sure I don't give a fuck about what happened to you last night or any other fucking night for that matter.'

The atmosphere changed from lighthearted to tense in a moment. I said to Dutch, 'Hold on, I told you last night it was no longer a problem, so just relax and stop berating people who accidentally offend you.'

'Yes, you're right. Sorry, Markey, just feeling a bit edgy about it, that's all.' Markey still had the look of a scolded child about him.

Right at that moment, in walked Sam and Barry. 'Fuck me,' exclaimed Kevin, 'you must have been up and out early for your walk.'

'Walk!! Out for a fucking walk,' replied Sam, 'we're just coming in from last night.' This brought wails of laughter and cries of delight from the assembled group as though welcoming returning heroes.

'Come on then, let's hear the story,' was the call from Don.

'Well, not much to tell,' began Sam. 'Him here'—gesticulating towards Barry—'said he knew of a place where we would be guaranteed a woman. He didn't tell me it was halfway to fucking Morecambe.'

'It wasn't that far,' put in Barry.

'It was way past Fleetwood,' was the response from Sam.

'Never mind the fucking geography, what happened, did you get any?' asked Don in an all too excited way.

'We went by taxi, we had two beers each from the coach, which sustained us on the journey. When we got inside, it was packed and most of them were indeed women. The beer was a bit on the expensive side but we downed a fair amount. Then I saw these two birds on their own sitting at a table near to our table.'

159

'Fucking hell, this is longer than *Crossroads*, get on with it,' called Kevin, showing a lot of irritable frustration.

'Look, if you don't want to hear this, you should not have inquired about it,' said Sam. Barry just sat there eating his breakfast.

Sam carried on with his tale. 'I went over and asked if Barry and myself could join them, to which they agreed. They were well turned out, very neat and tidy, lookers as well, aged about mid-forties. Anyway, after a few dances and some drinks, and by fuck, could they drink, they asked if we would escort them home.'

'Fucking hell,' interrupted Kevin again. 'Did you get any or what?'

'Simmer down, Kevin, you're going to cream your pants the way you're going,' shouted Don.

'Fuck off, you, I want to know what happened.'

'They shagged every which way you could imagine; we swapped over after about an hour and a half.'

Vic put in with, 'Don't you mean 10 minutes?' No one even smiled at his little witticism, they were that engrossed with Sam's story. I looked around, everyone was looking on with drooping mouths (I thought *poor lost souls, all of them*).

'Last thing I remember from last night,' said Sam, 'was this one seeing how far down my three-card she could put a lipstick ring.'

'Did you have another go this morning?' asked Brian.

'Ah, well, this morning it was a bit different,' said Sam. 'This morning, those two beautiful women of last night had turned into Wayne Rooney's uglier sisters.' The place roared.

Barry came in at this point in the story and said, 'It's always the case. I can honestly say I've never gone to bed with an ugly woman but, fuck me, I have woke up with a few.'

Wally came into the room requesting if anyone wanted extra sausage, the clamour for them was unbelievable. He had a large plate loaded with said sausages that he picked off for each individual who requested extras with his fingers, then confirming what I had witnessed before, proceeded to lick those fingers. I declined the offer. (Am I a bit squeamish for a lad's weekend away or what?)

Breakfast over, it was unanimously accepted, Sam and Barry's night had been the most spectacular of all the encounters of last night, at least the one's reported on this morning. Who knows what other secret stories may still be lurking in someone's memory?

Several blokes were still pestering Sam and Barry for the name and address of the venue they had been at last night when PK, who by now had regained his sense of humour, announced that the draw for the first round at the Waterloo would take place at 09:30 and that play would commence at 10.00 precisely. The time then was 09.25, it was reckoned to take 15 to 20 minutes to walk from where we were to the Waterloo.

Don and Brian had thought that much too far for a walk and decided to call a taxi. Jumbo and PK also joined them. Our team concluded that that amount of exercise was just what the doctor would recommend after last night's excesses. So off we set, with a good number of fellow travellers.

Ron was with the leading group, with Vic and Dennis just behind, another group of about six were behind them, with Dutch and myself some 20 metres back bringing up the rear.

We strolled rather than walked, the morning was quite cool with a light wind, more like what you call would a breeze. As we strolled, I asked Dutch how PK had ended up like that this morning. 'Don't you remember, last night he was snoring so loud that we had to shut him up.'

'Yes,' I said, 'I can recall Vic saying he was going to put a pillow over his head.'

'Well, that's exactly what he did,' replied Dutch, 'but he then rolled over and the pillow fell on the floor. As I bent down to pick it up, I saw his belt on his trousers, so using that we managed to attach it to him.' He went on to say, 'To be honest, I was going to remove it before I went to sleep, but well, sleep came a bit too quick.'

Just the memory of the situation had started me laughing again.

I then asked how his shoulder was. Not too bad was his reply, still not exactly right but OK. He then asked if Myfanwy and

David had managed to get to their hotel safely. I noted he used their correct names. 'Yeah, after you left, Ron and Mick got either side of Blodwyn, and the three of them carried each other the 400 or so yards to the hotel. They left me to struggle with Taffy on my own but I did manage.'

He then said something that made my head pop up, he said, 'She propositioned me last night.'

'You what? Fuck off,' I uttered.

'It's right,' he said, 'when we had that last dance. She told me he had arranged to go to the football match. Apparently, Blackpool are playing some team he supported.' He carried on with, 'She said she would be on her own all afternoon, and I could join her for a drink if I had a mind to.' He said, she went on to say, if it was too crowded or too noisy, they could always retire to their room.

'And are you taking up this offer?' I enquired.

'Can a dog lick his bollocks?' he replied. 'Course I'm going. I'd be very grateful if you kept that information to yourself. I don't want to broadcast it all around, remember I ain't Sam or Barry.'

'Say no more, it's our secret,' was my response.

We arrived at the Waterloo not many minutes before 10, paid our entrance fee and sat with the others. Ron, being there first had picked our seating area about halfway along the green right opposite the starting point. Good for viewing most of the green.

Satisfied with our lot, we settled down to watch the proceedings. It was noted our local representative Darren Baker from a Stafford club had drawn one of the favourites, a chap from Doncaster, they were one of the first four pairs on. Darren had taken one from each of the first two ends and was looking good.

The bloke from Doncaster hit form and was soon 12/4 up, it didn't look so good for Darren. At this point, Dennis said, 'I'm bloody freezing.' Being made aware of the cold, I realised just how cold I was. This sentiment was echoed all round.

On a suggestion by Vic, we all transferred to the lounge of the Waterloo. Inside the lounge there is a very large window looking out onto the bowling green. I ordered pints all round, (well, it was after 10.30, even if only just).

162

I must admit it was hard going, that first pint, but on a bloke's weekend away, stickability is the name of the game. Ron said, 'I ain't sure I wanted this.'

Vic said, 'What's want got to do with it? If we get the first one down, the second will be much less of a battle, and after that easy street.'

'There goes the voice of experience,' was the comment from Dennis.

'That of many battles over many years,' agreed Ron.

So, we settled into watching the day's bowls. Darren had made an excellent recovery and was only just behind at 15/17.

At about 11.15, Vic said, 'Come on, drink up, I'll get the next round in,' as all five of us downed the remains of our first drinks. Darren had lost but only just. With the score at 19/20 down, he had two scoring woods closest to the jack, match lie. His opponent, with his remaining wood, managed to drop it right on the jack to take the match.

The second pint was indeed more acceptable than the first but not by a lot.

It was Kevin who suggested moving round the corner to the CIU club, which had been a regular haunt on previous visits to the Waterloo, saying the drinks are so much cheaper there. This strategy was unanimously accepted, with a steady exit of our mob as drinks were finished.

By the time our little gang had drunk up and strolled the two or three hundred yards to the club, we arrived at the bar at exactly 12 o'clock. 'Time for some serious drinking,' claimed Dennis as he called the round.

It was Dutch who urged caution, saying, 'It's going to be a long afternoon, so I think we should keep it steady.'

A local brewery had a promotion going where if you buy two pints, you received a card with a question and six possible answers. Next to each answer was a box covered in a removable film. The idea was to pick out the correct answer and only remove the covering of its box; if you had selected correctly, the box revealed a tick, if wrong, a cross would be shown.

Dennis returned with five pints and two cards. Ron immediately complained that we had been short-changed as you could get two tickets with just four pints. 'Next round can be yours,' replied Dennis, 'you argue for the extra card.'

'Oh, OK, I will,' responded Ron.

Dennis read out the first question. 'How many times did Ivan Lendl win the men's singles title at Wimbledon?'

None
One
Two
Three
Four
Or more

'He did not win it very often,' said Dennis, 'so we can rule out the last two, or even the last three.'

'I can recall him beating Jimmy Connor,' was the input from Vic.

'No, didn't he beat McEnroe?' asked Dutch, and the debate had started. The noise level in the room was rising by the minute as each group debated the issues raised by their own questions and possible answers.

Ron suggested that he didn't believe he had won the event ever. In the end, Dennis took the decision and removed the film covering next to One, only to reveal an X.

'Fuck!!' was the response, as Dennis discarded the losing card. Everyone appeared to reach for their drinks before Dennis asked the second question. 'Which 16-year-old became the youngest goal scorer in the Premiership when he scored for Leeds in 2002?'

Kieran Dyer
Wayne Rooney
Michael Carrick
James Milner
David Nugent
Gareth Barry

164

Silence all round, Then Ron said, 'Rooney, he's the youngest player to score in the Premiership.' Silence again, as everyone sat there thinking.

'No, it can't be him, he never played for Leeds,' put in Dennis. He went on to say, 'Dyer was always a regular goal scorer wherever he played, it could be him.'

Ron came back with, 'I've never read anything regarding him being the youngest scorer.' To which Dennis agreed, as he felt whoever it was, they would have read about it somewhere.

While this little debate was going on, I heard a voice ask how many times Ivan Lendl had won Wimbledon. 'Not one, that's for sure I called.'

'Well, how many was it then?' came the reply.

'Hold on, where is that card with the question about the tennis?' I asked.

'Why?' asked Ron.

'Well, rub off all the answers and find out which one is correct.'

'You can't do that; it makes the card invalid.'

'So, what? It's a losing card so it doesn't matter, does it?'

'Oh, well, no I suppose not.' The next five minutes were spent searching for the discarded card. Suddenly Dennis remembered he had put it under his beer mat. I suspected last night's excess plus this morning drinking was already taking its toll.

The answer as it turned out to be, was 'None'. 'I told you it was none,' cried Ron with an air of jubilation: 'I said it was none but no one would listen.'

'No, you offered none as a possibility, which is not quite the same thing, is it?' countered Vic.

Ron came back with, 'No, maybe not, but if you remember when he became Andy Murray's new coach, it was pointed out quite a lot in the media that he hadn't won Wimbledon.'

'If you had said that in the first place, we might have accepted your answer,' was Vic's debate-ending statement.

Dutch butted in here and said, 'I hope this bickering isn't going to happen with every question we get. It's only a fucking glass that you get for a correct answer; it's hardly worth the bother.'

Ron and Vic both looked like they had been scolded by their mom and sat there staring at their drinks.

Dennis returned to the question of the youngest goal scorer. The answer came from Don, who called over, 'It's Milner.' This was quickly accepted as being correct.

Vic said, 'OK, Ron, get the next round in and see how many cards you can get.'

With a winning ticket in hand, Ron went to get the drinks. While he was at the bar, it was agreed that Dennis should hold all the invalid cards, thus allowing everyone to have a point of reference to answers for the quiz.

Ron returned with five pints, one glass trophy, and three competition cards, which he held aloft in a show of success and pride. He received cheers all round, the day was going fine.

The horse racing was now being shown on a television at the back of the room; it was fast becoming the focal point of a good number of our party.

With Dennis in charge of the questions, the beer starting to flow, newspapers had been obtained. With the racing pages to the front, the gambling started. The bowls and the Waterloo was firmly on the back burner.

The traffic flow to and from the bookies, just three doors down, slowly but surely increased.

With a loud cheer every time another glass was procured, which seemed to be with every card, Dennis had his system up and running, with practically all required answers recorded on a sheet of obtained paper.

Added to that, there was also the noise generated by the excitement or despondency of results from the horse racing on the TV screen. A lively afternoon was in store, almost certainly.

With all the comings and goings of the bookies run, I saw Dutch come out of the toilet and leave the club. I noted the time as being just after 1.30. He had acquired a round of drinks for our team before visiting the toilet. I had also noted he had not purchased a drink for himself.

No one else appeared to notice or be aware of his departure. I thought, *Smooth or what?* but didn't bring it to the attention of the room.

Sometime just after half past two, probably nearer three o'clock, there was suddenly an increase in excitement around the TV set. Upon investigation it transpired that Nick, a very regular investor with bookies, had an accumulator running. The first four of a six-horse bet had come in.

The talk was of three and a half grand already secured against £50 bets and possible winnings of 20 grand plus, so you can imagine the excitement.

Prior to this, I had said, 'Drink up. I'll get the round in.' It was at this point that first Ron asked where Dutch was, closely followed by Dennis making the same enquiry.

I suggested he was probably at the bookies. I said I would not get him a drink till he returned. Adding, 'You know Dutch, if a female is in there, he may be gone for some time.'

Nick was by now besieged by guys wishing to know his horses, so enabling them to place bets on those same horses. Nick being a superstitious bloke, as seems to be with most gambling folk, refused to give this information. Stating it would break his lucky run if he was to inform anyone of his selections.

I for my part stuck to my own selections, with much smaller amounts gambled, maximum stake on any one race just £5.

Ron being probably the most frequent user of bookmakers in our team, was the one taking our bet's round to the bookies, this time for the race that Nick's fifth selection in his accumulator was running. When he returned, Vic asked, 'Everything all right?'

'Yeah,' was the reply, but he had a puzzled look on his face.

Vic said, 'Well, something ain't right by the look on your face.'

'No,' he said, 'it's just that it was said that Dutch was at the bookies but he isn't there now, and he ain't here, so where is he? That's all I was wondering.'

Dennis put in with, 'I shouldn't worry; he's a big lad and can look after himself wherever he is.' I added he might have gone to have a look in at the bowls.

The noise level again rose as the next race started. Nick looked quite tense as the horses came round the last bend. My horse was pulling away in the lead. As they entered the last furlong, the chasing horses were closing in on my horse, Nick was out of his seat now, cheering on his horse, and as they approached the finishing line, it was neck and neck. It went to a photo finish. 'Who got it?' I asked; nobody was quite sure.

It was only realised then; I had backed the horse that was challenging Nick's accumulator. The atmosphere and the animosity towards me were instant. Not by Nick but people like Jumbo fucking Jennings, Don and PK, for that matter. As if my backing the horse had been the reason Nick's accumulator was about to possibly fold.

The result wasn't certain at this point but that didn't stop Jumbo, as main protagonist, mouthing off at me, saying, 'You fucking prize twat, why have you done that?'

I retorted with, 'Jumbo, you are talking like an idiot as usual, so I'll ignore the remark, owing to the fact you are fucking drunk.'

Jumbo's reaction to this was to say, 'You're all a bunch of cunts, all of your gang. You all think you're something special but you're nothing, just a crowd of cowards hiding behind Dutch.'

My thoughts were *Bloody hell, a lot of bitterness there. I wonder what that's all about?*

Vic by this time was right in front of Jumbo, who was still sat on his chair. He said, 'You're a big bloke, Jumbo, but you ain't very fit.' Michael Caine *Get Carter* was my thought and I started to laugh. Vic went on to say, 'If you use that sort of language at me again, I'll have you.'

Jumbo, puffing and spluttering, started to rise out of his chair. Vic put his two hands upon Jumbo's chest and gave him a huge shove. Jumbo, off-balance, goes back onto his chair, and with his weight and momentum, he and his chair go right over.

Vic is round and on him before he has chance to recover. Vic has his foot on Jumbo's throat, saying, 'Next time my foot is on your neck, I shall press so hard you won't breathe again, right.'

I was right with Vic; Dennis and Ron followed me. I said, 'Leave it, Vic, he ain't worth the bother.'

PK followed this with, 'Hold on, it was only said as a joke, there isn't any need for this.'

Vic said, 'Anybody call me a cunt and a coward had better be willing to back it up.'

Jumbo was still on his back on the floor, rocking around like a tortoise on its back. PK said, 'Yes, OK, that was a bit much, I'll agree, but we should all shake hands and settle down now. We've all had a drink and things get said, but no real harm has been done.'

As Jumbo finally got to his feet, still bumbling and spluttering, saying, 'You ain't heard the last of this.'

At that very moment, in walks Dutch. On hearing Jumbo's threat, he looks at him and just says, 'Oy, behave yourself.'

Jumbo picked up his chair and sat down, still trembling possibly through rage or probably through the effort of rising off the floor, but still mumbling to himself.

Dutch acquired a drink and sat in his former position, he commented on the number of glasses that we had accumulated. Then asked what was all that about. 'Oh, nothing much, Jumbo gobbing off as usual, about us lot in general and me in particular. Vic upended him and stood on his throat, that's all.'

'That's all, fuck me, I'd like to have seen that,' was his reply, accompanied by a roaring laugh.

'It was even funnier than that when it happened,' I said, laughing at the memory of Vic and his unintended Michael Caine impression.

Our afternoon in the club slowly fizzled out, the winning of glasses had long lost its appeal. My horse had got the verdict in the photo finish. The accumulator had collapsed, and the atmosphere in the room had changed from wildly enthusiastic to quiet and controlled.

At somewhat after 4 o'clock, Dennis suddenly said, 'That's me done for the afternoon. I'm going to look in at the bowls.' The idea was accepted all round.

As we left the club, I went into the bookies to collect my winnings. When I came out, Dutch was just leaving the club, having been left behind while finishing his drink. As we walked to the Waterloo, I asked, 'How did your afternoon go?'

'Well, now that's a tale to be told,' he said, 'I'll let you know next week at work.'

'Oh,' I said, 'does that mean it's good or does that mean not so good.'

'At work,' he replied.

The bowls had reached its climax as we arrived, the final was just about to end. The bloke from Doncaster was going to win at a canter. Darren fuelled by drink was now quite full of himself, telling anyone who would listen how good the bloke from Doncaster was and how he had been the only one to give him a good game.

I was by now feeling a little bit jaded. I slipped away from the Waterloo without saying anything to anyone. It was a fine late September afternoon, sunny and quite warm with just the gentlest breeze, unusually pleasant, especially for Blackpool.

I walked back to the seafront and turned left. Walking along the front at a good pace, I passed the Pleasure Beach and walked on. After about 20 minutes, I decided to turn back. I walked hard, all the way to the Tower. I then returned to Tolly Towers. I had been walking for a good hour and felt sweaty and in need of a shower.

On entering our room, I was greeted with, 'Where the fuck have you been? We nearly sent a search party out looking for you.'

'I only went for a stroll along the front.'

'Only a stroll, you've been gone hours.'

'I think you slightly exaggerated that statement,' I said, then added, 'I'm now going for a shit, shave, shower and a shampoo,' taking my toilet bag and towel, I departed, leaving them lounging on their beds.

There wasn't a bathroom on our floor, there was one on the 1st floor and one on the 3rd floor. I decided to try the third floor, only to find a queue. Well, when I say queue, there was one inside and two waiting outside. Fuck me, was my response. I immediately decided to try the first floor.

Great, no one waiting, but the room was occupied. I knocked and asked, 'How long you going to be?' It was Markey, he replied, 'Just a few minutes, won't be long.'

As I stood there waiting, a door down the corridor opened and out stepped Jumbo fucking Jennings. He stood by me as if in the queue, mumbling under his breath and looking extremely agitated. I thought *I'll wind him up a little bit*. I said, 'What oh, Jumbo, how's your health and temper now?'

His reply was, 'Tell that fuckwit mate of yours, it ain't over yet. If Dutch hadn't come in at that moment, I'd have had him.'

'It's about time you started to grow up and act your age,' was my response to his outburst. 'What did you think would happen when you go insulting people with the terms you used? If it hadn't been Vic, it would have been another of our crowd or even all of us if needed. Dutch hasn't been informed yet, that you included him in your tirade of abuse.'

Jumbo said, 'I ain't bothered about him either.'

I said, 'No, maybe not, but for the sake of the weekend, for all the blokes here and for your own peace of mind, you should make an apology at dinner tonight to everyone and say you were sorry for all the trouble you caused this afternoon.'

'Like fuck,' was his reply.

At this point, Markey vacated the bathroom. The bathroom was very basic, could be said to be a bit shabby but what the fuck, I was here now; let's get on with it.

Doing a full remit of ablutions took time. Jumbo waiting outside, started to get agitated again. He was banging on the door every few minutes, enquiring as to how long I would be. Even suggesting I was taking my time on purpose. He then resorted to insults, such as, 'What are you doing, are you playing with yourself again?' I at first had replied with smartarse replies but eventually stopped responding and did take my time just to annoy him as much as I could.

The abuse suddenly stopped, I listened with my ear close to the door and could hear a muffled conversation. Having completed my bathing routine, I quickly collected my toiletries into my bag, picked up my towel and opened the door, only to see Jumbo about to enter his room. I called, 'OK, Jumbo, I'm finished now, the bathroom's free.'

He responded with, 'Yeah, OK,' and carried on into his room.

I could hear whoever he had been in conversation with going up the stairs. Following the footsteps up the stairs, as I rounded onto the second-floor landing, PK was entering our room. I asked, 'Was that you speaking with Jumbo by the bathroom?'

'Yes,' he replied, 'Markey had come to the room and said Jumbo seemed to be spoiling for a set-to with whoever was in the bathroom, and someone should go and calm him down. These two volunteered me to go and have a word with him.'

'So, what was said?' asked Vic.

'I told him to stop shouting and banging doors as he was disturbing everyone, and that his behaviour and general mouthing off at people was spoiling the weekend.' PK went on saying, 'I told him if things didn't change for the better, I would have to consider putting it before the club committee.'

'What did he say to that,' I asked?

'He said it was fuck all to do with the club, and anyway he might report this afternoon's attack on him to the committee himself, so fuck off.'

'So, a successful bit of negotiation there,' was my comment. This statement relaxed the atmosphere and we all had a laugh. Time for dinner.

Our table was positioned close to a bay window and would seat eight. Three seated along each side, with one at each end. Our gang of five were joined by Fred and Harry. Dutch taking an end seat, Dennis sat opposite Vic, with Ron opposite me. Fred was sat next to Ron, with Harry taking the other end seat, leaving a spare place between Harry and me.

Wally came with a tray balanced on one hand with a number of bowls of soup on board. 'Who's for the soup?' he asked. I immediately indicated I was, hoping to get a dry thumb one. This achieved, I watched with my mouth gaping as Wally went through his routine of bowl, thumb in mouth, bowl, thumb in mouth. Nobody seemed bothered.

The room was full of blokes eating like they hadn't eaten for a week. I must confess I was very much in need of sustenance myself, as I hadn't had any food since breakfast.

It was Dennis who raised the subject of Jumbo, saying he ain't come down for his dinner. Vic's thought was he had stayed in his room sulking. Ron said for Jumbo to miss out on food, he must be dead; this raised a laugh all round. We carried on eating, not showing much concern.

172

There was a fair amount of chatting around the room as stories of the day's adventures were told. Harry was telling our table they had stayed at the Waterloo all day and how good the bowling had been; they had had a couple of hip flasks between them, which they had refilled on a number of occasions during the day.

Suddenly the room was washed with silence. On looking around, standing by the door was Jumbo. He stood there for a few seconds with all eyes on him. Then he spoke saying, 'Apparently, I've upset some of you this weekend with remarks that were only meant as a joke. For this I want to apologise. Sorry.' Then he added, 'But there are issues that I will have to deal with.'

Someone the other side of the room, Kevin, I think it was called, 'Sit down, Jumbo, and get your fucking dinner; no one's upset and no one needs an apology.' To which the room seemed to agree with murmurs such as 'yeah, get your dinner', and 'for fuck's sake relax a bit'.

Jumbo came over to our table where the only free dining place was, he grabbed the vacant chair and without saying a word went and sat at the table where Don, Brian, Bill and PK were sitting. An amount of giggling accompanied his actions, then everything settled down to the normal steady drone of chatter.

Our conversation turned to thoughts of what we might do this evening. Ron was in favour of seeking out Blodwyn, adding, 'She's lovely. I think I'm in love.'

Vic said, 'I don't think so, we don't want to just repeat last night.'

I looked towards Dutch, who was shaking his head very slightly with a look that sort of said 'no fucking chance'. Dennis intervened at this point saying, 'I agree with Vic, I think we should go south and seek out a different venue.'

Fred put in with an idea, saying on previous trips to the Waterloo, a number of our members had used a club called the Pear Tree, adding they always came back with exciting stories, plus it stays open very late. My response was to say, 'Yeah, we'll bear that in mind.'

Ron asked, 'How late is late?'

'Somewhat after two, I believe,' answered Fred.

'I don't think we'll be out that late, not after the last 24 hours we've had,' said Vic.

Saturday evening 25ᵗʰ Sept.

Seven forty-five found us walking along the seafront. We were travelling south at a very leisurely pace. The truth being none of us was in too much of a hurry to start drinking, our dinner still a little bit heavy in our stomachs. Plus, the day-long drinking slog in the workingmen's club. It had left us, or certainly me, feeling a little bit fragile.

We strolled as far as the Pleasure Beach. Considered taking a ride on the Big One but very quickly dismissed that proposition. After a short debate regarding the pleasures of the fair, we did an about turn and started to make our way back towards the centre.

Passing a bright-fronted, slightly gory looking place, Vic said, 'That looks exciting. Shall we give it a try?'

'Yeah, why not?' was the response from Ron. With no objection from anyone, Dennis stepped forward to enter the place. He was immediately stopped by the doorman requesting a £2 entrance fee.

I called, 'Whoa, hold on a minute, if we are going to pay £10 to go in there, we need to know if it's OK first.' I asked if we could go and have a look before handing over our money.

'One of you can have a look,' replied the doorman. Trusting my judgement more than any other of our mob, I volunteered to take a look.

When I came out, the doorman said, 'Everything alright, £10 and you're in.'

I said, 'Hold on, let me have a word with them.' I told them, 'It's all chrome and glass with flashing lights really, it's only a disco.' I then added, 'Mind you, it's full of totty. And all of them wearing less clothing than my wife wears in bed.'

Ron said, 'Here's my £2,' with a laugh, we moved on.

A hundred yards or so up the road was a proper pub, advertising one of our own home area beers, with Country and Western music.

Dutch said, 'I probably missed a round this afternoon, so I'll get them in.' Dennis spotted a table, only three chairs. Scrounging around the room, we were able to acquire another two chairs. It was slow going at first but with a familiar beer we soon settled into a steady drinking session.

By the time we were on our third drink, our demeanour was far more positive. The atmosphere in the place was getting wilder by the minute. We were by now singing along to the music, Ron was up on his chair playing air guitar. In short, we were all building for a party night.

At a table adjacent to ours, a group of young ladies (I use the term 'ladies' and 'young', come to that, very lightly) were apparently on a hen party weekend. Dressed in nurses' uniforms, they started taking photos of each other, in various groups and in any number of poses.

Dennis, making out he was Blackpool's equivalent of David Bailey, locally known as Bathe-it Daily (I don't think any of them understood his little joke), suggested he should take some group photos, enabling them all to be photographed together. This offer was seized upon very readily by the group of females. Dennis organised them into a quite formal group pose for the first one. He then got them into a more relaxed pose and took the second photo. He then said, 'OK, much the same again, please. Only this time can we have a bit more tit and thigh.'

The reaction to his suggestion was astonishing. Legs everywhere, buttons undone, flesh flashed all round. Dennis was clicking the camera as fast as his fingers would go. Ron jumped into the middle of this throng of female flesh, shouting, 'Get me in one.' The so-called ladies practically devoured him; Ron slowly surfaced with a huge grin on his face. Dennis had managed a good number of shots showing the mayhem.

Throughout all of this, Dutch had remained relaxed, could even be said to be slightly subdued; Vic had also remained a lot less involved than I might have expected. Both had laughed at

Dennis and Ron's exploits, but neither had shown the excitement or the involvement I thought the performances deserved.

For the rest of the evening, the hen party performed to their newfound admirers with ever more daring shenanigans, much to our delight and appreciation.

As last orders were called, it all seemed too quick, it felt like the night was still young. I said, 'I'm just beginning to feel in a party mood.'

'Shall I try for another round?' asked Ron.

'I think you're too late,' said Dennis.

'I'll give it a try anyway,' and Ron started to make his way to the bar.

'Don't get me one,' called Dutch. That was a call I didn't expect, I was even more surprised when Vic followed up with, 'Nor me.'

'You pair giving up on us?' I asked.

Vic said, 'I'm ready to return to Tolly's, if you want any more to drink, we can get it there.'

'Yeah, I suppose,' I replied.

Amazingly Ron returned with three pints, saying. 'I've had to promise the barmaid my body to get these.'

'What a let down for her that's going to be,' was the comment from Dennis. It was just one comment among many that addressed Ron's proud boast.

As I finished off my penultimate drink and as I was going to start Ron's acquired final drink, Dutch announced he'd had enough and was going to make his way back. I asked, 'Are you alright?'

He said, 'Yeah, I'm a bit tired, that's all.'

'OK, we'll see you back at the digs later.'

Vic finished off his drink and said, 'Hold on, I'll come with you.' As the two left the building, Ron was up dancing with the hen party.

When they returned to their seats, the leader of the entertainment informed everyone that the show was at an end. Ron and Dennis were in the middle of the eight females who made up the hen party, asking where they were going on to, had they got a night club in mind. One of them asked where are you going. Ron immediately answered the Pear Tree Club. 'Where's that?' was the next enquiry. Ron looked round for assistance. 'Don't look at me,' I said, 'I thought we were going back to base.'

'Bollocks to that,' said Ron, 'we're only just getting started, it is after all a Saturday night, and we are in Blackpool.' Dennis was nodding in agreement.

'OK, the Pear Tree Club it is,' I conceded.

Dennis came up with the idea that we should get a taxi, stating the driver would know where the club is. One of the hen party, Helen, the sister of the bride-to-be, said, 'There's too many of us for one taxi, would it be alright for some of us to come with you?' This request was readily agreed by our two heroes, who were now conducting negotiations with the hens.

Some minutes later found us outside. After a short conflab with two taxi drivers, we all piled into the said taxis. I found myself in a taxi with four of the hens. Helen, who had been lead negotiator with the taxi drivers, handed me £6 saying, 'That's our contribution towards the fare.' I enquired as to how much they had agreed to pay and was informed it would be £8. (I think I'd been taken to the cleaners there.) As I sat back squeezed between two of the hens on the back seat, I realised, when paying the taxi driver, I would also be coughing up the tip. Game, set and match to the hens.

At the door of the club, the doorman said it was £10 each to gain entrance. I said, 'Ten quid!! It's almost closing time. Can't we do a deal?'

'I don't do deals,' was his reply.

I said, 'Well, there's no way we are paying 10 quid for the short time we're going to spend here.'

As I began to walk away, he asked, 'How many of you are there?'

I answered, 'Eleven of us altogether.'

He then said, 'Hold on, I'll see if the gaffer's gone home yet.'

Two minutes later, he returned and said, 'He's gone. If you give me 15 quid between you, you're in.' Dennis quickly stepped forward and offered the money, I didn't say anything. I was going to offer 10 pounds, which I think he would have accepted.

They all filed in, ladies first, with me bringing up the rear. From the foyer was a corridor leading to double doors that opened into the main room. It was quite large with a stage on the opposite side and a dance floor in front of it. From the dance floor were two or three steps up to the seating area. The ladies commandeered a couple of tables on the right-hand side of these steps. Ron and Dennis were sat among them. The bar was round to my left, being as it was my round, I went directly to the bar.

As I ordered our drinks, Helen, who appeared to be chief honcho for the ladies, came up beside me and said, 'We've got a money pool, so we'll carry on drinking on our own if that's all right.'

'Oh yes, you carry on and party as you wish. You don't need to concern yourselves with us.' I then added, 'Oh, by the way, we had to pay £1.50 each to get in.'

'Right,' she replied, 'I'll go and get our money, that's £12 if my maths is correct,' and off she went.

A few seconds later, there was a tap on my shoulder, on turning around, who should be there but Brian. 'What's all this then, you lot pulled or what?' he teased.

'No, no, no, don't you start putting stories around like that,' I responded. 'It's only a hen party who asked for help to get in here. Me, being a gentleman of the old school, how could I refuse a request like that! What are you doing here, and who are you with?' I asked.

'We're all over there,' he said, pointing to the far side of the room.

'Who's all?' I enquired.

'Well, PK, Bill, Markey, Kevin, Don and Jumbo.'

'Oh, fucking hell, just make sure they all understand those women are not with us.'

It was right at this point that Helen came back. Grabbing hold of my arm, she said, 'Here you are, that's our entrance fee,' and handed me the money. She then went on to ask if I would help her with ordering their drinks. Brian eyebrows raised and he said 'right' and went back to the others, who were all standing up in an attempt to get a better view. (Oh shit.)

Drinks acquired, we returned to our seats. I asked Ron for his £1.50 and passed £13.50 to Dennis, saying, 'With your £1.50, that's the £15 entrance fee.'

'Great, well done,' was his only comment. Having paid the taxi driver £10 and telling him to keep the change, I considered it fair that I should be allowed to get away without paying my entrance fee. (I didn't flag this up to the others though.)

A few minutes later, I left our gang and went over to chat with the others, only to be greeted with accusations of inappropriate behaviour with calls such as 'you dirty old man' and 'I don't fancy yours'. PK asked, 'Where did you pick that lot up?'

I replied, 'Oh, they are what's known as groupies. When you're famous and good-looking like me, it's what happens all the time.'

'Bollocks,' was the response to that little statement.

The piss-taking carried on, which I mostly ignored. Instead, I turned to Jumbo and said, 'You in a better frame of mind?'

'What has happened to the other two meatheads from your gang?' was his response.

'Right, OK, no change there then. I see you're still as belligerent as ever.'

PK said, 'Take no notice; he's the worse for drink and doesn't mean anything by all of that.'

Jumbo then started to blubber, saying, 'Everyone is always picking on me, what have I ever done to anyone, nothing.' Everyone looked on in amazement.

Kin Hell, if that's what beer does to you, I think I'll pack it in, was my immediate thought. 'I'll leave you to it then,' is what I actually said.

On returning to my seat, I had another pint in front of me. I found myself sat with the same ladies as in the taxi. Helen did the introductions, Sandra and Jane as her best friends and Jane's sister Lisa. Why they thought I needed to know this information I've no idea. Next, I was asked who those other blokes across the room were. 'I don't really know them. We only met this afternoon at the bowls match.'

It was Helen who asked, 'Where did the tall, good-looking chap go?'

'I think he had a message saying his wife had turned up at the hotel we're staying at.'

'Oh, I see,' was the only response to that bit of information.

Ron arrived with another round of drinks. As he put them on the table, he asked the girls if they were going to dance. Helen, Jane and her sister Lisa all jumped up and went with Ron to the dance floor. Sandra for some reason stayed put. Dennis by now had joined Ron and the girls, all showing a lot of enthusiasm but not much style, particularly the two characters who were supposed to be with me.

The woman Sandra who was now sat alone with me, suddenly said, 'You're married, aren't you?'

'What makes you say that?' I asked.

'I can always tell,' she replied, 'there's something about married men that shows.'

'That must be useful, to be able to spot a married man.'

'Yes,' she replied, 'I'm a widow, my husband died a couple of years ago. So, I am well versed in spotting them, particularly when they try it on with me. Which is surprisingly regular, would you believe?'

'Oh, I believe,' I responded in a smarmy sort of way.

I was sat there thinking *I wonder what he died of? I bet he wasn't shagged to death, might have been bored to death though.* I then thought, *Should I get another round in? It is my turn.* As these thoughts were going through my head, she suddenly asked, 'Will you dance with me?'

'Oh, er, yeah, but I'll need to get the round in first if that's OK.'

'Yes, that's fine.'

'Can I get you one?'

'Well, yeah, ah, but no, I'd better stop with our group, but thank you all the same.'

As I stood at the bar, a thought went through my head, *I think she thinks I propositioned her when offering to buy her a drink, the look on her face seemed to find it very acceptable. Bloody hell, I'll never get rid of her now.*

She was halfway to the dance floor by the time I had put the drinks down. She had a look that suggested she was the cat that had got the cream. At the very moment, I joined her on the floor, the music stopped. I began to retrace my steps but was pulled back as a slow waltz started up. A dance promised, so a dance will be had, seemed to be the message.

Ron was getting to grips with Helen, Dennis was grappling with Jane, along with several other couples on the dance floor.

Sandra was rabbiting on about Julie the bride-to-be, saying she was 26 years old; she was 12 or 13 years younger than her sister Helen and herself. She twittered on about it being her first marriage and such things when there was an announcement over the sound system, saying my wife and kids were outside waiting to go home. Dennis looked up towards me with a surprised look on his face. No reaction from Ron at all. No one else was remotely interested in the announcement, as no one else knew who it was about.

I casually looked round and saw Brian and PK doubled up in laughter as if nothing else had ever been as funny. Looking a bit farther along, I could see the rest of the crew waving and gesticulating in some sort of victory dance. I responded with a none-too-discreet two-finger salute, which only appeared to up their celebration.

None of the aforementioned announcement or my reaction nor the sudden increase of noise had any effect on Sandra, who was still babbling on about the wedding. As my attention returned to her, she seemed to confuse it with me moving a little closer towards her and wrapped her arms even tighter around me.

When the music finally ended, I said, 'I need a drink,' and led her from the floor. I devoured my drink like it was my first of the night. Dennis then turned up with another round. Fortunately, he had acquired large Bacardis with one small bottle of Coke between us.

The night carried on in much the same way. The pairings became sort of set and acknowledged. I was really struggling to maintain concentration. So much so that at one time, watching Sandra go to the bar for their drinks, I was thinking she ain't so bad really, clean and tidy, not all that old, decent hair. Maybe I misjudged her. The saving grace was the thought in my head of Sam and his story of what he found with him this morning, plus the words *Beer Goggles*.

The end of the session found me having the last dance, once again wrapped in the arms of Sandra, still going on, this time about us getting a taxi of our own. She was saying, 'I'm feeling really horny. I've been on my own now for over two years, I really need a bloke.'

I responded with, 'Well, I've drunk more than a camel preparing for a three-week trek in the desert, so you may have to rely on Rampant Rabbit to console your ardour.' That little statement made me laugh, and surprisingly she joined in the laughter. (I don't think she really understood what I had said.)

The last thing I remember about the night was standing by the doors of the club saying to Ron and Dennis, 'Come on, while they are in the toilets, let's make a run for it.'

Sunday 26th Sept.

I was roused by the voice of Vic saying, 'I'm not going to call you again, it's almost 9 o'clock, if you don't get up now, you'll miss breakfast.'

I couldn't work out where I was or even who I was. I sat up on the side of my bed and thought my head was going to fall off. My trousers were on the floor, all crumpled by my feet. I still had my shirt from last night on. It was Dutch who said, 'What's all over your shirt? Is it blood?'

I looked down but couldn't quite see, so taking off my shirt and having a closer look, I cried out, 'Kin hell!! It's lipstick, the fucking bitch, what am I going to do now?' My two so-called friends were doubled up with laughing at my predicament. They then left the room to go for breakfast.

I couldn't remember much of what happened last night. On racking my brain, I could recall the woman Sandra dancing with me and the fact she was getting a little bit passionate about it.

I couldn't recall leaving the club or travelling back, and certainly no recollection of arriving back at the room. As I sat there wondering what to do with the shirt, I became aware of PK still on his top bunk snoring away and sleeping the sleep of the profoundly innocent.

The concern about my shirt had helped me regain a semblance of order in my mind. I splashed my face with water, cleaned my teeth, put a comb through my hair, put on a polo shirt and pulled on a pair of jeans. Decided to leave PK where he was in the land of nod, and went down for breakfast.

On entering the dining room, I was met with a cynical cheer from some of the guys who were at the Pear Tree last night. Choosing to ignore the cynicism, I took my seat at our table. A pot of tea was already there. 'OK if I have some of that tea?' I asked. Someone told me to help myself. As I poured the tea, I realised my hand had a slight tremor and thought, *Kin hell, what was I on last night?*

Wally came over and asked, 'Are you having cereal or are you ready for a full English?'

'I've no idea what I'm doing here at all,' I replied, then added, 'Yeah, OK, bring me a breakfast, I'll see what I can do with it.'

I sat there staring into my cup of tea. When I looked up, they were all looking at me. 'What?' I said.

'Come on, out with it, what happened then?' asked Vic.

'How the fuck should I know, I can't remember anything of last night.'

'That's a load of bollocks; you just don't want to let on, do you?' again from Vic.

Wally arrived with my breakfast. It had given me a moment before responding with, 'Think what you like but that's how it is.'

Right at that moment in walked Dennis closely followed by Ron. If I felt rough, they looked like they must feel as bad if not worse, especially Ron, who was squinting as if the light was giving him some problems.

'Ask these what happened,' I said, 'maybe they'll know the story of last night's events.' A new pot of tea had been acquired, Dennis was pouring it for Ron and himself, I requested he should do the same for me, I noticed his hands were shaking somewhat more than mine had.

When he put the pot down, he said, 'Don't ask me, I don't think I was there.'

How did he'—referring to me—'get lipstick all over his shirt?' asked Dutch.

Blank looks all round. 'Lipstick,' said Dennis. 'I don't know about lipstick; all I can remember is standing at that fish and chip van.' That caused me to show a surprised look, I couldn't remember any chip van. It all went quiet for a few moments, then Ron asked why we were running down that road.

'What road?' I asked. 'I don't know, I can recall running along a road. Whatever we were running from it couldn't have been very serious because we were all laughing.'

It all went quiet again, then Dutch said, 'Is that it then, nothing?'

'I believe it is,' I replied.

'So, when PK returned a long time before you, saying you had picked up some nurses and looked likely to be out for the night, he was a long way from the truth, was he?'

'I don't know what PK said or what he thought he saw, I don't remember anything like that happening. Ron said I was with a nurse; I wonder what happened to her? Maybe her husband turned up, perhaps that's why we were running,' I offered as an answer to both his questions.

PK entered the room; his arrival and his general demeanour immediately removed the attention away from our night of folly.

During this respite, I returned my attention to my breakfast but could not do justice to the effort to produce it. Ron and Dennis had both settled for buttered toast. On noticing this, I realised that was exactly what I should have done.

The end of breakfast signalled a debate on what the day's activity should be. I for my part would be happy to just find a bench along the front and sit there for at least four hours. Feeling this way, I took little or no part in the discussion that took place.

It was Markey's suggestion of a sand bowls competition, using sets of sand bowls owned by Wally. I say 'sets' as he had several, and the idea was to run two games simultaneously, this proposal gained widespread support. It was agreed Kevin and Markey would be organisers, 10.55 scratch out, 11.00 start was stipulated.

By the time we had sorted ourselves out and strolled to the by then marked-out playing area, we were only just in time to sign up for the game. Dutch declined the invitation to play, claiming his shoulder was not up to it and he didn't want to handicap his partner, whoever he was drawn to play with. A total of 24 had signed up, game on.

Twelve pairs were drawn, I was drawn with Bill Anderson. The first round consisted of four games between eight of the teams, with the four other teams being awarded a bye into the second round. Bill and I were fortunate in being one of the four gaining automatic promotion to the second round.

While the eight teams were being whittled down to four, I went and sat with Dutch, who had positioned himself on the parapet wall looking down on the playing area. Both Ron, who was paired with Don, and Vic, who was paired with Harry, were among the teams battling for a place in the second round. Dennis, coupled with young Liam, like me had secured a bye.

'Your shoulder giving you that much trouble?' I asked.

'No, not really, well yes, it's aching all the time now,' was his contradictory reply.

'That why you had an early night?'

'Partly, but with the constant ache it's wearing me down, I can't seem to get any respite from it. If that bloke was here now, I'd kick him in the bollocks instead of punching him.' This statement made us both laugh, and I thought, *Yeah, he'll be OK.*

He then asked, 'Right, what went on last night, and what were you running from?'

Having heard numerous thoughts and statements from Dennis and Ron, my memory of the evening had improved considerably. I replied, 'We, that is Ron, Dennis and me got pissed. Those females who were in that pub accompanied us to the Pear Tree Club where we got even more pissed. Those females also got pissed. They then attempted to take advantage of us, insisting we took them back to their digs, with the intention of having their wicked way with us. When they went to the toilet on the way out of the club, we ran off.'

He nearly fell off the wall laughing. 'Fucking hell, you ran off from a gang of women who were wanting an orgy with you,' he said, gasping for breath. 'Oh, dear me, that's the funniest story you've ever told me.'

I said, 'Maybe, but it's true.'

'You know, when you said my adventures were the only excitement in your life, that's the reason, you run off.' He once again started to laugh.

'Yeah, and when you said you envied my controlled life with nice wife and kids, I've probably got that because I do run off,' I replied. I then added, 'I've no idea why the other two ran, apart from me saying, quick while they are in there, let's run for it.' This time we both nearly fell because of uncontrolled laughter.

The games took somewhere around 15 to 20 minutes each. Ron was out in the first round. Vic went through to the second round. In the second round, both me and Dennis were defeated, Vic got through but lost in the semi-final. By the time the winners were declared (Paul and Brian) it was well after 1 o'clock.

Feeling slightly refreshed by the morning's activity, we retired to the same pub we had started in last night.

Still feeling a bit apprehensive of having a drink, I challenged myself with a remembered thought, *Stickability*, possibly the word of the weekend. I agreed to get the first drinks, pints all round. When I returned to the table with the drinks, Dutch was in the middle of telling the story of our last night's encounter with the nurses.

Vic found this very amusing. Ron, on the other hand, was well pissed off on hearing it was me who had instigated the flight from his nurse. 'I was well in there,' he complained, 'what did you do that for? Bloody hell, I'll never live this down, running off from a dead cert.'

'Listen,' I said, 'I think you're going to be in enough trouble during the next week or so, without any of last night's club activities getting back into the domain of Eileen.'

'What you mean by that, who's going to tell?' he asked.

'Well, think back to last night, just over there, you in the middle of all that female flesh having your photo taken.' His little face lit up at the memory of the occasion. 'In not so many days from now, those photos will be posted on Facebook for the world to see.'

'Facebook, what's that?' he asked.

'It's a site on the internet where people share with the world their lives. Plus, photos of holidays, parties, engagements, weddings or any little bit of excitement in their otherwise dull lives.'

Ron's response to this information was, 'No problem there, my missus doesn't use a computer and certainly doesn't know what Facebook is.'

'Maybe not but your niece Cheryl is a very frequent user. If she comes across photos of you in the midst of a bevy of female flesh, I'm quite sure Eileen will get to know of it.'

'Oh, shit, what do I do about it then?' he cried.

'Not a lot,' said Dennis. 'Just be thankful there won't be any real revelations to be spoken about at the club next week. Better to be laughed at for running away than have Eileen packing your bags for not.'

'My missus will pack my bags just for seeing those photos.'

'No, she won't, that's just a bit of fun in the middle of a pub, she won't pack your bags for what was only a bit of fun. She will give you a right bollocking and a very hard time for several days though.'

The next two hours were spent in a much more relaxed mode than yesterday afternoon's boisterous shenanigans. The drink still flowed but at a very leisurely rate. So much so that by the middle of the afternoon, I felt ready to take on the world again. We spent a lot of that time trying to convince Ron and probably ourselves, that things would be OK when we returned home. I'm not sure we were very successful. The only one who didn't seem concerned was Dutch, who to my mind and my knowledge had the most to be concerned about.

It was Vic who bought the afternoon to an abrupt end by stating he wished to go shopping, as he was going to take a little something back for his wife.

At first, his suggestion was ridiculed. But after a bit of consideration and a thought from Dennis that Ron would benefit from applying the same strategy, shopping was our next task. I was thinking, buying a little something for Doreen would be counterproductive. She would immediately assume me guilty of some misdemeanour if I started being so thoughtful. (Way out of character.)

So, I declined the invitation to go shopping and went for a walk along the prom. The weather was holding up well, it was a very pleasant afternoon. I strolled up just past the Tower. I actually sat on the same bench Ron and Taffy had sat on Friday evening. As I sat there reminiscing in my mind events of the weekend. Who should turn up but Blodwyn and Taffy.

It was Blodwyn who spoke first saying, 'Oh, hello, what are you doing up here on your own?'

'Ah, hello,' I responded, 'I'm just taking in the last of the summer sun, we're all off in an hour or so. Are you keeping alright?' I inquired. Taffy looked like he had no idea what was going on and seemed like he had never seen me before.

Blodwyn realising this said, 'This is one of the blokes who helped us get back to the hotel on Friday night. You remember, I told you about it.'

'Oh yes,' he said, making out he remembered, but it was quite obvious he had no recollection of Friday night at all.

Blodwyn sat on the bench and said to Taffy, 'Go and get some ice cream.' She then asked, 'Would you like an ice cream?'

'No, thank you, I've been drinking beer for the last couple of hours.' Taffy took off in search of ice-creams.

As soon as he was out of hearing distance, she asked, 'Is Dutch alright? I don't know if you are aware of him meeting me yesterday afternoon.'

'No,' I lied, 'I wasn't, he didn't say he'd run into you.'

'Well, yes, he did, but while we were talking, he had a very peculiar turn and almost passed out.'

'Whereabouts was this?' I asked.

'In my, er by er near our hotel,' she stammered her reply.

'I wonder what he was doing up there?' I asked, just to make her embarrassment a little more felt.

'I think he was taking in the afternoon sun, same as you are,' she replied with what might be termed as a slightly smug look at giving such a smart answer.

Touché, I thought, but said, 'Ah yeah, he probably was.'

Taffy returned with the ice-creams. As he sat there, he said, 'Actually, I can't remember much regarding Friday night.' While he was talking, a small amount of melting ice cream dripped onto his shirt. Blodwyn made a fuss over wiping it off. This action suddenly reminded me of the lipstick still on my shirt. So, I said my goodbyes and left.

Back at Tolly's place, I went to pick up our keys. There were around half of the guys already in the bar. Tolly had agreed to put on a light snack, a few sandwiches and such for everyone before we left. I was greeted with a chorus of 'Run Rabbit, Run Rabbit, Run, Run, Run'. It appeared the word had spread all round. Great!!! While at the bar I asked Molly if she had a hair dryer I could borrow. (Another mistake.) I left the bar to a barrage of abuse, mostly questioning my sexuality. My response was a raised middle finger accompanied with a line that went something like 'Well, your wives didn't seem to have any doubts.'

In the room, I rinsed the shirt with soap and water best I could. I then tried to dry it with the hair dryer. Not a successful task, I now had a wet, pink-stained shirt. Oh fuck it, I'll tell Doreen someone spilt some red wine on me, and then tried to clean it by tipping white wine over it and adding we were all very drunk. I bungled everything into my holdall, ready to leave for home.

As I was leaving the room, Vic and Dutch arrived. 'Good afternoon's shopping?' I asked. Their answer was just a load of grumbles. I thought, *Hmm, perhaps not.* 'I'll see you downstairs, I'm starving,' and off I went.

In the bar it was a bit more relaxed, or at least the goading of me had subsided. I acquired a plate with sandwiches, a couple sausage rolls with a cup of tea. I then sat at our usual table.

Harry and Fred were sat in their regular seats. Fred said, 'Look at them still drinking, I would have thought they might have had enough by now.'

189

'I don't think this lot will ever have had enough,' I replied. A simple 'no' was his reply as he sat there looking at them all with what can only be described as a sneering look of utter contempt.

Dennis came into the room, Ron followed him a few seconds later. Dennis got the sandwiches, Ron the teas, it was like they had worked out this routine before entering the room.

I enquired as to what they had bought from the shopping trip. Dennis said, 'Nothing much, they only seem to sell rubbish here. In the end I got a mug bearing the legend My Wife Rules OK.'

I said, 'Wow, classy or what.'

Ron said, 'She'll probably hit him over the head with it,' we all tittered about his wonderful gift.

'What did you get then, Ron?' was my next question.

'Well, I had second thoughts about buying anything. If I did buy her a present, she would be very suspicious of my motive.'

'My thoughts exactly,' I said.

When Vic and Dutch arrived, it was accompanied with statements such as, 'Have I really got to sit with blokes who run off from sexy women?' That one from Vic.

Ron hit back with, 'No, you don't have to, you could go and sit with Jumbo. Anyway, why have I got to sit with a bloke so frightened of his wife he has to buy her little presents whenever he's away for half an hour.'

'Now, ladies, let's not fall out over things that don't really matter,' said Dutch.

PK called for order and announced departure would be at 6.15, and no waiting for anyone so make sure you're not late. He went on to say it was intended to stop at a club South of Stoke, just off the M6. Adding, 'We've all had a good weekend, so please treat the club with some respect, they have always made us very welcome in the past, so don't spoil it.'

He then called for a round of applause and three cheers for Molly and Wally to show our appreciation for their unstinting effort in ensuring we had a good time. The drink-fuelled mob went ballistic with cheering and clapping like this pair had won a gold medal at the Olympics. It never got round to three cheers. Instead, they started singing.

Fare thee well, fare thee well, fare thee well, my delightful friends,
For we're off to Stoke-on-Trent, for that is our intent,
Singing Wally Tolly doodle all the way.

It was magic. They sang several verses, finishing off with Wally and Molly Tolly doodle all the way. Just brilliant.

The coach pulled up outside. A couple of the guys raced out to claim their preferred seats, the vast majority waited in line to shake hands and hug Molly and Wally. They all made a great show of it, most a little OTT.

I collected my bag, gave a wave to Molly and took my leave, I was closely followed by the other four. We sat in the same seats that we arrived in. The coach slowly filled. The time was now 6.22 and PK was doing a head count.

A disturbance started at the back of the coach and was spreading towards the front. Catcalls and whistles were being blasted out. By standing up and straining my neck to look through the window, I could see a group of women dressed as Hawaiian hula girls, with grass skirts, bright coloured bra tops, all topped off with garlands of flowers round their necks, and very little else.

The girls were giving as good as they got. Playing up to the audience on the coach, gesticulating and flashing, and the boys loved it.

Oh shit, I suddenly realised it was the hens. Looking round, Dennis was looking at me with his mouth wide open and eyes bulging out of his face. '*RON! Shut up*,' I bellowed. Too late, Ron was saying, 'That's my nurse.' As the realisation of what Ron had said slowly dawned on the coach, the noise level rose tenfold.

Blokes pulling at windows, desperately trying to make contact with the hens, just to inform them we were on board. I was, for my part, sitting very low in my seat, cringing with embarrassment.

Ron, not at all perturbed by the fact that the whole coachload was hellbent on causing as much embarrassment as possible, managed to open his window and called to them. I, having raised my head, saw the look of recognition suddenly appear on the one called Helen. As she grabbed the arm of the closest hen to her and pointed in Ron's direction, Lord be praised, the coach started to pull away.

Cries of 'stop' by several fellow passengers, Vic being loudest and most vocal of them all, plus Ron somehow seeming to think this was a good idea, added his voice to the protest against moving on, all to no avail. Barry, thank goodness, carried on. 'For fuck's sake, Ron, let it go.' He sat down, looking very dejected.

As we rolled on out of Blackpool, I sat quietly thinking, *Ah well, that's it now, my last chance of a shot at the old La Dolce Vita gone. I ran off.*

Ron must have been thinking along the same lines, said, 'That's it then, probably my last shot at a walk on the wild side. We ran off.'

For the next while, I sat there quietly thinking about all the tales Dutch had spouted and how I'd listened with an amount of envy, and thought, *I ran off.*

Maybe that was what this weekend had been about, me chasing my lost youth, and I ran off.

Well back to work tomorrow, knuckle down, get on with it and slowly drift on into old age. From that, I can't run off.

Let's get pissed.

We didn't get pissed; in fact, it was a very staid journey from Blackpool to the club in Stoke. I sat with a drink, quietly evaluating my life. Wondering if I was happy with my lot in life, could I have improved my role, my position, my station, or even just improved me. Looking around, Ron had nodded off. I removed his drink from his hand to prevent it spilling over him. Dutch was sitting with his eyes closed, occasionally sipping from his drink. Dennis and Mick were quietly chatting to each other. *Yes, our youth is well past.* As for the rest of the coach party, they were as noisy and boisterous as ever.

At the club we were made most welcome by a number of their committee. An area of seating had been reserved for our party. Entertainment was to be provided, and they hoped we would enjoy our evening.

Dutch got the round; he also acquired five cheese and onion baps, packets of crisps and various assorted nuts.

It was a very pleasant evening; the entertainment was a very good Matt Monro look-a-like tribute type guy. He did two spots; in between his performances, a game of bingo was called, which we joined in. (Didn't get a sniff at any of the winnings.)

The break from activities during the coach ride from Blackpool paid dividends; we were on good form drink wise. So much so come the end of the night, I, and I think the others were a little bit disappointed at having to call a halt to our weekend.

The run back down the M6 was as rowdy as at any time in the whole weekend, with singing, shouting and just pratting about by all on board. A great end to a superb weekend. All thoughts of lost youth back where they belong, out of mind.

Elizabeth was waiting when we arrived back at the club. She was not best pleased. 'When I agreed to ferry you and my mother about this weekend, I didn't expect to be acting as nursemaid to a load of drunken old biddies for 48 hours and then have to wait here till this time in the morning.'

'Yes, I'm sorry about being this late, I expected to be much earlier than this,' I offered as an apology.

'I've got to be at work in less than seven hours,' she berated.

'Yes, I am really sorry,' I once again apologised.

'It's about time you pair started to act your age and take some responsibility for yourselves.'

I did not add any comment, If I was supposed to feel guilty about not acting my age, I didn't. In fact, after my thoughts earlier in the day, I felt rather proud. Thinking, *Perhaps I have had a walk on the wild side.*

Doreen was asleep in bed when I arrived home, which was perhaps a good thing. From Elizabeth's comments, she had had more to drink than was necessary. Which would have meant she would have gone on and on about nothing till the early hours of the morning. This being the case, I retired to bed.

Monday 27th Sept.

At work that morning I was met by young Mickey, looking very pleased with himself. He informed me everything that could go wrong did go wrong. He had managed to fix every problem; he had received a phone call from old Billy thanking him and congratulating him on a valiant and effective performance over the last couple of days. He went on to say Billy had asked him to stay in post to update Dutch and me of the weekend's problems.

'Hasn't Dutch arrived yet?' I asked.

'No, I was expecting him to arrive before you, but no, not yet.' He had made the tea and poured one for me. While we sat with our tea, I asked if he had picked up the report sheets.

He had. 'Anything urgent?' I enquired.

'Only the auxiliary compressor in the paint shop panel spraying area. Shall I go and have a look at it?' he suggested.

'Don't you think you should go back to your own job?'

'No, it's OK. I've told our charge hand old Billy wants me to stop here and bring you pair up to date with things. Anyway, suppose Dutch doesn't report in.'

'Yeah OK, before you go charging off, what other problems are on the report sheets?'

'Only a bank of lights in Four Bay and some cladding lose in the wash bay.'

'Right, off you go, but don't get over involved with that compressor. If it needs more than just resetting come back and let me know.'

As he was leaving, Dutch arrived. 'Why is he still here?' was his first comment.

'He's only here to hand back the reins.' I then added, 'Go on then, fuck off and get that compressor sorted out.'

After Mick had left, I asked, 'What's all this then? You turning up late, that's got to be a first.'

'Yeah. Well, when I first woke up, I felt absolutely knackered, I ached all over, couldn't believe how much the weekend had taken out of me. It's made me realise I ain't as young as I was.'

'You sure you're OK for work today?' I asked.

194

'Yes, it was only 10 minutes or so, I had a shower and a bite to eat and now I'm fine.'

The day went well, young Mick sorted the compressor and returned to his own place of work. I fixed the lighting in Four Bay, Dutch set about re-fixing the cladding, which required some assistance from me to complete. By the middle of the afternoon, Blackpool and all that had happened during the weekend was well and truly behind us.

On arriving home, Doreen was fixing our evening meal. 'Hello, how's things gone with you today?' (I immediately thought, *Oh dear, something's amiss.*)

'Oh yes, everything was good,' I answered.

'And how was your weekend?' she added.

'OK, well, quite boring actually.'

'Oh, why was that?'

'Well, Friday night we had a couple of drinks at a pub just down the road from our digs. Saturday, we attended the Waterloo, then in the evening had a couple of drinks in a pub along the front. Sunday, we played sand bowls on the beach, on the way back home we stopped at a club up by Stafford. That's it really.'

'So, what's this then?' She threw my shirt, the one with the lipstick stains, to the floor right in front of me.

'Oh that, it's some spilt wine, I think.'

'Well, think again,' she said, 'it's lipstick.'

'Oh yeah, I remember, it was some of the guys buggering about, they borrowed the lipstick off Molly the hotel owner's wife and went into our room, found my shirt and did that.'

'So why say it was a wine stain?'

'I just forgot,' I stammered.

'Well, who tried to clean it?' she next asked.

'Well, I told them that if they didn't clean it off, I would tell you who had done it and they would have to explain it to you.'

'You expect me to believe that story?' she asked.

'Well yes, it's the truth. What are you accusing me of? Do you think if I had anything to hide, I would have brought it home in that state for you to find?'

She stared at me for several seconds waiting for me to crack. 'I shall ask about this at the club on Friday, and if I find you've lied to me, your life won't be worth living.'

While eating our meal, I casually asked, 'How did you get on at Silverdale Hall?'

'Great,' she replied, 'it's really nice there. I went in the sauna, had a facial scrub and a facial makeover. Can't you tell?'

'Oh yes, it's done wonders for you,' I said without betraying any of the intended sarcasm. 'Did you have a drink while you were there?'

'Yes, we had a glass of wine and a light snack as we rested in the quiet room.'

'What else happened over the weekend?'

'Not much, we went out for lunch on Sunday. I enjoyed that, it was all very pleasant.' Mmm, a slightly different story than Elizabeth had led me to believe, but I left it at that.

It was Wednesday lunchtime when Dutch suddenly asked, 'What happened about that lipstick-stained shirt?'

'Oh, bloody hell, she had a right go at me about it. First, I tried to say it was a wine stain but she knew it was lipstick. When I agreed it was lipstick and said someone from our party had smeared it on my shirt as a joke, she didn't believe me and asked why someone tried to clean it. I finished my side of the debate by saying if I had anything to hide, would I have left it for her to find. She finished all of the debate by saying she would ask questions at the club on Friday.'

He said, 'For a bloke who's been married as long as you have, you ain't very good at telling a lie, are you? The bit about the wine was rubbish, you shouldn't have gone there.'

'I know, but guilt got the better of me, I think.' Then I said, 'While we're on about confessions, you never elaborated on your Saturday afternoon escapade.'

'Well, surprisingly little to tell, actually. On my way to the hotel, I started to have second thoughts about the whole set-up. I think it's to do with what she (Karen) had done across me. When I arrived at the hotel, I went into the bar. She was standing at the far side, she raised her hand as if to say 'stop', she then put her finger to her lips. I stood quite still just looking around, I was wondering if Taffy was there. She slowly worked her way across the room and when close to me, said very quietly, "A lot of people in here know me. Don't speak, just go to the bar and get a drink, I'm in room 309," she then moved away.

'Having got a drink, I sat at a table, I was still having negative thoughts on this little dalliance. Eventually I went to room 309, knocked and went in. She was reclining on the bed in a flimsy, almost transparent negligee.'

I said, 'Wow, this is more like the stories of old.'

'Whoa,' he said, 'hold on, we haven't got anywhere yet.'

I said, 'So what happened?'

'Well, first, all thoughts of cancelling this little fuckfest were totally dismissed from my mind.'

'I should think so too,' I interjected.

He went on, 'I sat on the side of the bed and started to take off my shoes. Suddenly, a very peculiar feeling came over me. I felt I was floating away, everything seemed to be moving away from me. I became lightheaded and dizzy. In truth, I thought I was going to collapse.'

'Why didn't you say you had a problem when you came back in the club?'

'Wait a bit, I'll tell you what happened. Blodwyn started to panic, thinking I was going to be stuck there. She helped put my shoes back on and, still wearing next to nothing, ushered me out of her room. I didn't even cop a feel.'

'You were still up for it when you were at death's door, that's my boy,' I said, very nearly cheering.

He went on to say, he walked back along the front and sat on a bench for 10 minutes or so. Realising he was OK, he contemplated going back and giving her another go but thought that would be pushing the situation a little bit.

'Have you had any problems since?'

'No, only on Monday morning when I first woke, as I told you, I can't imagine what could have been the reason I had that turn.'

'You think it could have been anything to do with your shoulder problem?'

'No, no, no, it wasn't anything to do with that, my shoulder has been fine.'

I then told him of my meeting with Blodwyn and Taffy. Plus, the fact that Blodwyn got rid of Taffy to ask of his health and informed me of his problem. 'Why have you pretended to be interested, with all your, 'that's my boy' crap if you knew all about my afternoon?' he asked in a none too pleasant manner.

'I only knew you had a funny turn; I didn't know if it was "before", "during", or "after" the proposed event. My interest was very real. I hadn't said anything before for fear of embarrassing you.'

'Yeah, OK, I'm sorry. I shouldn't sound off like that. I should, and do, know you better than that,' he replied.

This conversation prompted me to ask, 'When do you get the results of your scan?'

'My scan, I've had the results from my scan. I'm now waiting for the results from the biopsy.'

'Oh yes, there's been that many tests, I can't keep up. When do you get the results?'

'They (the hospital) suggested I see my doctor in a week to 10 days. I've got an appointment sometime next week. I'm not quite sure exactly when but next week.'

'Well, it's quite obvious you have got some sort of problem, so make sure you do keep the appointment.'

'Yes, I think you are right,' was all he said.

Friday evening, Doreen and I were about 15 minutes later than usual. As we entered the club lounge, we were greeted with a chorus of Run Rabbit Run. Doreen did not react in the slightest, owing to the fact she did not realise the chant was aimed at me.

I ignored it completely, apart from a swift two-fingered salute from the back of Doreen, much to the satisfaction of the perpetrators, who greeted my salute with a rousing cheer. The thoughts in my head were, *What happened to the old comrades' binding commitment of what happens in Blackpool stays in Blackpool.*

We took our usual seats, drinks were obtained, no one made any comment on the welcoming chorus. Vic opened the conversation with, 'You recovered from the weekend?'

'Yes,' I replied, 'this is the first drink I've had since Sunday.'

'Doreen have anything to say about the weekend? Ours or theirs?' was his next comment.

'No, not really, we hardly mentioned it at all. Why, what were you expecting?' I realised all eyes were on me. 'What!!' I exclaimed. 'What am I supposed to say?'

'You do know about Saturday night, don't you?' put in Dennis.

'I remember most of that night, thank you very much,' I replied.

'Not ours, theirs. They all stopped at your house, drinking and partying till they all collapsed into your bedrooms.' The look on my face must have told them the answer to that question.

At that very moment, Doreen called across, 'Vic! What's the story behind the lipstick on his shirt?' A group of startled faces stared back at her. Not only from us guys but from the ladies as well. None of the ladies, it would appear, had heard anything about lipstick. Ron had visibly paled, Dennis seemed to have stopped breathing.

'Not now, Doreen,' I said, trying to defuse the situation.

'Shut up, you,' was her response to my request. 'Well, Vic?' she challenged.

Vic stammered, 'I don't know much about the er, erm.'

Dutch jumped in here and said, 'Vic was not involved with it. It was that lot over there. They borrowed lipstick off the missus of the hotel, thinking it was funny.' As he was saying this, he had stood up and had pointed straight at the gang over the other side of the room, the same gang who had sung the greeting chorus. Brian, Don, Kevin, PK, you know the usual suspects. The actions of Dutch made them realise they were being spoken of. The result of this encouraged them to all rise, cheering and gesticulating. Their actions, although not intending to, seemed to confirm their role in the plot Dutch had described.

A collective sigh of relief was practically audible from our side of the gathering as each side sat staring at the other. I broke the stare off by asking, 'Anyway, what's all this about you lot abusing my absence to drink all my alcohol, to use my house as a place to doss, and to fill your boots with my food?' Smiles all round from our side.

Doreen's reply was,' Oh shut up, you, you old tight arse.'

A roar of laughter from both sides of our divide seemed to end hostilities for the evening. Sometime later, we blokes transferred or perhaps I should say retreated, to the games room. In there, I was given a full run-down of the ladies' weekend.

Friday evening, after we had departed, they all gathered at the club as normal, and a fair amount of alcohol was consumed.

Saturday morning, all off to Silverdale, while there, several glasses of wine were consumed.

From the health spa, they went to a restaurant, where a lot of alcohol was consumed.

Doreen then invited them all to our house, where a huge amount of alcohol was consumed.

Sunday morning, had breakfast and tarted themselves up and went for lunch, followed by more alcohol.

To this information, I replied, 'Fuck me, it makes you proud to be married to women who can drink like that, don't it?'

On our journey home, Doreen suddenly asked, 'What was all that singing and shouting about when we first went in the club?'

'I've no idea,' I replied, 'you know that lot. They're all a bit doolally at the best of times.'

She then said, 'I think everyone enjoyed last weekend, don't you?'

'Well, from what I've heard, you lot certainly did. How come you didn't say anything?'

'I didn't think anything happened that warranted a mention.'

'That's my girl, play it really cool,' was all I could think of saying.

As we arrived home, she said, 'Barbara is very worried about Dutch.'

'Oh, why's that then?'

'Apparently, every evening when he's returned home from work, he's just more or less collapsed onto the settee and sleeps for a couple of hours, or sometimes even longer.'

'He seemed to be OK tonight,' I said.

'I know, but she said he'd had a couple of hours before they came out.'

'Yeah, but I've been known to have a kip after work, it's not that unusual.'

'Yes, but not every night, and certainly not before having a shower and eating your dinner.'

'He's got an appointment next week to get the results of his biopsy. Oh, and there was a blood test as well,' I informed her.

'I hope everything is alright,' she said with a look of anguish that said she didn't believe her hopes were going to be realised.

Dutch turned up really late on Saturday morning. It was very nearly half past eight when he arrived. 'What's all this then?' I asked.

'Don't know, I just felt well fucked, I nearly didn't come at all. But for the fact that we have to do a shakedown of the extractor filters in the brake-shoe shop, I don't think I would have bothered.'

'I could have managed if you've got that much of a problem.'

'Yeah, you probably could have, but it is difficult, heavy and very awkward to deal with on your own. So here I am, let's do it.'

The work was completed without any incidents. Dutch had coped well and had not shown any signs of fatigue or distress.

It was almost 1 o'clock by the time we returned to our workshop. I said, 'OK, that will do for today. You go and get washed up. I'll make the tea.'

Dutch asked, 'Are you finishing now or what?'

'No, I've got a bank of sockets out in the machine shop. I'll have a cuppa then take a look at them before I leave.'

'I'll sort them, make up for being late this morning,' was the response from Dutch.

'No, no, you have a cup of tea then fuck off and I'll see you Monday morning, OK?'

'You sure?'

'Yes, I'm sure.'

'OK then, I'll go, see yah.'

I arrived at work to find Dutch already there, with tea made, report sheets collected and him looking all bright and breezy. 'Blimey, you look your bouncing best,' I said with genuine pleasure.

'Yes, I feel a thousand per cent better, I think it must have been a chill or one of them virus things doctors say you've got when they don't know what else to say.'

Work went well throughout the morning and at our lunch break he told me of his weekend. He said while at work Saturday morning he'd realised he was feeling more himself, stronger, more alert, felt ready to take the world on. 'That's why I was prepared to sort out the problem with those sockets in the machine shop.'

After work he went to his own house, did some cleaning and tidying, spent a couple of hours in the garden preparing it ready for the oncoming winter. On Sunday he and Barbara had gone over to Bridgnorth. They had walked along the river, had a pub lunch; all in all, a very pleasant time.

'Great.' I said, 'I'm glad you're back to your old self, I was beginning to be a bit concerned about your general health.'

Quite late in the afternoon, I heard a call over the tannoy, requesting Dutch to the garage office to answer a telephone call. Nothing unusual in that apart from the fact there was only about 20 minutes left of the working day.

Back at our base, I had almost completed the clearing away of tools and equipment when Dutch returned. Anything interesting?' I enquired.

'What?' he responded in an all too nonchalant manner.

'The telephone call.'

'No, not really. Well, I'm not sure. It was Barbara calling to let me know my doctor has been in touch to say he wants to see me tonight. I had an appointment with him on the 6th Oct, which is Wednesday, but he has bought it forward to tonight for reasons only he understands.'

'OK, go and get yourself off, I'll finish everything around here,' I said. Three minutes later, he was gone.

Next morning, Dutch was already there as usual, tea made and he was going through the report sheets. 'Any major problems in that lot?' I asked as I took off my coat and climbed into my overalls.

'No, just the usual array of minor items requiring some attention.'

While drinking my tea, I suddenly remembered his appointment. 'How's it go then, last night at the doctors?'

'A right load of bollocks, that's what it was. I told him as soon as I entered his room. I told him, whatever my problem was, it's all gone now. I told him I didn't need any treatments as everything was alright now. Do you know what? Him and the fucking hospital between them have only gone and booked me in, they've booked a fucking bed for me and expect me to be in for a few fucking days. And Barbara is insisting I go along with this plan of theirs.'

'On what grounds do they think you need to be in hospital?' I asked.

'Well, he said the biopsy seemed to show no problem in my lungs, the blood test, on the other hand, was showing an abnormality in the platelet count, whatever that's supposed to mean.'

'I haven't a clue what it means,' I replied. 'The only way to find out is to go along with this little plan, and I'm sure all will be revealed.'

'Yes, I suppose I don't have much choice really,' he said. 'Let's get on with our work, then after lunch I'll go and tell the manager I shall be out for a couple of days.'

'Why don't you leave all this to me? We haven't got that much on. Go and see the manager, he'll be in his office by now. Give him all the details, and go prepare for your incarceration.'

'It ain't prison, you know.'

'You wait till you're in there before you come to that conclusion.' We both had a laugh at that remark.

He went on to say, 'No, I'm not having time off for no reason. I feel well enough to work so work I will. I'll see Billy this afternoon, like I said.'

It was the middle of the afternoon when Dutch went to see the manager. Well over an hour later, he returned to our workshop

I was just beginning to finish for the day, 'Good grief, that was longer than I expected,' I said.

'Yeah, me and you both,' he replied.

'Billy OK with your news?' I asked.

'Well, he gave me a lecture on blood in general and platelets in particular. He reckons low readings of platelets could indicate a serious problem. He was also of the opinion I should have had the day off sick. I told him that when the blood was taken for the test, I was a little bit under par, but since then I feel everything has righted itself. He had said he didn't think it worked like that and I should be very careful of what I do.'

'And that took an hour and half, did it?' I asked.

'No, he rambled on about his life, work, how much he relied on the people who worked for him, us two in particular and a whole range of subjects. I got the distinct impression he's a bit lonely.'

'I think you're probably right, but enough of all that, off you go. Make sure Barbara keeps in touch and lets me know what is going on.'

'Yeah, she will. Oh, just one more thing before I go, don't let anyone mess with my lockers unless you've heard from me, OK?'

'Yes, off you go, no one will mess with anything belonging to you. See you next week.'

The following day, quite early, I was summoned to the manager's office. 'What are we going to do about all this?' he asked.

'I presume you mean Dutch and his problem,' I answered.

'Yes, but that problem now creates a problem for us, doesn't it?'

'Does it? I'm not sure we have a problem, not yet anyway. Dutch is quite sure he'll be back at work next week.'

'Maybe he does think that, but you do realise a low platelet count could indicate a serious illness?'

I said, 'Well, hold on, let's not write him off yet. He's only in there for tests. Shall we wait for the outcome of those before making any major changes to our procedures?'

'Of course, we wait for the outcome of his test. However, we need to understand our position in a worst-case scenario. All I'm asking is that we give some thought as to how we cover all eventualities.'

Bill then went on to say, 'I had quite a conversation with him yesterday. I now realise I didn't really know him. For all the times I've spoken with him, it always only related to work. You had suggested some weeks ago that he was a lot more than I credited as being, and yesterday I found that out.'

He said Dutch had spoken about his life, his work, and about the people who were presently employed in the company, showing a lot of understanding and even compassion of the nature of a number of characters within the company. Quite an eye-opener.

I said, 'You know I socialise quite a lot with him and his partner and can tell you he is a top bloke both at work and play. He can be relied on and trusted, he would never let you down in any circumstance. It's just the way he is.'

After saying I understood his worry but thought Dutch would be back next week, I said, 'At the moment, I can manage everything on my own as we've no big projects and are just ticking over. Only concerns, fleet on the road, heating and lighting around the garage.' I also said, 'If we do hit problems, I'm sure we will find answers.' I then left.

By the time I'd wrapped everything up on Friday, I was about half an hour later than normal finishing work. At home, Doreen greeted me with, 'I've been talking to Barbara.'

'Oh, have you? Great, what has she got to say?' I asked reluctantly, knowing I'm going to get a ten-minute ear-bashing about everything and nothing.

She started with, 'Barbara hasn't been to the hospital yet today. She said they've done loads of tests and he won't be out till they get the results from them. They may have to do more tests then, depending on the results of the first group of tests. So, it's very unlikely he will be out soon.'

'Yeah, well, that's what we expected, ain't it?' I then added, 'I'm going for a shower,' before she could start again.

As I walked upstairs, she followed me. Going at full throttle, telling me what Barbara had said about the weekend and how well Dutch had been, how he didn't think he had a problem, and what a waste of time all this fuss was.

By now, I was stripped off ready for my shower and said, 'OK, just leave it there, save it till we get to the club tonight, then you can tell everyone. Now bugger off and let me have my shower in peace, OK.'

'I was only telling you what Barbara had to say.'

'Yes, now sod off.'

'Huh, you in a bad mood again,' she said and left.

At the club everyone was shocked by the news. Doreen was in her element, relaying all the details. Some known and some assumed. Eventually, Chris was able to butt in and asked, 'Is he allowed visitors?' (*That will be the last thing he will want*, was my thought).

I put in with, 'He might be out sometime during the weekend. So, I think it's wait and see on that one.' This seemed to satisfy all parties.

I worked till about 1.30 on Saturday, then spent a couple of hours sorting out the garden, cutting back various shrubs and suchlike work that needed doing before winter really sets in.

Doreen came out to me, I suppose it was around 4 o'clock, and said Barbara had phoned to say Dutch was home. 'Great,' I said, 'I told you he'd be out this weekend. He'll be back at work on Monday, I'll bet.'

'I don't think so,' said Doreen, 'he's got to rest at home over the weekend. Then next week he's to attend the day clinic at the hospital for more tests. It's likely he will have to be there each day all the week.'

I asked, 'Are they going out for a drink tonight?'

'Don't be so silly, you come out with the most stupid statements.'

'That's because I practice a lot, I'm quite fluent in stupidity. Pray tell me why "are they going out tonight" is such a stupid statement?'

'He's been in hospital, hasn't he?'

'Yes, but now he's out, so why shouldn't they go out?'

'Why don't you ring him if you're that bothered?' she said as if to finish the debate.

I said, 'I only asked as a precursor to a suggestion that any time you are speaking with Barbara, you might ask if she and Dutch would like to go out, or indeed if Dutch can't make it for any reason at all, would she herself like to have a break and go for a drink, or just visit us here or anything to just give her a rest from the continual pressure she must be under.'

'Well, why didn't you say that instead of the stupid statements you come out with?'

'Yes, you're absolutely right as usual. Where is my dinner?' was my final statement.

Monday 11th Oct.

That Monday and most of the week for that matter, I was plagued with requests for information regarding Dutch from the vast majority of our work colleagues. They all showed genuine concern for his welfare.

Among those showing concern was the manager, though I think his concerns were as much for the wellbeing of his garage as for Dutch. (Though I might be doing him an injustice.) He made contact with me mid-morning, making the usual enquiries of Dutch, his health, and his general disposition, and being told it was probable that Dutch would be off work all this week, possibly longer.

He was of the opinion the problem could be greater than I apparently thought. 'That's a bit glass half empty thinking, ain't it, boss?' I said.

'You may think so, but I think it's being realistic. After all, he is having these tests, it would appear there is some doubt as to the exact problem, but low platelet count indicates a major illness, maybe even cancer of some sort.'

'Oh, fuck me, Bill, don't say that,' was my only response.

Bill went on to say he was going to arrange for young Mick Reynolds to work with me. I told him Mick was a good kid and an excellent worker but what was really needed was a bloke with building and construction skills.

'Long-term requirements may be just that, but let's see how this all pans out first, shall we? I've got a few ideas to put forward whatever the final outcome is.' After this statement, he left me to get on with what I was doing.

Mick's a nice lad and, as I said, a good worker but working with him wasn't the same as working with Dutch. He rattled on about his life outside working hours, his mates and the 'bits of skirt' as he referred to all the young females he always nearly pulled. To be quite honest, they were always very keen on him, but he never quite managed to land his catch. I was beginning to think he'd never actually done the most delightful of deeds. Ever.

The upshot of it all was Mick being overjoyed at once again working for our department. Me, well my thoughts were, in the past if Dutch had been on holiday or absent for any reason, I would cope on my own, and vice-versa; should I be absent for whatever reason, Dutch would cope. I couldn't make too much fuss about the arrangement; it had been my idea originally to bring in Mick as extra cover.

On Wednesday evening after dinner, I made a phone call to Dutch just to check on his wellbeing. He was his usual upbeat self, sounding confident and saying everything will be back to normal very soon. I asked if he would be going for a pint any evening this week.

His positive stance diminished somewhat as he declined the offer. Saying tomorrow at the hospital they were going to give him an intravenous, drip-fed very strong antibiotic. 'What's that for?' I enquired.

'Oh, I don't know, you know how hospitals work, if in doubt, bang in some antibodies.'

We rattled on for a while about work, family and such things, then after a while, I said, 'OK, look after yourself, do what the doctors ask of you, and I'll speak to you again soon.'

I was a little bit late getting home from work on Friday. Looking forward to going to the club, I said to Doreen, 'I'll go and have a shave and shower while you prepare my food.'

She replied, 'I've just spoke to Barbara.'

I said, 'Leave it for now, I'm in a bit of a rush,' and shot off upstairs.

On the way to the club, Doreen once again started to tell me what Barbara had spoken about on the phone this afternoon. She had said it appeared Dutch had some sort of an infection to the membrane surrounding his lungs.

In the club our usual gang had gathered, Doreen was in her element, informing everyone of the plight of Dutch. The conversation rolled on, discussing how serious his problem was, or could be, or even might be.

Eventually, Vic suggested a game of snooker, seconded by Dennis, so we four men departed to the games room. In the games room, Ron asked how serious this problem with Dutch was.

I responded with, 'Well, inflammation of the membrane is what's known as pleurisy. And owing to the fact he is already on a heavy load of penicillin, I think this time next week he'll be right here ready for a game of snooker. Come on, let's play.'

At precisely the same time we returned to the lounge, PK and Joan were patrolling the area. Joan with notepad, PK doing the spiel. 'What's all this then?' asked Vic. Joan informed our team that the sports presentation dinner would be on 19th November and they were getting an idea of numbers.

This information received all-round approval from our gang. Dennis asked how much the tickets were. PK said, 'We don't know yet, but we expect it to be about £5 depending on what support we get.'

He then asked if Dutch would be putting in an appearance. This led the ladies and Doreen, in particular, bursting forth with the full report on Dutch and his health. I just said, 'Yes, put him down as a definite two,' to Joan.

Monday 18th Oct.

The following week at work, I told the manager of the treatment Dutch was receiving and said, 'So with a bit of luck, he could be back sooner rather than later.'

'Yes, well, we'll wait and see,' was his only comment.

Work was drifting along nice and steady that week, no real emergencies, just a steady flow of the usual problems.

Early afternoon on Thursday, I was working in the main body repair shop when a call came over the tannoy system requesting me to report to the bus-wash bay. While I was still tidying up the job in hand, and not more than two minutes after the first call, a further call came from the tannoy requesting my immediate presence in the wash bay.

At that, I dropped everything and hurried over to the indicated area, realising it must be a major problem.

As I rounded the wall of the bus wash bay entrance, I heard a loud voice call, *'Whoa, don't move that, get out of there now!'* I thought, *I know that voice,* sure enough, it was Dutch. He was calling to Mick, who was in the cab of a bus that had been driven into the wall separating the fuel bay from the wash bay. Demolishing a considerable amount of said wall. The bus appeared to be jammed into the resulting gap.

'What's all this then?' I asked of Dutch. 'This is a real pleasant surprise; I really was not expecting to see you.'

'It's fortunate I turned up when I did; that fucking idiot was just trying to reverse that bus out of that hole in the wall. The whole building would have likely come down; it requires some support to the roof first.'

'Yes,' I said,' er, well done. Anyhow, how are you, are you OK?'

'Well, I was until that little incident, it seems to have set me back a bit.'

'OK, you go and sit in the shop and relax. I'll go and sort out this lot; we'll then have a cuppa and a chat.'

Mick said, 'It was a driver that did this, not me.'

'That's OK,' I said, 'no one is blaming you, are they?'

'No, but the way he went on, it seemed that he thought I'd done it.'

'No, he didn't, he was only concerned that moving the bus could result in the building coming down.'

'Really?' was Mick's surprised and embarrassed response.

'Yes, that was his only concern. Here's what I want you to do. Go to the garage office and raise an order number to the tool hire place in Bridgetown for sixteen 20-foot acrow props and 20 heavy-duty scaffold boards. Then phone the company and request immediate delivery of that equipment, and impress on them the need for some real urgency. Then come and see me in our workshop.'

Back at the workshop, Dutch was just sat there looking quite fragile. 'Not put the kettle on yet then?' I commented.

'No, I was just waiting for you to arrive, I'll do it now.'

'It's alright, I've got it,' I said as I took the kettle and topped it up with water. 'What brings you here at this time of day? No treatment at the hospital today or what?'

'Yeah, I've been at the hospital all morning. Had my treatment and a conversation with the specialist. He has said he intends to finish with the antibiotics today.'

'Oh, is that a good sign or not?' I interjected.

'Well, I'm not really sure. On Monday, I'm due more tests, and on the outcome of those, he will decide if he puts me on a course of radiotherapy.'

'Radiotherapy,' I repeated. 'Why, what are they suggesting is the matter with you?'

'The official diagnosis is it's too early to say, or that's what I'm being told. I now believe they are suspecting a cancer or something,' he said in a quite matter-of-fact way.

'Cancer. What makes you think that?'

'Well, actually, it's what I've thought for some time now.'

'Oh! And have you put that thought to them?'

'Yes, several times,' he replied.

'And what was their response?'

'Only that it is not certain yet, the test procedures suggest some other complications, whatever that may mean.'

'Fuck me, I hope they know what they are about,' I said as we sat there just looking at one another. 'What's Barbara's take on all of this?'

'Oh nothing, I haven't spoken with her about my theory, and until they confirm the diagnosis, I don't intend worrying her with it.'

'No, perhaps you're right,' I agreed.

'I would be grateful if you kept these kinds of thoughts just between us,' he said with a look that was kind of pleading.

'Goes without saying,' I replied.

While still sitting there with our tea, the manager walked in. 'Ah hello, Dutch,' and shook his hand with what seemed genuine pleasure. 'Ready to start back?' he said in a joking sort of way.

'I just popped in to see if my position was still open,' Dutch jokingly responded.

'Always will be,' replied the manager. 'Now what's happening out there?' he asked.

'Props to support the roof are on their way.'

At this point, Dutch said, 'I can see you're busy. I'll leave you to it, see ya, ta-ra.'

The manager said, 'Yes, OK, keep in touch, bye.'

I said, 'If you fancy a drink anytime during the weekend, give me a call, right?' and away he went.

'Right, back to business,' said the manager.

I explained, 'We intended to support the roof with the props. Remove all the loose brickwork, remove the vehicle to the body-shop. Clean the area up of any other debris. Then hang a tarpaulin across the gap to prevent any water spray from the wash bay entering the fuel bay, which would cause the floor to be slippery, making an accident similar to the one that started all these problems likely. The garage will then be fully operational. We can then consider the best way to reinstate the wall permanently.'

'How long before I get my garage back?' asked the manager.

'Well, it's almost 3 o'clock, so if the props arrive within the next 10 minutes, everything should be up and running by 4.30ish.'

'OK, I'll leave it with you while I go and check on the state of the driver who is responsible for all this.'

I then said, 'It's just this situation that I was referring to when I suggested we required someone with building experience to replace Dutch.'

'Don't start with the politics, not now,' he said and left. I thought, *And fuck you too.*

When I returned to the scene of the incident, Mick had seconded a couple of garage cleaners to assist in cleaning and tidying the area. 'Oh, well done, that's exactly what was required.' Just then, the props and boards arrived, the four of us set about getting the job done.

It was somewhat later than anticipated when we finally finished, but everything was functioning and operational. What we had discovered as we removed the loose brickwork above the bus was a fairly substantial RSJ supporting the roof. So there had not been any possibility of the roof collapsing after all. *I suppose better safe than sorry*, I thought.

At home, I mentioned to Doreen the fact that Dutch had popped into work this afternoon. 'Hasn't he been to the hospital for his treatment?' she exclaimed.

'Of course he has, it's just the hospital has said the treatment he was having has finished. He has to wait till Monday for some more tests, then they will decide what to do next.'

'That sounds promising, doesn't it?'

'Well, let's wait and see, shall we, before we pronounce the all-clear of his ailments.'

'I know, but it does sound hopeful. Shall I ring Barbara, see what she thinks?'

'No, I think you should leave it till after the results of Monday's tests. If you do want to ring her, ask if she and Dutch would like to go for a drink at the club or anywhere else anytime over the weekend, but make sure you don't push too much. Make sure you let her lead on any discussion on his health issues, and don't offer an opinion.' 'Oh, shut up, you, don't you think I know how to talk to people?'

'No comment,' was my only comment.

Friday evening, a full team was in attendance. Doreen seemed delighted to be leading the conversation on Barbara and Dutch until Chris interrupted her flow by saying, 'I spoke with Barbara this evening and she said they might pop in here tonight.' Doreen seemed a bit crestfallen by this revelation.

Separate of their conversation, we blokes had been discussing the forthcoming weekend's sport. From my position, I was aware that Paul Lee had entered the room; he had gone over to the table of the usual gang of mischief-makers, consisting of Brian, Kevin, Don, Markey and Sam.

They seemed to get very excited about something that was being passed around them; it looked like a card of some sort. The noise level suddenly rose; attention was quickly directed to our table. I, not knowing what was going on but suspecting a potential problem, suggested we retire to the games room.

Ron asked, 'Aren't we a bit early?'

'No, it's just about the right time now, I think,' was my reply.

Vic said, 'I'll get a round in before I go in.' Dennis offered to give him a hand, but Vic said, 'No, it'll be OK; go and reserve a table. I won't be a minute.'

As soon as we were in the games room, I said, 'Something's amiss. I think a problem is brewing.'

'How do you mean?' asked Ron, looking rather perplexed.

'Well, while we were sat in there just now, Paul Lee came in with something in his hand and went directly to Don and all that crowd. As they viewed whatever it was, it raised a lot of excitement and an amount of interest in our direction.'

Dennis was all for going and finding out what it was all about. I thought it better to wait till we could get one of them alone and ask quietly what was going on.

A table was acquired, and as we set it up, Vic came in as said, 'Is something going on? Only PK came up to me and said, "You're in trouble now, aren't you?" Anyone know what he's on about?'

Then in walked Jumbo fucking Jennings, he took hold of a snooker ball and slung it up the table, bouncing it off the top cushion in quite an aggressive manner and said, *'Gotcha!'* to a chorus of 'Fuck off, fat cunt.' He strolled back out with a big grin on his face.

The game progressed in a very subdued atmosphere. It was Ron who first cracked after missing a comparatively easy shot. 'I can't concentrate. I'm going to find out what's going on.'

Right at that moment, in walked PK selling sports night presentation tickets. 'Just the bloke we want to see. What's going on?' asked Dennis.

'Let me deal with these tickets first, then I'll explain all the excitement.'

'Fuck the tickets,' said Vic, 'tell us what fucking Jumbo's jumping about.'

'No, I must concentrate on one thing at a time. Now, who wants what? They are £7:50 each. For that, you get a cooked meal and a sweet, a show consisting of a comedian, and a group with a very good female lead singer. Plus, the presentation.'

'Yeah, OK, I'll have two tickets,' said Vic. 'Do you want the money tonight?'

'Well, yes, if you've got it, but next week will be OK if you give a firm commitment tonight.'

Vic handed over his £15. I asked for four saying I'd have two for Dutch, and I'd pay next week. Dennis had two also saying he would pay next week. Ron asked for two, saying he would pay next week. As each had made their requests, tickets were handed over. PK recorded all transactions in a book. Then said to Ron before handing him his tickets, 'I think you should speak with your wife before you commit much further.'

Ron went white. 'Why? What's going on?'

PK then explained what had happened. Apparently, Paul Lee's daughter had a friend on a website called Facebook, and one of her followers, as he believed they are called, had a follower who had come across some photos of a hen party in Blackpool. Along with the photos was a request for information regarding various persons in these shots, claiming they are believed to have come from our area.

Paul's daughter, knowing her dad had recently been in Blackpool for a weekend, asked if he recognised the bloke in the photo. Paul immediately recognised who it was and, without letting on, asked if he could take it to the club to see if anyone could assist in the identification. Hence all the excitement out there.

'What's it got to do with Jumbo?' asked Vic.

'God knows,' replied PK as he handed two tickets to Ron and left.

Ron sat down on a chair and said, 'You know what the photo is; it's that one you took,' glaring at Dennis.

Dennis countered with, 'I took quite a few, actually. It isn't my fault if they have turned up here.'

I said, 'Listen, we've got to get our story straight before it gets back to the ladies out there. You remember the first week after the trip when that lot were singing Run Rabbit Run. That's what happened, OK. We've got proof that we ran away, right.'

Ron was saying, 'It's alright for you, it's me in the—'

At that moment, Eileen's head came round the door and said, 'Oi you,' looking directly at Ron, 'out here, right now.'

Ron called back equally aggressive, 'Wait a bit, we're busy, I'll be out there in a minute.'

Eileen responded with, 'You'll come out here right now.'

Ron just said quietly and controlled, 'In a minute.'

Vic, believing it was nothing to do with him, was finding it all very amusing, and led our party out of the games room.

We sat in our seats, looking at four very unfriendly faces. Eileen thrust the photo forward and just said, *'Explain.'*

Vic picked it up first and looked with a big smile on his face. Passing it to Dennis, who with great boldness said, 'I took this,' and passed it to me. It was indeed the photo of Ron in the middle of all the hens. I handed it to Ron, whose only reaction was, *'Wow!'*

I started with, 'Hold on, it's not what you think.'

Eileen jumped in and said, 'Not you, him.'

I carried on with, 'Well, we were all there, and you want an explanation, so if you just give me a chance, I'll put you in the picture.' We all laughed at my little play on words. (Well, the blokes did anyway.) The four faces opposite remained very dour.

'Now cast your minds back to that first week after Blackpool. That lot over there were singing 'Run Rabbit Run' at us all that evening, remember? Well, that was because we were in a pub, the same pub as that hen party. They requested assistance in taking some photos. Dennis here, ever the gentleman, offered help. One of the hens grabbed Ron and dragged him into the middle of the melee. Also, being a gentleman of the old school, he went along with their rough inner-city ways and thus said photo has been produced. The reason that lot were singing is, having the apparent morals of tomcats themselves, they thought it very amusing that we – being very much in love with our wives – ran off.'

The eight of us sat there in total silence, just looking at each other for what seemed like quite a long time. I eventually asked, looking directly at Doreen, 'No comment?' Then said, 'Is it alright if we go and finish our game of snooker now?'

'When you've got a round in, yes,' was the only command from Chris.

A round was acquired and us blokes reassembled in the games room. We stood there for a while just looking at one another. Dennis said, 'I think we got away with it, don't you?'

Ron complained, 'It's alright for you lot. I'm the one in the photo.'

Vic's comment was, 'It's nothing to do with me. I went back to Tolly's, remember.' He seemed rather pleased with himself for that fact.

Dennis was quite defiant, 'All we need to do is stick to the line "we ran away" as backed up by the gang of singers.' At that, we continued with our game of snooker.

Dutch and Barbara had not put in an appearance. I mentioned this to Doreen on the way home. 'No,' she said, 'Chris had phoned Barbara earlier in the evening and had been told Dutch had completed his present course of treatments and was to undergo more tests. Chris had then asked if they would be out tonight, to which Barbara had said they possibly might.'

After a moment of silence, she asked, 'Is that where the lipstick came from?'

'Now you've had all that explained, why bring it all up again now?'

'None of us believe a word of what you said. It was all too pat, all too glib. All too easily said, it just flowed out of you like a rehearsed line of bullshit that you are so well renowned for.'

'And that's the considered opinion of you all, is it?'

'Yes,' was her direct answer.

'Well, thank you. I expect you put up a good argument in my defence, did you?'

'No,' she replied,' it was me that said all of that, they only agreed.'

'Fucking great,' I said, which got no response at all, which considering the language was very unusual.

Saturday morning, work was calm. A steady flow of work as pre-planned with the manager. We had agreed the rebuilding of the damaged wall should be put out to contractors. The driver that had had the collision had been disciplined. More and larger Max Speed signs were to be displayed, and a more frequent inspection of floor surfaces should take place. A number of other items were attended to, all in all, a quiet, steady morning.

I finished work at about 1.30 and went to the club. As I went into the bar, Vic was calling a pint, he doubled the order and we sat down. After a short while, Paul came over. He started by saying he wanted to apologise about last night when he had entered the club with the photo, he had not intended it to be passed around all the club and certainly not put on the noticeboard as had happened.

I said, 'Yeah, but what happened to the old comrade's code of what happens away from home stays away from home?'

'Yes, it was a mistake, a bad error of judgement on my part; it had only been intended as a bit of a laugh. I'm really sorry it got a bit out of hand.'

Vic's take on it was he should have realised that the mob in this club, given a chance to kick someone, would not stop kicking. They couldn't tell the difference between a joke and a fucking pantomime.

I said I thought he and some of the others could go some way to alleviate the problems they had created by offering an explanation of the situation to the wives of our group. In particular the fact they were all there, it was all innocent, and the fact that when the hens had become too demanding, we had indeed run off. He could also add that it was very amusing to all club members at the time.

Paul agreed, he said he would certainly do that and try to encourage one or two of the others to follow the same line. He then offered to buy a drink as recompense for our discomfort, which we accepted.

Over the weekend, I spoke with Dennis and Ron. Explaining what had transpired and that with a little bit of luck, things would settle down after next week. Ron told me Eileen had said Doreen didn't believe a word of what I had said and that she was inclined to agree with her. She had gone on to say, 'If ever it turns out to be false, it might mean the end of some marriages.'

'Hang on in there, keep to the quoted line,' was the only advice I could offer.

I had also spoken with Dutch. After running through Friday night's debacle, he had been laughing like a drain and said it was the best medicine he had received. He went on to say, 'You haven't done anything wrong, just tell the whole truth, it'll give them a good laugh.'

'Yeah, thanks for that little pearl of wisdom,' was my response.

Monday 25th Oct.

At work, the manager informed me a contractor had been selected for the wall rebuild. He requested that I liaise with them and give instruction of procedure while they are on site. He said they were to start on Wednesday.

While we were in conversation, he went on to say he understood my concerns regarding a replacement for Dutch and when, or even if, the time arrives for a decision, he will consult with me. I let him know my main worry was the reaction of Mick if he failed to secure a role in our setup after all that he had done for us this summer. The manager replied, 'If or when.'

Ron phoned on Wednesday evening. His story was, he and Dennis had been in the club last night, just for a quiet drink. Jumbo Jennings had turned up and started taking the piss and saying, 'Don't think you've got away with it, it ain't over yet.'

I said, 'I'll tell you what I'm going to do as soon as I see Jumbo on Friday night. I'm going to tell him I'm asking the committee to cancel his membership of the club and ban him indefinitely. I will also let him know I have the backing of most of the club bowlers and most of the committee. See if that threat slows him down a bit.'

Ron's take on it all was that Jumbo would still go ahead with whatever he was planning.

I thought, *It's unlikely he would be able to acquire any more photos as I don't think he's computer literate. So, it could be his threats and his aggressive rhetoric are just smoke blowing out of his arse.*

Doreen had been reasonably subdued all week, polite to me at all times but not over-friendly any of the time.

It was in this frame of mind that we entered the club on Friday evening. We were first to arrive. I went to the bar to order our drinks; I asked the bar steward if Jumbo was in. He replied that he wasn't in at the moment but had been in several times during the week.

As I put our drinks down on our table, Ron and Dennis plus their wives arrived. I went back to the bar with the guys and said, 'How goes it with the ladies?'

'Oh, very fragile in my case,' said Dennis.

'Likewise,' said Ron.

'I've made enquiries regarding the whereabouts of Jumbo; I've been told he's not in the club yet.' I went on to say, 'As soon as Vic gets here, we'll retreat to the games room where we can discuss our plight without the fear of being overheard.'

The girls were already conspiring, with heads bent close whispering.

As we sat down, they sat up. We all just sat there without speaking for what seemed an age. Vic and Chris were exceptionally late to the point where Ron, breaking the silence, said, 'I don't think they are going to make it tonight.'

Right at that moment, they walked in. Ron said, 'My round. I'll get them in.' As he and Vic went to the bar, Paul Lee approached. *Oh good, I hope he makes it sound sincere and logical,* was my thought.

Paul, looking very worried or even a bit frightened, said, 'That lot out there ain't anything to do with me.'

'What are you on about?' asked Dennis.

'Those photos on the board in the foyer.'

Realising action was required, I immediately went to rise with the intention of removing the evidence. Too late, Chris, who had only just arrived and had not taken her seat, stood directly in front of me, obstructing my path. She then gestured for the ladies to make haste to investigate the situation.

Feeling somewhat defeated, Dennis and myself just sat there. Ron and Vic returned with the drinks and asked what was going on. After having a quick update on what Paul had said and the ladies' rapid response, Ron went visibly pale. He said, 'I thought this would be all behind us by now.'

Vic, still feeling blameless, smiled and said, 'It can't be that bad; nothing happened.'

We just sat there, one smiling, three looking forlorn. The moment of reckoning soon transpired. The ladies returned with what looked like a number of photos.

They sat all across the back of the seating bay, all four looked distraught. We blokes just sat there, still three sorry-looking, one with a half-smile.

It was Chris who opened up with, *'You lying bastard!'* This aimed straight at Vic.

His response was, 'Who me? What have I done?'

Chris carried on by saying in a whinging, whining, it wasn't me, childlike, mimicking way, 'You went back to the digs and had nothing to do with any of this. And do you know what? Like an idiot, I believed you.'

'I did,' protested Vic.

'Well, what's this?' Chris skimmed a photo across the table.

It landed close to me; I picked it up and looked. Oh my God, it was of the coach outside Tolly's place and showed Vic leaning out of the window, reaching down and passing or receiving a note of some sort from one of the Hawaiian hula-clad hens. In the next window was the face of Ron with a beaming smile on his face. I passed it on.

Vic said, 'It wasn't like that.'

'Yeah, so you said,' replied Chris.

Eileen was next. *'You ran away?* It looks like you spent the whole weekend with them. They show you with them in three

221

different places. I believe they show Friday night, Saturday night and Sunday at your digs. Do these photos tell a lie? Were they staying at your digs? Because that's what I believe.' With that, she threw the remaining photos towards us blokes, scattering them everywhere. June started to cry. Doreen just stared at me with a look of total evil.

My response was, 'I don't know what these photos show. I can only reiterate; whatever they show and whatever you believe is a total misconception of the whole situation. If you will allow me and my colleagues a few minutes to view the evidence, we will try to resolve this conflict.'

'To come up with more bullshit,' was the retort from Chris.

'Whatever,' I replied as I collected the scattered photos. 'Come on, guys.'

Dennis said, 'I'm taking her home. I don't think she's at all well.'

Ron said, 'We should check all the photos first.' To this, Dennis agreed.

We sat at a table in the bar. All present members of the club seemed to be interested in our dilemma, they watched on without any comment at all.

The photos were very damning indeed. Two were of Ron in the middle of the hens; the first was the original, the second, though similar, showed the hens flashing much more flesh. The next four photos were taken at the Pear Tree Club. One was of Ron and Dennis sitting at a table with several of the hens. One of me at a table with just the one hen, can't recall her name. One was of the dance floor, showing Ron and Dennis with a group of the hens.

The last of these four photos was the most damning of all (well, to me in particular). It was of the dance floor with me in the foreground, locked in an embrace with the same hen I was at the table with. We appeared to be looking into each other's eyes as if in a very intimate moment. In the background of the photo was Dennis in close combat with a hen and Ron in a similarly compromising position.

These photos, along with the one outside Tolly's place, did seem to tell a story that was inconsistent with the true facts.

222

Vic said, 'I wasn't in the club; these photos show that. So how come I'm being blamed for something I didn't do?'

Dennis came back with, 'None of us did anything, yet we are all being blamed for something we didn't do.' My input was the photo of Vic hanging out of the coach was possibly the most damning of them all. It showed a continuity of contact between the parties.

'What was all that about, the note?' asked Ron.

'I don't know,' answered Vic. 'What happened was, I pushed myself out of the window, she ran forward, reaching up with the note, shouting "pass this to..." and I thought she said "Dave". The coach had started to move before I could take it from her, so who knows what it might have been.'

'Who the fuck is Dave?' asked Ron. As we all looked at each other, a thought ran through my mind. *Had I said to any of them that I was a Dave?* Which I have probably done before, but being too pissed at the time, I don't know the truth of that fact.

'So, what do we do now?' asked Ron.

'I was given some advice recently,' I said. 'Just tell the truth; you did nothing wrong. So that's what I shall do; tell the truth, the whole truth, and nothing but the truth, so help me God.'

'You've got no chance of any help from him.' said Vic, 'but it's about all we can do. Make sure we all tell the whole truth and it needs to be the same truth.'

Dennis said, 'Are we all agreed? Right, I'll go and take her home. I bid you all a good night and good luck.'

Vic, believing Dennis had adopted the right strategy, followed suit.

Ron said, 'I don't know what to do; what you going to do?'

'Me?' I said, 'I'm going to get another drink, then I'm going to find out who put those fucking photos out there.'

Back in the lounge, Eileen and Doreen were still sat there looking not best pleased. 'Another drink?' I asked.

"No, I'll get my own,' replied Doreen.

'Now pack that in, you know all this is a storm in a beer glass, don't you? So have another drink while I go and sort it all out.'

'Don't you start fighting with anybody over this, I know you.'

223

'See, you do care,' was my parting shot.

Leaving Ron and the two ladies with drinks in our regular drinking bay, I went over to the table where the usual suspects sat. 'Can I join you for a while?' I asked.

'Oh, I don't know,' replied Don, 'we don't want you bringing your trouble with you over here.' Knowing what had happened, they all roared with laughter.

I said, 'Yes, very droll, and it's OK for you lot to have a laugh, but at the end of the day, someone needs to supply some answers.'

Kevin then said, 'Yes, bringing it out into the open like that is past a joke.'

At that, they all seemed to become more serious. Brian next added, 'That was a dirty trick to play. I know we all had a good laugh about it at the time, but it should have stayed there in Blackpool.'

'So!!' I asked, 'Who is responsible?'

Paul said, 'That one last week was me. I've admitted to that and I've apologised, but I don't know anything about this as I've already said.'

I carried on by saying, 'I would put it all down to Jumbo, but I don't think he knows how to use a computer.'

It was Markey who said, 'Maybe not, but I bet he knows someone who does.'

'If any of you hear, and it's only facts that I need, not rumour. I'd be very grateful.'

As I left their table, PK was doing his rounds collecting money for the sports night presentation tickets. 'Are you paying anything in this week?' was his request of me.

'Yeah, four tickets. Thirty pounds, correct?' I counted out the money. While he was recording the transaction, I asked if he was aware of tonight's debacle.

He looked up with a look of concern on his face and said, 'No, what has happened?'

I gave him a full run-down of the evening's events plus the reaction of our wives; his reaction was of surprise. He said, 'That's out of order, especially after last week's performance. What has Paul got to say about it this time?'

'He denies having any knowledge of this lot, and I think I believe him,' I responded. 'I do, however, intend to find out who is responsible, and I shall expect you and the committee to do something about it.'

'Like what?' he asked.

'Like an indefinite suspension from the club,' I shot back at him.

'That's a bit harsh, ain't it?'

'Not if marriages break up as a consequence of their action.'

'It won't come to that, will it?' PK asked.

'It very well might do,' I replied. I then added, 'We'll leave it at that for now, I'll speak with you again when I have proof of the culprit.'

When I returned to the lounge, Doreen and Eileen were sitting alone, still looking quite glum. 'Where's Ron?' I asked. I received no reply. 'Look,' I said, 'I know those photos could be interpreted as a total betrayal by us blokes, but I do assure you that is not the case. Nothing happened, nothing went on, it was just a couple of innocent moments caught on a camera. They do not tell the truth of an innocent weekend.'

Eileen just replied, 'He's gone in there,' indicating the games room. Doreen did not respond. (I thought *And fuck you too*) and went to find Ron.

Ron was in the middle of a game with Bill Anderson. I only acknowledged the two, then sat and watched their game. Ron won a close battle; Bill suggested I play the winner.

'You OK, Ron?' I enquired.

'Yeah, I couldn't stop in there with them pair; they just sat whispering to one another and totally ignoring me, so I came in here.'

'Yeah, I got much the same treatment.' I went on to say, 'I didn't get much useful information out of any of that crowd. Though they are sympathetic to our plight, they aren't aware of who is responsible for the photos.' I told him I'd had a word with PK letting him know we would expect action to be taken against anyone found responsible for all of this.

'A peculiar thing happened as I entered this room,' said Ron. 'Young Liam was in here with Kevin's son. He took one look at me and shot out of the door. Do you think there was any significance in his action?'

'I couldn't say, but bear it in mind,' I replied.

Ron wanted to know what he was supposed to do with Eileen. She wouldn't even talk to him, never mind listen to him.

'Give her the truth and keep repeating it; we'll get a few of the guys to tell the same. Hopefully, she and the rest of the wives will get the message.'

On the way home, I started to tell Doreen the full story, but she interrupted me, saying, 'Save it, I'm not interested in anything you have to say anymore. I've had all I can take of your lying cheating ways.'

'Well, bollocks then,' was my closing statement. (Still eloquent as ever, me, eh.)

Towards the end of work on Saturday morning, I made a phone call to Dutch. He was very amused by my story of Friday night's debacle.

I said, 'It's all right for you, you who went closest to breaking the sacred trust. How come you're the only one not in trouble?'

'I know how the game is played. I've done it on a regular basis for a good number of years now.'

I said, 'Yeah, I must learn the secret.'

'It's simple; you don't let anyone you don't trust completely know what goes on,' was his reply.

'Knowing you know how it plays, how would you like to explain to our wives the whole story?'

'Fuck off,' was his reply to this little idea.

'Why not? You know the truth, it was you who said just tell the truth, you did nothing wrong, and you really thought we were rather pathetic. What's more, they'll listen to you.'

'As long as you don't expect me to divulge my feeble little dalliance, I suppose I could try to win them over,' he eventually agreed.

Saturday evening, Doreen refused to go out, which was a first as far as I could remember. Vic was staying at home; Dennis was visiting his son's family and probably babysitting for the evening. Ron said he didn't know what to do, Eileen still wasn't communicating in any shape or form. He'd had to get his own meals. 'If I go out, it'll only worsen the situation.'

So, I ended up on my own in the Boat. There were a number of people in the pub

I knew and spoke with. Most only seemed interested in why I was on my own. It was a question I gave numerous answers to, the sum total amounting to 'bugger off and mind your own business', not necessarily using those exact words but nonetheless expressing that meaning.

Ron finally walked in somewhat after 10 o'clock. He'd been to visit an elderly cousin who was on his last legs. He said he wouldn't be staying long as he didn't want to antagonise the situation at home any more than it already was. He went on to say Eileen seemed to think he was the ringleader in all the shenanigans as he was in all the photos.

I let him know I had spoken to Dutch, and he was going to convey the full true story to all the wives. 'They will accept the story if it comes from him, I hope,' I said.

Ron said, 'Yeah, I think you're right, they will. Why they should accept his word more than mine is beyond my understanding. Especially when you consider, he is the biggest rogue of all.'

'Yeah, but that's life, as they say,' was my final observation on the subject.

Sunday morning, I was back at work, contemplating staying there the whole of the day rather than face the misery that beckons at home.

It was around 11.30, Mick and I were doing an oil change and full service on the tyre bay compressor. The garage shift foreman came and said there was a phone call for me in the garage office.

It was Dutch. He asked if I was up for a drink at the club this lunchtime. 'Has Kylie popped her cherry? You bet I am,' I replied. 'The question is, are you OK? What about your medicine and your treatment, is that an issue?'

'No, everything is under control. I'll give all relevant information at the club.'

'Great, I'll pick you up, that OK?' I asked.

'Yeah, that's fine, what time?'

'12.15 do? Good, see you outside my door.'

'You are at Barbara's, aren't you?'

'Yes, where else would I be?'

'Yeah, where else indeed? Bye.' At that, I rang off.

I let Mick know I was to have a liquid lunch with Dutch. He was extremely pleased that Dutch was well enough to be out and about. His mood changed slightly when he realised Dutch might be returning to work.

He said he was OK to carry on with the work in hand, if any problems arose, he knew where to find me.

I left work at 12 o'clock. I was at Barbara's door spot on the arranged time. Barbara was not at home, which surprised me just a little bit.

On the way to the club, Dutch gave me a rundown of his treatment and the progress he thought he was making. The treatment was to run for three weeks. He had been told he might suffer some side effects such as headaches, nausea and maybe some skin irritation. He went on to say, his only discomfort was a slight feeling of sickness on Wednesday evening, otherwise everything was going swimmingly.

In all honesty, he looked OK, maybe a slight look of weariness about his face but not very much. The weight loss, though not considerable, I think helped in his look of wellbeing.

He was greeted at the club like a returning hero. All the euphoria was very genuine, it took quite a few minutes to get a drink and settle into our seats.

As we settled in, I asked, 'How's Barbara?'

'Fine,' he replied.

'She out for the day?' I enquired.

'Don't you know?' he said with a look of astonishment.

'No,' I replied in a somewhat over-careful way.

'She's out to lunch with your wife.'

'Well, fuck me, when was all this arranged?'

'Well, after you phoned yesterday, I told Barbara the full story of how you were picked up by those ladies, and how you were used by them to get into that club, how they drank more than they ought, how they started to flirt and get raunchy and how you ran away.' He went on to say, 'Barbara fell off her chair laughing. Like I said at the time, best medicine I've received.'

'I personally don't see the joke.' I said in a mock affronted way.

He went on to say he'd also explained the fact that purely by chance, they had passed by as we were just leaving our hotel and how all the coach had reacted when it was realised they were the bunch of women we had run from.

'Ah! So now I'm the laughing-stock of your household as well as the entire club; thanks, mate.'

'Yep,' he said, 'I wouldn't be surprised if it doesn't make the BBC news before too long.'

This was the sort of banter I'd been missing while Dutch has been off work.

'So, the only people not laughing about this are our wives. Can you do something about that?' I asked.

'Already done,' he replied. 'Why do you think Barbara is at lunch with them?'

'Them?' I asked. 'You mean they have all gone out to lunch?'

'All barring June, apparently, she's staying at her daughter's. But, yes, the rest are all together at lunch right now, hopefully hearing the full story and laughing about it as much as everyone else.'

'I don't care what the rest say about you, I think you're a prince among men.'

To which he replied, 'Like fuck you do.'

Some half an hour after we had arrived, Paul Lee came in the club; he purchased a drink and approached our area. Looking a little bit sheepish, he said, 'Can I have a quiet word?'

'Yes, sure, sit down.' I gestured to a seat at our table.

He said, 'I don't know quite how to say this. but our Liam acquired those photos.'

'*Liam!!*' I cried, 'What the fuck did he think he was doing?'

'Before you go of the deep end,' Paul said, 'let me give you all the details. He was asked to get them, in fact he was bribed into getting them, someone offered to pay him £2 for each photo he could get hold of. He was told it was only a joke. Look how everyone laughed last week at just one photo; think how much more they will laugh if you can get hold of a load. He said he received £20.'

'Off who? Off who?' I pushed for the information.

'Jumbo,' was the answer.

'*Jumbo Fucking Jennings!*' I repeated.

'OK, Paul, thanks for that information.'

Paul said, 'There's no need to give Liam a hard time over this. I've given him a big enough bollocking already and told him to keep away from the club till it's all sorted.'

My take on this was, 'I don't blame Liam, he's only a young lad, and he was led astray by a big mouth arrogant twat. It's him I mean to get even with. So don't be too hard on him and tell him he will not be held accountable.'

Paul said, 'Thanks, and once again, sorry. I still feel guilty for starting all this off in the first place.'

'Yeah, well, we'll leave it at that for now and see how it all pans out.'

When Paul had left our table, Dutch said, 'Mind how you deal with this, it won't take much to set all these lot against you if you overreact. If I was you, I'd wait and see how the wives behave after their lunch together.'

'Yes, you are probably right, but he has got to know of my displeasure, and I aim to take him to task regarding his role in all of this.'

We let it lie after that and spoke of Dutch and his progress at the hospital. We spoke about work; we spoke about Barbara and his ongoing relationship with her and generally put the world to rights. Just another steady Sunday lunchtime session.

We didn't drink much, in fact we only had a couple of pints. I was suddenly aware that his concentration level was beginning to waver. On inquiring if he was alright, he said, 'Yeah, I'm OK, a little tired perhaps, but not too bad.'

We finished our drinks and left to much shaking of hands and see yer soons. It took longer to get out than it had taken to get in.

At Barbara's house, I could see her car was not on the drive and assumed the ladies were still at lunch. Dutch invited me in. I declined his offer on the grounds that I needed to return to work to check on young Mick.

The real reason was, I didn't want to be there when Barbara returned. (It might be bad news.) Plus, the fact I could see Dutch, for all his bravado and insistence he was OK, was in fact very weary and in need of a rest. So, I bade him farewell and said, 'I'll give you a ring in the week.'

I did pop into work; Mick had actually left. The work in hand had all been completed and everything was in order. I hung around for about an hour, filling in worksheets, timesheets and all other relevant paperwork. Eventually came the time to go home. No matter how much I delayed, it was inevitable that I had to face the demon that dwelt within.

On entering the house, I was greeted by a woman with a big smile on her face. *Most probably drink induced. Still, it looks like a good sign, but I'll play it cool.* 'No dinner cooking?' I asked, raising my nose in the air and sniffing.

'No, I'm not cooking today,' was the reply.

'Oh, bloody hell, you're not still holding on to that attitude, are you?'

'I'm not holding any attitude as you term it; I don't hold any sort of a grudge, *ever*.' Then after a short moment, said, 'Guess where I've been?'

I replied, 'I'm not sure I'm in the mood to play guessing games. So, if you must, just go ahead and tell me.'

'I've been out for my lunch.'

'Oh, it's alright for some, while others are out toiling to earn a crust, you just swan off to lunch. What brought that about?' I asked.

'Well,' she said as she started on a long and winding tale about her lunchtime activity. Of which I was already fully aware. Although it was quite amusing to hear how she saw the whole event now.

When she had completed her narrative, she came over to me and kissed me and said, 'Sorry for doubting you.'

'I'm not sure it's that easy to get back in my good books,' I said. 'What you need to do now is get me some food while I go and shave and shower, then if you ask very nicely, I'll let you spend the rest of the afternoon in bed with me.'

Monday 1st Nov.

Mick was keen to hear of Dutch and how he had fared over lunch yesterday and, in particular, if he would be returning to work in the near future. I explained that he had been very well and we'd had a very good time. I further explained that after a couple of hours he did seem to tire and began to show signs of fatigue, and in my opinion, it would be some time yet before he would return to work.

Mick had mixed emotions to the news on Dutch; pleased he was getting on so well, sad that he was poorly enough to keep him away from work for so long. But also glad to be staying on in his present role.

The manager, on receiving a similar report of Dutch from me, viewed the news in a very philosophical way, saying, 'I never expected it to be any different to that.'

Tuesday evening, I went to the club with the express view of having a word with PK. The first person I saw as I entered the door was in fact the very same man I was seeking. 'I want a word with you,' was my opening line.

'Yeah, OK,' he replied, 'if you can give me 10 minutes, I'll come and see you.'

Who should walk in while I was still standing at the bar with my drink but Vic and Ron. 'Blimey, I wasn't expecting you pair to be in here tonight,' I said and bought them a drink each.

As we sat down, Vic asked how the ladies were. Ron said after they all went out for lunch on Sunday, Eileen seemed to be in a better frame of mind, not much but certainly better. I let them know I had spoken with Dutch, he had spoken with Barbara, she had organised the lunch to inform them all of the true facts about Blackpool and the hens. Vic thought it incongruous that Barbara and Dutch, particularly Dutch, should be believed when his words had not been acceptable. Ron said that's exactly what he thought when he said he was going to ask them. I said, 'And I'll repeat what I said then. If that's the way the world works, I'll go along with it.'

Suddenly I realised neither of them knew the role Jumbo Jennings had played in this saga. I related all the facts as put to me by Paul. Vic's response was predictable. 'The bastards, they're going to pay for this.'

I said, 'Well, Liam is only young and was easily led, in fact bribed into his role, so some leeway should be afforded him.' I went on to say, 'I've already requested a meeting with the club president; he should be along at any moment.'

We were on our next drink by the time PK arrived at our table. I outlined our case for action to be taken against Jumbo. Vic said, 'We expect real action against him, because if you don't, we will.'

PK was very cautious in his response to my complaint. He thought we were overreacting. Jumbo had been a member of the club for a lot longer than 20 years. In all that time, there had never been an occasion to bring him before the committee. So, it would be difficult to present a case to remove his membership. He also pointed out that Jumbo had been in receipt of an actual physical assault perpetrated by the persons now pressing for his ban.

He went on to say he did not advise taking matters into our own hands. That could result in people being banned.

Ron asked, 'So what happens now?'

PK replied, 'He will be called before the committee and told he is not to use the club noticeboard to carry out his personal vendettas.' He then added, 'I am prepared to give him a verbal warning against any other misdemeanour perpetrated on the premises.'

Ron thought it was too light a punishment, saying, 'My wife hasn't spoken to me for nearly a week.'

Vic said, 'Same here.'

PK replied, 'Well, maybe he did you a favour.' We all had a laugh at that, and the mood lightened considerably.

* * *

Friday evening found us with a much-depleted crew. No Dutch or Barbara and no Dennis and June. The wives had been in constant touch all week. Barbara had let them know Dutch was struggling with his treatment; he seemed to be having greater reactions to it this week, certainly more so than the first week.

June had been told the story of last weekend, and right now, it was generally accepted that Blackpool was indeed mostly just innocent horseplay. June's take on this was innocent or not, he was still dancing with a woman in his arms behind her back, so he was going to carry on suffering for a while longer.

The atmosphere around our seating bay was relaxed and, for the most part, friendly. We blokes were chuckling and smirking about Dennis and his perceived problems.

Suddenly there was a hush right across the room. I looked round, standing by the door was Jumbo fucking Jennings. He looked over at me and hollered, 'Oi, fucking big mouth, you bin trying to get me banned from the club. What's the matter; you lost your sense of humour or what?'

I responded with, 'Shut your big fat gob and sit down, because if you speak to me like that again, I'll take you outside and knock seven shades of shit out of you, as big as you are.'

He came roaring across the room at me with surprising speed, shouting, 'Why you little cunt, I'll rip your fucking head off.'

Quickly getting up, I took hold of a nearby chair and slid it under his feet. At that precise split second, he threw a punch, catching me on the side of my head.

It sent me tumbling backwards, and I seemed to partially black out. As I crashed into the bar and collapsed onto the floor, I saw through one ring of light (it all seemed to happen in slow motion) the sight of Jumbo becoming entangled with the chair. At the very same time, his trousers began to fall down. Making a grab to stop them falling left him with no hands to save him as he fell. With his hands on his trousers and his leg tangled in the chair, his face smashed right into the legs of the piano.

A deathly hush came over the room, save for the groaning of Jumbo. Vic, quickly followed by Ron, rushed over to help me up. As I rose, my head cleared quickly. I said, 'I'm OK.'

Ron, looking round at Jumbo still on the floor, said, 'Look at his leg, it's broken.' By now a number of people were assisting Jumbo. An ambulance was called. Apart from a broken leg, Jumbo had also sustained a cut above his eye and what looked like a broken nose. He was being attended to by a couple of ladies who claimed to have done a First Aid course. We blokes sat down in our seats. The ladies all looked shocked.

Doreen said, 'Couldn't you have ignored him, just this once?'

'That's right, blame me again. I was the one who was attacked, remember?' I countered.

'Oh yes, I forgot, it's never your fault, is it?' was her retort.

Paramedics arrived, patched up Jumbo, transferred him to an ambulance and off to hospital.

As he was being taken out of the building, PK came over and said, 'I warned you about taking matters into your own hand, didn't I? You'll now have to appear before the committee. 7.30 Wednesday evening has been pencilled in, that OK?'

'Hold on,' said Ron, 'Jumbo attacked us.'

'Us?' put in PK.

'Well, him actually,' said Ron. 'He flattened him with a punch to the head.'

'Save it for the committee,' offered PK. 'In fact, if you have a view on the incident, put it in writing for the committee to deliberate over.'

Vic pointed out that over half the committee were in the room and, as such, were in fact witnesses to the incident. PK's reply was, 'See you on Wednesday.'

On the way home, Doreen would not let up.' You go from bad to worse, it never seems to stop; problems just follow you around, why is that? Are you a troublemaker, or is it that you are just thick, because that's what I'm beginning to think?' (And on and on she goes.) I just ignored her ranting.

Over the weekend, reports on Dutch were not good. He was not responding to the treatment very well. Doctors were concerned and thought there may be an unidentified complication.

I spoke with him late on Sunday afternoon. His thoughts on everyone's concerns were, 'Well, they have always been aware there might be side effects. My situation was no different than expected.'

He then asked what I thought I was doing with Jumbo and said, 'I told you to be careful in how you handled it.'

I said, 'I didn't have much choice.'

'There's always a choice,' he replied.

Monday 8th Nov.

'I thought there might be,' was the manager's response to the idea that there seemed to be complications with the treatment Dutch was receiving. 'It's going to be a long haul getting him back to full health.' He seemed pleased his line of thought was proving to be correct.

Young Mick had requested the second half of the week off, starting Wednesday, and said he would not be available over the weekend. This was OK by me, as I was quite happy to work on my own. Well, for a few days certainly.

Wednesday, I had cause to have a change of opinion. My workload was heavy. Everything that could go wrong, did go wrong. To the point I was almost late for my appointment with the club committee.

I went directly to the club from work; I arrived a couple of minutes later than the appointed time. I knocked on the office door and walked in as PK called, 'Come.' I nearly pissed myself laughing at the pretentiousness of it all.

They, the committee, were sat behind along the table on a raised stage. Level with the centre of this table, and some three feet below them was a single chair. With a sweep of his arm, PK gestured I should sit there. I said, 'What's all this, the fucking Inquisition?'

PK opened with, 'We take a very serious view of this incident. A member of the club has been hospitalised after becoming involved in a fracas in the lounge bar of the club. We are attempting to conduct an investigation and believe you will be able to enlighten the committee as to what took place.'

'The big fat twat punched me in the head then fell over a chair. End of,' was my statement of the incident.

'There was more to it than that, surely?' asked PK.

'Not as I recall,' I said.

Derrick Smethurst, club secretary, butted in and said, 'I have received a couple of letters from witnesses who were at the scene of the incident.' PK asked him to read them out.

One of the letters was from Vic; the other from Ron. Both letters were word-for-word exactly the same, stating that Jumbo had come into the room shouting out that he was going to rip someone's head off, using extraordinarily foul language, then proceeded to throw a punch, at which time he fell over a chair.

Derrick followed on to say, 'It would look like an amount of collusion has taken place in the production of these,' as he waved the letters above his head.

I said, 'Maybe, but they tell the truth. If you want confirmation of that fact, several members of your committee were present at the time of the incident. Ask them.'

Phil Earl (committee member) stood up and said, 'I believe something about knocking several shades of something out of somebody was uttered as a threat against Mr Jennings.'

'Fuck off. Have you seen the size of him? He must be twice the size of me; who in their right mind is going to take any notice of me issuing a threat like that?'

PK said, 'Could you moderate your language. These are formal procedures, and minutes are recorded for future reference.'

'Yes,' I replied, 'I'm sorry about that, but I do think you're taking a fucking liberty here.' A number of the committee broke into a laugh at that statement.

PK said, 'I give up.'

I was asked to wait in the bar, allowing the committee to deliberate on what was now known of the incident. I would be called back in a short while to be told the outcome.

In the bar, I found the only people there were Fred and Harry (always together, those two). I offered to buy them a drink, they both declined, owing to the fact they were working later on in the evening. When I told them what I was doing at the club at that time of the evening, they started to laugh and said they had heard I'd given Jumbo a right seeing too. 'Bloody hell, no,' I protested, 'what happened to him was nothing short of an accident.' With stories like that going around, no wonder the committee were so uppity.

Eventually I was summoned back up to the committee room. PK opened by saying, 'For all your protest and stated innocence, it is absolutely certain that you did issue a challenge to Mr Jennings. I'm also aware there has been a long-running feud between the pair of you.'

'Not of my making,' I interjected.

PK carried on (totally ignoring what I had said), 'It is also quite certain that Mr Jennings did come at you and throw a punch. All this has got to stop. You are to be issued with a written warning. Any more unacceptable behaviour will result in a substantial ban. You are dismissed, thank you.'

At that, we all retired to the bar. The ambience around the committee members in the bar was altogether different. They reverted from pompous prats to the normal obnoxious prats we all know and love.

Don offered me a pint. I said, 'Go on then, but I'm only stopping for one as I've been out of the house from very early this morning.'

'Yeah, that's OK, it's your usual trick, have a drink, then run.'

My reply to that was 'bollocks' (everything back to normal).

I put it to them all that they should ensure that Jumbo behaved himself and not harass me anymore. It was Kevin who said, 'Harass you; I don't think you'll have any worries there, he ain't going to try anything on with you anymore, *Rocky*.' The whole committee roared.

'Oh, bloody hell, that's the way it's going to be, is it?' I left and went home.

Work on Thursday and Friday was every bit as hectic as Wednesday. When discussing the coming weekend's work with the manager, I very nearly suggested that we hold back all but the most essential requirements, but suddenly realised next Friday is sports presentation night. When more will be drunk than really ought.

Consequently, come Friday evening, I was a little below par. Arriving home from work, I had a light meal, followed by a shave and shower. I then reclined on the bed and must have dozed off. Next thing I know is Doreen telling me she's ready to go out.

My reaction was, 'Oh bloody hell; why have you let me doss here this long?'

'Don't start gobbing off at me this early in the evening,' she replied, 'just get yourself ready and let's go.'

It took me quite a while to stir myself into action, toilet, dress, and present as ready. Result being we were about three-quarters of an hour late getting to the club.

As we entered the club, PK was in the foyer, and as Doreen went on into the lounge, I stopped and asked him if he had heard anything of Jumbo. 'Yes, I saw him yesterday, no it was Wednesday, feeling very sorry for himself; milking the situation for all it's worth. He's using a wheelchair to get around.'

'Is he!' I was quite surprised by his statement.

'Well, with his weight, I think the medical people thought it best,' said PK. 'I'm wondering if he is considering making a compensation claim against the club,' added PK.

'Surely it was all of his own making, wasn't it?' I asked.

'Maybe, but you know how solicitors are these days with their "No win, no fee" claims,' said PK.

I left it at that and proceeded into the lounge where I was greeted by a rhythmic chant of ROCKY, ROCKY, ROCKY by the gang of the usual suspects; they followed this with roars of laughter, presumably in appreciation of their own perceived wit.

I, choosing to ignore their little performance, went and sat in our usual bay, where a drink had already been acquired for me. Doreen asked, 'Do you always have to make such a spectacle of yourself everywhere we go?'

I looked at her with a blank expression and answered, 'Yes.'

Our gang, finding the spectacle presented by the usual suspects and Doreen's remarks at me all very amusing, were laughing and in good spirits. When I say our gang, I really mean Vic and Chris and Ron and Eileen. Dennis and June were once again missing, and of course there was no Dutch or Barbara.

I informed the assembled crew of my dealings with the committee. They all seemed surprised a formal written warning had been issued. I explained it was due to Jumbo being hospitalised and the possibility of further action being taken. The issuing of an official warning was only to cover their arses should any action be forthcoming.

At that, we gentlemen retired to the games room. Markey joined to make up a foursome and we played some snooker.

Over the weekend, Barbara spoke with Doreen a couple of times, expressing a good deal of concern over the treatment Dutch was receiving and even more concern with his seeming lack of progress to the point that she now feared losing him altogether.

Doreen was quite shaken by this revelation, asking me what I thought. I responded by saying, 'Well, of course she's worried, I'm beginning to believe his problem is probably a bit more serious than I first believed, but he's a big strong bloke, and I have absolutely no doubt he will win through.'

I went on to say, 'She's probably a bit depressed by the strain of it all. Remember, she's already lost a husband and fears history will repeat itself. She just needs to tell this to someone and to hear some reassuring words back. So, when you speak with her next, be upbeat and positive, tell her what I've just said; he's strong, he's having the best treatment, medical people now know how to handle such cases. It's pretty much run of the mill stuff nowadays, so you don't think there's too much to worry about.'

My reassuring words did little to alleviate her concerns, and she still felt we should do something. She was unrelenting with her demands, even if it was only to send a get-well card or some flowers, anything to let Barbara know she wasn't on her own in this.

I'd said I didn't think he would appreciate flowers or even a card for that matter, it ain't a bloke thing. But by Sunday evening, I relented and said, 'I'll call him on the phone, see if there's anything they require.'

When I called, Barbara answered. I asked if she was OK, she replied she was fine. I said, 'Look, if you ever want to get out for a break, with or without Dutch, you're always welcome here, just for a chat or a break from your routine. Anytime at all, don't forget we're here.'

'Yes, I know that, thank you.'

I then asked, 'Is he available?'

'Just a minute, I'll get him.'

'Now what do you want?' was his opening line.

'What oh, matey, you sound like your old self. How goes it?' I asked.

'I'm good,' was his reply, 'how's the situation with Jumbo and the club?'

I tell him of my meeting with the committee and the sheer folly of it all, and of Jumbo and his wheelchair and of the ROCKY chant. All of which had him guffawing with laughter. He said, 'That's great, I love to hear all these little yarns. You know when you used to say your only excitement was my adventures in life, well the roles are reversed now, don't you think?'

I said, 'Yeah, but my stories are very tame in comparison with the tales you would tell.'

'But not anywhere near as funny,' he replied.

'It's the way I tell em,' I countered.

I then said, 'Right, let's get serious for a moment, when are you likely to be back at work?'

'Bad news there, I'm afraid,' he answered.

'Oh, what's that then?'

'Well, on Friday, the consultant came to see me. When I told you a couple of weeks ago of a complication, it turns out the complication is asbestos. They are now saying it's a mesothelioma.'

'And what exactly is that?' I asked.

'It's a cancerous tumour as a result of exposure to asbestos.'

'Oh, fuck me,' I said, 'so that's what Barbara's upset about.'

'No, I haven't told her, and I'd appreciate if you would keep it to yourself till I know how successful the treatment is going to be.'

I said, 'I think you're going to have to tell her. I think she has a right to know.'

'No, she's already lost a main man in her life. I don't want her to start thinking she might lose another. But to finish on a high,

I fully intend to beat this and come out the other end totally clear of these problems.'

'Good,' I said, 'I'm with you all the way on that.'

He then said something that surprised me, he said, 'If I believed in God, I'd think it was his way of making me pay for all the bad things I've done.'

'God!! I can't imagine you've ever done anything that would incur his wrath. Any amount of husbands maybe, but not God's,' was my honest answer.

'That's what you may think,' he replied in a much more lighthearted tone.

I then asked, 'Now what about Friday?'

'What about Friday?' he replied.

'It's the sports presentation night. Will you be able to attend?'

'It all depends on what is decided at the hospital. If they carry on with the radiotherapy, I'll probably be there. If they change my treatment and put me on chemotherapy, it depends on how it affects me. If they decide to operate, which is a possibility, I probably won't be there. So, it's a bit up in the air at the moment.'

'Is it likely they will operate?' I asked.

'It's one of the possibilities put forward by the consultant on Friday. They are to do more blood tests and a scan, then a decision will be made on the action to be taken.' He then said, 'I'll pay for the tickets either way.'

I told him what I had agreed with PK. 'If you weren't able to attend, he'd return the money, so don't worry about it, OK.'

'No, it's alright. I'll pay whatever the outcome, tell PK it's not a problem.'

'Righty-oh, we'll leave it at that then,' I said, 'I'll give you a ring during the week for a progress report and we'll see how it goes.' At that, I rang off, feeling very troubled about the conversation and his revelation. It is a whole new concept now regarding his illness. Asbestos!!! Where from, and even more concerning, who's next?

I couldn't tell Doreen as Dutch had asked that it be kept from Barbara. Never mind what her reaction would be to my situation and involvement with contaminated areas at work. Best keep it to myself for as long as possible.

Monday 15th Nov.

Mick was back from his break and very full of himself. His little break had been to Somerset. He and his mates had been involved in a football tournament. They hadn't won but had done quite well. His euphoria was brought about by his meeting with a young lady (not a bit of skirt, you notice, but a young lady). She, it appears, is the sister of one of his teammates. Not one of his regular close mates, just a teammate. Apparently, the guy's family all went on this little jaunt.

Mick said he'd clocked her the moment she boarded the coach. He had then worked a flanker (as he put it) and very quickly manoeuvred the situation to ensure she finished up sitting with him. They hit it off right from the start, and hung around together the whole time they were away. Her name was Jennifer Tomkins, she was known as Jenny to everyone. He would be seeing her on Wednesday evening but was not sure yet where he would take her.

I said, 'That's great, now put it all to the back of your mind and let's get on with some work.'

My own mind was racing with thoughts of what I was going to say to the manager regarding Dutch, or more importantly, about asbestos.

To a very large extent, asbestos had been replaced in practically all areas of our buildings. I decided I would identify and list all remaining asbestos sites. I would then set up a regular inspection of such sites and record its stability. First, I set up for a consultation with the manager to discuss the issue.

He agreed to see me at 11.30. I knocked and he summoned me in. 'Yes, what can I do for you?' was his opening.

I said, 'Well, a *good morning* always goes down well.'

'Oh, it's going to be one of those sorts of conflabs, is it?' he replied in a not too friendly tone.

'Only a joke, boss,' I said, 'if you've got other problems, my enquiry will keep.'

'No, no, I'm sorry if I sounded a bit offhand, I'll start again. Good morning, what can I do for you?'

'Well, now that you ask, I was wondering what the company policy is regarding asbestos.'

'Er, enlighten me, if you would,' he replied.

'Well, I know it's a very contentious issue, and I'm aware that over the years most has been removed from our premises, but small amounts still remain.'

'Oh! How much and where?' he asked.

'Well, in the boiler house under the old tram sheds, some of the lagging is asbestos. When we had that survey done by that company of so-called experts, they had said that as it was all neatly sealed, it was acceptable to leave it in situ. So, it has been left. The cladding of the steam cleaning compound, though covered in so much shit and sludge it makes it unrecognisable, is also asbestos.

'I also believe that in the roof space above the bus station canteen, some asbestos would be found, and maybe a few other areas around our sites.'

'What bought all this about?' the manager asked.

'Just me being diligent in my job,' I replied.

'What, after all this time? Something must have triggered your interest, what was that?'

'You must figure me as being a cynical bastard, ah boss.'

'Yes, to a greater or lesser degree, always put yourself first. I don't think you would do it above anyone else's interest. But I digress, what I think we should do now is list all known asbestos areas, and I will take it to the directors for a decision and means of funding removal of same.'

'Already in hand, list being made up as we speak,' I informed him.

'So why this little tete-a-tete?' he asked.

'I never put into practice anything I haven't cleared with you, boss, you know that.'

'No comment,' was his reply as I left his office.

At break time on Wednesday morning, I mentioned to Mick his date tonight and asked if he had it all planned. 'Yeah, it's all sorted,' he replied in a very melancholy way.

I said, 'Now hold on a bit, you'll overwhelm her with your excitement if you're not careful. What's the matter, you gone off her or what?'

'No, it's nothing like that,' he said. 'It's just I worry as to how I move things on.'

'Oh, I see, you want to get your jollies, and you're worried she will reject you and kick you into touch when you try it on with her. Is that what you are panicking about?'

'Yes, something like that, only with other girls it never seemed to matter. But with Jen, I think I'm a bit frightened. She's a real nice girl and I can't stop thinking about her. I don't want to upset her in any way. I don't know how to handle it, how to move it forward. Will I upset her? Is she as fond of me as I am of her? Does she want me to move in on her? How am I supposed to know that?'

'Fuck me, here's me thinking all you kids go around shagging one another like it's going to be rationed, when really you don't know the first thing about it. Or am I being cynical and it's *love* you don't know anything about? Yes, I think that's what your problem is.

'First thing you must realise and I think you do realise, is the female of the species likes and wants sex every bit as much as you. But, and it's a big but, what they want from a long-term partner is tenderness, gentleness, thoughtfulness and most of all, trust.

'So just be nice to her, treat her with respect, go slowly and let nature take its course. Remember you've got nothing to prove, be yourself and get to know each other. It's still very early days, time will see everything sort itself out.'

'Do you think so? I hope so. You ought to see her; she's absolutely gorgeous.'

Bloody hell, the kid's got no chance, she'll take him and make mincemeat out of him, in a couple of years' time he'll be as much under control as the rest of us married blokes. Then he really will have to worry as to how he gets his jollies.

Thursday, the smile on his face and his general demeanour said it all. 'Good night then, was it?' I asked.

'The best ever,' he replied.

'Don't tell me you had your evil way with her?'

'No, nothing like that, well not quite anyway.'

'Oh, so what was so great about it then?'

'Everything, I took her for a meal at that Italian restaurant at the top of the town.'

'And!' I prompted.

'Then we went for a drink at the Boat.'

'You keep away from the Boat,' I said, 'I use there. But carry on; what made it such a wonderful night?'

'Well, like everything. She said she had been thinking about me all week and could hardly wait for our date. She'd told all her mates and the people she works with, they all seemed to be pleased for her.'

'So, what made it such a wonderful night?' I repeated.

'I told her all about you, and how you had given me advice, and how you made me laugh when you berate people, and they are all a little bit frightened of you but that you're really soft-hearted and pleasant to know.'

'God give me strength. Don't you go spreading that little story around; people will start to believe they can ignore me when I chunter at them. Anyway, I'm glad it all went well, now it's time for work.'

Every break for the rest of the week, it was *Jenny this* and *Jenny that*, I finally said, 'For fuck's sake, Mick, give it a rest, I feel like I've been giving her one all week, having heard so much about her.'

'Don't say things like that about her, you,' he answered in an aggressive tone.

'Ooh, a bit touchy, aren't we? Big mistake getting all possessive like that, not good at all,' I said.

'Bollocks,' was his short answer as he departed to get on with some work. *What the fuck. Am I bothered? No. It's Friday, and tonight is party time at the sports presentation supper.*

Knowing we were to consume a considerable amount of alcohol, our daughter transported us to the club. It was intended we would return by taxi. We arrived quite early, quarter to seven actually. Tables had been reserved for the bowls section.

I immediately claimed an area of eight seats for our team. Most of the usual crew were already settled in, a couple of them with their wives, now that's a rare sight make no mistake. By 7 o'clock all our team had arrived and a serious drinking session had started. At 7.30, the proceedings commenced, starting with the presentation of awards.

First up, the football, runners-up in their league, top goal scorer, player of the year and so on. Followed by the pigeon flyers, with winners of many categories and competitions, which had little or no meaning to me, being given various awards.

Suddenly, Derrick Smethurst – who, as club secretary and not involved in any sporting activity in the club, was judged as totally impartial and was acting as MC – announced Best Old Bird In Show, then called out my name. Everyone looked at me, including the pigeon-flying fraternity.

Derrick looked at me. I looked at Doreen and said, 'What her?' The place roared.

Doreen, having not been following the progression of the presentation, asked, 'What are you on about now? Shut up and stop making a fool of yourself.'

Derrick, looking down at his paperwork, realised he had misread his script and with a red face called out the correct name. All too late, the room had erupted. Eventually, control was restored and the ceremony carried on.

Our little group did very well. Ron was runner-up in the darts singles. Dennis won the club Open Cribbage Competition. Vic & Ron won the Bagatelle Doubles and Vic was runner-up in the snooker.

With a bottle of whisky for a win and half a bottle for a runner-up spot, our table was already looking well supplied.

It eventually came around to the bowls presentations. To do the honours, Joan as bowls secretary, was called to act as MC for this part of the presentation. The roll of honour was as follows.

1. Best Average Saturday Wolverhampton Works League, Brian Holmes.
2. Best Average Sunday Walsall league, Paul Lee.
3. Best Average Monday Willenhall League, Markey Mason.
4. Best Average Thursday Cannock League, Vic Davies.
5. Opening Day knockout Cup Winner, Pete Kenyon. Runner-up, Vic Davies.
6. Captains and Officials Shield Winner, Joan Hutton. Runner-up, Ron Mitchell.
7. Singles Knockout Cup Winner, Markey Mason. Runner-up, Brian Holmes.
8. Doubles Knockout Shield Winners, Vic Davis and Ron Mitchell.
9. Bowlers, Bowler of the year, Liam Lee.

At this point, Joan relinquished her position at centre stage, and Derrick continued as MC, announcing.

Sports Person of the Year: Craig Johnson. (One of the footballers.)

He then said, 'We now come to a special award, one that has not been presented before. The club committee, along with the sports administrators of the club, all agreed that the situation warranted this action. For outstanding service to the club, with particular reference to the bowls section, for dedication, strong leadership, and total commitment under very difficult personal circumstances, it is my great pleasure to offer this special award to Haakon Van De Enks, commonly known to us all as Dutch.'

The whole room stood as one to applaud the announcement; it went on for some time.

As the applause died down, Derrick said, 'I note his understandable absence, and call upon Joan Hutton to step up and receive the award on his behalf, knowing she will pass on all our good wishes along with this trophy.'

As Joan stood to approach the presentation area, the main entrance door to the room opened and in walked Barbara closely followed by Dutch.

An absolute silence covered the room, Joan stood stock still. Two seconds later, the applause erupted. Barbara, noting where we were sat, made her way over to our area. Vic and Dennis made haste and acquired two chairs. I noticed PK, who was stationed by the door, go into close conversation with Dutch. Joan remained standing, awaiting instruction from PK or anyone who might know what the next move should be.

The applause and general hullabaloo slowly died down. Dutch looked towards Derrick and said, 'Fuck off !!! are you taking the piss or what?' Then to great support from the room, stepped forward and received his award.

Barbara's response was, 'Nothing changes, does it?'

My thoughts went along the lines of: You might not think there's much change, but looking at Dutch, for the first time, I realised he was extremely ill. He looked to have lost at least two stone, his face was very drawn and pinched looking, and he seemed to be slightly hunched forward as he walked.

Having said that, his response to his award and his general demeanour were typical Dutch. Big, brash and aggressive.

Derrick had announced the end of the presentation and that the food would be distributed shortly. It was better than expected. Pate with toast or soup and bap as a starter. A choice of main meal, turkey or beef with all the trimmings, and a choice of sweet, apple pie and custard or fresh fruit and ice cream.

For all the activity going on, the evening seemed, well, a bit flat, a bit subdued, as far as my recollections of presentation nights go. On reflection, it was early yet, they were still clearing the aftermath of the meal.

As our area was cleared of debris, Vic opened the first bottle of whisky and said, 'OK, let's get this party started.' On looking around, I could see similar actions taking place at other tables.

Dutch, who was sat next to me, asked if I would get a round of drinks and some mixers to go with the whisky, offering me two twenty notes. He said, 'If I go up there, I'll get lumbered with answering all sorts of enquiries.' He went on to say, 'I need to get a round in now as we may not be staying very much longer.'

I said, 'You don't need to get a round in, you've only been here a short while.'

'Please,' he said with a look that was truly pleading.

Taken aback and feeling shocked, I suppose, by this sudden realisation of his predicament, I just said, 'Yeah, OK.'

By the time I'd returned with the drinks, half the bottle of whisky had gone. The noise level had increased considerably. Vic realising June and Chris were drinking gin said, 'I'm going to try and swap a bottle of whisky for a bottle of gin over the bar.' This bold plan received a lot of scepticism, but with loud cheers of support for his nerve or, more likely, his cheek, off he went.

He returned not many minutes later brandishing a bottle of gin. This received a standing ovation from our group. On realisation of what had happened, only what can be described as a stampede started with other groups racing to the bar to attempt similar transactions. Total chaos reigned around the bar for a number of minutes. PK was in the middle of it all, trying to restore order. He eventually went to the stage and announced over the sound system that the exchange of drinks over the bar was not an acceptable arrangement, so could everyone please stop making such requests. This little bit of control did not go down very well at all, and was greeted with boos, jeers, and the skimming of beer mats at the club president. He responded by uttering, 'Fuck off, the lot of you.' This little statement received the biggest cheer of the night so far.

The next indication the party had really started happened while a number of ladies, the females from our group among them, were dancing to one of these tunes that ladies in particular seem to know, where they all assemble in lines and move their hands and arms in unison up and down their bodies then jump and turn at right angles. Into the middle of this performance appeared a chap known as Chips. I believe he is a carpenter (chippy, chips, see, I think), on his back, break dancing, or at least what he considered to be break dancing.

The dancing ladies for the most part tended to ignore him. That is except Doreen, who left the floor and returned to her seat chuntering about drunken yobs spoiling everybody's night. Nobody took any notice of her ramblings, especially me.

Suddenly, as this bloke Chips spun round on his back, he caught the leg of one of these so-called ladies. She being quite a sizable young thing, lifted her sizable leg and put her dainty little foot in the middle of his back and gave him a God almighty shove. He goes arse over apex into the stage. A great cheer went up from the assembled crowd showing approval of her performance. Chips' girlfriend took a different view of things and launched herself at said sizable young thing, who dispatched said girlfriend into the same area as Chips with a thunderous right hook. More cheers and shrieks of joy from the watching crowd. Several members of the committee rush in and restore order.

I think, *Who wants to stop at home watching telly when there are performances like this going on?*

The comedian was next on stage. His main problem was the audience were funnier than he was. He started OK. A tale about a North American Indian kid named Two Dogs Shagging, and one about a bloke named Wankbreak. But as his act progressed and members of the audience needed to visit the toilet, he started to make lighthearted remarks regarding their persona. What a mistake to make. This lot had been around the block a few too many times to be intimidated by little witticisms and could be relied upon to give back better than they receive. Each reply was greeted by huge amounts of laughter. At first the comedian laughed along with these remarks. Slowly but surely, he lost patience with these smartarse retorts and started to get agitated. He started using obscenities and bemoaning, 'It's like working at Paddington fucking Station with you lot.'

Dennis said, 'He's losing them.'

Vic added, 'They're gonna have him any time now.'

At that very moment, a bread roll flew past his right ear. He turned and picked it up, and ever the funny man said, 'Four more of these and two fish, I could feed you all again.' As he began to laugh at his own little funny, a barrage of bread buns, baps and rolls peppered his area of the stage. 'Aw, fuck it,' was all he said and left the stage to great roars of delight from the audience.

The entertainments secretary of the club was now on stage berating the section of the crowed that had seemed to lead the onslaught. Accusing them of bringing the club into disrepute, making it difficult to book acts in the future. Nobody was listening.

Throughout the evening I'd kept an eye on Dutch to ensure he was faring OK. He had not consumed much of his meal and was still only on his second drink while the rest of us were on our seventh pint, plus a liberal amount of whisky. In fairness, he had had a drop of the hard stuff himself. He had laughed along with all the shenanigans that had been displayed in abundance this evening and did seem to be enjoying it all.

At just after 10 o'clock, the group were back on stage, all our females were on the dance floor, Ron had gone to get another round of drinks. Dutch announced he was off to the toilet. As I sat watching the dancers, Barbara suddenly broke away and went out towards the toilet area. A minute or so later, she came back into the room and came around behind me; stooping down, she whispered, 'We're going now.' She added, 'He wants to leave quietly,' saying if it was realised that he was going, he'd be pressurised to stay or have another drink. 'Rather than that, he asked me to say he'll be in touch.'

'OK, I understand,' was all I said. Wondering when his next appearance at the club might be.

The evening carried on in much the same mode, noisy, boisterous and a little bit wild. For the most part, it was all good-humoured fun. Of our party, Dennis had behaved impeccably, with June keeping an ever-watchful eye on him. He was not totally exonerated of the Blackpool saga. Vic spent a good deal of the evening chasing after various committee members, expressing his opinion that the comedian should not be paid for what he described as an abomination of an act.

Ron, with the drink beginning to get the better of him, was in the midst of a bevy of young things, strutting his stuff like he belonged there. Eileen suddenly realised what was going on, strutted her stuff into the middle of the floor. Grabbed Ron by his shirt front and dragged him back to his seat. Saying, 'You're out with me, so you dance with me. You aren't in Blackpool.' She then added, 'You pile into these situations when I'm here, I can only imagine what you're like when on your own.'

Ron's take on the situation was, 'It's only a bit of fun, I ain't doing anything wrong. Nothing was said last year when I danced with Karen.' This was said with a look of triumph and a big smirk.

Eileen responded with, 'Well, there I could see your imagination was so much greater than your ability, so no problem.' The ladies of our group greeted this comment with loud cheers and laughter. Even we blokes were impressed by her response. (I certainly was.)

With the drink slowly dulling my senses, the evening came to a close when Doreen informed me our taxi had arrived. I don't recall much of the journey home, apart from the constant chatter of the dear beloved. What she was on about, I've no idea.

Saturday morning, I arrived at work somewhat after 9 o'clock. I was greeted by Mick saying, 'Oh, so you've made it then.'

'Only in body, not in mind or spirit,' I replied.

Monday 22nd Nov.

After Friday night's exploits, the weekend work had been accomplished mainly due to the fortitude displayed by Mick. I did thank him. I also let him know I was very grateful; he had recognised the situation and got on with things without referring to me or my state of health. 'It's what I'm here for, ain't it?' was his nonchalant reply.

'Nevertheless, it was a job well done. I'll see that the manager is made aware of the fact, OK.'

During our afternoon tea break, Sammie from the garage office popped into our compound and informed me Mr Williamson requested that I meet with him tomorrow at 11 o'clock to discuss his report to the board early next month.

At home that evening, Doreen asked if I had had any contact with Dutch since Friday. When I said I hadn't, she said she thought I should call him or Barbara. I was a bit reluctant to make contact. 'I might get news I don't want to hear.'

'What makes you think that?'

'Well, how do you think he looked the other night?'

'Yes, one or two passed remarks about him. But that should not stop you checking to see if he is alright.'

'Yes, I know, but couldn't you call Barbara, just for a chat.'

'Ooh, you really are pathetic. I can't imagine how you get on at work.'

'It amazes me as well,' I replied.

Half an hour or so later, I was writing up some notes ready for my meeting with the manager. Doreen came in and informed me she had been on the phone with Barbara. They had really enjoyed Friday evening and had had a good laugh, but Dutch didn't want to hang around very long as he found it all a bit tiring owing to the medication he was on. She went on to say he had struggled with things quite a lot over the weekend and felt Friday evening had taken more out of him than he had expected. But for all that, he was still glad he had gone along.

Barbara had said they hoped his treatment would start to show some positive progress during the next week or so. I asked, 'Did she say whether he is to start chemotherapy or anything?'

'Chemotherapy!! Why would he have chemotherapy?' Doreen bellowed out, 'What do you know that you haven't told me?'

Oh fuck, what have I said? was my immediate thought. I responded with, 'No, nothing, I just thought they may have changed his medication, that's all.'

'You think he's got cancer, don't you?' she said. Then went on, 'I've been thinking that for some time now.'

I said, 'Well, the fact is we don't really know anything, do we, so let's keep all these thoughts to ourselves, shall we, and wait for more definite notification of the situation.'

Next morning, I had my meeting with the manager. I had produced a report on the asbestos, its whereabouts and general condition. Added into the report, I made comments regarding the outcome of the summer maintenance programme, the general state of all the buildings, floors, pit areas, lighting and heating, in fact all aspects of the garage. I also gave a report on the progress of Michael Reynolds and how successful he had proved to be. Stating I still had some reservations regarding our ability to cope with any construction projects that may crop up.

My main concern was what to say about Dutch. Should I inform the manager of his asbestos-related problem or not say anything. I decided to keep it to myself and say nothing. Knowing that when it finally did come out, the manager would believe I had indeed let him down.

The manager spent quite a while reading the report, then said, 'Right, thank you, that says just about everything I need.' He then informed me he had also asked the traffic superintendent for a report on all aspects and proposals for the future requirements and was to have a meeting with him later on in the day.

He then went on to say what he intended to put to the board regarding me and my role in the business. First, he would recommend removal of all asbestos as soon as possible, as he feels that is a very urgent requirement. He would ask for funding to reposition or at least upgrade the steam cleaning facility. He also would like to see the bus wash replaced or modified.

He then said, 'Now we come to you.'

'Me?' I said. What do you mean me?'

'I am going to suggest that you be made assistant manager with a view to training you up to take over when I retire. This will allow Mick to carry on in your role with Dutch if he is able to return; if not, we would be able to recruit a buildings trade person.'

I wasn't quite sure what to say. My thoughts were, *I waste my time talking to this bloke. I'm sure he doesn't hear a fucking word I say.* What I did say was, 'OK, let's see what happens. By the way, when exactly is your meeting with the board?'

'Next week on Thursday, which is the 2nd of December, I believe.'

'Is that it, can I take my leave now?' was my parting shot as I removed myself from his office without receiving a reply.

He was busy scribbling away making notes, actually on the bottom of my report.

While walking back to our workshop, my mind was racing. My statement, 'let's see what happens,' was received by him as acceptance of my agreement to go along with his plan of promoting me to assistant manager.

For the rest of the day, my mind was preoccupied by thoughts of my meeting with the manager. *Why didn't I object to his plans regarding me? I can't let Mick know what his plans are, he'll take it as confirmation of his permanent position in our section. What would I say to Dutch? Would I lose money?*

By the end of the day, I had decided the best course of action would be to arrange to see the manager tomorrow and tell him I'm too old to start a new career and that he needs to come up with a different plan.

At home that evening, I spoke with Doreen about my day and in particular my meeting with the manager. When I informed her of his intention of pushing for me to become assistant manager, she was overjoyed, saying, 'It's about time your efforts for that company were recognised, maybe now you will be able to have more time off.'

I said, 'Hold on a bit. I'm too old to take on new responsibilities like that, so I'm going to see him tomorrow and tell him to find someone else.'

'You'll do no such thing; it's the best thing that could have happened. If you think you're too old to manage people, you're not, but you are getting too old to work all the hours you do, and all the lifting and the climbing. So, you just have a rethink, right.' At that, she sat back and just stared at me as if daring me to challenge her opinion.

I just said, 'Yes, it is something to think about, I suppose.'

I retreated behind a newspaper. I sat there pretending to read, realising how right she was, and in so many ways.

The garage manager was not sought or spoken to the next day, nor at any time during the rest of the week. The acceptance of the idea of being pushed into management was constantly on my mind, I started to find the prospect quite appealing. So much so that by the end of the week, I had become extremely keen on the idea.

On Thursday evening, Doreen informed me she had had a call from Barbara. Dutch had been put on a course of chemotherapy. He had apparently started it on Tuesday. When asked what his problems were that deemed chemotherapy necessary, Barbara had responded by saying, 'The doctor had said it was a stubborn little growth that they were finding difficult to subdue.'

I said, 'What the fuck's that supposed to mean?'

To which she answered, 'Do you have to use that sort of language?'

I said, 'Well, it sounds like to me they are just being fobbed off.'

Friday evening, as we were preparing for our evening out, Doreen let me know that she and Elizabeth were going to Oxford tomorrow, and with April were spending the rest of the weekend Christmas shopping. 'Oh, great, and who's going to tend to my needs?' I enquired. 'You,' was the sharp reply.

A full team were at the club, apart from Barbara and Dutch. It was all relaxed and very normal until Doreen mentioned chemotherapy. The reaction of Chris was explosive. 'Chemo!' she practically screamed, 'is it cancer, is that what he's got? How come it's took till now to find out. Somebody should be charged with neglect.'

This retort seemed to encourage the other females of the group to spout off similar tirades of abuse against the medical profession and their failure of Dutch.

We blokes just looked on with some disbelief at the emotion that was being displayed. It was Vic who bravely interrupted their squalling by saying, 'Excuse me, but don't you think you're getting a bit carried away? They have now identified his problem; he's having the best of care. Let's leave the dramatics till we have something to be dramatic about.'

'You don't have any feelings for others, do you? None of you do, do you? You're all the same, men.' This was June letting off at us blokes.

Ron said, 'Shall we retire to the snooker room?' With that, we departed.

'What was all that about?' asked Dennis.

'Fucked if I know, let's play,' was my input.

On the way home, I asked Doreen what she thought about the response of Chris and for that matter the others, on the news of Dutch. She said she was very surprised by the reaction of them all, especially after they had seen Dutch on Friday and knew how ill he was. But it seemed to be a genuine shock when they heard 'chemo' closely followed by 'cancer'. So she supposed it was understandable. I said, 'Yes, maybe.'

Next morning, Doreen along with Elizabeth took off for their weekend shopping. I went to work. I had decided, owing to the fact that I was on my own all weekend, to commit myself to a good number of hours at work. I had discussed with the manager my situation, and we had agreed a schedule to suit that situation. Mick could only commit to four hours on Saturday as he had football duties to perform.

Halfway through the morning, I retired to the canteen for breakfast, thinking, *The only way I'm going to get fed this weekend is by eating out. So, breakfast now, and in the evening, a meal at the Boat.*

We worked hard all morning (apart from breakfast that is), Mick left at midday. I carried on into the afternoon. I became quite involved in what I was doing, so much so that by the time I looked around, thinking I'd have a cuppa, I realised it was pitch black outside. When I checked the time, it was quarter to six.

By the time I had put all the equipment away and cleaned myself up, closed up the shop and arrived at the Boat it was well turned seven. I ordered a pint and chose a meal from the menu. My choice was steak (medium rare) with mixed seasonal veg.

After my meal, I ordered another pint and sat in the lounge bar reading the *Sporting Star* that had been on the bar, and although it was still only early evening, I suddenly felt extremely fatigued. I was just thinking of calling it a night. Who should walk in but Eileen and Ron. 'I wasn't expecting you to be in here,' said Eileen.

Ron said, 'What are you drinking?'

'No,' I said, 'I'm still on my way home from work.'

258

A couple of pints or so later I said, 'That's it, I'm off home.'

Ron said, 'OK, we're moving on to the club anyway.'

I took the *Sporting Star* with me. At home, I sat with a cup of tea, reading. When I woke up, it was two thirty. I went to bed.

Sunday morning found me a little bit late at work, alone again. Mick had apparently phoned in early to say he had been injured playing football yesterday and needed a couple of days off. It was no problem for me; I was more than capable of completing what work remained of our weekend schedule.

My first task was to seek out Colin Edwards, a first-class mechanic, and arrange with him to give my car a service. This was a regular ploy while working on Sundays, and done with stealth, and certainly without the knowledge of any of the management.

I didn't have a breakfast; I worked straight through till lunchtime and retired to the canteen to have a cooked Sunday roast. I finished off with a cup of tea and a read of a Sunday paper.

As I strolled back to our shop, I was thinking *I'd better check on my car soon. I've only another hour or so to complete the weekend's work. Complete the paperwork, then home to await the arrival of my beloved wife and have my ears assaulted by tales of exciting shopping. Oh, what a wonderful life I lead.*

As I entered our workshop, someone was messing around with our personal lockers. I called out, 'What the fuck do you think you're doing?'

The figure let out a startled cry and swung round. 'Fucking hell, you gave me a fright,' said Dutch. From the back, I had not realised it was him. He did not look good.

'What's all this then?' I asked.

His reply was, 'Where is your car?'

'Colin Edwards is doing a service on it.'

'Oh yes, of course,' was his deep in thought comment.

'So, I'll ask again. What's all this, after a job or what?'

'No, I didn't think anyone was here. I wondered why the door was not locked,' he said once again in a deep in thought kind of way.

'Can I get you a cuppa or anything?' I asked.

'No, I'm off now,' he replied.

259

'Have you got everything you came for? Is there anything I can get for you? Have you driven here on your own?' I asked all these questions and only received a shake of the head in reply. He seemed very preoccupied.

'You worked very late yesterday, didn't you? Major problem or what?'

'Why? Were you here yesterday as well?'

'We only passed by.'

'We? Is Barbara with you?'

'Yes, but don't let her know you're here, I told her you were away today. That's the reason I couldn't ask you to do what I needed to get done.'

'And what did you need to get done?' I asked.

'Well, the way I feel now, I'm not sure how long, if at all, before I'll be back, so I needed to sort out a few things.'

'Chemo not going well?' I asked.

'No,' was his curt reply.

After he'd gone, I was left wondering what it had all been about. He and, for that matter, Barbara had obviously been around the depot a number of times over the weekend. He had been quite alarmed at being discovered in the shop and had been very pensive during our little conflab.

He was messing around his spare locker, it's something to do with that. He's been very mysterious about that locker and its contents ever since he acquired it. That was about the time Karen left. Fuck me, he didn't put her in there, did he? was a thought that passed through my mind. *It was big enough to accommodate her body, but no, there would be a very strong smell by now. Anyhow I saw her letter saying she had gone away.*

I completed the assigned work and went home. Doreen and Elizabeth arrived home a lot earlier than anticipated. Elizabeth well pissed off with having to ferry them around all weekend, plus her mother's constant bleating about anything and everything, said, 'That's it, I'm not stopping. I'm off home. I've got work tomorrow.'

Doreen asked, 'Did you have a good weekend?'

'It was fine,' I replied and added, 'Welcome back.' She immediately went into a long-drawn-out yarn about their expedition. I watched the television, hardly hearing a word.

Monday 29th Nov.

Mick called me around mid-morning, informing me he had twisted his ankle and slightly strained his ligament. He said he would not be playing football again till into the New Year but felt he would be OK for work by Wednesday. I let him know it was alright, but I didn't want him back if he wasn't ready. I didn't want him hobbling about being a danger to himself or anyone else for that matter.

I didn't discuss the situation with the manager. In fact, I didn't discuss anything with the manager, he wasn't seeing anyone for a couple of days, he was totally wrapped up in producing his report to the board of directors.

Mick returned on Wednesday. He still carried a slight limp but seemed OK for work.

That same evening at home, Doreen informed me Barbara had been in touch. Telling her she was very worried about Dutch. The chemotherapy treatment was distressing him a great deal. He was hurting all over, in practically every joint, and his breathing was much laboured. 'I know, I saw him on Sunday—'

'You never said,' she interrupted.

'No, I didn't,' I replied and carried on. 'Although he didn't complain about any discomfort, he did look extremely fragile. He, for the first time, spoke about how long it was going to be before he would be able to resume work, he also added *if ever.*'

'What did he mean by that?' she asked.

'I don't know. He seemed to think there were things that needed finalising. What those things were, he never said. In fact, the whole episode of Sunday was strange, with no real explanation.'

The next morning, the day of the manager's meeting with the board, I didn't expect to see him around. What I did wonder was what time he would be back. I contacted Sammie and asked what she knew of his intended schedule. She informed me his meeting was to start around 11 o'clock, it was intended to include lunch and carry on into the afternoon; she said he was not expected back on site today.

With the situation as it was, I said, 'OK, I'll just carry on, let me know if any problems arise and I'll speak with him tomorrow.'

When I arrived home that evening, Doreen was in a high of state anxiety. She greeted me with, 'What happened then, have you got the job?'

'Whoa, what happened to "good evening, oh husband of mine"?' I managed to get in.

'Never mind all your witticisms, I've been sat here all afternoon waiting for a phone call from you.'

'Well, there is no news, the manager has not returned from his meeting. So, nothing.'

On Friday morning I was told the manager would not be seeing anyone today; he intended to use the day and the weekend to contemplate the issues and information coming from the meeting with the directors yesterday.

I spent a lot of the day trying to figure out what the manager's dilemma was and how it might affect my future. Finally, I thought, *Fuck it, it's Friday. I'll arrange the weekend work schedule and see the manager sometime next week when, or if he sees fit.*

From the moment I walked through the door at home till we arrived at the club, Doreen had been constantly going on asking question after question regarding the situation with the manager and my position. To which I could only reply, *'I don't know.'* As we pulled onto the club car park, I finally said, 'For fuck's sake, give it a rest, we'll know all there is to know next week, so no more, OK.'

'That's your answer to every problem, bad language,' she stated.

In the club, Vic got the drinks in. As we said all our hellos and how are you all, Doreen's demeanour prompted a response from Ron saying, 'Do I detect an atmosphere?'

'Er, no,' I replied.

'Yes,' was the input from Doreen, 'it's him and his big gob again.'

'Not really the case,' I managed to get in before she could say anything more. I went on to say, 'We were just debating Dutch and what if anything we could or should do for him.'

This prompted a long discussion on Dutch, his illness, and what if anything could be done for them. During this discussion, I realised my wife and her friends were off on another jaunt tomorrow to Chester for more Christmas shopping. (I was wondering if she had any intention of telling me.) The information was only disclosed when Chris let it be known she had asked Barbara if she wished to be included. She had apparently declined the offer as she didn't think Dutch could cope with a full day on his own.

Dennis and June had turned up while the discussion had been in progress, us blokes decided it was time to get some snooker practice in, but before we departed, Chris had let it be known, her and Vic were going on a cruise over the Christmas period. This news was greeted with a lot of excitement by all the ladies, who very quickly entered into a tighter huddle to discuss the whys and wherefores of this little expedition. We lads took our leave.

The tables were all fully booked so we played darts.

On the journey home, Doreen said, 'What do you think about Vic and Chris going on that cruise?'

I said, 'It's great, very nice, I think they will enjoy it.'

'Why don't we ever do things like that?'

'Well, one of the reasons is, I've got a wife who wishes to travel all over the country every weekend shopping. Don't you think there are enough shops around our area without travelling all over the cosmos in search of places to spend money?'

'They are all going,' she replied.

'I don't think any of them were in Oxford and surrounding areas last week, were they?'

'That was different,' was her closing statement.

'Anyway, while we're on the subject, what do you want from me for Christmas?' I politely asked.

'Nothing,' was her immediate sullen reply.

Saturday was to be a relatively easy morning; without the manager's input, I had only arranged the cleaning and the shake down of the extractor unit in the brake-shoe shop. This work requires special safety clothing to be worn. We wear disposable overalls, safety goggles, and double filter face masks, owing to the fact there is a lot of potentially dangerous dust around this apparatus.

It was just after 12.30 when we had completed the task in hand and disposed of all the hazardous waste into the correct waste bins. Mick was keen to be on his way. Although not playing, he was very committed to the team and needed to show his support, so he left as soon as he could get his coat on.

I completed the necessary paperwork, signed off the job sheets and called it a day as well. I decided (owing to the fact that Doreen was gadding off shopping) to pop into the club and have a pint.

In the bar were the usual crew of bowlers, Brian, Kevin, Don, Will and Paul. I don't think they're ever not in.

But I digress, I acquired a drink and went and sat with them. After the usual greetings and some small talk, the conversation moved onto Dutch. I think it was Don who first mentioned him, asking how he was as he didn't look very good at the sports presentation do. When I said he wasn't faring very well with the chemotherapy treatment, the reaction was quite surprising. I then realised they would not have known just how serious his problem was.

'What sort of cancer has he got?' Brian almost demanded to know.

'The way it was told to me was that it was a stubborn little growth at the top of his right lung,' I replied.

At this point we were joined by PK. On receiving the news of Dutch, he said, 'I thought as much when I saw him at the do the other night.'

The discussion then went the way of most discussions in bars all over the world. What the best treatment 'would be' or 'should be' as they all turned into world-leading experts on cancer. Very soon, Dutch and his very real problem subsided, and the normal piss-taking of every comment made by anyone and everyone took over.

As the general chinwag continued, who should walk in? None other than Jumbo Jennings. Well, I say walk in, he actually was still in a wheelchair. 'Blimey, Jumbo,' I said, 'you still riding about in that?'

'Shut it, twat, this thing ain't over, not by a long way,' he spat out with a lot of venom at me.

'Tell him, Chairman, if he speaks to me like that again, you'll ban him. Either that or I'll break his other leg.'

This statement I directed at the assembled gang. They all roared their appreciation of my comment. As the laughter continued, PK jumped in and said, 'Pack it in, the pair of you, or you will both be banned, possibly forever.'

Jumbo, still glaring at me, went to the other side of the room.

Me, I just laughed along with the rest of the guys. Deep down, I was thinking, *He is going to keep on making trouble or even doing some physical harm towards me.*

A DUTCH MASTER PART THREE

Monday 6th December

Neither Mick nor I worked on Sunday. I didn't receive any calls, so assumed everything was in order. First thing this morning, it all seemed to be just that. Round about 9.30, things suddenly changed. First a call to inform us, the lights in 3 Bay had all gone out, quickly followed by a second call saying the compressor in the tin smiths had failed, then immediately a call telling us a brush shaft on the bus wash was badly bent, putting it out of action.

OK, I then suggested to Mick that he should look at the lighting problem and do a quick fix on that. I, in the meantime, would check on the bent shaft to see what could be done. After a quick check, I realised it would have to be changed. At this point, Sammie informed me the manager wanted to see me. I told her, 'I can't see him just yet as we have a number of problems going on around the garage.'

Mick returned after a short while, saying he had managed to disconnect an offending light fitting and switched the rest on, all OK. I said, 'Right, get the brushes off the shaft, fit them to a spare shaft that we have got, it's along the wall by our workshop, while I go and check on the compressor.' I found that the starter had failed and required changing.

It was over an hour before I got back to Mick; he had roped in a couple of the cleaners to assist him. Having removed and refitted the brushes, he was now attempting to remove the offending shaft.

I informed him I had to go and see the manager; he should carry on as he was doing, if he hit any problems, he should let me know.

On my way to the manager's office, Sammie accosted me and said, 'He's not in a very good mood.'

I knocked and waited; it was a good few seconds before he called, 'Come in.' When I entered, he exploded. 'Who do you think you are?' he practically screamed at me. I just stood there, mouth open with a look of astonishment on my face. 'I am the manager here. When I request someone to attend me in my office, I do not expect to be told he's too busy.'

'I'm really sorry, boss, it wasn't like that at all. The garage was practically at a standstill, and I thought it was better to get things sorted before coming here to have a chat with you.'

'Oh, you thought, did you? If you had thought at all, you should have thought, "I'll go and tell the manager what is happening and make arrangements with him", which would have only taken a few minutes. No major hold-up to the garage repairs. Leaving me to be getting on with something useful.'

'Yes, boss, I am really sorry. I'll make sure nothing like this happens again,' I bumbled out.

'I don't suppose it will,' he replied, looking down at the paper in front of him.

When he looked up, he said, 'Right, the director's report. First, a contractor will be appointed to remove all asbestos; they are to do an investigation around all our buildings, identifying and removing all found areas of offending material. I received a severe reprimand for not having this accomplished before now. The contract has already been issued; the contractor will be on site today. You will liaise with them. Right?

'Second, a replacement for me will not be sought from within the company. It will be advertised nationwide, seeking a university graduate with a degree.'

'When is this going to happen?' I asked.

'Now,' was his curt reply.

'Bloody hell, that's a bit rushed, ain't it, where does it leave you?' I hurriedly asked.

'I'm to be pensioned off at the end of the financial year.'

We just sat there for what seemed an age. He suddenly said, 'It was indicated that you could still apply if you were still interested.'

'Oh, thanks,' I said. I then asked, 'Was any of this expected?'

'No,' he replied, 'but I suppose I should have realised it was an option.'

'How do you feel now you've had time to digest the situation?' I enquired.

'Still a bit numb,' he said, looking completely washed out.

'I'll go and lookout for these contractors then, OK?'

He dismissed me with a wave of his hand, which seemed to say *yes, fuck off.*

I spent the rest of the day in a bit of a haze. The thoughts running through my head were, *What will Doreen have to say about it all? Quite a lot, no doubt. This degree-educated person will have very different ideas of how things are done. Will I get along with him, or even her? Oh fuck, please.*

I was concerned about what, if anything, I should say to Mick. What would Dutch think or have to say about it all?

On arriving home, all was peaceful and serene. Suddenly Doreen asked, 'Have you had a word with Mr Williamson?'

'Yes,' was my only comment.

'Well?'

'Well, what?'

'What's he had to say?'

'Not a lot; the board rejected every one of his ideas. Not only that, they are making him redundant as of next March.'

'So, you get the job.'

'No, I might be redundant with him.'

'*What!*' she exclaimed, 'they can't do that.'

I took quite some time going through what I'd been told and tried my best to explain what it all meant. Well, as much as I understood the situation. 'So, you can still get the manager's job then,' was her take on what had been said.

'No, not really. I'm too old and not qualified for what they are looking for.'

'You said they had asked you to apply for the post.'

'Once again, NO. They let it be known that I was free to apply if I considered I would be able to fill the criteria of the advert. Which I can't, end of.'

She sat very quietly for a long time. Then said, 'But you will put in an application, won't you? Just in case, you never know. If you don't, you might always regret it.' I didn't reply, she seemed more down with the situation than the manager was.

Throughout the next few days, she was preoccupied with the manager's role. She constantly came out with sayings like, 'it's not right', 'they can't do this sort of thing', 'surely there is something you can do?' All of which prompted a 'hmm' from me as a reply.

By Thursday evening, fed up with her going on, I said, 'I'm going to call Dutch and put him in the picture.'

'Oh, you can't do that,' she bleated out.

'What do you mean, can't?' I asked.

'I forgot to say, I had a phone call from Barbara this afternoon. Dutch has had some sort of relapse and has gone back into hospital. He apparently was having great difficulty in breathing.'

'Oh, dear me, when was this?'

'She phoned around mid-afternoon, about 3 o'clock. She had called an ambulance this morning because he was having so much trouble with his breathing.'

'Bloody hell, I'd better give her a call,' I said.

'Don't do that. Barbara said she would ring us as soon as she knew what was happening.'

'OK, I suppose I'd better leave it till she gets in contact with us.'

Next day, I was regularly bothered in my mind as to what was happening to Dutch. I didn't speak to or even see the manager at any time during the week. I told Mick only that the manager thought there were going to be major changes.

It was getting on for 4 o'clock, we were thinking about wrapping things up for the day. I received a call over the intercom to attend the garage office. It was a phone call from Doreen to say Barbara had called to say Dutch had a collapsed lung. I said, 'Alright, leave it there, I'll speak to you when I get home.'

Upon arriving home, I found Doreen in a high state of anxiety, fretting about Dutch and his predicament. I said, 'Whoa, ease up a bit, he's in hospital. They know all about collapsed lungs, they are more than capable of re-inflating a lung. I would think they do it several times a week, so stop worrying.'

'Barbara sounded so worried though, I think we should do something.'

'There's not a lot we can do, is there? All I can do is to phone her and have a reassuring little chat.' When I called, there was no answer, she was still probably at the hospital. I decided not to call on her mobile phone. I did say I would try again later.

After I'd bathed and dressed, ready for a night out, I did indeed call Barbara again. This time she did answer. I said, 'What does he think he's doing now?'

She gave a little nervous laugh and said, 'Oh, we were very frightened when it happened, I think Dutch thought it was the end. We have been comforted by the hospital and their reaction to his situation. What they intend to do is suspend his chemo treatment for a while and then hopefully inflate his lung.'

'Good,' I said, 'you've got to have a bit of faith in the doctors, they do this sort of thing day in, day out. I think by the end of the weekend, you'll be all smiles again.'

I then asked if she would fancy going out to the club with Doreen and myself. She declined the offer on the grounds she was pretty well exhausted by the past few days.

At the club, all the talk was of Dutch and his ongoing problems. The debate ranged from how long before he recovers to will he be able to play bowls next season, when will he be able to work, even to will he survive.

Eileen put forward a suggestion that the club should do something to help Barbara and Dutch. 'Like what?' asked Chris.

'Well, raise some money,' said Eileen. 'With a collection or a raffle.' At that, Eileen, Chris and June all went over to PK to put him in the picture and inform him of their thoughts.

Ron said, 'Are we going to play tonight or what?' It was agreed all round that we should. Dennis went to get a round of drinks in, Ron and Vic went to secure a table. Leaving Doreen and myself.

'Don't think you're going anywhere till they get back,' was her very adamant statement.

'I'm playing snooker in there. Why don't you go over to them if you don't want to be on your own?'

'No, I'm not in favour of what they're proposing, I think it will only embarrass them.'

'Yes, I think you are probably right.' I went to the games room.

The game was set up, and I'd played my shot, a little bit of conscience must have hit me because I went and had a peek through the door to see if Doreen was OK on her own. Well, fuck me, she was sitting chatting with none other than Jumbo fucking Jennings. I carried on watching just to make sure he wasn't being aggressive or belligerent in any way. They actually looked quite amiable. At that, I was called back to the table for my shot.

I hadn't made any comment on the little incident, and no one else did throughout the rest of the evening.

On the way home, I casually asked, 'What did Jumbo have to say for himself?'

'Oh, did you see that?'

'Yes, I did. I took a look to make sure you were alright on your own and was very surprised. What did he have to say?'

'Oh, nothing much. He only said his animosity towards you didn't mean he felt any bitterness towards me. In fact, he thought I was a very nice and pleasant person. He said he couldn't understand why I was with you.'

I said, 'Jumbo knows words like animosity? Kin hell,' I laughed.

The weekend work, once again sorted without any input from the manager, was not too hectic. Both Mick and I cruised through the whole weekend without incident. My overriding thoughts were of Jumbo fucking Jennings having the hots for my missus. That will be the butt of a few tales to be told over the next weeks.

When I arrived home, mid to late afternoon, Doreen was sat looking very pensive. 'You OK?' I inquired.

'I'm not too sure,' she replied.

'Why what's happened?'

'Barbara's phoned saying they have had a go at inflating his lung but had limited success.'

'What's that supposed to mean?' I asked.

'Well, they weren't totally happy with the result. He is to rest for a while, they will try again later, possibly tomorrow.'

'Shit, that don't sound good, does it?'

Monday 13th December

Around mid-morning I was summoned to the manager's office. I walked in and said, 'Morning, boss,' and sat on the opposite side of his desk, facing him. He just sat for what seemed like a long time to me. I sat there with what I felt was a neutral look on my face.

He suddenly said, 'I want to apologise for what happened last week. I had been taken by complete surprise at the directors meeting. So much so that I think I was probably in shock. Since then, I've given it a lot of thought. I'm quite annoyed with myself for not seeing this coming. I should have realised this was one of the options. Now, after fretting over the situation for a number of days, my wife and I have come to accept the fact that I am to retire. I will not be making any more major decisions. Apart from seeing through the removal of asbestos. By the way, how is that going?'

'Quite well by all appearances, they seem to be very professional, closing off areas, using a lot of safety equipment, and getting on with the job without any hassle.'

Good,' said the manager. He went on to say, his priorities now were to secure an acceptable payoff and plan his retirement. To help him plan this retirement, he would be taking some of his outstanding holidays that were due to him. So as from this coming weekend he would be on holiday till Tuesday 4th January. 'Do you think you'll be able to cope while I'm away?' he asked.

'Well, yes, boss, unless there is a major catastrophe that requires big expenditure, I'm sure we'll cope.'

'If anything like that happens, I'm sure a board member will be on hand to facilitate all requirements.'

I noted he never put himself forward, a board member, yes, but not himself. Not only that, but he had started to use university graduate speak (facilitate). Bloody hell, this is the future.

'Are you going to apply for this position?' he suddenly asked.

'Not much point,' I replied.

'Are you going to be agreeable to a younger, less knowledgeable person taking over?' he ventured.

'That's progress for you,' was my response.

'I'll speak with you towards the weekend before I leave. Is everything covered for the Christmas period?' he prompted.

'Yes, I think we'll operate the same as every other Christmas,' I replied. Thinking, *As if you give a flying fuck.*

'Good,' was his actual response.

When I left, I had the distinct feeling that he indeed did not give a flying fuck. In his head, and heart for that matter, he had already retired.

At home that evening, Doreen informed me she had spoken with Barbara. The news was not totally good. The hospital had inflated the damaged lung for Dutch but were unsure it would hold. He had been put on a support ventilator to assist his breathing. Hopefully, in a couple of days, he should be able to cope without it.

Next day, things at work seemed to just drift along. I heard nothing from the manager, which made me feel a little bit lonely if I'm honest. On the realisation of this, I was a bit surprised. Mick just coasted through the days, seemingly unaware of any change in procedure. To be honest, his mind is totally occupied with thoughts of his young lady friend. He had confided in me that he was contemplating presenting said lady friend with an engagement ring at Christmas and asked what I thought.

When I enquired, did it matter what I thought? He said, 'Well, yes, I'm not sure whether it's too soon or not. So yes, I would value your opinion very much.'

'If you're so unsure, don't do it, it is too soon. Why don't you buy her an eternity ring instead?'

'*Yes! That's it,*' he practically shouted. 'How come you and Dutch know all the answers?' he asked, standing there with a very big smile on his face.

I didn't answer that little enquiry. I just thought, *if only.*

At home that evening, Doreen had once again been in contact with Barbara, no real change in the situation. Doreen's concerns over Barbara's predicament had not abated.

By Wednesday evening, with the situation unchanged, I rang Barbara and said I would go and visit Dutch in hospital. She got quite agitated at this suggestion, saying, 'He doesn't want anyone to see him in his present state.'

I said, 'OK, I understand what you're saying,' which seemed to pacify her.

After my phone chat with Barbara, Doreen pestered me for details of our conversation. Upon gaining the knowledge I had suggested going to visit him and being requested not to, she said, 'Do you think she is just trying to protect him?'

'No, knowing Dutch like I do, I can well imagine him telling her to keep people away. I think if it were me, I'd do exactly the same.'

Nevertheless, after work on Thursday, I went immediately to the hospital. Although afternoon visiting had finished and evening visiting was yet to start, I, after giving a bit of a sob story regarding commitment to work, was allowed onto the ward.

I'm not sure what I was expecting to see, or in this case, nearly not see. I had almost walked past him when I heard a rasping voice say, 'What are you doing here?' with a gasp for air after each and every utterance. I just stood there and looked, hardly believing what was before me.

'I've come to see you,' I managed to splutter out, trying to look calm and unflustered. 'You seem better than I expected,' I lied. Two-thirds of his hair had gone, his face appeared to be half the size it had previously been. The way he was slumped into his chair made him look quite small and very fragile.

'Same old bullshitter,' he rasped, 'nothing changes with you, does it?'

'Nor with you and your swift retorts,' I countered. 'Anyway, it's good to find you in such good spirits.'

'Yeah,' he said, 'but it's all a bit of a show. Truth is I feel absolutely knackered.'

'Yeah, well, sit back and just relax. I'll update you on things in the outside world.' I gave him quick rundown of things at work.

Missing out the manager's debacle and the asbestos clear-up. He was very amused to hear of Mick's Christmas plans for his lady friend. When I spoke about Jumbo's attempted wooing of Doreen, he almost suffered a seizure for lack of breath while trying to laugh.

I had to assist him in applying his oxygen mask. After a few minutes, he was sufficiently recovered to say, 'It will be the death of me if you don't stop telling me tales of this sort.'

I said, 'Yeah, I can see that now, sorry. Anyhow that's it for my news, now how about you, what are their plans for you?'

He was finding it a real struggle to converse with me. He managed to get out the fact that the consultant was now talking about a possible lung transplant. If and when, no one was very sure.

I, realising he was extremely fatigued by my visit, wished him well and said I would look in on him in a few days' time. I shook his oh so very limp hand and said goodbye. The main thought occupying my mind was, *Will he still be with us in a few days' time?* I had to admonish myself for that thought, thinking, *Of course he'll be here, he's Dutch; big, brash, tough Dutch.*

I hadn't told Doreen of my intention to visit the hospital, consequently she didn't ask why I'd arrived home at that particular time. She is quite aware of my irregular hours at work. During the evening, she suddenly said, 'You're very quiet tonight, anything happened?'

'I've been to the hospital to see Dutch.'

'Why didn't you say? I would've liked to go.'

'That's why I didn't say anything. He doesn't want any visitors.'

'Then why did you go?'

'Because I needed to.'

'Well, how was he?' she asked in an almost aggressive fashion.

'Not good,' I responded, 'I had to assist him with his oxygen mask while I was there.'

'Why, what happened?'

'He got very short of breath, and I was on hand, so I assisted, that's all.' I then said, 'Don't let on tomorrow night that I went to

275

see him. It will only encourage them to believe that it is OK for them all to make a visit.'

At work on Friday, thoughts of Dutch and his plight were constantly on my mind. I didn't refer to my hospital visit to Mick or anyone else for that matter.

My expectation of being summoned to the manager's office never materialised. What did materialise was a note from him handed to me by Sammie. The note stated he was sorry not to have had time to chat with me, but you know how things get, busy, busy, busy. He had gone on to say if any major problems arose to call the Director of Engineering Mr George Kane. Added to this was a telephone number on which the director could be contacted.

It ended with, *Wishing you and yours a Happy Christmas and a prosperous New Year.*

PS. Which is more than I can hope for myself.

Jesus. This ain't on. He may be put out somewhat, but he can't just leave and expect me to take up the reins. I can imagine the director's response if I call him. He'd sack me for incompetence and the boss for dereliction of duty. As that's what I consider his reaction is.

Back in our shop, Mick was saying he didn't want to stay late tomorrow as he and Jenny were going Christmas shopping. 'Yeah, I'm also only planning an easy weekend.' Adding, 'The manager hasn't left any particular instructions, so we'll do the small tools and oil changes on a couple of compressors. Then call it a day, right.'

As we busied ourselves preparing for the evening out, Doreen suddenly produced a sizable package to take with us to the club. 'What's all that?' I exclaimed.

'I need to hand out our Christmas cards and presents, that's all.'

That evening at the club, a full team had assembled. The main topic of conversation was naturally Dutch. Eileen had been in touch with Barbara and gave a word-for-word account of their conversation. Then June gives a narrative of her telephone chat with Barbara that was not dissimilar to Eileen's. This was closely followed by Chris, who was also very eager to add her knowledge of Dutch and his plight. If I hadn't known better, I might have thought they were competing as to who had his interests most at heart. Or perhaps I'm just cynically minded.

Then Doreen, not to be outdone, came in with, 'He went to see Dutch last night.' I gave her a look with tight thin lips and raised eyes that sort of said, *Why?*

June was first to react, 'Is he having visitors, what are the times for his ward?'

Chris immediately states, 'Barbara told me he was to have no visitors.'

They all sat looking at me as if I was some sort of lying cheating ogre. 'What?' I said at them all.

Chris said, 'Why are you visiting him if there are no visitors allowed?'

'Well,' I started, with my brain in overdrive. 'I didn't actually make a visit as such. I had to take some paperwork that required his signature for his sick pay. Yes, while I was there, I did speak with him. It's not that there aren't any visitors allowed, it's just that he's very fragile, weak and feeling quite wretched and does not want anyone to see him like that, OK?'

The general consensus was, it was understandable that he did not want visitors if he felt so poorly. I quickly put in with, 'Are you all packed ready for your cruise?' with the aim of changing the subject, which proved successful. Chris went into full detail of the itinerary and descriptions of ship and cabin. The ensuing discussion lasted quite some time.

As her sales like spiel of their cruise tailed off, Doreen swiftly produced her bag of Christmas cards and such, then started to distribute said items. This appeared to spark action all across the room. It was Ron who said, 'Is this where we remove ourselves to the games room?' Which is exactly what happened.

The evening ended with everyone wishing Chris and Vic a good holiday then a Happy Christmas and New Year to everybody else.

Work on Saturday was as planned and quite quickly accomplished. I had arranged to meet up with my daughter in town. The intention was to do all my Christmas shopping.

'First things first,' suggested Elizabeth, 'coffee.'

As we sat with our drinks, I said, 'Right, what does your mother expect for Christmas?'

'I don't know,' was the response.

'Oh!' says me. 'Well, what are you expecting to receive?' I ask.

'Mother's already got that sorted. Tommy, sorted. April, sorted. Daniel, the same.'

'So, what are you here for?' I venture to ask.

'To make sure whatever you buy for Mother is adequate and appropriate.'

'Like what?'

'Up to you,' was her reply.

'Yes, that's very helpful. When I asked your mother what she would like, she replied, "Oh, I don't know, we could do with some new carpet on the stairs."'

Her response to that was, 'No, you need to buy her something personal.'

'OK, I'll go to a jewellers and see if there is anything that you think is appropriate.' It finished up with me paying a small fortune for a Gucci watch. My thoughts were, *Fuck me, all that money just to know the time.* I actually said thank you to Elizabeth for her assistance. I had half expected to see young Mick and his potential bride, but they were not to be seen.

Monday 20th December

This week would mainly be aimed at ensuring we were ready and able to cover Christmas. If called upon, we needed to be able to deal with any emergency quickly and efficiently. Allowing a swift return to our holiday. With this in mind, I had produced a list of items that would enable us to achieve the desired effect. Namely:

(1) BOARDS OF ASSORTED SIZES to board up damaged windows or doors and such.

(2) HOSES OF ASSORTED SIZES for leaks of water or air.

278

(3) FUEL PUMP HOSE AND NOZZLE.
(4) FUEL PUMP SPARE MOTOR.
(5) ASSORTMENT OF SCREWS, NAILS, BOLTS & NUTS.
(6) ASSORTMENT OF JUBILEE CLIPS.
(7) CABLE TIES, ASSORTED CLAMPS AND ROPES.
(8) TARPAULINS OF ASSORTED SIZES.
(9) AND ANYTHING ELSE YOU CAN THINK OF.

At our mid-morning break, I put it to Mick that over Tuesday and Wednesday, he could busy himself with assembling these items in sufficient quantities to cover all our requirements.

I then asked how he had fared with shopping over the weekend, as I hadn't seen him around town on Saturday. He said, 'No. I didn't shop in town. At Jenny's suggestion. we went to Birmingham, to the jewellery quarter.' He said, 'Fuck me, they don't half ask for ridiculous prices.'

'You and me both,' I added, 'it's the cost of romance, or at least in my case, the cost of a bit of peace.'

On Tuesday, after a reasonably quiet day, I went to visit Dutch. Same as last week, I arrived between afternoon and evening visiting times, again blagging my way in.

He was in his bed, eyes closed, looking very old, tired, drained of strength and spirit. I was thinking of just leaving so as not to burden him with any activity. His eyes suddenly opened. 'Hello, mate,' he very quietly and gently said.

'Hi,' I responded, 'just popped in to see what progress had been made. How are things progressing, any news?' Trying my hardest to be positive and upbeat.

He made a valiant effort to raise himself up. I offered to assist; he declined my offer, insisting he could manage. This he did finally accomplish. I did however lift his pillow and procure an extra, just to support him.

In his rearranged position, he did seem more his old self. He then went on to tell me the consultant had indicated that rather than wait for a transplant donor, it might be better to remove his diseased lung. He'd said lots of people had lived very near-normal lives with just one working lung. He had gone on to say, in the longer term, if a suitable donor lung became available, a transplant could then be considered.

I suggested it was very good news, but when were they going to do it?

The consultant had said between Christmas and the New Year, they quite often had a quiet spell; that might be the ideal time to get him in theatre. 'So, I'm provisionally booked for a week tomorrow. I'm on a food supplement and over the next week, need to gain a bit of weight and strength before they will perform the operation.' All this said between gasps of oxygen from his mask.

I said, 'That's good to hear. Make sure you get these supplements and eat as much as you can over the holiday period.'

'No worries there, I've already told them I'm ready and will be in the theatre on that day.'

Because of his positive outlook, I decided to tell him about the manager's situation. I explained the manager was to be pensioned off. To which he responded with a, 'Wow! I bet he didn't see that coming.'

I went on to say, 'Neither of us will be considered as his replacement. The position is to be advertised requesting applicants to have a degree in business studies or some sort of equivalent degree. This is all to happen between now and the end of March. So, in three months, we'll have a new gaffer.'

'That's OK, it won't take long to train him up for the job, will it?' he rasped.

'Him? What if it's a her?' I put in.

'In that case, I won't be back,' was his comment, said with an almost smile. Very PC, Dutch and me both, as you no doubt are already aware.

He had put on his oxygen mask; he then lay back looking quite relaxed. I was about to ask if he was going to be allowed home for Christmas when I realised he had drifted off to sleep. I left, whispering I would see him sometime over the holiday period.

As I was going away, I became slightly agitated, having not wished him a Happy Christmas. The debate going on in my head was, *How can you wish anyone a Happy Christmas when it was so obvious their Christmas was going to be anything but a happy one?*

I had not told Doreen of my hospital visit, nor was I about to tell anyone else. Wednesday, once again, was a steady day. Mick was quite happy with progress on his preparations for our Christmas emergencies.

The whole establishment seemed to be relaxing into the Christmas spirit. I was cleaning the electric distribution boards at the bottom of 3 bay when a call came over the PA system for me to report to the manager's office. My thought was, *What the fuck has happened now?*

Arriving at the manager's office, seeing the door slightly ajar, knowing the manager was not in, I just barged right in. Waiting inside was none other than the Director of Engineering, Mr George Kane himself. 'Oh! Good morning, sir,' was the utterance that came out of my mouth.

'Good morning, I'm George Kane, Engineering Director.'

'Yes, I am aware of who you are, sir,' I interjected, 'it's that I was not expecting you to be making a visit.'

'No, sorry about that, it was on a sudden impulse. I realised you were rudderless going into the festive season and felt I should put in an appearance to assure myself that all was well. Bill had said you were the person to contact should I require any knowledge or assistance.'

'Oh, did he, that was very kind of him,' I said with a hint of cynicism.

'Why? Is he wrong with his opinion?'

'No, I don't suppose so. It just seems to be taken for granted that I'll be there to pick up the slack when anyone else just stops pulling.'

'Is this about not promoting you to Bill's position?'

'No, I had already let it be known I thought I was too old to be starting a new career.'

'Mr Williamson didn't think so, he spoke very highly of you. He thought you would be a shoo-in for the role.'

'Yeah, but no reward to show,' I said.

'It *is* about you not being given the role then,' he said triumphantly.

'OK, yes, if you want to put it like that,' I agreed with a half-smile on my face, just to show I wasn't all that despondent.

'Right,' he said, 'we'll take a tour of the conurbation if we may.'

'Er, could you give me just two minutes to let my apprentice know the situation? He will be able to cope as long as he knows what is happening.'

As soon as I got out, I sought out Sammie and asked her to contact all departments to let them know the director was on site. 'Already done,' was her reply.

'Good girl,' was my slightly patronising response. 'And Mick?'

'Will do.'

Back at the manager's office, I suggested, 'All under control, shall we proceed?'

As we began the tour of the site, he suddenly asked about Dutch, not by name but as your regular assistant, saying, 'He's off on long-term sick or so I've been led to believe.'

'Yes, he is very ill. It's cancer.'

'Is he likely to return sometime in the future? Or should we be thinking of letting him go?'

The thought going through my head was, *You callous bastard.* What my reply was, 'There are a good many employees here who I would let go if on long-term sick, but Dutch is not one of them. If there is the slightest chance that he will return, I think it's what we should be hoping for.'

'Is it because he is a friend stroke mate, or because he really merits your support?'

'Some blokes lead, some follow. Dutch is a leader; people will follow him every time. He is strong mentally and physically. What he has done for this company is priceless. Turning out at all hours, day or night if needed. Yes, he is a mate and a friend, we work together and socialise together. Yes, I may be a bit biased in my opinion. What you will find, though, is most people at this unit and anyone else who knows him will be of the same opinion. He is the type of person you want on your side.'

'If he's as good as that, we'd better hope he can return.' That was his final comment on the subject. No more was mentioned about Dutch.

As we progressed around the site, I made introductions with all section heads. It was almost unbelievable the number of enquiries after Dutch that were made. I am quite sure Mr Kane was aware of the interest being shown but did not comment.

After completion of the tour, Mr Kane thanked me and said he had full confidence in the business being able to function during Mr Williamson's absence. He went on to say I should carry on doing what I had been doing for the last few days. If any problems arose that might require his input, please contact his secretary. She was always able to contact him. He checked I had her phone number.

Then wishing me a Merry Christmas, he took his leave. As he was leaving, he suddenly said, 'Please pass on to Dutch my sincere and heartfelt wishes for a quick recovery from his health problems.'

'Will do,' I responded.

Returning to our shop, Mick was full of curiosity. 'What's he got to say?'

'About what?' I enquired.

'Everything, like Billy just fucking off like that. Or, who's supposed to run things while he's away. Did he say anything about me and my situation?'

'What makes you think Billy, I think you meant Mr Williamson, the manager, just fucked off as you put it? Mr Williamson applied for holiday leave, and his application was granted. As to who runs the business while he's away, a good manager always makes contingencies to cover his absence. As for you, he doesn't even know you exist.'

Mick stood with his mouth open, then asked, 'Didn't you tell him what a good job I'm doing?'

'No,' was my blunt reply. I then said, 'I never lie to a director, so how could I say that?' said with a big smile on my face.

Lots of thoughts went through my mind during the rest of the day. Was the director satisfied with his visit, was he impressed or disappointed in my contribution? Would it have any bearing on my future role in the company? These were all questions with no answers but nevertheless constantly revolved around in my head. As to what Doreen's take on it all would be, I shuddered to think.

At home that evening, on receiving the news of the director's visit, Doreen's demeanour was as expected: OTT. Did you tell him, did he say, will it, do you think, and on and on and on. I don't think I got a word in.

Thursday evening, April and Daniel arrived, they along with Tommy were to stay with us over the festive season. Tommy wouldn't arrive till late tomorrow, as work commitment governed his festive break. Or possibly a celebration drink with work colleagues delayed him. (Which is more likely.)

Friday, Christmas Eve, the main response from Mick was, 'What time are we working till?'

My reply to his regular enquiry, 'When all the work is completed.'

Most of the departments, what I mean by that is all of the garage departments, had started early at 06:00hrs, with the intention of working straight through till 12.30, then allowing all the staff to relax and celebrate. Mick's dilemma was how to get back with his mates in the auto-electrician's department.

I, having spoken with Eddie their foreman, already knew they planned to finish at 12.30 and retire to the Boat. Where it had been arranged for a buffet to be laid on. I had also been invited to join their little shindig.

Work had been very light all morning, as expected. At around quarter past twelve, Mick asked if it would be OK for him to go back to his old department to celebrate the forthcoming festivities. It was at that point I told him I had been invited and offered to give him a lift to the Boat. Mick was absolutely delighted but asked why I hadn't said so earlier. My response was, 'When at work, we concentrate on work, when at play, we play hard. The two don't mix.'

It was a pleasant little session. The electrical section consisted of five guys. Two who were approaching retiring age, Jim and Harry, two middle-aged, Bill and Dave. Plus, an apprentice, Tony.

Along with the foreman, Eddie, Mick and myself made up a very tidy drinking group.

There were several other groups from work in the pub and a very good atmosphere soon built up. A lot of enquiries regarding Dutch were made to me, which I just casually passed off with, 'Oh, he's fine and showing some improvement.'

I only had a couple of drinks, thinking, *It's going to be a long hard slog over the festive season so pace yourself.* The rest of the group drank as if it was their last chance.

At about 2.30, I took my leave, accompanied with calls of 'Quitter' and, 'you're showing your age ain't yeah?' To which I replied, 'Merry Christmas, everyone.' The place had become quite boisterous.

My first port of call was back at work, just to satisfy myself all was well. The tinsmiths were partying in their workshop in a reasonably controlled way. The refuelling guys were all at their station, most had a drink in hand. As the shift foreman wasn't due on till 6 o'clock, I suggested they should take great care with their drinking as we did not want any mishaps at this time of the year.

With everything else in order, I made my way to the hospital. Dutch had been moved to a small side-room on his own. 'What's all this then? A private room, things are looking up.'

Barbara, who was sat in an armchair at the side of his bed, said, 'It's so he can be prepared for his operation.'

'It's more likely that the rest of the ward wanted him out of the way,' was my jocular response.

'That is a possibility,' replied Barbara.

'So, how are things?' I asked.

Dutch said with laboured breath, 'OK, I think I'm ready for it now. I really think this is going to be successful.'

'Great, that sounds very positive.' His demeanour seemed very upbeat. His look belied that fact. He was very drawn and frail-looking.

Barbara then told me they had asked if he could go home for Christmas Day but had been told No as they needed to monitor him in preparation for the operation. She then apologised for not accepting our invitation to Christmas dinner.

'No need to apologise, it's all understood. The invitation is still there for any part of the day or of the holiday, should you have need.' Before leaving, I produced a bottle of whisky. Wishing them both all the best and hoping it all went well. Barbara pointed out that the medical people wouldn't allow him to drink any spirits before his treatment. I said, 'Well, it's there for when he's recovered, maybe New Year.'

At home, Tommy had arrived and retired to his bedroom for forty winks. Doreen and April were busy in the kitchen, I was asked (no, instructed) to take Daniel out to the park. I pointed out that it was very nearly dark. 'Well, take him to a McDonalds or somewhere.' So, off we went. My thoughts were, *When do I get to rest my weary head?*

We had a pleasant hour or so in town. The atmosphere all around town was very seasonal, with lots of decorative lights, and Christmas carols being played from practically every establishment. A lot of people milling around. Last minute shopping. Making their way home from work, or more likely from a drinking den of one sort or another. Quite a number knowing me from work or from pubs, or even from bowls, called out Christmas greetings. Some asking after Dutch and his health. All these greetings prompted Daniel to ask, 'Does everybody know you, Grandad?'

'So it would seem,' I replied.

On arriving home, I had a shower and lay on the bed; at last, I could get my forty winks. After what seemed like about four winks, never mind forty to me, Doreen was asking what we were doing tonight.

I replied, 'It's Friday, so I shall be going to the club.'

She then informed me, 'April is staying in with Daniel. Tom is ready and asking what the plan for the evening is.'

'Are you ready?' I inquired.

'I've only got to finish putting my makeup on.'

'OK, give me five minutes and we can be off.'

At the club, we sat in our usual seats, which amazingly were vacant as the club was full to bursting point. Soon after we arrived, Eileen and Ron appeared. Dennis and June were spending Christmas with their daughter down Bristol way. Chris and Vic were on their cruise. So, a very depleted team tonight. Then, very much to our surprise, who should turn up but our daughter Elizabeth.

A neat little team for a Christmas eve, it reflected the team set for our Christmas lunch, if April and Daniel were added. Eileen and Ron were to join us for dinner as their son had gone into France somewhere to spend his Christmas with a girlfriend of some sort.

After about three-quarters of an hour, Doreen, along with Eileen and Elizabeth, went into the assembly room, hoping to find seating for all of us. There was a DJ and a karaoke, with people dancing along with the music. A regular party night.

After a number of minutes, Elizabeth came and said they had acquired a table and four chairs, which they intended to hang on to. She went on to say, if we were to join them, another two chairs could possibly be acquired. 'OK, we'll be in shortly.'

When we had finished our drinks, we headed for the big room. Tommy went to get the round in; Ron and myself scoured the club looking for a couple of stools. Ron finally found two in the bar; we settled down to enjoy the spectacle, and what a spectacle it was.

There were some surprisingly good performances. There were also some surprisingly bad. The dance floor was always full, the crowd cheered and applauded all performances, good or bad.

The highlight of the evening, for me at any rate, was the gang of usual suspects, namely Don, Kevin, Markey, Brian and Sam, leading the room in a rendition of 'The Twelve Days of Christmas'. Not the regular well-known one but a Black Country version that had five sniffs of snuff, four Jack-bannocks, three flat caps, two clay pipes, and a jug of um med brew. Added to this list, somewhere along the lines were some willing whippets, some big strong 'osses and some tasty faggots. All in all, brilliant.

The night ended with me planning with Ron to meet up in the Boat at around midday, have a couple of drinks before returning to our house.

I was awakened by Doreen informing me, 'It's Christmas Day and time to get up; everyone else is downstairs opening up presents.'

By the time I had washed and dressed, I arrived downstairs to find what seemed like acres of wrapping paper strewn all over the house. April presented me with an egg and bacon sandwich and a cup of tea. My euphoria was beyond description, by far the best Christmas present of all.

After breakfast, I opened my wrapped presents, a tie, a pair of socks, a couple of woollen pullovers, a pair of trainers for next season's bowls from Doreen. I faked raptures of joy with each and every opening. My thoughts were, *I work extremely hard all year and end up with all this crap*, miserable old git that I am.

Daniel had more presents than you would have thought possible. His main item was a gleaming red bike. Among other items he received were a football, football boots, a football shirt (Walsall, of course), much to his disappointment; he had requested Man United. (Not in my house.)

Doreen said, 'If you clear all the rubbish away, I'll make a cup of tea.'

'Great, I'll have some whisky in mine,' was my reply. Just as I threw the last of the rubbish out, who should arrive but Ron and Eileen. 'You want one of these?' I asked.

Ron said, 'Yeah, smells just like Christmas.'

Eileen said it was a bit early in the day for her.

'Anyway, I thought it was to be midday in the Boat.'

'So did I,' answered Ron, 'but those two had had their heads together and decided otherwise.'

Eileen then put in with, 'Doreen wasn't sure she wanted to be at the Boat this lunchtime, neither did I. We decided this would be the best option, you lot could go to the pub, we would stay here and have a drink if we wanted to.'

In the end Ron, Tommy and myself went to the pub. There was a fine Christmas feel about the place, with many a seasonal greeting floating across the air. A good percentage of drinkers in Christmas jumpers. (I've never had one, never felt it was quite me.)

Tommy got the round in. I let it be known I only intended to have a couple, as I felt it was probably going to be a long day. After a short while, Ron's brother-in-law, Paul, turned up with his father-in-law, John. I knew both quite well and they joined our little team. A session was in the making.

While at the bar getting my round in, I was able to see into the saloon bar; there, sitting all alone, was Jumbo Jennings. With the Christmas spirit getting the better of me, I asked the barman to take a pint of whatever Jumbo was drinking over to him with season's greetings from me.

I watched on as the barman took over the drink and relayed my greetings. Jumbo lifted his drink and offered a drinker's salute my way. I acknowledged his raised glass with a nod of my head. He then called through, saying, 'Don't think this goes any way towards clearing our little issue.'

I replied, 'Merry Christmas, Jumbo,' and sat down.

Our Tommy, who had witnessed this little charade, asked, 'What was that all about?'

'Oh, just a bit of bowler's banter,' I replied. (I was actually thinking, *The twat is never going to let it go*.)

Our lunchtime session finished with me, well, all of us, having slightly more to drink than had been intended. On arriving home, we were informed that dinner was ready to be served. I carved the turkey, then popped the cork of the champagne, a very nice Veuve Clicquot. A bit ostentatious, but well it's Christmas only once a year. We pulled crackers, put on fancy hats, tucked in and had a very pleasant meal. As well as the champagne, there were a couple of red and a couple of white wines. Consequently, by the end of the meal, the atmosphere was quite boisterous but happy and very pleasant.

A Christmas pudding then appeared; it was universally rejected but not before a bottle of brandy was offered up. A liberal amount was poured over the pudding, it was then lit, a full rendition of 'We Wish You a Merry Christmas' rang around the house.

First Tommy, then Daniel, closely followed by me, then Ron, all changed our minds and decided to have some pudding. There was cream or custard to go with it. I went with the cream, followed by a rather large brandy. I then retired to my favourite armchair and promptly fell asleep.

Sometime later, I awoke with a start. Dutch had been declared free of cancer; in fact, he hadn't had cancer. He had been studying to be a surgeon while at the hospital. Now he was about to perform his first operation. It was on someone close to me; I wasn't sure, but it may even have been me.

Looking around, Ron and Eileen were asleep on the small settee, with Doreen spread along the large settee. Reality came flooding back to me, it was Christmas Day. The house was very quiet. *What a strange dream, it must have been them sprouts.* I went for a cup of tea. In the dining room, Elizabeth and Daniel were playing a board game.

With my tea, I sat at the table and joined in. As ever when playing these types of games with the kids, I quite openly cheat. Their accusations and my feigned protest of innocence soon raised the noise level in the house.

Ron was first to rouse. He came and said, 'I think we're off shortly.'

I replied, 'Rubbish, the night is young as yet. Sit in here, I'll get you a drink.'

'Just a cup of tea then.' Ron, as ever, quite easily persuaded.

Ron suggested we should play a card game; this was agreed all round. Before we got very far into the game, Eileen came in and said, 'I thought we were going?'

Ron countered with, 'If we go home now, what are we going to do? We'll only sit and watch the telly, and there's only the same old rubbish as last year.'

Eileen, not to be overruled, came back with, 'If you start drinking again, we won't be able to get home at all.'

I put in with, 'Eileen, relax, it's Christmas. I'll make sure you get home safe.'

'You,' said Eileen, 'you'll be lucky if you can find your own bed.' This brought howls of laughter from everybody, including me.

Soon after this, Doreen inquired, 'Does anyone want anything to eat?' This request was declined by all. I suggested another cup of tea, this time with some whisky in it.

At that very moment, Tommy came in and said, 'That sounds like a very good idea.'

In no time at all, a Christmas evening party was in full swing. Drinking, eating, gambling, records being played, dancing and singing. Wow!

I awoke, I did find my bed. Whether by myself or with assistance, I know not. A cup of tea and a bowl of porridge later, still not feeling anywhere near 100%. Doreen, looking fresh and controlled, said, 'You were putting it away a bit last night, weren't you?'

'It's Christmas, isn't it?' was my retort.

'Maybe, but still,' she replied, 'a bottle and half of whisky.'

'I wasn't the only one drinking,' I said defensively.

Daniel was on the carpet, colouring in a book. I enquired of Doreen if I was expected to keep him amused for the rest of the holiday. Only to be told, Tommy, April and Daniel were going out for the day. Apparently to the Black Country Museum, always a good outing.

My response was, 'Great, a real lazy day for me.' The house had been tided, everything put away. I read the papers, watched sport on the TV, and had my real lazy day. Late in the afternoon, a visitor arrived, it was Barbara. She told of Dutch and his Christmas, how all the hospital staff indulged and pampered him. She said his son, Robert, had spent an hour there, along with his two grandchildren. This made me feel very guilty. Instead of drinking, eating and generally whooping it up, I should perhaps have gone and spent some time with him. *Too late now, I'll go tomorrow.*

I had not said any of this out loud, but then Barbara ended all speculation regarding visits by saying he was to have no visits from anyone from now and until after his operation. This was to prevent any possible infection being transferred to him. She herself would be allowed limited access but not any physical contact, and she must wear a face mask while in his area.

She left with our good wishes and hopes that everything went well. I said, 'Tell him he's needed back at work, that should cheer him up,' and she was gone.

Sitting there, just the two of us, deep in thought, thinking of Dutch. I suddenly said, 'I should have gone.'

Doreen responded with, 'Gone where?'

'To the hospital yesterday. Me, I should have gone. I feel guilty. I didn't know what to say when Barbara was going on about everyone who was there.'

'You don't have to feel guilty at all, it's not all about you, you know. His family come before you. It's only right and proper that his family were there. They certainly didn't need you getting in the way.'

'Yeah, you're probably right,' and there I let it lie.

Monday 27th December

It was officially Boxing Day. Daniel asked if it would be alright to go and play football. After breakfast, we went down to the small park area just off our road. I set up two road cones that were by the fence, these became our goal posts. I marked out a penalty spot and we spent an hour taking penalties.

I said, 'Had enough?' Daniel agreed. I said, 'Come on then, in the car, we'll go and check out what's going on at work.'

While driving along in the car, Daniel suddenly asked, 'What time am I going to the pantomime?'

'What pantomime?' was my response.

'Mom and Dad are taking me, and Grandma's also going.'

'Are they?' This is all news to me. 'Don't worry, I'll get you back in plenty of time.'

I parked up at the garage, everywhere was very quiet. A couple of guys working the bus wash waved over to me, I went to our little office and called home. Doreen answered. 'What's all this pantomime business?'

'We're going to Wolverhampton to see the panto.'

'Why wasn't I told about this?'

'Why, you didn't want to go, did you?'

'No, but it might have been nice to have been asked or even just consulted about it.'

'Well, you weren't, you didn't want to go, so what's the problem?'

'No, nothing, what time are you planning to leave?'

'Around 4 o'clock. Where are you now?' she asked.

At work.'

'Where's Daniel?'

'Here with me.'

'What are you doing at work?'

'Phoning you to find out what time you're going to the panto.'

'Oh shut up.' She then hung up.

At that very precise moment, who should walk in but Mick. 'What are you doing here?' he asked.

'Just passing by,' I replied. 'The real question, perhaps, is, what are you doing here?'

'Number 2 fuel pump nozzle had broken, and I received a call from the shift foreman, so here I am.'

'I never received any calls,' I uttered in a seemingly belligerent manor.

'Well, er no,' said Mick. 'I spoke with the shift foreman on Friday and said if any minor problems arose, to call me, as you had your family visiting over the holiday period.'

'Thanks for that, not that it would have been all that much of a problem, but thanks all the same.'

Mick went on to say he had gone to the hospital yesterday to see Dutch but was turned away when told he wasn't family. I said, 'Yeah, so I understand.'

'Is he really that poorly?'

'No, it's not that, it's only a precaution against the spread of any infection.'

Back home, everyone was rushing around, looking for hats, scarf and gloves. Eventually, they were off. The pantomime awaits. Me, I was left all alone with just my thoughts. My thoughts were, *I've let him down again. Everybody is there for him bar me, what a mate to have. Not only that, it now looks like Mick has took over at work, issuing instructions on who should do callouts. He's getting more like Dutch than Dutch.*

I went to the club for a few bevvies.

The club seemed quite busy; the car park was almost full. I went into the lounge, called a pint and sat in our usual seating area. It seemed most members were in the concert room.

As I sat there, all quiet and relaxed. I was thinking, *Is this what people mean when they say they have had a nice but quiet Christmas? I don't think I've ever had a quiet Christmas; this year has been the closest I've ever come to a quiet festive season.*

Just then, Fred and Harry came into the lounge, went to the bar and ordered their drinks and approached me. 'Is it OK to sit with you?' Harry asked.

'Yeah,' I replied, 'make yourselves at home.'

'It's not often that you're in here on your own,' he continued.

'No,' I explained, 'the family have all gone off to a pantomime.'

'Which one?' asked Harry.

'Wolverhampton,' I replied. It then went quiet, as if nothing else needed to be said.

I then blurted out, 'How was your Christmas?'

To which Fred answered, 'Nice but quiet.'

Harry said, 'Yes, nice but quiet.'

I just said, 'Yes, that's the way it should be,' and thought, *Why the fuck did I ask that?*

Fred went on to ask about Dutch. I told them he was to have an operation Wednesday and that the medical staff seemed very positive regarding the outcome. 'Will he be bowling next season?' Inquired Harry.

'It's a bit early to say yet, but hopefully at some time during the season he will,' I ventured.

At that very moment in walked Ron. 'Here he is.' was his cry, as though he had been searching for me. 'What are you doing here, where's Doreen?'

'One question at a time, please,' and said, 'she's at the panto in Wolverhampton.'

To which Ron asked, 'Is she playing the part of the Dame?' and burst into a fit of laughter at his little witticism. I must own up that I laughed too and thought, *Hallo, Ron's having a good night.*

He then asked, 'Are you coming in? We're all in there.'

In the big room, indeed everyone did seem to be there, well most of the bowls section anyway. Ron said, 'I'll get you a drink.' Season's greetings came from practically everyone, plus calls of 'late again' and 'oversleep, did you?' All offering a handshake.

I eventually arrived where Eileen was sitting with two spare chairs. 'I've been saving these for you.' Then realising I was on my own, asked, 'Where is Doreen?' at the very time Ron turned up with my drink.

He at once chimed in with, 'She's at the panto in Wolvo, she's playing one of the ugly sisters.' All within hearing distance howled with delight, seeming to think it was the funniest thing ever. Ron looked pleased with himself.

Eileen said, 'Shut up, you, and sit down.' Which he did, still looking pleased.

I didn't enter the spirit of the evening quite as enthusiastically as the rest of the gang; apparently, a large percentage of them had been at it all day long. Nevertheless, I had a very good evening.

Driving home, I began thinking, *Maybe that's where I'm heading, nice but quiet as I slowly age.*

As I approached our house, it was lit up with lights on in all of the windows and loud music vibrating those said windows. I went in to be greeted by a house full of partying people.

I was first greeted by my daughter. 'Hi, Dad, where have you been? We expected you to be here when we arrived.'

'It's Boxing Day evening, where do you expect I've been?' I replied.

'Yeah, I suppose I should have known you'd be out,' was her retort.

'Anyway, what's all this about?' I asked.

'Tommy phoned me this evening and wanted to know if I had anything planned tonight, as when they would be leaving the theatre it would be a bit late for going anywhere. Having told him I had a group of friends round, he suggested we all came round here and have a bit of a session. After consulting my team, we agreed. Finding no one here, we set to, rearranged the furniture, and set up for a bit of a do.

'As they all arrived back from the panto, Steve and Wendy from across the street were returning from the pub. They had been to the Star and Garter. Found it very dull and decided to return home a bit early. Mother invited them in for a drink.

'Twenty minutes later, Tommy went to get some more drinks from the boot of his car when Tony from next door was just pulling onto his drive, and he invited him and Kath to join the party. So, here we all are.'

'Great, am I to be extended an invite?' I asked.

'It's your house,' she replied.

'Is it? I sometimes wonder.'

'Well, you've always said, all of this is not yours but ours, the family, have you not?'

'Yees,' I replied slowly, then said, 'can I have a drink?'

After saying hello, to everybody, I eventually found Doreen in the kitchen still preparing food for everyone. 'Enjoy the show?'

'Yes, it was quite excellent and very funny. Daniel laughed so much all the way through, he really did have a good time.'

'Great,' I said, 'now pack all this in and come and relax with a drink. Elizabeth and Tom set this up, so they should do the entertaining.'

I seemed to spend most of the night sat at the dining table with Tony from next door and a bottle of Jonny Walker (Black Label).

What time I eventually called it a day, I've no idea. So much for nice but quiet, some chance.

Next day, Tommy and April took Daniel to visit some old friends that Tommy had known from his youth. They said they would be late getting back.

With it still being bank holiday, Doreen and myself were determined to have a quiet day. Elizabeth had rung and said she intended to hit the sales, and did we want to join her? 'No,' was the firm but polite reply. 'Oh, alright then,' was her reaction. She and her friends had made a good job of clearing up after last night's little rave.

Doreen and I had breakfast and read the papers in almost perfect silence. Tommy and his team departed shortly after midday. A final tidy up, then we settled ourselves in front of the telly and watched a film, *From Here to Eternity*. I had seen the film before, so it was easy watching. My mind drifted onto Dutch and his preparation for tomorrow. I suggested to Doreen that she should ring Barbara later, she said, 'Why don't you ring?'

I answered, 'I don't want to seem anxious.'

Doreen did ring Barbara; everything was going well. Dutch was quite relaxed about things; he had been given a sedative and had gone to sleep.

Asked how their Christmas had been, Barbara had answered that it was fraught with worry about the operation. Doreen had said, yes, she understood that and wished them both good luck, saying we would be thinking of them.

Back at work on the Wednesday morning, all was quiet and in order. I went through the motions of checking the site. There was only a skeleton crew on throughout the plant. Cleaning, fuelling and emergency repairs only were the order of the day. Mick had booked the rest of the week off to pamper his young lady. Which allowed me a very relaxing stint.

Throughout this calm and comfortable day, my mind regularly would stray to Dutch, trying to envisage what would be happening at that moment. As the day went on, I became more apprehensive and in need of some assurance that all was well.

I called it a day as early as deemed acceptable. Upon reaching home, I gabbled out to Doreen, 'Have you heard anything? Any phone calls?'

She, looking somewhat astonished, said, 'Hello, and how was your day?'

'Oh, yes, sorry.' Then added, 'Has Barbara phoned?'

'No, she had said she would let us know as soon as she had any news.'

'Give her a call,' I suggested.

'No, she'll let us know when she's ready.'

'They must know something by now; it's got to be bad news or we would have heard,' I reasoned.

Ignoring me, she went on to say that April, Tom and Daniel had gone to the Aeroplane Museum at Cosford. I had a shower and my evening meal, still feeling a bit on edge.

It was about quarter to seven when the phone rang.

'There you go, the call you've been waiting for,' she stated in a triumphant manner as if she was some way responsible for it ringing at that particular moment.

'Can you answer it?' I asked.

'It's the call you've been waiting for, so answer it,' she replied with an amount of hostility.

'I can't,' I replied.

'You're such a wimp at times,' she said with an equal amount of hostility, then picked up the phone. Her side of the conversation went as follows. 'Hello, Barbara, how's things? Oh good, that's great news. (Me! 'Let me have a word.') Doreen, 'Wait a bit.' She went on, 'I suppose you're ready for a good rest now?' The phone was eventually passed on to me, but not until Doreen had ridiculed my wimpish reaction to the phone ringing.

'Hello, Barbara, good news then?'

'Yes, I am so relieved,' she said. She then went on to say that the surgeon had gone out of his way to speak with her. Saying he was very pleased with the operation, it had gone as well as was possible, better than he had dared hope. There was no sign of any spread or any other infection in the other lung. Everything was perfect. Dutch now just needed rest to aid the healing process. She followed on to say he had been heavily sedated and must be kept quiet and very relaxed.

'How long for his recovery?' I asked.

'Well, he'll be sedated and on a ventilator for a number of days till the wounds start to knit. After that, it will be a long, drawn-out battle back to fitness, running into months rather than weeks. But that's OK. God willing, we'll get there.'

'That's great, I'm glad it's all gone so well. Anything you want or need, let me know. Just make sure you let me know as soon as it's allowable for visiting.'

Thursday was very routine, all quiet, no major trauma, not a lot happening. I had wondered if the manager might put in an appearance. On reflection, I thought most unlikely. As it turned out, he didn't.

At home, Doreen gave a full narrative of her day. Tommy, April and Daniel had gone to Telford shopping, and also visiting a museum of some sort called Ingenuity. Elizabeth had been round, and was still there when Barbara had called in. While they were sitting with tea and biscuits, Eileen had phoned saying they would

298

be at the club tomorrow night, also Dennis and June were back from Bristol and they would be there.

My response to this was, 'Oh, I'm so glad you've had an exciting day.' Said in a very sarcastic way.

To which she said a very ladylike, 'Bollocks.'

I said, 'Doreen, language like that's not you, are you out of sorts?'

'I was alright till you come along with your snide ways.'

'Yes, sorry, you're right, I shouldn't be like that.'

I'm wondering, *What is the matter with me being like that? Perhaps it's the post-Christmas blues. Bloody hell, if I'm like that now, how will I be towards the end of January? I shudder to think.*

Back at work on Friday (New Year's Eve). Who should turn up but Mick. 'What are you doing here?' I asked.

'I'm fed up, totally pissed off with life,' he replied.

'Well, hold on, there's only room for one in that position and I've already taken that, so what do you want?'

'Will it be OK for me to be at work today?'

'Oh, I don't know, you're booked off on holiday, aren't you? I don't think I've got the authority to sanction a change like that. But tell me what has happened.'

'I don't really know. It's her, she suddenly said she felt things were going too fast and that we should slow down a bit. I mean, what's that all about?' He just sat there looking all forlorn and dejected.

I said, 'If you're asking me to explain a woman's mind, forget it, they are beyond understanding.' He just grunted. I asked, 'Are you seeing her tonight?'

He replied, 'Yes; we're going to her parents' club to celebrate the New Year.'

'Well,' I said, 'get her away from her mom and dad as soon as possible, get a few drinks down her, not too much though. When you are away in a secluded spot, give her some very rough sex, not love, but with a lot of lust and passion. Fuck her till she squeals. If it's a squeal of fear and dread, it's all over. But if it's a squeal of fulfilment and joy, she's yours forever.'

'You really think so?' he asked.

'What do I know? You said a couple of weeks ago I had all the answers. Well, the reality is I know fuck all.'

'So, what do I do?' he asked with real bewilderment.

'Just play it by ear, pretend you didn't hear nor even notice she's having this emotional turmoil. If she should raise the subject again, say it's the weather or time of the year. Or claim you thought it was PMT. But as I said before, what the fuck do I know? Anyway, back to what we do about you being here. We can service the large roller shutter doors, that's a two-handed job. I can then claim that I requested your attendance, OK.'

We deeply involved ourselves in the servicing of the doors and time rolled by quite quickly. During the day, I had spoken about Dutch and how successful his operation had been. Mick had inquired if I thought he would return to work and how soon that would be. I had replied, I wasn't sure that he would return; if he did it wouldn't be for several months. Mick had then asked what his position would be if he did return. He then went on to say, 'Don't get me wrong. I'm very pleased everything went well for him, but I just wonder where I will fit in the scheme of things.'

My take on this situation seemed to set Mick back on his heels a bit. I ventured to say, 'In a couple of months or so, everything may have changed. We'll have a new boss. He or she will have very different ideas about how it all works. It could be that none of us will fit in the scheme of things.'

Mick said, 'Do you really think that's likely to happen?'

'What the fuck do I know?' I once again uttered... 'If I knew the future, I would be a rich man.'

Work complete, we ended the working day by wishing each other a Happy New Year, I also wished Mick good luck with his lady friend. Then went home.

Tommy, along with April and Daniel, had once again gone to meet up with his old friends from way back to celebrate the New Year. Saying he would probably see us later on. I had acquired tickets for all of our family to cover all eventualities. So, no problem with that scenario.

300

Doreen and myself arrived at the club at around 7 o'clock. Elizabeth had said she would drive there in her own car, as she thought she would want to leave long before her mother and I would be prepared to leave.

Dennis, June, Ron and Eileen were already seated and seemed well-entrenched for an exciting night. (Hopefully.) Dennis went to get our drinks, June gave us a rundown of their Christmas, matched by Eileen's narrative of our festive frivolities. Doreen seemed a bit peeved at not being able to get her two-pennyworth in. All was saved by Dennis returning with our drinks and asking how Dutch was faring after his operation. This became the running theme of the night, with many enquiries from any number of club members, showing a great deal of interest in his wellbeing. All were well pleased that he was considered to be doing well.

Elizabeth arrived at about 8 o'clock. Ron immediately offered his seat and said, 'While I'm up, I'll get the round in.' I beckoned her over to sit by her mother and I took the stool that had been acquired earlier.

The room was beginning to buzz. A DJ had managed to fill the floor with dancers. There was also a young female vocalist, who was quite good and extremely attractive, with a somewhat revealing outfit. This led to any number of calls from the more inebriated in the audience to 'get em off and get them out for the lads'. Then the one that received most reaction from the crowd. 'Bring on the donkey.' Half the crowd roared with laughter, the other half were demanding the perpetrator to shut his gob, but mainly he should be banned from the club. The girl herself had just laughed off all of the comments.

When I said one half did this and the other half did that, I was not including the females of our group. Who, led by Eileen asked, 'What's he on about a donkey for?' Backed up by June, who stated, 'They get dafter by the day in here, I think it's the amount they all drink.' Doreen just looked to me with a look of bewilderment. Me, I just thought, *I'm not going to explain.*

Apart from the entertainment, food had been laid on by way of a running buffet. There was rice, plus beef curry, and what was labelled as chilli con carne, this label was possibly debatable.

There was also chips, sausage and beans for the more sensitive pallet. Not a bad spread for a New Year's Eve.

The night was swinging along very nicely. Lots of food, lots of drinking, all in good company. During the conversation, Vic and Chris were mentioned. Dennis was of the opinion that Vic was seated at the captain's table telling him how to run his ship. Ron's take on the subject was rather than being best mates with the captain, he was more likely to be being keelhauled. This was greeted with much laughter and nods of agreement as being the more likely scenario.

The evening carried on in this sort of atmosphere, everyone having a pleasant time. Tommy arrived at about quarter past ten. April had dropped him off and had gone on home with Daniel. He was too tired to see the rest of the night out.

For all of the frivolity of the evening, I didn't feel I was having the best of New Year's Eve. There was no particular reason for feeling this way. Outwardly, I think I seemed to be having a good time, but somewhere in my head was a fragment of apprehension.

Suddenly it was midnight, everyone was singing 'Auld Lang Syne'. Followed by hugs and kisses and shouts of Happy New Year. As things settled down, the bar reopened, Tommy came back with a bottle of whisky and any number of glasses. Elizabeth said, 'I think this is where I leave.' With kisses and hugs all round, plus Happy New Year again, she departed.

A session then started as the team hit the whisky. June immediately complained that she was drinking gin and did not want to change to whisky. Dennis said, 'Hold it right there,' he went to the bar and returned with two large gins and a number of mixers and said, 'Here, get stuck into them.'

June looked at him with a look that said, *you'll pay for that* but uttered, 'I won't drink all of that.'

To which Dennis answered, 'Drink whatever you want and leave the rest, I'm sure someone will be able to manage it.'

With that, we all carried on with the night. I'm not very sure how things went from there on. I seem to relate to the fact that Ron supplied a further bottle of whisky. My memory of the rest of the night is somewhat impaired. I'm aware we had to wait an age for a taxi, but somehow, we did arrive home. At what time I've no idea, I did make it to bed.

In what seemed like five seconds after my head hit the pillow, Doreen was saying, 'Are you awake? There's a phone call for you, someone named Bob.'

'Oh fuck, it ain't work, is it?'

'There's no need for that sort of language at this time of the morning. You just can't stop, can you? The chap said it was important.'

'OK, tell him I'll be just a minute. Make me a cup of tea, would you please.'

'Hello, who's calling?'

'It's Robert. Dutch's son.'

'Oh, hi, Happy New Year.'

'Not really,' he replied, 'it's my dad. He's dead.'

'*What?*'

'Just after midnight.'

'*No!* Oh *fuck!*' I practically screamed out. The phone was hung up at the other end.

I sat on my chair at the dining table, not a thought in my head. It was as if my brain had shut down and did not want to function. Doreen arrived with my cup of tea. 'I don't think you should go to work; you're not in a fit state to be at work.'

'It wasn't work.'

'Who was it then?'

'The eldest son of Dutch.'

'What did he want?'

'He told me Dutch has died.'

'No, that can't be true. Are you having me on?'

'Do you think it's the sort of thing I would joke about?'

'Oh dear, what should we do?'

'Nothing,' I replied, 'there's nothing that can be done to change the situation.'

'I think I should ring Barbara.'

'No, leave them for a while, let them grieve alone, at their own pace.'

'I'll have to let Eileen and June know.'

'If that's what you feel you should, but suggest they leave Barbara alone, just for a few hours.'

I spent the hours that followed in deep thought. It seemed only a few weeks ago that it all started. *Yes, it was last Easter. Yes, it was when Karen buggered off. He had some time off work. When he returned, he started to complain of a problem with his shoulder. Dear oh dear, just nine months. Now he's dead. Never in my wildest thoughts did I imagine this outcome. He's dead.*

These sorts of thoughts kept going around and around in my head. *He didn't make 50, didn't even get his half-century. Dead, it doesn't feel real. It's not fair; bloody murderers, paedophiles, rapists and all sorts of ne'er-do-wells manage to exist. Why him?*

As I wrestled with my thoughts, Doreen came and said Eileen had just called, saying she had called Barbara. Robert's wife had answered, she had said Barbara had had a sedative off the doctor and was now resting and did not want to speak with anyone. I just gave a heavy sigh and said, 'I've got nothing to say.' (To myself, I bemoaned, *For Christ's sake.*)

Late in the afternoon, coming up to five or thereabout, Ron phoned. 'What a shocker,' was his opening line.

'Yeah,' I replied, 'what a shock.'

He went on to say, 'He was supposed to be on the mend, I can't believe it.'

'No, an unbelievable shock,' I answered. I couldn't think of anything else to say.

'Are you going to be out this evening?' was his next enquiry, to which he added Dennis had called him to say he was going to the club, but June didn't want to go. He would be there, and Eileen had decided to stop at home as well.

'Yeah, OK, Tommy and me will see you there.'

Half six, quarter to seven, the phone rang again. Doreen answered; she looked through the hallway door to me and silently mouthed 'Barbara' then shut the door. After two or three minutes, the door opened, and she gesticulated for me to take the phone. I could see she was in a very upset state but just took the phone.

'Hello, Barbara, you OK?'

'Why? Why? Is it me?' she sobbed down the phone.

I could only say, 'No, it's not you, don't put any blame on yourself. In situations like this, it's natural to feel some guilt.'

'It feels worse than the last time. I don't think I can cope with it again,' she said' still sobbing in a near uncontrolled way.

'Look to your family and friends, keep them close; we're always here and will help in every way we can.' I went on to say, 'I don't have any of the answers, and I surely don't know words that can comfort you at present. What I want to say now is, as soon as you feel you can, start a folder and record everything and anything that any of the hospital staff say to you. Keep a record of what they say, who said it, what time it was said and what the date was when it was said. Not wanting to add to your already stressed situation, but try and start as soon as possible. I say this because answers are going to be required. You're in the police, you know the importance of accurate evidence.'

'Yes,' she said, 'I'm sure there will be an investigation, but at the moment my mind is just a blank.'

'OK, let's leave it there. Have you anything to help you sleep?'

'Yes,' she replied.

'Good, have a warm drink, take the tablets and get as much rest as you can over the rest of the weekend.' I went on to say, 'I'll try not to disturb you, but please call me if there is anything that you need, anything at all.'

At that she started uncontrolled sobbing again and put the phone down. I, likewise, put the phone down and felt very near to sobbing myself. Doreen looked at me and said, 'OK?'

I said, 'I don't think anything will ever be OK again.'

She flung her arms around my neck and started to gently weep. I said, 'It's alright, sweetheart, let it all out,' as a tear rolled down my cheek. We remained embraced for a couple of minutes until I gave her a gentle kiss that said I understood, then offered to make her a cup of tea.

Tommy and I entered the club at around quarter to eight. Neither Ron nor Dennis had arrived, in fact the club was very much quieter than most Saturday nights. We sat in our usual seats; Tommy went to the bar to get the drinks. A couple of the bowls squad who were in their regular position acknowledged our presence with a raised glass and a call of Happy New Year. Seemingly to have forgotten we were in the club last night.

Dennis and Ron arrived some five or six minutes after ourselves. Tommy got their drinks while we commiserated with each other.

We sat huddled close together, speaking in hushed tones of our feelings and of our wives and family's thoughts and feelings. I suppose, to an outsider, we may have looked quite a forlorn group. As I looked up, the bowls group had expanded and looked to be a full team, at that very same time, PK walked in and went to join them. Looking over, he called, 'What's the matter with you lot, someone died?' The bowls crew roared with laughter.

I said to our group, 'Let's go and join them and spread the news.'

Ron asked if it was OK to join the group. Brian said, 'Only if you cheer up a bit.' That raised a few titters.

Our group all seemed to look to me to open the dialogue. 'Well, there is some bad news, very bad news. In the very early hours of this morning, Dutch passed away.' I looked up, a sea of disbelieving faces staring back in deathly silence.

After what seemed an age, Mark said, 'Dead, you mean he's dead?'

Don then said, 'You were saying last night he was on the mend.'

PK then said, 'I didn't know, I was only making a joke.' To be honest, he did look mortified.

Then the questions started. How, what, who? Our Tommy came in with, 'There are no answers at the moment. His son Robert, who some of you might know, rang this morning with the news. He was too upset to give any details; it seems none of the family are ready to talk with anyone either.'

Once again, we sat in silence. Then, after several minutes, good old reliable Ken stated, 'Dutch wouldn't want us to be this miserable on a Saturday night, let's go to the big room and listen to the music and celebrate his all too short life.'

The celebration of his all too short life was every bit as subdued as in the lounge, with everyone speaking in low voices. This, in part, was due to the fact that shortly after we entered the concert room, PK was on stage informing everyone of the demise of Dutch. This news shocked the whole room into a similar state as the bowls squad.

It took more than an hour for the atmosphere to begin to lift. The main reason for this rise was the effect of drink and the slow realisation that nothing would change the situation.

I didn't drink much, certainly not compared with that of the regular crew, who drank like any other Saturday night. They were all out to celebrate the life of Dutch. Any number of toasts were called in his honour. Like, 'Dutch, the best team captain the club ever had,' 'Dutch, here's to a top, top man. RIP.' Then we had, 'Dutch, not one of the best but the best.' On and on it went, each one trying to outdo the last one, all done in high spirit and halfway to comedy.

In the midst of all this, up rolled Jumbo Jennings, still in his wheelchair. He said, 'Despite all that's happened, I liked Dutch, had a lot of time and respect for him. Will you please pass on my condolences to his family?'

I said, 'I'll certainly pass on your thoughts, thank you.'

Ron put in with, 'Good on you, Jumbo.'

As he moved away, Dennis said, 'He's got a nerve. My missus hasn't forgiven me yet for those photos, brings them up every time we have a disagreement.'

This started howls of laughter from all in hearing range and only added to this so-called celebration of the life of Dutch.

Sunday morning, it was to be a quiet day. April and Daniel were packing, Tommy was having a lie in. They were going home later today. We had a roast beef and Yorkie lunch, followed by apple pie and custard. One hour later, they were gone. Festive break over.

Doreen was reclining on the sofa, I was sprawled into my large armchair, the sound on the TV set was down low, the whole house was tranquil. I was in and out of the land of nod, with all sorts of thoughts going through my mind.

Suddenly I was snapped back to reality by the chimes of the doorbell. Looking at the clock, it was close to 6 o'clock. Doreen opened her eyes and said, 'What was that?'

'The doorbell,' I replied.

'Who can that be?' she asked.

'How the hell should I know,' I answered as I went to the door.

Upon opening the door, I got the surprise of my life, it was Barbara with Robert.

I said, 'Wow, come on in,' and put my arms around her. She immediately broke down crying. I escorted her to the sofa and sat her down. Doreen was straight in with a comforting hug. I shook hands with Robert and asked, 'You OK?'

'No, not really,' was his reply.

Barbara said, 'I'm sorry to drop in on you like this, but I just had to get out and talk to someone.'

'No need to be sorry; you know you're always welcome here. So come in, sit down and relax. You're among friends. A drink, anybody? Tea, coffee, or would you like something a little bit stronger?' Robert requested coffee, stating he was driving. Barbara's preference was also coffee and Doreen the same. Me, I went for tea.

When I arrived back in the lounge with the drinks, there was a very sombre atmosphere in the room. Doreen, speaking very softly, was saying how sorry she was. She went on, saying what a wonderful person Dutch was, how good-looking he was, how charming he had always been and how much he was going to be missed, not by just her and me but by everyone that knew him.

As I handed the drinks around, I offered a drop of fortification, whisky, brandy or even gin to go in their drinks. Doreen went for the brandy, Robert declined on the grounds he was driving. Barbara also half-heartedly declined, saying she had been taking various drugs and sedatives and wasn't sure it would be wise to mix alcohol with them. Doreen asked, 'When did you last have any medication?'

'Well, actually none since last night, but might need some tonight.'

'I think you should have some, purely medicinal, of course,' said Doreen. This raised a little titter around the room.

'Oh, go on then, just a small amount then,' said Barbara. I myself settled for a drop of whisky.

Whether it was Doreen's eulogising about Dutch or the effect of the brandy, but 10 minutes later, Barbara's demeanour seemed much improved. She started to talk about Dutch.

She was saying how pleased she was that everyone thought well of him and spoke in such high regard about him. As she herself, though probably biased, thought him the best person anyone could wish to meet. She went on to say she was extremely pleased that we could talk of him, as everyone had seemed to shy away from saying anything about him, and all she wanted to do was talk about him. Then she broke down crying again.

Me, I didn't know what to say or do. Doreen knew exactly what to say and do; she just carried on talking to her, saying, 'Yes, we understand that you would want to talk about him. When we wondered how you were getting on, we had said that's what you would want to do and how people find it hard to do that in these circumstances.'

I don't remember any conversations that went along like that. Credit to Doreen though, she knows what to say and when to say it. She then got a packet of tissues and offered them to Barbara. Barbara's response was to say, 'I'm sorry about this, but I can't help it.'

I said, 'No, don't be sorry, it's no more than we expected. In fact, we would have been surprised if you didn't show your emotions.'

After a short while, she gained control and said, 'I worry he'll be forgotten, and nobody but me will remember he ever existed.'

'That won't happen, this is Dutch we're talking about.' At the very mention of his name, she broke down again. This time I kept on talking. 'He will not be forgotten, not in my lifetime, nor his family's.' I looked over at Robert, he just nodded his head. I realised he was battling to maintain control of his emotions; he had not said a word since he sat down. 'He's very much appreciated at work. At the club, the news sent everyone into disbelieving shock. It took well over an hour before spirits revived enough to be able to suggest Dutch would not want them to be permanently dejected. They decided to celebrate his life. Which they did in style. It was also put forward that a competition should be arranged as a memorial to his memory. So, I think he will be remembered for a very long time to come.'

Barbara, having regained her composure, asked, 'Are they really going to do that?'

'Oh yes, it's not official yet, but it will happen, so many people have good memories of him.'

She then said, 'I don't want to go into detail, but I have a very vivid memory of the first time I ever saw him. I thought he was *magnificent*.'

I thought, *Yes, I'm not going to say anything on that subject. I don't want her to realise how he would relay on to me all his sexual adventures at that time. But yes, I can recall his very vivid narrative of the event.*

What I did do was to ask if anyone would like another drink. Barbara replied, 'No thank you, we've taken up enough of your time, I think we should be off.'

'Nonsense, our time is your time. So don't think you're impinging on us at any time ever.'

'Yes, I do know that and I thank you for it. Still, I don't want to abuse your kindness.'

'It's not kindness, it's friendship,' was my comment.

I then said, 'Before you go, what has the hospital had to say?'

'Nothing,' was her reply. 'I think that's why I had to get out.' She went on to say she had called and asked to speak to the surgeon. She was told he wasn't available and was passed on to the ward sister.

She was told by the sister, the surgeon would not be allowed to say anything to her till after the post-mortem and not then if an inquiry needed to be held. She went on to say any questions or enquiries should be directed to herself.

When asked what had happened, she had replied, 'I cannot say anything till after the post-mortem.' Asked when the post-mortem would be, she said, 'Hopefully sometime next week.'

Barbara started to weep once again, saying, 'They won't tell me anything, I'll never find out what happened to him.'

Doreen took over saying, 'It's still the holiday period and they're only staffed with holiday cover. The nurse is probably only saying what the hospital have told them to say in this sort of circumstance. I don't think they'll keep anything from you.'

I added, 'It's very understandable there should be a post-mortem, and they will be very guarded as to what they say till the outcome is clear.'

'Yes, I suppose so,' was her reply. They left shortly after.

I said to Doreen, 'I think this is going to run and run, there will have to be an inquest. His death was so unexpected. He was doing unbelievably well; something must have gone very, very wrong.'

Monday 3rd January

It was New Year's Bank Holiday Monday, Christmas suddenly seemed so very long ago, yet we were still in the holiday season. Doreen was, as usual, moaning, this time about the state of the house, plus the fact all the bed linen needed to be changed and washed. I said, 'Whoa, life ain't that bad, you go and strip the beds, then put it all in the washer. I'll tidy up and put all the furniture back in its place. Then we'll go out and get some lunch somewhere.'

An hour and half or so later, we were off driving. Doreen asked, 'Where are we going?'

'I've no idea, I think if we just head towards Bridgnorth, there are plenty of pubs down that way. I'm sure we'll find one that will suit you, OK?'

'Mm,' was the only response I got.

As we were driving along, I suddenly thought of work. I hadn't heard from them, not once all holiday long. I know Mick had made arrangements for all calls to go to him, but, well I would have thought he might have kept me informed as to what was going on. Mm, perhaps not.

After a pleasant leisurely lunch, we ambled our way back home, by which time it was late afternoon. Doreen said, 'That's it. I'm doing nothing for at least a couple of hours.' She then pointed out the answering machine on the phone was flashing.

I immediately thought, *Work*. It was, in fact, two messages, urgent work perhaps. No, the first was Vic saying, 'We're back,' nothing else. The second was Ron, inquiring, as it was still holiday time, were we out for a drink tonight? Also Chris and Vic were back and said they would be at the club.

I rang Ron back and said, 'Yes, OK, we'll be there.' Ron informed me nothing had been said to Vic regarding Dutch.

At the club, Ron, Eileen, Dennis and June were already there. As we settled down, Doreen gave a rundown of Barbara's visit in quiet, hushed tones. Suddenly, could be heard someone singing 'Sailor stop your roaming, come home to me.' Enter Vic and Chris. Ron said, 'OK, Petula, stop that row, and I'll get you a drink.' Greetings and hugs all round, and with lots of Happy New Years, our Intrepid Travellers were welcomed home.

Chris gave a very comprehensive rundown of their adventure, with regular interruptions of questions and enquiries, enabling us to share the pleasure of their cruise. As the euphoria slowly subsided, Vic asked, 'How was your Christmas?' A sudden silence hit the group. Vic looked startled and said, '*What?*'

Dennis (God bless his soul) took up the conversation and said, 'Christmas was OK, but the New Year not so good. Dutch didn't make it.'

'What do you mean, didn't make it, make what?' asked Chris.

Dennis, looking around as if requiring assistance, carried on, saying, 'Well, actually, he did make New Year but only just. He died a quarter past midnight.'

After what seemed like minutes but was only a couple of seconds, Chris very quietly murmured, 'No,' then seemed to explode, '*No!*' and started weeping. She was comforted by June and Eileen, who were either side of her. Doreen just looked at me with raised eyebrows as if to say *I didn't expect that.*

Vic, seemingly not all that concerned with Chris's dilemma, asked what happened. Dennis once again took up the dialogue saying, 'His operation went very well, and everything seemed positive. Then early New Year's Day, the call came saying he'd passed on. Since then, we've been told there's to be an autopsy sometime this week, and nobody's saying anything till the results are posted.'

Vic said, 'Something has gone very wrong here, I would think a very large dose of compensation will be sought.'

Doreen then piped up, 'Whatever compensation is offered, it still won't bring him back, will it?' She went on to say, 'That's if there's any compensation to pay. It mightn't be anyone is to blame.'

The rest of the evening seemed to revolve around what could or might have happened. Chris was in a much more controlled state as the evening rolled on and expressed strong opinions supporting the idea that someone had messed up, adding that she herself had never trusted that hospital. We didn't stay late, as it was back to work in the morning.

Mick was devastated by the news of Dutch, totally floored. He sat there, very quiet; he went very pale, I was about to be concerned for him. He then said, 'You said he was OK, everything had gone well, it just needed time for him to be up and about.' He went on to say, 'I never expected this, never, I can't believe it.'

I thought for a moment he was going to start weeping. After a couple of minutes, he suddenly said, 'So, I suppose we will just have to get on with it then.'

I said, 'Yes, that's about the size of the situation.'

I suggested he should do the garage inspection and fend off any inquiries as to what happened to Dutch by saying there's to be an autopsy; nothing will be known till that has been completed.

I would go to the garage office, put in our timesheets and completed worksheets. Tell them of the death of Dutch. I also needed to make an appointment with the manager as soon as he arrived.

Just as I was leaving, Mick blurted out, 'When you see the manager, ask him—'

At this, I put my hand up and said, 'Hold on, this is not the time or occasion to ask the manager about future happenings. He is not going to make any more decisions about anything. In a few weeks, the new manager will be here, and all will be sorted then.'

He said, 'I was only going to say make sure he knows I covered the holiday period.'

I nodded and said, 'Yes, I know what you were only going to ask.'

In the garage office, the news was received with stone stares of disbelief. Then Sam burst out crying and ran to the toilets. The rest of the crew in there, when recovered from the initial shock, asked the usual, what, when, how. I just told them what I'd suggested Mick should say to all enquiries.

Samantha returned, still dabbing her eyes, I wasn't sure how to proceed. I just quietly said to her, 'I need to inform the manager as soon as he arrives. Could you let him know I wish to see him.'

She replied, 'He's here already. He arrived very early, before me actually.' At that she rang his office, and when he answered, she immediately told him of Dutch's demise. She then went on to say I was waiting to see him.

In the manager's office, he stood up and offered his hand, which I shook. He went on to say how shocked he was and how sad that it had turned out this way. He said Dutch was as fine a person as he'd ever known. Saying he'd only recently become aware of his ability and potential as a leader of men. I said, 'Thank you. I will pass on your thoughts to his family.'

'Apart from all this, how was your break?' I asked.

'Quite agreeable,' he replied. 'After the shock of the board's decision to terminate my role in the company, Mrs Williamson and myself discussed our future. She is employed as a secretary with a large company in Aldridge. I intend to negotiate a retirement /redundancy package deal, and she will be doing the same. If we are successful, we can look forward to an adventurous and exciting retirement. Once we had agreed our course of action, the rest of the Christmas break was very pleasant.'

I then gave a résumé of all our activities during his absence, including the visit of Mr Kane. I went on to ask, 'Any comment or instruction?'

'No,' he replied and added, 'I shan't be issuing much in the way of instructions from now on. That is unless I have anything from on high to relay to you.' At that, I took my leave.

Back at our workshop, all that concerned Mick was if I had told old Billy of his involvement over the Christmas break and had he said anything about his future role in the company. I explained to him, Billy, as he liked to call the manager, had been told of his gallant involvement over the holiday period but had not offered any comment. As for his future role, 'Billy, as you like to call him, doesn't give a tuppeny-fuck.'

The rest of the week passed by without much happening at work. Similarly, the evening at home passed quietly without incident.

Friday evening, Doreen told me she had spoken with Barbara. Owing to the holiday period, the autopsy wouldn't be held till Monday. Its findings would be released on Tuesday or possibly later if there were any complications.

At the club, things were back to normal. The usual crew in situ, plenty of chatter from happy conversations all around the room. Our own conversation was frequently interrupted by various members requesting information regarding Dutch. Such as, what happened, what's going to happen next, when's the funeral, etc., etc., etc.

Then the club president, PK, turns up. Very formally said, 'On behalf of myself and my family and the club and all its members, could you please pass on our sincere condolence to Barbara and the rest of his family.'

Ron said, 'Yeah, will do.'

Chris, with a look of disdain at Ron, said, 'Thank you, Peter, for your kind thoughts so elegantly put. I will make sure your message will be passed on to all his family.'

Ron said, 'I've just said that.'

PK, with his eyebrows raised, said, 'Yes, thanks.'

Vic then asked him, 'Want a drink?'

PK said, 'Yes, I will, thank you.'

While Vic got a round in, PK said, 'Keep me informed as to the progress of events and the funeral date.' He went on to say, 'I'll post bulletins on the noticeboard to keep all the members informed.'

At work, and everywhere else for that matter, all was back to normal. The holiday period well and truly behind us. Heads down, for a hard slog through till Easter. Hadn't heard anything from the manager since we spoke last week about Dutch; that was alright by me, keep it nice and quiet, just how I like it.

At break time that morning, it all changed. Or I thought it was about to change. Sammie called to inform me the manager wanted to see me right away. 'Aye-up, here we go,' I said, 'the balloons about to go up,' as I made my way to his office.

I gently knocked on his door. 'Come in,' was his immediate response. 'A-ha, just the man.' *Blimey, he's turned into Alan Partridge,* I thought. 'I'm going to be out for the rest of the day. I'm meeting with the directors to discuss my severance pay and probably won't be back. Is everything in order?'

'Yes, sir, everything's fine, all very much routine.'

'Good,' was his absentminded sort of response. He then produced an envelope and said, 'Could you please pass this on to Haakon's family with my sincere condolences.' He then added, 'He will surely be missed by all that knew him.'

I only answered, 'Will do,' then left.

It was just before noon on Wednesday when I next received a call to say I was needed in the manager's office. I'm thinking, *Bloody hell ain't he got anybody to talk to again?* as I approached the office. I gave a double tap on the door and was immediately beckoned in by none other than Mr Kane. 'Oh, good morning, sir,' I blurted out.

'Yes,' he said, 'I want to speak with you regarding our friend Dutch. Mr Williamson told the board on Monday of his demise. When we spoke before Christmas, you spoke in such glowing terms of Dutch that I wondered if it was just rhetoric. On our tour of the conurbation, I was aware of all the seemingly genuine enquiries of Dutch and his wellbeing. Then Mr Williamson spoke in such high praise of his qualities and his contribution to the running of the unit that I felt that I, on behalf of the company, should pay our respects on his passing. Would you kindly pass this card of sympathy along with our condolences to his family?'

I told him of the post-mortem that had taken place earlier in the week and that the findings were due to be released sometime today. I went on to say, I thought it likely an inquiry would have to be held. As the operation had been deemed a success, rendering his death somewhat unexpected. He asked to be kept informed of progress and kind of dismissed me in a way that only director type of people can.

On arriving home, my very first utterance was, 'Have you heard anything?'

Doreen, being equally anxious, instead of moaning about my greeting with some sort of sarcastic comment, replied, 'No, nothing.' We didn't pursue that conversation, not at that time anyway.

I had a shower, then my evening meal, sat back to read the paper. My mind was still fully engaged on the results from the post-mortem. 'Should we phone, or what?' I asked of Doreen.

'No,' was her short answer. 'We're not family; we're not entitled to know till they are good and ready to tell us.'

'Yeah, you're probably right. Only I've got a couple bereavement cards for his relatives from work.'

'Well, we should wait till Barbara gets in touch, so you'll just have to wait,' said like it was the final word on the subject.

It was well into the evening, gone 9 o'clock. I was thinking, *We're not going to hear anything tonight, if nothing has been heard by tomorrow evening, I will contact Barbara regardless of what she says.* Suddenly the phone rings. It is Barbara. 'Ah, hallo, how's things with you?' I asked, trying not to sound anxious.

'Not all that well, really,' she replied. 'I'm somewhat confused.'

'Why, what have they said?'

'Well, first of all, it was asbestos that was responsible for his problems. The operation was successful; his aftercare was correctly planned and executed. The cause of death was a bleed of the internal wound that flooded his lung.' At this she started to cry.

I waited a while for her to regain her composure. She said, 'Sorry about that.'

I said, 'No need to be sorry, it's all OK.'

She then said, 'I'm meeting with the ward sister and a member of the management board tomorrow to discuss the post-mortem and future developments.'

'Have you got anyone to go with you? You'll need someone to take notes. Do you think you should have some sort of legal representation?'

She informed me that Robert would be with her, they were going to request the meeting be recorded. She also told me she had spoken with her Police Federation representative, who was going to attempt to arrange some legal support.

'Good,' was my response, 'you seem to have an element of control of the situation, make sure you keep it that way. By the way, I've got a couple of sympathy cards from senior management, one from the board of directors, no less, to pass on to you.'

'That's nice,' she said with a bit of a croak in her voice as she seemed to start to break up again. She then rapidly said, 'I'll be in touch,' and hung up.

We did not receive any news of the meeting during Thursday. Both Doreen and I thought it would be too intrusive to call Barbara. Better to wait till she contacted us.

On arriving home on Friday evening, Doreen greeted me with the news that Barbara had been in touch. 'Great, what's the outcome of their discussion at the hospital?'

'There's going to be an inquest,' she replied.

'Any information as to what happened?' I asked.

'Only what we already know, the wound had bled, it caused heart failure.'

'Is that it?' I asked.

'Well, it seems he became agitated and restless, and this movement had a detrimental effect on the internal wound.'

'So, the inquest is to determine what triggered his agitated state, I presume,' was my take on the issue. *Considering he was supposedly heavily sedated* was my thought.

What could be considered a full team was in situ on Friday evening. All the ladies of the group had been in touch with Barbara. When I say in touch with Barbara, it became evident that

318

Robert had been answering the calls. I suspect in order to shield Barbara from the avalanche of calls they were probably receiving.

First Chris, 'All his stitches came undone. That surgeon needs to be reported and struck off.'

Followed by June, 'He drowned in his own blood, you know.'

Then Eileen came in with, 'That doctor had boasted the operation had been perfect and he was well on his way to recovery.'

Vic puts in with, 'Yes, he's got some answering to do, a big claim will be aimed at him.'

This kind of talk went on for quite some time. Doreen looked at me with a quizzical look. I put my forefinger to my lips with a slight shake of my head, more or less saying, *keep out of this.*

After a while, good old Ron asked, 'Are we playing snooker tonight?' This enabled us guys to escape the cackling of the females.

On the way home, I said to Doreen, 'I'm glad you kept out of the whinging about the surgeon.'

'Yes,' she replied, 'I told them Barbara had phoned and said he had become restless, which had caused his stitches to break.'

'What was their reaction to that little bombshell?'

'Nothing, no one passed any comment.'

Monday 17th Jan.

At work on Monday, after a reasonably quiet and easy weekend, it was Mick who was first to ask the question, 'When's the funeral?'

My response was, 'I've no idea. Nothing has been said about it. Everybody has been totally absorbed in the post-mortem and now the inquiry.' I then add, 'I'm not sure what the procedure is for releasing bodies in these situations.'

I was also asked the same question by the manager and two or three other people during the day. Consequently, when arriving home, it was that question that was on my mind. I asked Doreen if, in any of her conversations, had there been any mention of the funeral. 'No,' she replied, 'nothing at all. Why do you ask?'

'I have had several enquiries as to the date and details of the event, that's all.'

Later on, Doreen suddenly said, 'We haven't had any contact with Barbara since before the weekend. I think I'll give her a call.'

I suggested she could mention the funeral. Her response was, 'I'll see how the conversation goes.'

I was making some adjustments to a hinge on a kitchen cupboard door when Doreen came and said, 'I've just spoke with Barbara.'

'Hold on a minute, let me clear my tools and equipment away, make a cup of tea, then we can sit and talk about it all.'

It had been advised that a solicitor should be appointed to oversee all the requirements necessary for the inquest. Until all parties were satisfied that that had been achieved, it would not be permissible to have the body released. Nor would it be possible to issue a death certificate. 'Good,' was my response, at least it seemed the situation was being taken very serious by all concerned.

Doreen, later on, eventually informed me that Barbara and Robert were meeting with the solicitor that had been engaged through the Police Federation on Wednesday morning.

Throughout the rest of that evening and most of the following day, my mind was full, wondering, if not worrying, about the timing and the supposed details of his final moments. While we were singing and dancing, celebrating the New Year, Dutch was slipping away. Where were the hospital staff? Were they with him, or singing and dancing like most of the population? Why did he become restless, at that particular time, when supposedly heavily sedated?

I know when I had a camera scan down my throat some years ago, they anesthetised me with Valium and I didn't feel or remember anything. Having said that, when I came to my senses, I was actually drinking a cup of tea. (*What do I know about people being sedated? Nothing.*)

With these sorts of thoughts going round and round in my head, I decided to have a chat with Robert before he and Barbara met with the solicitor. I thought it better to relay my concerns to Bob rather than Barbara as I felt he might be less emotional in discussing the situation.

320

At home later that evening, I rang Bob, only to be informed he was out and wouldn't be back till late. With no other course open, I called Barbara. What I found was, Barbara, rather than being emotional, was quite forthcoming in her attitude to the situation.

She felt the sorrow of her loss had changed to anger at what she now realised was an overwhelming belief that his death was wholly preventable.

'That's precisely what I'm calling about,' I interjected. 'For some time now, I've been concerned about the timing of events. Such as on the stroke of midnight of the New Year, when practically all the world was in party mode. Was there a party mood at the hospital? Was there a party on the ward or in the vicinity of the ward? Were all the nurses at their station? Was there a fireworks display anywhere near his ward? Had all his medicines been given at the correct time?

'I ask all this, owing to the fact that he woke up enough to move when supposedly in an induced coma. How's that possible? My thoughts are, only if his medicines have been neglected and some sort of noise disturbs him.'

I was suddenly aware that Barbara was distressed and crying. 'Oh, I'm very sorry for that,' I uttered.

'No,' she replied, 'it's just that I'm so pleased you think like that because it's the type of thoughts that I've been having. I thought I was the only one, I thought I was going out of my mind thinking things like that.'

'No, not at all,' I went on to say, 'it's why I phoned this evening. Tomorrow when you meet with your solicitor, these are the questions you want answers to. Make sure he understands your concerns. Talk it over with Robert before the meeting, be sure you both know what you require. Good luck, and don't let him take an easier option.'

I left it at that and didn't get a report back on Wednesday evening. By Thursday evening, I was getting slightly anxious. I felt I couldn't chase after information as I was not really entitled to any.

It was close to 9 o'clock when the phone rang. It was Bob, he told me Barbara was feeling a bit down, as the solicitor had not seemed all that impressed with their take on the situation. He had said: You can't go throwing accusations around of hospital staff not doing their duty without any evidence.

After a moment's deliberation, I responded with, 'Well, he is perfectly correct, but that's not what we are saying. What we are saying is that it's a likely scenario and to make sure the evidence is available to prove or disprove our concerns.'

'Well, that is the argument we put back to him, and I think he understands our concerns, but Barbara was still disappointed with his show of indifference.'

'I suppose it is part of his role to keep a balanced view,' I said. 'Just make sure you keep the pressure on whenever you have meetings with him.' I signed off by saying, 'Tell Barbara to keep her chin up; we'll get there.'

Friday evening, a team of eight had gathered, it seemed to me to be a bit jaded. The main topic of conversation revolved around Barbara's solicitor and how useless he was. For my part, I kept out of it, I said nothing.

I was just about to suggest we went to the snooker room when the bowls secretary Joan approached. 'What are you all looking so serious about?' was her opening remark. She was immediately engrossed in conversation with the females of our group. Topic of conversation: *Dutch*. Such was the intensity of this conversation, us blokes were totally redundant. Dennis suggested a game of snooker. As we began to rise, Joan suddenly said, 'Hold on, you lot, it's you I came to chat with.'

'You won't get much chance of that with this lot,' put in Vic, gesturing towards our spouses.

Joan carried on, totally ignoring Vic's remark, 'I hope to have the bowls AGM somewhat earlier than last year. Owing to the fact there's a change in the lease of the green.'

'When are we opening the green?' asked Vic.

'Will the subs be going up?' asked Ron before Joan could take a breath.

'All these things get sorted at the AGM,' she replied, 'that's what AGMs are for.'

'Yeah,' said Ron, 'OK, when?'

Joan was of the opinion that Tuesday 22 February would be satisfactory, giving time to sort any problems with the lease plus all other issues.

'OK, no problems with that,' I ventured, receiving nods from our guys to the snooker.

It was June who spoke up with, 'It'll be around the same time as the funeral, won't it?'

Blank stares looked back at her. Dennis said, 'Yeah, maybe,' and with that we went to play snooker.

Monday 24th Jan.

Work was steady, no emergencies, no panics, no manager, very conspicuous by his absence and his non-involvement in events. Mick was still totally confused by the female of the species. (As if all us blokes aren't.) And life carried on, even without Dutch.

I had made the conscious decision to distance myself from Barbara and Dutch's family and their discussions with the hospital. It really wasn't any of my business. I felt I'd done my part and satisfied myself his death was being suitably investigated. I had not let him down.

Tuesday, Doreen, along with Eileen and Chris, took Barbara for lunch. Consequently, Tuesday evening, I was bombarded with gossip on an unbelievable number of subjects. The only item I took interest in was Barbara becoming impressed with the solicitor, plus the fact that they hoped to be in a position to issue the death certificate sometime next week.

Well into the morning on Thursday, I was repairing one of the floodlights on the car park adjacent to the manager's parking spot when lo and behold, he turned up. 'I was about to report that as soon as I arrived this morning. I noticed it last night as I was on my way home,' he added.

'Yes, someone else also noticed and put in a report sheet. Everything in order?' I enquired.

'Things seem to be moving in the right direction regarding my departure,' was his comeback.

'Oh good,' was my response.

'I've been in consultation with the financial guys regarding my payoff.'

Once again, my response was, 'Oh, good, all go well?' I asked. (My thoughts were, *It's got fuck all to do with me, why am I hearing this?*)

'Yes, thank you,' was his reply to my question. He then went on to say, 'While at head office, I spoke with Mr Kane, who let me know the interviews for the manager's post are to be next Thursday.'

'They aren't waiting around, are they?' was my comment.

'No,' he replied,' between you and me, I think they headhunted the person they wanted and have been successful.' With a self-satisfied look on his face, he took his leave of me.

That conversation must have been playing on my mind as Mick suddenly asked, 'Is there a problem?'

'No, why?' I asked.

'Well, you've been very distracted and withdrawn over the past hour or so. I just wondered if I'd done something wrong.'

'No, no, it's me, just daydreaming and having thoughts drifting through my mind. I've been speaking to the manager regarding the progress to replace him.'

'We haven't had much out of him lately, have we? Is he OK?' asked Mick.

'Yes,' was my only reply.

My thoughts had been *Uni educated, degrees in civil engineering and business management, headhunted. Is that the sort of bloke I will be able to get along with? Still making the assumption it's a guy.* I'm also wondering what Dutch would have made of this situation. I reckoned he would have said, 'We'll treat him much the same as he treats us, as I've always done with people.'

Friday evening at the club, Ron, Vic, myself plus our other halves were in attendance. June and Dennis had gone visiting their daughter in Bristol for a few days. The topic of conversation was of course Barbara and her pursuit of justice for Dutch.

Suddenly Chris asked me, 'Are you going to be at the inquest?'

'Me, no, why should I be there?' I answered.

'I think one of us should attend to make sure all the incidents and events are put forward and noted before any conclusions are arrived at.'

I said, 'I don't think it works like that, it's the solicitor's job to see all evidence is produced.'

Chris replied, 'I don't care. I want to be there.'

At that moment, PK entered our area. 'Hi guys, how are things?'

Vic butted in with, 'Good. You?'

PK answered, 'Yes, fine.'

Ron asked, 'All set for the AGM?'

'Well, that's really why I'm here. Are you up for re-election as captain for Thursday's team?'

Ron, looking very pleased with himself, said, 'Yeah, but ain't it up to a vote at the meeting?'

'Just a formality,' replied PK.

As he was leaving, Vic asked, 'What date is the green opening?'

'No idea,' was his response to that question, and he was gone. We made our way to the games room.

On our way home, I asked,' What did anyone have to say?'

Doreen's response surprised me somewhat. 'Oh! Chris went on and on about what had happened to Dutch and how the hospital should pay and the surgeon must be held responsible.' She went on to say, 'You would have thought it was her husband the way she went on.' Doreen carried on saying, 'She then started on about Barbara, saying she thought she was a bit dopey for allowing it to happen in the first place. She then said, "Why should she have everything? She wasn't even engaged, let alone married to him."'

Doreen then said, 'Eileen looked at me with raised eyebrows and a puzzled look on her face but neither of us said anything.' Doreen went on to say, 'Chris seemed quite disturbed and emotional, I even thought she was going to cry.'

I said, 'Poor old Chris, you do realise she's carried a torch for Dutch for a long, long time. She needs to be very careful as to what she says and does, as it could make a lot of problems for herself and others.'

Work over the weekend went well enough. I arranged a programme myself. The manager had not shown any interest in having an input. He had, in fact, suggested I should take charge and do whatever needed to be done. The situation suited me very well, as in actual fact, it was no different to what always happened, apart from the manager's stamp of approval. Work in general just drifted along, no major projects taken on, No capital spending. Job just drifting along. Only real concern, make sure the fleet gets into service.... *I don't half miss Dutch.*

Monday 31st January

Monday evening, Ron phoned. He was a little bit uncertain about him being propelled into the role of captain for Thursdays. Asking what if they don't want him, what if he can't get a team together?

'Hold on a bit,' I interjected, 'if you're not wanted, you'll be rejected at the AGM. But why would they not want you as captain? You did an excellent job last season.'

'Yes,' he replied, 'but I was only there because Dutch had said so. Nobody was going to object to that situation.'

'Ron, you're selling yourself short here. You did an excellent job, appreciated by all. Anyway, you know the team are always happy for anyone to be captain as long as it's not themselves.' I went on to say, 'You can get Vic to be vice-captain again, no problem.'

He came back with, 'Ooh, I'm not sure what's going on there. Eileen was telling me while we were playing snooker, Chris was going on about Barbara in a very disparaging way, as though she had an interest in the termination of Dutch and his estate.'

I said, 'I shouldn't worry too much about that. Chris had feelings for Dutch that were only in her mind. I think she is grieving silently and feels very alone. Vic won't notice, and if he did, I don't think he would be very bothered. With him, life will just carry on as ever.'

'You think that's what it is? Eileen thought perhaps something had been going on.'

'No, no, only in her dreams,' I once again reiterated.

'Only Eileen has been talking to June, telling her all about Friday's performance. Between them they came to a conclusion that something might have gone on.'

Oh, the rumour drums are beating at full blast. Wow, this need's nipping in the bud, was my take on this situation. My advice to Ron was to ask Eileen to ring June and tell her, on reflection and speaking with me and Doreen, she now thinks it's all only in Chris's imagination.

'Yeah, I think you are probably right,' said Ron.

'So, that was the real reason you called, nothing to do with the bowls then.'

'Well, yes and no,' came back Ron. 'I'm still somewhat concerned about the reaction to the assumption of me being captain just on the nod of PK.'

'I don't think you have anything to worry about there,' was my parting comment.

It was after work on Thursday; as I finished my dinner, Doreen suddenly said, 'Oh, Barbara called earlier on, she wants you to give her a call as she wishes to ask a favour of you.'

'What favour?'

'I don't know, phone and ask.'

I did give Barbara a call. When she answered, she was quite apologetic about having asked for me to give her a call. Saying she was aware of how busy I was at work and such. I said, 'I've never been too busy to react to your call, so never worry about that. Now how can I help you?'

'Well,' she said, 'I've been trying to work out and put some organisation into the funeral arrangements. One of my thoughts was, who should do the eulogy? My mind is telling me there is only one person who can do it, and that's you.'

That statement was met with absolute silence. 'Hello, are you there?' she asked.

My mind was in total turmoil. 'Yes,' I replied, 'I'm still here... but don't know what to say.'

'Oh, I'm sorry, I should not have asked. If it's a problem, it's OK.'

'No, it's not that, I would like to do it. In fact, I want to do it. It's just I don't know if I could hold it all together without falling apart.'

She responded by saying, 'Do you want to leave it for now and think about it?'

'No, if I stop to think about things, I'll talk myself out of it. So, put it down to me, it will be done.'

'Are you sure?'

'Most definitely,' I replied, giving the statement an amount of assurance that was not necessarily felt.

Friday morning, all seemed to be going well, work was mainly routine, no major, or for that matter, minor problems. Around mid-morning, as I was returning to our workshop from the spray booth area, my mind full of the funeral and in turmoil about what I should say about Dutch. When suddenly, standing before me was the manager.

'Oh, hello,' I half spluttered with surprise, 'you looking for me?'

'No, not really,' he said. 'I'm just strolling around the place. looking at what is going on.'

'What, a few twangs of regret at having to leave,' I ventured.

'No, no, I've no regrets on that score. I think boredom is a more likely suspect for my little meander around the site.' He then said, 'By the way, we held the interviews for my replacement yesterday.'

'Oh yes, anyone any good?' I inquired.

'Yes,' he replied, 'two male and one female, all very good.'

'And!!' I added, asking for more details.

'Are you at all busy?' he asked.

'No, not particularly,' I replied.

'Good.' He then suggested I take my tools and equipment back to the workshop and report to him in his office.

On my arrival at his office, he said, 'Take a seat,' then offered me a cup of tea, which I gratefully accepted. He opened by saying he wanted to apologise for his lack of support over the last few weeks. He said he had found it very difficult to involve himself or concentrate on any work issues and now felt a bit guilty. 'So, how are things progressing?'

'Well, first of all, I don't think you need to apologise to me. I quite understand your reluctance to get involved. Things have been ticking over quite well, our problems have been mostly seasonal, weather-related, such as frozen water pipes around the bus wash area. We also had a problem with the fuelling points and had to make extra heating available.

'The only other sticky point was the heating in the body-shop failed, and the union guy got himself involved. Telling me if the temperature wasn't up to 60 degrees in the next 10 minutes, he would call his men out. I'd asked how come it was too cold for his blokes to work but not for me. "It's your job," he replied. I said, "If it had been Dutch standing here and you had said that, he'd have put you through that exit door and I ain't sure that he would have bothered to open it first." He replied, "That may be so but he ain't, so get on with it." I came very close to getting physical with him myself, but let it go. The heating was fixed, and everything settled down.'

He said, 'It's not your role to negotiate with union reps, and it's certainly not his to harass workers doing their best to alleviate problems.' He went on to say he would have a quiet word with him.

'Good,' I said.

I then asked, 'What about the selection committee, did they make a selection?'

'If they did,' he replied, 'they did not confide in me. I was asked my thoughts on each of the candidates. I'd said they were all very good. The young female, well-educated but lacked experience. The more mature guy was not that much younger than me. The final guy seemed well qualified and of the right age and experience, and as such would be my preference.

'The young lady from HR suggested that as a forward-looking company, we should give a serious amount of thought to employing a female in this type of role. Mr Kane then said, "Thank you very much for your contribution. I will now deliberate for a while on what's been considered today. I will then consult with my fellow directors. We will then reconvene, if my conclusion is acceptable, the position will be offered to the successful candidate. On acceptance, it can be announced hopefully by Friday next week."'

'It won't be the female, will it?' I asked with some trepidation.

'I've no idea,' he replied, 'but I think the young man I put forward as my favourite is the one who has been headhunted.'

329

'I do hope you're right. Dutch would not have been very happy with a female boss.'

'I don't think we need to take that into consideration, now do we?'

The mention of Dutch prompted him to ask what the situation regarding the funeral was. I explained what had happened over the last few weeks, leaving out the role asbestos had played. He would be long gone by the time the problem arrived with the company. No need to alarm him with it or give him the dilemma of informing the company or not.

He then asked, 'What date is the funeral?' I said I expected to be informed of that later today or at least over the weekend.

I went on to say I'd been asked to do the eulogy and I was struggling to come up with the right words. At this, he reached into his desk drawer and produced a pamphlet. 'Here you are,' he said, 'this should give you some help.' He handed it to me, it was titled 'Making Speeches for All Occasions'. A quick glance identified a page for eulogies.

I said, 'Wow! Thanks, that's great.'

He added, 'I've found it very useful over the years.'

Feeling we were getting on more as friends than gaffer and subordinate, I ventured to ask how the negotiations regarding his departure were going. He looked at me for a second or two, so much so, I thought he was going to tell me to fuck off and mind my own business. But no, he was quite forthcoming and said everything had gone extremely well, he had secured a redundancy/retirement package of which he was very pleased. He also informed me his wife had a very similar payoff; the pair of them were very happy with their situation. I said I was very pleased for them. I shook his hand and wished him and his wife a very happy retirement and left.

We entered the club at about our usual time. No one leapt on me requesting information regarding funeral arrangements, which was unusual.

A full team were present, all seemed to have expectant looks on their faces. I looked back and said, 'What?'

It was Eileen who opened up with, 'You're doing the sermon at the funeral then, aren't you?'

'It seems that way,' I answered.

'Is the date OK with you?' This was still Eileen.

'What date?' I enquired.

'The date of the funeral,' still Eileen.

'I didn't know there was a date for the funeral.'

June came in with, 'We've all spoken with Barbara today; she's told us all that you're doing the speech at the funeral and that it's to be on Thursday the 24th.'

'Oh, great,' I interjected. I went on, 'Yes, I have agreed with Barbara to do the eulogy, but at that time, a date for the funeral had not been set. So, thank you for that information. Doreen, make a note.'

The thoughts in my head were, *No wonder I wasn't bombarded by people on my entrance, they already knew.* At that, PK arrived on the scene. 'If you can let me know all the details of the funeral, I will post a note on the board.'

'Ah, PK. Good evening to you as well,' I prompted.

'Oh, yes,' he replied, 'good evening.'

Eileen piped in with, 'It's on the 24th.'

'Yes, but time and place and any other information will be needed.'

'He's doing the speech,' said June, nodding towards me.

'You doing the eulogy? Always tricky, I've got a pamphlet advising on giving this sort of spiel.'

'Oh, good, that will be very helpful.' I didn't say anything about already having one.

'Yeah, it's somewhere in the office. I'll find it out and let you have it before you leave, OK.'

So, everything sorted, apart from my little speech. Oh, bloody hell. why did I agree to that?

Throughout the weekend and well into the next, my mind was forever engaged with thoughts about my role at the funeral. I read both pamphlets. Both different but very similar in content. Quite helpful, more of what not to say rather than what to say.

331

MONDAY 7th February

Throughout the weekend, I had come to the conclusion that I should make a note of any thoughts I might have regarding Dutch and the guff I would probably spout at his funeral. Armed with that thought, plus a notebook and pen, I was more relaxed going about business at work and at home, for that matter.

It was Wednesday when I next spoke with the manager. He informed me the directors had reached a conclusion and selected the young man that he had favoured. He told this as though it was on his recommendation. He seemed quite proud in a self-congratulatory way. I, at this point, asked if this was the bloke who was headhunted. This momentarily flustered him. He very quickly regained his composure and said, 'I'm not sure that ever was the case. It was only an assumption on my part that he could have been sought after like that.'

'Oh, I see,' was my seemingly disbelieving response.

He went on to say he was a 34-year-old with a degree in civil engineering, plus a degree in business studies. His name was Cameron Montgomery.

I said, 'Fuck me, that's a mouthful, ain't it. Do we call him Monty?'

'I don't think he's the sort to take kindly to nicknames,' was the manager's reply. He went on to say, 'Don't breathe a word of this to anyone, a formal announcement will be made in a week or so. The guy will then be brought to the site and introduced to all sometime later.'

When Doreen and I arrived at the club on Friday evening, Eileen was sitting alone in our seating area. 'Where's Ron?' asked Doreen.

'Over there with that lot,' comes from Eileen, with a hint of being pissed off, sitting there without a drink. That lot being Joan, PK and Markie. I went to the bar.

While at the bar, Vic arrived. 'Where's Chris?'

'Over there with that lot.' Said with an air of assumption of everything being quite normal.

When they finally returned to the fold, Ron said without a prompt, 'Executive meeting to prepare for the AGM.' (With an exaggerated air of importance and a big smile.)

At that, all faces turned to Chris. She then goes into a long, drawn-out dialogue regarding her discussions with Barbara of the funeral arrangements. Then the debate with PK as to the information to be posted on the board.

The information to be put on the board is.

OUR DUTCH

FUNERAL 24TH FEB.

13:30 FROM THE HOUSE. 14:00 STREETLY CREMATORIUM. FAMILY FLOWERS ONLY. DONATIONS CAN BE MADE. ALL DONATIONS WILL GO TO MACMILLAN NURSES. FOLLOWING THE SERVICE, A BIG CELEBRATION OF HIS LIFE WILL TAKE PLACE IN THE MAIN ASSEMBLY ROOM HERE AT THE CLUB. ALL ARE INVITED.

In the games room, Ron informed us of his little tete-a-tete with the bowls captains. Joan had asked what form of tribute should be put forward to commemorate Dutch. He said, 'They all looked to me as if I would know.' When asked what he had put forward, he said, 'I'll talk with you pair and let them know.'

I explained to them that I had spoken with Barbara some weeks back. She had been upset and wondering if he would be very soon forgotten. I had suggested it was most unlikely he would ever be forgotten, and I understood a competition was to be arranged in his honour.

Vic then put in with the idea that our group should purchase a trophy, perhaps a shield of some sort. It could be named The Dutch Summer Open Plate or something similar. 'Brilliant,' cried Ron, 'I'll put that forward to go on the agenda at the AGM.'

'Slow down a bit. I think we should consult with Barbara first. Particularly regarding the purchasing of a trophy. She might want an input. Well, that's my thinking.'

It was agreed that I, as I had already broached the subject with Barbara, should discuss the idea with her and find her thoughts on the issue.

Throughout the weekend, my mind was preoccupied with thoughts of writing and then delivering the eulogy. I made copious notes, with a commitment to do a full write up in the middle of the week.

I did, however, manage a chat with Barbara. I put to her our proposal, that our group of friends wished to purchase a trophy for a club competition named in his honour. Her response was, 'Well, you having spoken of this previously, I have had a chat with Robert, he was very keen to have this happen. Between us, we concluded that we as a family would like to finance the whole project.'

'Right,' I said, 'OK, I'll put that to the club members at the AGM in a couple of weeks, leave it with me.'

Young Mick, in the meantime, was preoccupied with what to do for the sweet little Jenny; it was Valentine's Day on Monday. He asked me. My advice was: a card, some flowers, and a few inches of what's in your trousers. (Always very helpful, me.)

Monday 14th Feb.

During the morning, the manager sought me out. He told me he had had words with the union rep for the body-shop, who had at first denied any altercation. 'When challenged with having a clear the air meeting with you in my office, he claimed he was only concerned with getting the heating restored and might have been a bit overzealous. He is very anxious to offer you an apology, OK?'

At lunchtime, I asked Mick, 'How things go with your loved one on this Valentine's Day?'

'I more or less did what you suggested, card, big flowers; as for the rest, mind your own.' (I thought, *Not much of a story. I don't half miss Dutch.*)

On Wednesday evening, I met up with Vic, Ron and Dennis at the club. During our ramblings, I informed them of my chat with Barbara. Saying she was more than pleased with the club commemorating Dutch this way. She had spoken with Robert and had come to the conclusion that their family would like to fund the project.

Ron thought the club itself would feel it was their duty to honour Dutch. Vic put it forward that it would be for the members at the AGM to conclude who does what, so we should leave it till then.

Dennis then suggested, 'Maybe the club should ask the league to run a competition in his name.' Vic considered this a brilliant idea and would put it to the meeting himself.

Ron wanted to know why Dennis was involved in suggesting things for the bowls AGM. (Said in a humorous way.) At this, Dennis surprised us all by saying, 'I've acquired a set of woods.' He sat there with a sizable grin while three astonished faces stared back.

'And this gives you the right to influence our AGM. You've got a set of woods?' said Ron.

Dennis then said, 'Yeah, I'm looking for a team to join this season.'

'Done,' fires in Vic, 'as soon as the green opens, me and you practice every night, OK.'

'Are you coming to the meeting, it's next week. Because, if you are, you could put forward your suggestion of a league competition yourself,' suggested Ron.

I had what I believed to be an acceptable dialogue put together, ready for next Thursday. I was a bit more relaxed now that was accomplished.

Sometime during Friday, I ran into Samantha, the girl from the garage office. She told me that Mr Williamson had requested her to arrange transport for members of staff wishing to attend the funeral. Saying he had agreed with department heads to release up to 50 per cent of their staff. She was to collect names and numbers. And discuss with the traffic superintendent. I told her I had booked the day off, but young Mick would be aboard.

Friday evening was all about Dennis playing bowls. Very early on, Joan was sought, asked how Dennis could become a member of the bowls section of the club. She was of the opinion it should be put before the members at the AGM where it could be proposed, seconded and voted on, also recorded in the minutes, making it very official.

This was greeted with glee by us guys. Not quite as much by our female companions. With comments like, 'You won't be seeing much of him this summer,' that was Chris to June, nodded at by the other two.

We, the guys, went to the games room, where we continued our conversation of the AGM. The funeral wasn't mentioned. The ladies, according to Doreen later on, discussed clothing and what they were wearing for the funeral.

During the weekend, Mick expressed his disappointment at not being able to be at the wake for Dutch, as he was his closest work colleague. I explained, we needed to offer as much cover for the company as possible. He could go to the funeral on the provided bus, return on said bus. Check all was well; if or when all is in order, he could leave and come to the club and ask for me. If required at work, they had been given the phone number of the club, and one of us would have to respond. 'By this, I mean you. This has been agreed with the manager.'

Monday 21st Feb.

Going constantly through my mind were the words I was to deliver on Thursday. I was determined to commit it to memory. It was to be delivered as if spontaneous. It needed to be heartfelt and sincere.

I arrived for the AGM. Astonishingly, the room was packed. I think I'd mentioned before, only about eight or ten would normally be in attendance. Tonight, 30 or more. Wow. I wasn't late, but some of this crowd seemed to have been here for some time, having apparently demolished a fair quantity of drinks between them. This promised to be a lively evening.

I sat with our usual crew. 'How about this for a crowd then?' I said.

Vic spoke first, 'Yeah, I hope they all behave. Jumbo's over there.'

'Still in his wheelchair, for fuck-sake. He's milking that a bit, ain't he,' added Dennis.

At 8 o'clock, spot on the dot, PK called the meeting to order with a sharp knock on his table. 'Good evening, gentlemen. Oh! Er! and er lady,' with a nod towards Joan.

He then requested a minute's silence to honour absent friends; this was observed faultlessly.

The rest of the agenda was then followed, the minutes of the last meeting, financial report, plus the setting of subs (payments towards securing bowls section). Selection of officials, then captains of each team. Green opening date agreed (19th March), pushed to be as early as possible by Vic.

Then on to Other Business. Joan said, 'There has been huge interest throughout the whole of the club, not just the bowls section but the whole club to honour Dutch.'

Ron immediately got to his feet and said, 'As vice-captain to Dutch and to subsequently relieve him of the role of captain, I would like to put forward an idea that we, his closest friends, have had. That is that we would like to sponsor a tournament. In so much, we will purchase a shield for said tournament and have it called The Dutch Summer Plate. Open to the whole membership of the club.'

A round of applause started by Vic rang around the room. As the applause subsided, Joan, holding up her hand as if to say *hold your horses*, said, 'Well, the problem with that is the club itself wishes to promote a contest in his honour.'

This was my cue to rise to my feet. I informed the meeting that having been in conversation with his family, they had expressed a wish to sponsor an event in his memory.

The room went very quiet as everyone seemed to mull over how could we not go with his family's request.

After a very few seconds, which seemed much longer, Dennis got to his feet and put forward a thought. 'With so many propositions on the floor, could I suggest, we his close friends along with his family promote a club event. With the club arranging and sponsoring a league-wide event in his memory.' Once again, the room fell silent.

PK broke the silence, saying, 'I think that's a very good idea. I will, along with Joan, speak with the league management committee.'

At this, Jumbo Jennings shouts up. 'Who the fuck is he? How long have we had non-members putting things forward, telling us how to run our club?'

Dennis answered by saying, 'Shut your gob, Jumbo, my missus hasn't forgiven me yet for those photos.'

Jumbo came back with, 'You and your gang think you're something special, well you ain't, you're a bunch of pricks.'

Vic, not accepting this, said, 'Have a care, Jumbo, throwing insults around like that might keep you in that wheelchair a good bit longer.'

At this, Jumbo leapt to his feet with the intention of attacking someone. PK roared, 'JUMBO,' which stopped him in his tracks, and he sat down. Once again, the room was silenced.

I felt I must intervene. I said, 'Look, that's enough. I know Jumbo's a cantankerous, disagreeable, bad-tempered chap, but goading him is never going to suppress him. I would like to say let's leave it there, it's finished, it's over, OK.'

Jumbo looking very glum, said, 'No, it ain't finished, it won't be over till you've been sitting in one of these for a couple of months,' gesturing to his wheelchair.

As the room went quiet again, all in the room looked at me. I stared Jumbo in the eye and just uttered, 'Twat.' After a few seconds, I added, 'And stop chatting up my wife; she's far too much woman for the likes of you.' This remark bought the house down. The mood of the room lightened a lot.

I then called for the chairman to move the meeting on. 'First, though, can I have it in the minutes that with just the slightest provocation, Jumbo Jennings did leap from his wheelchair with no hint of any injury.'

Another bout of sniggering around the room. Jumbo's reply was, 'Bollocks you.'

The meeting continued. It was left with the officers to make the arrangements for a Memorial Competition or competitions in honour of Dutch. Dennis accepted as a member of the bowls section. The remark regarding Jumbo and his athletic prowess wasn't recorded in the minutes.

At the conclusion of the meeting, the chairman reminded everyone, 'It's the funeral on Thursday. I hope people who attend are better behaved and we don't have any silliness hindering proceedings. Meeting closed.'

With everyone settled back in their usual places, the evening continued. Our conversation was first drinks and congrats to Dennis. Then the piss-taking of Jumbo and his general disposition. Any number of club members came and passed comments, such as, 'He doesn't like you lot, does he?' Also, 'He still blames you for his problems,' and several other similar comments. What was noticeable, none of them seemed to think he was wrong.

The next morning at work, Mick was still bemoaning the fact he wasn't able to remain with the funeral and had to return to work. My take on the issue was, 'You want to be with this department, and that's how it goes in this department.'

Later in the day, the manager informed me the replacement manager was to be on site sometime next week. 'Oh great,' I replied, 'I'm looking forward to meeting him.'

He inquired if everything was settled ready for tomorrow and added, 'A vehicle has been made available for members of staff to attend.'

I said, 'Yes, but you do know I've booked a day off.'

'Oh, of course, yes,' was his suddenly remembered reply. 'Is Mick all sorted and ready?' he asked with a confused look on his face.

'Yes, we spoke about it last week and agreed the arrangement.'

'Ah yes, that's right,' was his comment as he took his leave.

I thought, *He's either going senile or really doesn't give a fuck, and I think it's the latter.*

* * *

It was funeral day, and from the moment I awoke, I felt tense and somewhat apprehensive. Doreen was all of a flummoxes. While having breakfast, I said, 'I need something to relax me.'

Doreen added, 'If we feel like this, how is Barbara coping?'

'I don't know, but I'm having some whisky in my tea.'

Doreen's retort was, 'Likewise,' and pushed her cup towards me.

By the time we were spruced up, suitably attired, we found ourselves 10 minutes too early. We had elected to follow the funeral cortege from the house, so time was not so critical. Another whisky was in order, purely medicinal, of course.

We parked a good number of yards up the road from the house, owing to the fact that the road was already quite crowded. The cortege had not yet arrived. Doreen thought we should go and present ourselves in the house. Robert was the first to greet us. I shook his hand, he said, 'I'm glad you're here.' Then asked, 'You got your script?' Which received a nod from me. 'I can't thank you enough for volunteering to do the eulogy, otherwise it would have been down to me. I'm not sure I would have been able to do it.'

I only said, 'No problem.'

Doreen went into the front room. When I looked in, they were hugging and somewhat tearful. I gave Barbara a hug and said, 'Stick with it; it'll all be OK.'

Following the hearse at a very leisurely pace, I was still going through my spiel in my head. We were in quite a long line of traffic, so very little concentration was required.

At the crematorium was a huge crowd. I found it difficult to park. Noticing Dennis's car, I parked right behind it. Blocking him in, but that was no problem.

The funeral director had been advised of my role. He ensured seats for Doreen and myself were kept free directly behind the family by the gangway.

The chapel was packed, people were standing two deep down each side of the seating area. There were reported to be several dozen standing outside.

Sitting there, as it all went quiet, looking at the coffin, I suddenly felt quite emotional. I thought, *Oh sod, get a grip.*

The vicar stood at his lectern and said, Welcome, I see we have a very large turnout to say a final farewell to Haakon.'

A lone voice from the back called, 'His name is Dutch.' It was Brian, a slight murmur was heard. I thought, *Oh no, don't let it kick off, not in here.*

The vicar, after a very faint pause, carried on. 'We gather here not only to say farewell but also to celebrate the life of Haakon.'

This time it was Don who called out, 'His name is Dutch, call him that, will you please?' This was followed by several cries of 'yes'. The vicar, now somewhat flustered, turned to Barbara with a look that said *help.*

Barbara, able to smile with the break in tension this pantomime has brought to the chapel, faced the congregation and nodded a yes. Followed by a round of applause.

The vicar, now seeming more relaxed, proceeded with the service. Eventually, I was beckoned to the lectern.

I opened with, 'Haakon Van De Enks,' raising the flat of my hand towards the gang of bowlers at the rear of the chapel, suggesting they didn't interrupt. This prompted a little snigger from the congregation. 'Quite a large name for one who can only be described as a colossus among us: Dutch. Yes, he was big in body, big in mind. Hard as diamonds, Tough as teak. Gentle as a lover's caress. Soft as a small child's cuddle. He was all of this and more.

'Fair, kind, honest to all who deserved it. He would scold stupidity. He did not suffer fools. He was a natural leader, a friend, once a friend, always a friend. He wasn't a moody sort of person. He didn't fall out with people, he just said it as it was. His disposition, his confidence made him good to be around. And to use a term that was used on the noticeboard in the club, he was OUR DUTCH. For this is how he was thought to be. He belonged to us all. Or, perhaps we all felt we belonged to him. He certainly grabbed life and shook it till it went his way. And when the vicar referred to celebrating his life, it certainly will need a big celebration to do justice to that life.

'He never spoke ill of those who passed through his life. I refer here to his first wife, Shirley, who he always seemed to hold

341

in the highest regard. Also, his children, of whom he was extremely proud. It was his lust for life; he couldn't resist, that was the cause of him breaking from them.

'Dutch, to me, was a friend, a very good friend. We socialised together, played sports together, along with others who are among us today.' I might add, a "yes" was heard to come from the area of the bowls crew. 'He was also a work colleague. It's as a work colleague that I will miss him most. He did lead an extraordinarily hectic life but never ever failed to turn up and deliver top-level service. He could be exceptionally funny when giving accounts of his adventures and escapades in this wilder side of life. I often claimed this was the only real excitement in my life. Many is the time I've been bent double with laughter at his narratives.

'His meeting up with Barbara had quite an effect on him. He seemed to acquire an inner peace, much more relaxed in himself and in his surroundings. I think, or more than that, I believe, he had at last found his soul mate.

'OUR DUTCH. Not *one* of the greatest, but *the greatest*.
'He was the best:

AN ORIGINAL DUTCH MASTER.

'Thank you.'

I sat down, feeling very agitated. Was only slightly aware of the vicar requesting a round of applause. My mind was in turmoil. I had not done justice to him; I had gone off script right from the start. The Haakon business had thrown me. I panicked. I rambled. I should have had notes. Oh, what a twat.

Suddenly, with the service almost over. The coffin started to lower and curtains began to draw around. Robert called out, 'See you, Dad.' This cracked everyone up.

Doreen, using her handkerchief, was dabbing her eyes, along with any number of others. I had a large lump in my throat, I was struggling for control.

Service over, I thanked the vicar. He said, 'You did very well, it was a very good speech.'

Barbara, along with Robert, his brother and two sisters, stood in line to thank people for attending. Doreen was first; she gave Barbara a big hug, saying, 'I thought it went very well, you did him proud.'

Barbara then turned to me, put her arms around me, and said, 'You were the star.' She went on, 'I was alright till you referred to us as soul mates; that's when it all hit me.'

I could see she was crying again. I just said, 'Sorry,' and moved on.

Standing outside, our group, the eight of us, gathered together. All a bit quiet, feeling the effects of the afternoon's proceedings. It was Vic who opened up with, 'You did well there, I know it isn't easy. I thought your Dutch Master bit was a stroke of genius.' As he was saying this, I was aware that he, Ron and Chris, who were all standing opposite me in our little circle, were actually looking over my shoulder.

I felt a slight tap, and someone said, 'Excuse me.'

On turning round, I said, 'Oh, hello,' and stepped back a couple of paces. 'Hello, Mrs McDonald.'

'Ruth, please,' she said. 'I hope you don't mind me being here?'

'No, I believe all are welcome. Is your husband with you?' I asked, looking around, 'Or are you on your own?'

'No, just me, you would not find him here; he had a low opinion of Dutch. I only came to check if our Karen would show up. Having arrived with the funeral cortege, I never had time to see who was here.' Ruth, claiming to have scanned the whole congregation, said, 'No, she's not here.' She then asked, 'Have you heard anything? You never mentioned our Karen's role in his life. Did Dutch ever mention anything?'

'No, no, and no,' I replied. 'Are you staying on for a drink?' I enquired.

'No, there's nothing for me around here anymore.' With that, she left.

As I watched her returning to her car, who should turn up but young Mick. 'What's going on with you and her?' he asked with a big grin all over his face. 'I've only seen her twice, and both times she's been all over you.'

'Yeah, some chance,' I replied. Then asked, 'Everything OK at work?'

'Yeah, well was when I left. Anyway, got to go, we're off now, see you later at the club, OK.'

As I returned to our group, Ron, Dennis and, for that matter, Vic, were still looking towards Mrs McDonald, getting into her car. Chris comes out with, 'Who's that, is that the girl from work Doreen was on about going out with Dutch?'

'No, she is not, and Doreen wants to keep her mouth shut.' This said while giving Doreen a bit of a stern look.

Ron, with a disbelieving look on his face, said, 'It ain't another one of his conquests, is it?'

I replied, 'I have been led to believe he had carnal knowledge of the young lady, yes.'

The funeral cars were preparing to leave. Vic made the first move, 'Come on, let's go.' We all made off to our cars.

As soon as we were in the car, Doreen started. 'OK, who is she?'

'I told you, a friend of Dutch.'

'Like you said. So, how does she know you?'

'She doesn't.'

'Yes she does, she came right up to you, tapped you on the shoulder, you turn around, say hello and move away. Then spend several minutes in conversation. To me, that says she's more than just a friend of Dutch.'

'OK, if I tell you, you must keep it to yourself, not like you did with the information about the office girl.'

Doreen jumped in, saying, 'I only said—'

'Whoa!' I hollered, 'I know what you only, but nevertheless, you had it open, right? Well, this time, keep it shut, do you understand?'

'Yes, OK,' was her defeated reply, followed by, 'So, who is she?'

'Well, actually, she's Karen's sister.'

'Well, why didn't you just say?' Suddenly, she asked, 'So how does she know you so well?'

'She doesn't.'

'I think we've already established she does,' she stated, with a very satisfied look on her face.

'If you must know, and I really mean keep it to yourself, she came to the garage looking for Dutch when he was away on holiday. Because he wasn't available, she spoke with me. She was seeking news of Karen and her whereabouts as she had had no contact with her since she left Dutch. I presume she still hasn't.'

'Yeah, I'll believe you, though thousands wouldn't,' she replied. 'But I don't see why I can't tell the others.'

'Because!!' was all I said.

Doreen and I were among the last to arrive back at the club. Consequently, the car park was once again full. We had to park way over the back, by the bowling green. This gave Doreen something else to chunter on about as we entered the club. 'Where have you been?' from Eileen.

'Where haven't we been?' from Doreen.

'Great, let's settle down and celebrate the life of Dutch,' from me.

The volume of noise, rising from a very quiet beginning, slowly but surely built a pleasant atmosphere. After a few minutes, I went over to Barbara. She was sat at a table with other members of the family.

'Hi, everything alright?'

'Yes,' she replied, 'I'm beginning to feel more relaxed now.'

'Good,' I replied, 'I thought it went quite well, or as good as these events can be said to go.'

She then said, 'Thank you for your part, I think everyone appreciated your sentiment.'

She then said, 'I would like to thank everyone for their thoughts and condolences. Do you think that will be possible?'

I said, 'I'll get the chairman to come over, you tell him what you require, and I'm sure he'll arrange it.'

Robert approached me, shook my hand, said, 'Well done and thank you.' He then asked, 'Can I introduce you to my mother?'

'By all means,' I replied. An attractive woman, attractive in an understated way, if you know what I mean, was introduced to me.

She opened by saying, 'Hello, I've heard a good deal about you.'

'Not all bad, I hope,' was my hopefully witty remark.

'No!' she said in a seemingly surprised way. 'Quite the opposite.' (So, it wasn't at all witty.) 'I want to thank you for what you said of the regard Dutch had for me and our family. I had always known his feelings for us, but it was nice to know he had confided it to others.'

As I re-joined Doreen, who was sat all alone, the others having gone walkabout, as in circulating, who should arrive but Mick. 'Oh, great, you made it; everything OK at work?' As I said this, I realised he had a pretty, very young lady with him.

'Well, hello,' I said in a very lecherous kind of way. Adding, 'And who do we have here?'

Mick said, 'This is my friend Jenny. I hope it's not a problem me bringing her. It's because she has heard so much about Dutch, she felt it right to be here.'

'Yes, of course, she's very welcome.' She sat by Doreen, who immediately engaged her in conversation. I get the drinks.

The afternoon drifted into evening. Barbara made a short speech. The evening drifted into the night; it was done.

Doreen contacted our daughter to come and drive us home. A task that was well beyond either of us.

Throughout Friday and the weekend, I felt the loss of Dutch a great deal. Mick was OK as a worker but was too young to give the mental stimulation and support that at times I needed.

He hadn't been to a funeral before and wondered if it was typical of funerals, having people calling out. I said, 'Not usual but not unheard of.' He asked what my thoughts were of Jenny. 'I thought she was a very nice, sweet girl; also my wife was quite taken by her.'

His thoughts regarding my wife surprised me somewhat. She was a lot different to what he had imagined. She was very nice, very pleasant, attractive, and a pleasure to be with. My reaction to this was, 'Why, what did you think I was married to?'

'Well, the way you go on about her, I expected her to be quite fierce and aggressive.'

I replied, 'Can't think why you should have thought that.'

Apart from a complex problem with a vehicle lift in the body-shop, all was routine.

It was later in the morning when Samantha informed me Mr Williamson had requested her to let all department heads know that Mr Kane, Director of Engineering, would be on site tomorrow with the new manager.

When this information was relayed to Mick, his only thought was, 'Will I have a chance to ask him what my role will be?'

It was getting on towards 11 o'clock. I was installing replacement controls in the steam cleaning area. The visiting dignitaries seemed to descend upon me suddenly out of nowhere. Introductions were made. 'Pleased to meet you, Mr Montgomery, looking forward to working with you.'

He said, 'Likewise.' Then added, 'I've been told you are the "go-to" man for info and answers.'

'Is that so?' I replied. 'If that's the situation, I might seek a salary increase.' Hoping no one would be offended by my attempt at humour.

'I fink that will need some fought,' came from him. (*Fink, fought, oh my God he's got a speech impediment.*)

Now that's going to lead to some piss-taking. There'll be no controlling Mick, nor half the blokes in the garage. Fuck me, this is all we need.

I have some sympathy for speech problems. When a child of about 11, the school doctor asked me, 'Have you always had a lisp?' I'm thinking, *What fucking lisp, what's he on about.*

The upshot was I was sent to the school clinic. My problem was with 'S's'. This was very quickly dealt with. What annoyed me was that in all my 11 years, no one had bothered to tell me I had a lisp. I was wondering if poor old Cameron had ever been told. If not, was it down to me to tell him? Bloody great!!

Wednesday evening, while relaxing after dinner, there's a ringing of the doorbell. Oh, who's come to bloody disturb me now? Miserable old sod that I'm becoming. Doreen answered the door.' Oh, hello,' I hear, 'come on in.' It's Robert.

'Hi, how are you?' I asked.

'I'm good,' he replied. 'How's Barbara?'

'Not too bad, seems to be improving each day.'

Doreen asked, 'Would you like a drink?'

'Yes please, I'll have a coffee if that's alright.'

As Doreen left the room, Bob produced a six by four envelope from his pocket. Said, 'Sorry for the secrecy, but Dad gave me this a few days before his operation, asking me, in the event of him not getting through, to be very sure it got to you. He emphasised the fact it was to be unobserved.' Bob then gave me a quizzical look as if to say, *I don't know.*

I just nodded and put it in my pocket. Just then, Doreen came back with the drinks. We chatted about the funeral, the day in general, promised to keep in touch. Bob left.

Doreen enquired, 'What was that about? What did he say while I was in the kitchen?'

'Not a lot, just the day and how it went.' When she retired to bed, I said, 'I'll be up in a minute.'

I took a look at the envelope. On it, a single word, my name. It contained a new shiny key and a note. The note said: MAKE SURE YOU ARE ON YOUR OWN, VERY ALONE, WHEN YOU USE THIS. READ THE LETTER BEFORE YOU DO ANYTHING ELSE.

I surmised the key was for his mysterious locker. A feeling of trepidation accompanied this thought. *What the Hell can it be?*

The feeling of trepidation turned to curiosity.

In bed, my mind would not stop racing through various scenarios and possibilities. Could not nod off, suddenly thought, *Whoa! Slow down, must be patient. Need to get Mick out of the way. Leave it till the weekend. Far fewer people around.* Next thing I knew, it was time to get up.

Thursday and Friday dragged like never before. Mick seemed to sense my unease, asking on numerous occasions if things were alright.

As we discussed our weekend work requirements, Mick asked if it would be OK if he only worked Saturday morning, as he had a number of commitments to attend to. I pretended disappointment, saying, 'You know what's expected on this department.'

He claimed, 'It's the only time since Christmas.' On this point, I capitulated and accepted his request.

I had convinced myself that Sunday afternoon would be the perfect time to open this mysterious locker. Saturday morning was seemingly long. I realised the locker would be open as soon as Mick departed. Then he was gone.

I locked the door to our workshop, took the key out, and approached the locker. Realising my heart was beating very fast and what seemed to me very loud, thinking, *I hope it's not anything gruesome*. It was open. An A4 sized brown envelope fell towards me; startled, I stepped back as I caught it.

Left there inside were two large canvass holdall-type bags, standing on their sides, one on top of the other. Above these, there was a briefcase. Holding on to the envelope, I forced a small opening in one of the bags. *Oh fuck*. Not bothering to close the bag, I closed the door to the locker and refitted the lock.

I made a cup of tea. Then sat down and opened the envelope. I found four or five sheets of A4. All seemingly full of script. I sat with my tea and read.

Hi

If you are reading this, it means I've moved on into oblivion.

I'm sorry having to drop this mess on you. I did not know who else I could leave it with. I always regarded you as the most logical, thoughtful and street-smart bloke around. So, you're selected as the only person I can trust to sort this mess out. Whatever conclusion you arrive at, I'm sure it will be the best for all concerned.

What follows is to my recollection a faithful narration of all events in this sorry saga.

It all started if you remember last Easter. I had taken the weekend off. Intending to visit my mother, who lives in Banbury. It was her Eightieth Birthday on the Saturday. The intention had been for Karen and I to spend the weekend there. At the very last minute, some sort of emergency cropped up at Karen's place of employment. She said she would have to cry off, as she had to go into work and help sort out the problem. She had suggested I went on my own and if at all possible, she would join me on Sunday.

I arrived at Mother's at just about midday. She was in very good spirits, but disappointed that Karen had not been able to be there. Mother and Karen had always got on well together. They regularly teamed up when teasing me about something or other, and always seemed happy when together.

I gave her our Card and Present. I let her know it was my intention to take her for a meal at her regular watering hole, thinking that would brighten her day. Only to be told she had made arrangements to have a Party with a group of friends from the Bingo Club.

She had said I was welcome to join them if I wished, the thought of spending an evening with a gang of old Geriatrics was more than I was prepared to risk.

So, after a cup of tea and a biscuit, I set off to return home. At about 3-45 I turned into our street. I noticed a car parked on my drive, it was very similar to my car in size and colour. Karen's car wasn't there, which made me think she would still be at work.

I parked on that spare ground at the end of our street and walked the 50 or so yards to our house. I very quietly let myself in, only to find the hallway full of assorted travel bags.

With my mind in a whirl as to what was going on. I could hear the unmistakable rhythmic sound of shagging coming from upstairs. I crept up the stairs as quietly as I could and opened the bedroom door.

The sight that greeted my eyes was of that LYING CHEATING DIRTY FILTHY FUCKING SLUT OF A BITCH, STARK BOLLOCK NAKED. Straddled across a fucking bloke. Riding him as if she was Frankie fucking Dettori coming up the final furlong at Epsom.

Whether I made a sound, or not, I don't know, but she turned her head and looked over her left shoulder. Without even slowing down, never mind stopping, she said, Oh fucking hell! What are you doing back here?

She just turned back to the job in hand, as if nothing else mattered. I stepped up towards her back right side and hit her so very, very hard to the side of her head with my right-hand fist. Her head went right over, I thought it was coming off. She just seemed to collapse making a sort of "UURGH" sound and then lay very still.

Lover Boy, was up on his feet in a split second. He launched himself at me with both arms reaching forward. I stepped slightly to my right, catching his left arm and using his momentum swung him round a full circle and half finishing with smashing him head-first into the wall.

Trembling with rage I went downstairs. I felt like I wanted to scream at the world. I thought I'll go and smash his car; no, I'll go and kick his bollocks so hard they'll never be any use again. I had all these stupid random thoughts going through my head.

351

It was then I noticed the letter, propped up against a vase on the coffee table, an envelope with just DUTCH written on the front. As I read, my anger subsided and I began to sob.

After a very few seconds, I suddenly got real mad at them again and decided, if she wanted to leave, she should go right now, naked if that's the way they still are.

I ran up the stairs, as I entered the bedroom, they were both in exactly the same position as I'd left them. A quick check confirmed they were both DEAD!!! Her with what seemed to be a broken neck. Him with a smashed skull, OH FUCK WHAT HAVE I DONE!!!

I started to go downstairs thinking, I'll have to call the Police. That's it my life is over. (Nobody knows). I'll spend the rest of my days in jail. (Nobody Knows) I picked up the phone and started to ring. 99(NOBODY KNOWS). I put down the phone. Wait a minute, what am I doing? Why should my life be over just because of these two bastards; I've got the note that says they've gone away. Come on, think it through, what can be done to sort this mess out.

I went into self-preservation mode. Survival instinct just took over.

I went back to the bedroom. Wrapped each body in a sheet and lay them on the bedroom floor. One each side of the bed.

Next, I removed the travel bags from the hall and put them in the spare back bedroom. The two Holdalls and the Briefcase, that were in the lounge, were so much heavier than I expected, I put in the cupboard under the stairs.

I then turned to the problem of the car on my drive. I realised immediately that it required hiding someplace where it could remain undetected for several weeks. I first thought a Railway Station car park. I then found his keys.

Before I started off, I put on an old reversible raincoat that I've had in the wardrobe for years, and an old black cap, along with a pair of leather driving gloves.

I then drove his car to the top of the road, to where my car was parked. I transferred my clothes that I'd took for my weekend away, into the back of his car. They were in a kitbag type of carrier, the sort that can be held as a holdall or used as a knapsack.

As I drove away, I was thinking of Lichfield Trent Valley Station car park. I suddenly realised Traffic Wardens probably patrol around that area. Shit, where the fuck can I put it? BIRMINGHAM AIRPORT, yes.

The route I took was aimed at being as camera free as possible. I went over Bar Beacon, through Erdington, on to Tyburn, then along the Collector Road and into the long stay car park of the Airport.

I parked quite central, slightly to the back and a bit over to the far side from the main entrance road into the Airport.

Pulling my cap down over my face and the collar of my raincoat turned up, I caught the airport bus down to the Departure entrance. I went into the Departure lounge and on into the toilets. In there I reversed the raincoat so the light side was now showing. I changed my black flat cap for a light cap that was in my bag as part of my weekend walking attire. Carrying my bag as a holdall I went out through the arrivals door and took the bus to the International Railway Station.

At the station, I purchased a ticket to Manchester, I was told it would be through in 25 minutes, perfect.

On the Station, I first had a cup of tea, to use up some of the time. I then went into the toilets and again changed my clothing This time I changed from the raincoat and put on a Hooded Fleece, I also changed my shoes for a pair of trainers and my cap for a baseball cap. I then used the bag as a knapsack.

I waited for the train to be announced over the intercom, I then left the toilets and boarded the Train.

The next stop was Birmingham New Street where I got off the train. I left the Station with my hood down and with my baseball cap back on carrying the bag as a holdall again.

I walked to the Bus-stop and took the Bus back to town. From there, got the Bus home.

The bus dropped me at the top of our road just after Ten O'clock.

Had it really been six hours from when I'd first arrived home? One minute it seems like forever, then the next it felt like minutes. I drove to the Queens Head. I needed a drink but not company. I wanted to be seen but not be involved with people, the Queens Head was just about right.

Inside, when I ordered my drink, Dave the Barman asked where is the wife? I said, Oh, she left me. He took this as a joke and gave a laugh, which suited me just fine. I only stayed for two drinks then left for home.

From the moment I realised they were dead; my mind had been in a whirl as to what I should do with the Bodies. The plan that slowly formulated in my mind went along the lines of, I was already in the process of putting down a base for my new shed. Take the footings down another couple of feet or maybe an extra three feet and that's where they can go.

My neighbours, Trevor and Kath were away for the Easter week, in a caravan out Yarmouth way, with their kids. So, no interference from them.

The old couple the other side might be a problem, knowing how nosey they can be. So, some care must be taken on that front.

That night I couldn't go upstairs, So, I lay on the settee. For as tired as I was, I could not sleep. My mind was in a constant whirl. How could this be happening to me, why is this happening to me? Am I doing the right thing? can I get away with it? What if his family or friends know about this association!!! Fuck me, I hadn't given that one a thought.

It was Three O'clock in the morning, I decided to try once more to sleep. Resting on the settee, my mind still would not stop running various scenarios as to what might happen. Nobody knows became everybody knows.

I finally came to the conclusion, it didn't matter who knew, the note said they went away.

By Five-Thirty, I decided to stir myself, I went to the kitchen, made some tea, thought I must try to eat something, made some toast. I realised I was indeed hungry.

After the tea and toast, I felt a little more relaxed, the fact I had the note gave me a bit more confidence that I could get through this. It was at this point that for some reason the bowls AGM popped into my mind, can't just not attend, that would raise interest in my situation. Better write to the secretary asking to be excused. I'll do that now.

I already had the new base for my shed dug-out and the shuttering in place. What I intended to do, was to dig two trenches inside of this area to accommodate the bodies. I was very anxious to get started but knew if I started too early it would create an interest from the old chap next door. So, a nine-thirty start would be about right.

It was very nerve wracking waiting for time to pass. Realising I was still hungry I cooked a full English, mainly to pass the time. I tried eating it but anxiety had taken my appetite. So, I finished off the letter for the bowls and went out to post it.

On my return, it was just after Nine O'clock, I just couldn't wait any longer. I began assembling tools and equipment and made a start. It wasn't till after Eleven that the chap next door showed any interest, and then it was only to call, "Still at it then?" It was me that engaged him in conversation, asking, Haven't you gone anywhere for the holiday? He informed me his Daughter and Son in law are taking him and his Wife out for the day tomorrow (Monday). Oh, great I replied, have a good time won't you. I left it at that and carried on digging.

For most of the day I was at it, knowing I wouldn't be able to move the bodies till the next day when the old pair would be out, So, I took my time. I actually dug somewhat deeper than I had originally intended, but finally called it a day.

I had a shower, and ate the remains of my breakfast. Adrenalin was still running high I found it hard to relax.

That night even after all the hard physical work I found it impossible to sleep. I may well have dropped off for a short while on a few occasions throughout the night but it was not what you would call a restful night.

Next morning, I was out as soon as I thought the DIY. Stores were open. I went to several and purchased two bags of lime from each. I had eight bags in all when I arrived back home.

After confirming the old couple were indeed out, I laid each body in separate trenches. I placed the clothes of each one in the trench to which they had been allotted and covered them with a very liberal amount of lime.

I became aware I had tears streaming down my face while I accomplished this task. I found It so much more wearing than I ever thought anything could be.

I had the concrete mixer going full tilt for the rest of the day. The Sand, Cement and Aggregate, I had originally obtained for the base had been nearly half used. Would have to acquire more, no problem.

Tuesday, I had to return to work. If you remember, I kept well out of the way. At lunch time I made a swift visit home, just to check nothing was amiss. I also ordered more sand, Cement and Aggregate, to be delivered on Wednesday morning.

On Tuesday evening and all through the night for that matter I worried about the delivery and would the blokes delivering be inquisitive and start nosing around the site.

At about 4:30 Wednesday morning I made the decision to go to work. Must keep everything as normal as possible. I could get Photostat copies of the note; Pass it on to her Sister, that will take care of her and the family. I'll lock the back gate, which should deter the Delivery Men from being inquisitive.

With my mind much settled by these thoughts, I decided to relax for an hour or so, wash and shave by then it will be time for work. I sat down to relax and of all things, nodded off.

I awoke with a start. It was 7: 40. Oh shit, keep everything as normal as possible, must get to work on time.

Driving to work, I realised I felt wrecked. How am I going to be able to put down the base for the shed? I can't sleep, apart from the odd hour. When I wake from short naps I feel worse than before I nodded off. In the evenings, after work there are only a couple of hours of daylight left. It just can't be done.

As a consequence, when I arrived at work, I felt quite wretched and know I must have looked wretched too. I had by then realised I would have to tell you of my problems, or at least some of my problems. I also knew I needed to take some time away from work.

I want at this point to thank you for the understanding you showed to my distress. Also, you were able to keep the extent of my problems quiet for so long. I also appreciated that you did not press for a more detailed account of my predicament. And your assistance with the photocopying. THANK YOU

From work I went directly to the Doctors. Explained the situation regarding my wife leaving me. He prescribed sleeping tablets and gave me a Box-Note for three weeks. I arrived home just as the building material was being delivered. Things seemed to have started to go my way.

All that day I slogged away; the mixer never stopped. I kept going on adrenalin alone. It was into the evening when I was finally satisfied the base was as good as it was ever going to be.

I took a shower, had some food, took a double dose of sleeping pills and went to sleep. It was just 8:30.

I slept a very deep sleep. It was 6:45 when I awoke. I immediately began to fret about what I had done. How things should have been handled different. Should I have called the Police. With a hundred

357

random thoughts running through my head, I thought I might be going mad.

Throughout that day I must have checked the base a hundred times. I had decided to leave it till the weekend before erecting the shed on the base. During Thursday and Friday, I checked and double checked the base and the sections of the shed. I was really uncomfortable as to how to fill my time I felt a real need to keep myself busy.

On Friday evening I thought about Trevor and Kate returning home the next day. I didn't want to be there and have to explain that she had left me. I made the decision to go out during both Saturday and Sunday, then, set about erecting the shed on Monday, when everyone was at work.

Saturday, I drove into the Peak District and walked the Dove-Dale Valley. On Sunday, I went out to Iron-Bridge and strolled alongside the Severn.

On Monday morning after everyone had gone off to work and school, I got started on the shed. With the floor down, the sides up and the end sections fixed. I was contemplating a cup of tea. When PANIC!! I had forgotten the bags under the stairs. Oh shit, they should have been buried under the concrete base. What the fuck do I do now?

I came to the conclusion the only course I could take was to burn the bags and their contents. This thought was quickly ruled out. Where there's fire, there's smoke. Great Plumes of smoke drifting across the neighbourhood would soon attract attention, bringing all sorts of authoritative bodies poking noses in.

In a high state of anxiety, I sat with a cup of tea, fretting about my ability to control events. Why had I not remembered the bags under the stairs. The Briefcase, what's in that?

The Briefcase had combination locks. Taking a screwdriver, I forced both locks and opened the case; FUCK ME!! MONEY. Tens of Thousands, oh shit what do I do with this? I then started to worry as to where it had come from. She had sold her car but wouldn't have received this amount. Has she sold the house? She couldn't do that without my signature.

The Holdalls were a lot heavier than you would expect. I opened one of them. Holy Cow, more money, not tens of thousands but Hundreds of thousands. I quickly opened the other Holdall which was also stuffed full of money.

Now this will be sought after. I must get rid of these bags, or certainly get them away from my house. How and where is the problem. I sat in a very flustered state. Couldn't think of any course of action I could take. Where could I dispose of this money, it must run to Millions.

I fretted away the rest of the day. I couldn't carry on with the shed, couldn't concentrate. What am I going to do, where am I going to move it? Eventually late into the evening I took sleeping pills and went to bed.

When I awoke next morning, my mind was still in turmoil. As I lay there, my mind racing, it suddenly dawned on me, WORK, I can hide it at work. I spent most of the day contemplating how I could achieve this idea. Where at work could I hide it, when can I do it?

Not wanting any witnesses to my act of stealth, I decided to take it on Saturday afternoon. Sit in my car and wait for you to leave. I could put it into my personal locker. I had a new formidable lock that I had intended to use for my shed that could be used to secure the locker. I knew of spare lockers around the site I would be able to use on my return to work to store my working clothes.

The following day, I carried on erecting the shed. When I came to lift the roof section, I found it quite difficult. During my struggle with the roof, was the time I first experienced problems with my shoulder. Which we now know was the beginning of my demise. The rest, as they say, is history.

By now having read this letter, you will have decided to hand this letter and the money over to the Police. This is almost certainly the right thing to do.

Before you take this action, PLEASE remember I did not want this to happen. I did not want to hurt her, it was a reaction, it was frustration and pure disappointment at her actions. I am truly sorry for my part in her end.

His demise was all of his own making. First messing about with someone who I regarded as mine. Secondly, having the cheek to launch himself at me, I was only defending myself.

The act of covering it all up was on reflection probably wrong and was an act of panic.

I don't want to leave this world with everyone thinking ill of me.

By this I particularly mean my Mother, my Children, my Ex-Wife and most of all Barbara. Do whatever you can to shield them from the worst of this, or at least make sure they get to know the sorrow I feel at having let them all down.

I know you realise what regrets I had. You seemed to understand my reluctance at being in the company of others. You accepted my displeasure at the mention of her name. I don't think you understood my anger at the subject of him, (I did not know who he was until the discovery of the car. That also explains the money). Nor did you understand my fear of the Police in Blackpool. My reluctance to sell my house and my reluctance of letting Barbara move in must have caused some confusion in your mind. I am aware of the pressure I frequently put you under during my bad spells and thank you for accommodating my mood swings.

Just remember, It's a lot of money. No one knows where it is. No one seems to be looking for it. If you can come up with an idea as to how you can convert it into usable currency. It's yours to have.

I hope all this is not too much to ask of you. And sincerely wish you, your Wife and family a good life.

THANKS AGAIN

DUTCH

OH MY GOD!

EPILOGUE

What am I supposed to do? What is expected of me? I don't know what to do. How do I tell Barbara? How do I tell Robert or any of his family?

Hand it all over to the police, let them sort all that. It's the only thing to do.

What about work, who's going to explain everything to them, me?

What about the club? What about the Memorial Trophies? That must be sorted ASAP. Down to me again.

How do I go about shielding them from the worst of it all? I don't know.

I'm now remembering: *It's a lot of money. Nobody knows. Nobody is looking for it. If I don't tell, I don't have to explain anything to anyone.*

Could I do that? Can I secrete the money away somewhere secure, act as if none of this ever happened? Hmm, I'm not all that sure.

Having stopped and given it some thought. I was of the opinion, the smartest thing to do now was to take about five grand. Me and little wifey could go and lie on a beach somewhere very warm. Think all this through.

If I am able to come up with an idea as to how to convert the money to usable currency, I'll think about letting you know.

Who are you? What's your name? I hear you asking, realising my name has never been mentioned throughout this little piece of history. Well, my name is not important. I refer you to the front cover. As you will see, it says *A Story as Told by Baz.*

* * *

I only know Baz as Baz. Whether it's his real name, I know not. What Baz says is that all names of the characters have been changed. That's if indeed they were real in the first place. He says, if anyone thinks they recognise a character or themselves, they should think of it as self-flattery.

He gives the reason for all this subterfuge. Should an under-utilised plod read this, his thoughts may turn to promotion. Believing he might gain a few brownie points by instigating an investigation in an endeavour to locate the money.

So, mum's the word all round, OK?

See ya!